Val McDermid is a top ten bestseller, translated into more than thirty languages, with over two million copies sold in the UK and over ten million worldwide. She has written twenty-five bestselling novels, most recently *The Retribution*.

She has won many awards internationally, including the CWA Gold Dagger for best crime novel of the year and the Stonewall Writer of the Year Award. In 2011, Val was the recipient of the Pioneer Award at the 23rd Annual Lambda Literary Awards.

In 2010, she was awarded the prestigious CWA Cartier Diamond Dagger. This followed her induction into the Hall of Fame at the ITV3 Crime Thriller Awards in 2009, the same year in which she was elected to an Honorary Fellowship at St Hilda's College, Oxford.

Also by Val McDermid

A Place of Execution
Killing the Shadows
The Distant Echo
The Grave Tattoo
A Darker Domain
Trick of the Dark

TONY HILL NOVELS

The Mermaids Singing
The Wire in the Blood
The Last Temptation
The Torment of Others
Beneath the Bleeding
Fever of the Bone
The Retribution

KATE BRANNIGAN NOVELS

Dead Beat
Kick Back
Crack Down
Clean Break
Blue Genes
Star Struck

LINDSAY GORDON NOVELS

Report for Murder
Common Murder
Final Edition
Union Jack
Booked for Murder
Hostage to Murder

SHORT STORY COLLECTIONS

The Writing on the Wall
Stranded

NON-FICTION

A Suitable Job for a Woman

THE
VANISHING POINT

VAL McDERMID

Little, Brown

LITTLE, BROWN

First published in Great Britain in 2012 by Little, Brown

Copyright © Val McDermid 2012

The moral right of the author has been asserted.

*All characters and events in this publication, other than those
clearly in the public domain, are fictitious and any resemblance
to real persons, living or dead, is purely coincidental.*

A CIP catalogue record for this book
is available from the British Library.

Hardback ISBN 978-1-4087-0321-2
Trade Paperback ISBN 978-1-4087-0322-9

Typeset in Meridien by M Rules
Printed and bound in Great Britain by
Clays Ltd, St Ives plc

Papers used by Little, Brown are from well-managed forests
and other responsible sources.

MIX
Paper from
responsible sources
FSC® C104740

Little, Brown
An imprint of
Little, Brown Book Group
100 Victoria Embankment
London EC4Y 0DY

An Hachette UK Company
www.hachette.co.uk

www.littlebrown.co.uk

For the ones who got away while I was writing this book –
Davina McDermid, Sue Carroll and Reginald Hill.
Without all of you, in your very different ways,
I would never have made it this far.
Your absence is a constant presence.

Acknowledgements

It's a learning curve, this writing business. Every book teaches me something about the world as well as the craft. And so I have a roster of people I need to thank:

Jon and Ruth Jordan for too many things to mention, but in particular this time for passing me on to a contact without whom this book would never have got started. Thanks for giving me the heads-up, Timm.

Linda Watson-Brown and Michael Robotham for sharing their experiences of donning the white sheet.

Kelly Smith for Detroit.

Professor Sue Black for the blood and for www.million-foramorgue.com.

Paula Tyler for giving me access to her encyclopaedic knowledge of family law.

The book doesn't get from me to you without help. There's a whole team of enthusiastic people at Gregory & Co, Little, Brown, Grove Atlantic and HarperCollins Canada who play a crucial role in making sure everything works the way it's supposed to. In particular, I am indebted to Jane Gregory, Stephanie Glencross, Anne O'Brien and the inspirational David Shelley, whose passion infects us all.

And finally a big shout out to my family and friends, whose support I never take for granted. Thank you for cherishing me till the pips squeak.

If you come to fame not knowing who you are, it will define you.

OPRAH WINFREY

PART 1

flight

1

O'Hare Airport, Chicago

Stephanie Harker was just about old enough to remember when air travel had been exciting. She glanced down at the five-year-old fiddling with the tape stretched between the movable pillars that marked out the snaking line waiting to go through security. Jimmy would never know that feeling. He'd grow up to associate flying with tedium and the mounting irritation that came from dealing with people who were variously bored, dismissive or just plain rude. Jimmy seemed to sense her eyes on him and he looked up, his expression tentative and wary. 'Can we go in the pool tonight?' he asked, his voice tinged with the expectation of refusal.

'Course we can,' Stephanie said.

'Even if the plane's late?' There was no sign that her words had allayed his anxiety.

'Even if the plane's late. The house has its own pool. Right outside the living room. It doesn't matter how late we get in, you can have a swim.'

He frowned, weighing her response, then nodded. 'OK.'

They shuffled forward a few more feet. Changing planes in America infuriated Stephanie. When you arrived by plane, you'd already been through security at least once. Sometimes twice. In most other countries, when you transferred to an onward flight, you didn't have to go through a second screening. You were already airside. You'd been declared secure, the authorities figured. No need to go through the whole rigmarole yet another time.

But America was different. America was always different. In America, she suspected, they didn't trust any other country on the planet to have proper airport security. So when you arrived in the US for a connecting flight, you had to emerge from airside to landside then, whoop-de-doo, you got to stand in a queue all over again to go through the same process you'd already endured to get on the first bloody plane. Sometimes even losing that bargain bottle of mandarin vodka you'd picked up on special offer at the duty free on the way out because you'd forgotten you'd have a second security examination where they'd be imposing the rule about liquids. Even liquids you'd bought in a bloody airport. Bastards.

As if that wasn't irritating enough, the latest American version of the security pat-down nudged the outer limits of what Stephanie considered sexual assault. She'd become a connoisseur of the thoroughness of security personnel, thanks to the screws and plate that had held her left leg together for the past ten years. There was no consistency in the actions of the women who moved in to check her over after the metal detector had beeped and flashed. At one extreme, in Madrid she'd been neither patted down nor wanded. Rome was perfunctory, Berlin efficient. But in America, the thoroughness bordered on offensiveness, the backs of hands bumping breasts and butting against her like a clumsy teenage boy. It was uncomfortable and humiliating.

Another few feet. But now the line ahead was moving

steadily. Slowly, but steadily. Jimmy swung under the tape at the point where the queue rounded the mark and bounced in front of her. 'I beat you,' he said.

'So you did.' Stephanie disengaged a hand from the carry-on bags to rumple his thick black hair. At least the frustrations of the journey were a distraction from worrying about holidaying with her son. Her nostrils flared as the unfamiliar phrase stuttered in her head. Holidaying with her son. How long would it be before that stopped sounding freakish, outlandish, impossible? In California, they'd be surrounded by normal families. Jimmy and her, they were anything but a normal family. And this was a trip she never expected to be making. *Please, let it not go wrong.*

'Can I sit beside the window again?' Jimmy tugged at her elbow. 'Can I, Steph?'

'As long as you promise not to open it in mid-flight.'

He gave her a suspicious look then grinned. 'Would I get sucked out into space if I did?'

'Yup. You'd be the boy in the moon.' She waved him onward. They'd picked up speed and were almost at the point where they'd have to load their bags and the contents of their pockets into a plastic tray to pass through the X-ray scanner. Stephanie caught sight of a large Perspex enclosure beyond the metal detector and pursed her lips. 'Remember what I told you, Jimmy,' she said firmly. 'You know I'll set off the alarms and then I'll have to stay inside that clear box until somebody checks me over. You're not allowed in with me.'

He pouted. 'Why not?'

'It's the rules. Don't worry,' she added, seeing the troubled look in his eyes. 'Nothing bad's going to happen to me. You wait by the luggage belt, OK? Don't go anywhere, just wait till I come out on the other side. Do you understand?'

Now he was avoiding her eye. Maybe he felt she was talking

down to him. It was so hard to pitch things at the right level. 'I'll guard the bags,' he said. 'So nobody can steal them.'

'Great.'

The man ahead of them in the queue shrugged out of his suit jacket and folded it into a tray. Off with his shoes, then his belt. He opened his laptop bag and removed the computer, laying it in a second tray. He nodded towards them, indicating he was done. 'No dignity in travel these days,' he said with a grim smile.

'You ready, Jimmy?' Stephanie stepped forward and grabbed a plastic tray. 'That's an important job you've got, the guarding bit.' She loaded their stuff, checked Jimmy's pockets then shooed him through the metal detector ahead of her. He turned to watch as the machine beeped, the red lights lit up and the beefy Transport Security Agency operative indicated the Perspex pen.

'Female officer,' he called out, chins and belly wobbling. 'Wait inside the box, ma'am.' He pointed to the enclosure, a couple of metres long by a metre wide. The outlines of two feet were painted on the floor. A plastic chair sat against one wall. A wooden plinth contained a hand-held metal detector. Jimmy's eyes widened as Stephanie walked in. She waved him towards the conveyor belt where their possessions were slowly emerging from the scanner.

'Wait for me,' she mouthed, giving him a thumbs-up.

Jimmy turned away and moved to the end of the conveyor belt, staking out their plastic trays. Stephanie looked around impatiently. There were three or four female TSA officers in sight, but none of them seemed eager to deal with her. Thank goodness she and Jimmy weren't rushing to make a connection. Knowing what US transfers were like these days, she'd deliberately left plenty of time between their flights.

She looked back at Jimmy. One of the TSA agents appeared to be talking to him. A tall man in black uniform trousers and blue shirt. But something was off-kilter. Stephanie frowned. He was wearing a cap, that was what it was. None of the other TSA people wore anything on their heads. As she watched, the man reached for Jimmy's hand.

For a split second, Stephanie couldn't believe what she was seeing. The man was leading a compliant Jimmy away from the security area towards the concourse where dozens of people were milling back and forth. Not a backward glance from either of them.

'Jimmy,' she shouted. 'Jimmy, come back here.' Her voice rose in pitch, but it was deadened by the Perspex enclosure. Neither the man nor the child broke step. Worried now, Stephanie banged on the side of the box, gesturing towards the concourse. 'My kid,' she shouted. 'Somebody's taken my kid.'

Her words seemed to have no impact but her actions did. Two agents moved towards the box, not towards Jimmy. They were oblivious to what was happening behind them. Frantic, Stephanie thrust aside the voice in her head telling her she was crazy and made a run for it.

She'd barely made it out of the Perspex box when one of the agents grabbed her arm, saying something that didn't register. His grip slowed her but it didn't stop her. The prospect of losing Jimmy pushed her over her normal limits. The officer snatched at her with his other hand and without thinking, Stephanie whirled round and smashed her fist into his face. 'They're kidnapping my kid,' she yelled.

Blood flowed from the guard's nose, but he held on tight. Now Stephanie could only see the man's hat. Jimmy was lost in the crowd. Panic gave her strength and she dragged the guard behind her. Dimly, she was aware of other officers drawing weapons and shouting at her, but her focus was total. 'Jimmy,' she screamed.

By now, another guard had grabbed her waist, trying to

wrestle her to the ground. 'Get down on the floor,' he yelled. 'On the floor, now.' She kicked out, raking her heel down his shin.

The raised voices blurred into a meaningless noise as a third TSA officer joined battle, throwing himself on her back. Stephanie felt her knees buckle as she crumpled to the floor. 'My boy,' she mumbled, reaching for the pocket where she'd put their boarding passes. Suddenly the bodies restraining her melted away and she was free. Confused but relieved they were finally paying attention, Stephanie pushed herself one-handed to her knees.

That was when they tasered her.

2

Everything happened at once. Excruciating agony flashed along nerves, dancing synapses sending devastating messages to muscles. Stephanie's collapse was instantaneous, a complete system failure, like the flick of a switch. Her mind raced in confusion, unable to make sense of the pain and the total loss of physical control. The one impulse that remained was the need to communicate what had happened.

She was convinced she was shouting Jimmy's name, even as she hit the ground hard. But what she heard was a meaningless mangle of sound, the kind of dream-mumble people made when they were having a nightmare.

As suddenly as the pain had hit, it disappeared. Stephanie raised her head, bewildered. She paid no attention to the ring of Transport Security Administration officers surrounding her at a cautious distance. She was oblivious to the rubbernecking passengers, their exclamations or their camera phones. She strained to see Jimmy and caught a glimpse of his bright red Arsenal shirt next to the black and blue of a TSA uniform. They were turning off the main concourse, disappearing from sight. Ignoring the residual ache in her muscles, Stephanie pushed herself upright and launched herself in the crucial direction, a primal roar emerging from her throat.

She didn't even complete the first stride. This time, the taser blast was longer, the disarticulation more thorough. This time, once the initial disabling effect was over, she remained disorientated and weak. Two officers hauled her to her feet and dragged her down the concourse in the direction opposite to where she'd last seen Jimmy. With the last of her energy, Stephanie tried to struggle free.

'Give it up,' one of the officers restraining her yelled.

'Cuff her,' a second, more authoritative voice said.

Stephanie felt her arms yanked behind her and the cold bracelet of metal handcuffs closed round each wrist. Now they were moving more quickly, hustling her down a side hallway and through a door. They dropped her on a plastic chair, her arms uncomfortably pulled over its back. Her head felt like the gears were slipping their cogs. She couldn't get a grip on her thoughts.

A stocky Hispanic woman in TSA uniform stepped in front of her. Her expression was rock hard and grim but her eyes seemed considering. 'You'll feel confused for a while. It'll pass. You're not dying. You're not even hurt. Not like my colleague with the busted nose. Do not attempt to leave this room. You will be prevented if you do.'

'Someone kidnapped my son.' The words came out thick and slurred. She sounded drunk and incomprehensible to her own ears. She couldn't even focus enough to read the woman's name badge.

'I'll be back to interview you shortly,' the woman said, following her colleagues towards the door.

'Wait,' Stephanie yelled. 'My boy. Somebody took my boy.'

The woman didn't even break stride on her way out.

Now the overwhelming sensation in Stephanie's body was the cold clutch of fear in her chest. Never mind what the taser had done to her body and her mind. Terror was all she understood at that moment. Her initial panic had altered, taking with it the urgency for flight or fight. Now the apprehension felt like a chill lump in her chest, weighing down her heart and making it hard to breathe. As thoughts and emotions tumbled inside her, Stephanie forced herself to focus on one solid piece of information. Someone had walked away from the security area with Jimmy. A stranger had whisked him away without a ripple in the surface of normality. How could that have happened? And why wouldn't they listen to her?

She had to get out of there, had to make someone in authority understand that something terrible had happened, was still happening right now. Stephanie struggled against the back of the chair, trying to release her arms. But the more she wrestled against the rigid plastic, the more trammelled she felt. At last, she realised the design of the chair meant she couldn't push her arms far enough behind her to clear its back. The fact that it was bolted to the floor meant she couldn't even get to her feet and take it with her like some bizarre turtle shell.

She'd no sooner reached that conclusion than the woman who had spoken to her walked back into the room. She was followed by a lanky middle-aged man in the now-familiar TSA uniform who sat down opposite Stephanie without greeting her. Greying dark hair in an immaculate crew cut framed a face that was all hollows and angles, like something constructed from a kid's magnet modelling kit. His eyes were cold, his mouth and chin too weak for the image he was trying to project. His name badge read Randall Parton and there were two gold stripes on the shoulder board of his blue shirt. Stephanie was relieved to find she could make sense of what she was seeing this time around.

'Somebody kidnapped my boy,' she said, urgency tumbling her words together. 'You need to sound the alert. Tell the cops. Whatever it is you do when a stranger steals a kid.'

Parton kept up the stony stare. 'What is your name?' he said. Stephanie recognised the tight twang of New England in his speech.

'My name? Stephanie Harker. But that's not important. What's important—'

'We decide what's important round here.' Parton straightened his shoulders inside his neatly ironed shirt. 'And what's important right now is that you are a security risk.'

'That's crazy. I'm the victim here.'

'From where I'm standing, my officer is the victim here. The officer you assaulted in your attempt to escape the security screening area before you could be searched. After you had set off the metal detector.' Behind him, Stephanie could see the woman shift from one foot to the other, as if she was uncomfortable in the moment.

'I set off the metal detector because I have a metal plate and three screws in my left leg. I was in a bad car accident ten years ago. I always set off the detectors.'

'And as of now we have no way of determining the truth of that. Now what we need to establish before we go any further is that you are no risk to my country or my team. We require that you submit to a thorough search.'

Stephanie felt pressure building up inside her head, as if a blood vessel was about to burst behind her eyes. 'This is crazy. What are my rights here?'

'It's not my job to inform you of your legal rights. It's my job to maintain airport security.'

'So why aren't you searching for the kidnapper who stole my son? Jesus Christ.'

'There's no need for language like that. For all I know this story of a kidnap is an elaborate ruse. I'm still waiting for you to confirm you will submit to a thorough body search.'

'I'm confirming nothing till you start dealing with what has happened to Jimmy, you idiot. Where's your boss? I want to talk to someone in authority here. Get these handcuffs off me. I want a lawyer.'

Parton's lips compressed in a tight smile that had nothing to do with humour. 'Non-US citizens selected for a longer interview generally do not have the right to an attorney.' There was more than a hint of triumph in his voice.

The woman officer cleared her throat and took a step forward. Lia Lopez, according to her name badge. 'Randall, she's talking about an abducted kid. She has the right to an attorney if we're asking her about anything other than immigration status or security.'

Parton swung his head round portentously, as if it were as heavy as a bowling ball. 'Which, as of right now, we are not doing, Lopez.' He held the glare for a long moment then turned back to Stephanie. 'You need to confirm your consent,' he repeated.

'Am I legally required to submit to a search?' It had dawned on Stephanie that if this idiot wasn't going to listen to her, somehow she had to get in front of someone who would. And quickly.

'Are you refusing to confirm?'

'No, I'm seeking clarification. Am I legally obliged to submit to a search? Or can I refuse?'

'You're not helping yourself here.' There was a pale pink flush on Parton's cheeks, as if he'd been out in a cold wind.

'I don't know the law here. As you have already noticed, I am not a US citizen. I'm simply trying to establish what my rights are.'

Parton's head jutted forward, aggressive as a farmyard rooster. 'You're refusing to confirm your consent to a search? Right?'

'Do you actually know the law? Do you actually know what my rights are? I want to talk to someone in authority, someone who knows what's what.'

'Listen, lady. You wanna play smartass, I'm not going to play your game. If you don't give me the answers I'm looking for, the next person you'll be talking to will be from the FBI. And that's a whole other ball game.' He pushed back from the table and turned to Lopez. 'What have we got on her ID?'

Lopez muttered something into her radio and turned away. Parton spoke again, obscuring the other conversation. 'Like I said, you're not helping yourself here. You assaulted one of my officers. That's all we know. Nobody witnessed any incident. Nobody reported a child being abducted. All I know, lady, is that you just went crazy on us. Why the hell did you break out of the box? Why did you assault that officer?'

Answering that question once had achieved nothing. There was no reason to suppose that repeating herself would take them any further forward. If she could have folded her arms across her chest, that's what Stephanie would have done. There was no available body language for her to convey 'enough'. She swallowed her panic, cocked her head and met his eye. 'Am I legally obliged to answer that question?'

Exasperated, Parton slapped his hands on the tabletop. Lopez moved forward and said, 'She entered the US half an hour ago here in Chicago. She came in on a flight from London Heathrow.' She cleared her throat. 'She was accompanied by a minor child.'

The silence expanded to fill the space available. In a voice cold with rage, Stephanie said, 'Now can we get a real law-enforcement official in here?'

3

Parton's bluster did not survive Lopez's information. He ordered the cuffs to be removed, but couldn't resist barking at her. 'Keep your hands out of your pockets. And don't use your phone.'

'I don't have my phone. It's in a plastic box with all the other stuff that went through the X-ray machine. Which presumably includes Jimmy's backpack. All you had to do to establish I was telling the truth was to take a look at what was sitting on the scanner belt.' Stephanie didn't even try to hide her disdain.

Parton said nothing more on his way out of the room. Lopez gave her a rueful smile. 'Is he going to get someone in here who can do something about my child being kidnapped?' Stephanie demanded, rubbing her wrists.

Lopez looked away as the door opened. A TSA officer brought two grey plastic trays into the room and dropped them on the floor. Stephanie could see that one contained her carry-on bag, while the other held her jacket, shoes, toiletries in clear plastic for easy examination and the assorted jumble of items from pockets. 'Wait,' she said. 'There should be another. With Jimmy's backpack and his hoodie.'

The officer shrugged one shoulder. 'That's all there is.' He closed the door behind him.

The absence of Jimmy's possessions sent a fresh shiver of fear through Stephanie. Somehow, that spoke of chilling calculation, a targeted move rather than a spontaneous random selection. She had never been more aware of time passing. 'Does nobody have any sense of urgency round here?' she demanded. 'Do you have children? Would you not be losing your mind if somebody kidnapped your child and nobody paid any attention?'

Lopez looked uncomfortable. 'You have to be patient. We've got a job to do and it's got a very narrow focus. We're obliged to act inside tight limits. And I shouldn't even be talking to you.'

Stephanie put her head in her hands. 'Every minute that passes, Jimmy's in danger. I promised . . . I promised . . .' Her voice stuck in her throat. Her fear and rage couldn't maintain their adrenalin-fuelled level for ever. Now it was her sense of failure that choked her. She'd given her word. And it seemed her word was worthless.

Being posted to the Chicago Field Office had felt like a promotion to Special Agent Vivian McKuras. But when they sent her out on permanent attachment to the office at the airport, she understood that she was actually being punished for the sins of her previous boss. Jeff was now serving time in a federal penitentiary for his novel methods of funding his gambling addiction. She'd known there was something off with him, but she'd thought it was to do with his marriage, not a surreptitious arrangement with the local mob. A fine detective she'd turned out to be.

To an outsider, the airport posting might have looked like a plum job, out there on the front line against the terrorists seeking to undermine the American way of life. The perfect place for an agent to redeem herself, to show she was really a class act. The reality was about as unglamorous as it could get. Most of the people pulled out of the line by the TSA were about as close to terrorists as her grandmother. On second thoughts, that wasn't such a great analogy. Her grandmother could get pretty fired up these days about Scottish independence. Never mind that she'd left Rutherglen when she was five months old.

The problem for Vivian McKuras was boredom. Every interview she'd carried out as the result of a TSA stop had been entirely pointless. Mostly she'd known within three minutes that the men, women and children detained for her attention were, in terms of the security of the state, entirely harmless. Disabled veterans, the incontinent elderly and the Sikh with the black plastic copy of a ceremonial dagger were not going to hijack a plane or raze the airport to the ground. And on the few occasions when she thought further investigation was merited, protocol required that she bring the Chicago office into the circle. Her potential suspect would be whisked off for questioning by officers who had fewer black marks on their record than she.

The tedium was killing her. So many times in the past weeks she'd stood in the shower composing her letter of resignation from the Bureau. But always she came back to the practicalities. What else could she do for a living? There was a recession on. Nobody was hiring. They especially weren't hiring people who had no vocational training. Five years in the FBI didn't qualify you for anything except more of the same. And more of the same was precisely what she didn't want.

And now, just to make her day complete, Randall Parton was walking through her office door. Vivian had tried not to let the instinctive dislike she'd taken to Parton interfere with their professional relationship. But it was hard, given the perfect storm of arrogance and stupidity that had been obvious at their first encounter and at every one since.

'Agent McKuras,' he said with a sharp nod of greeting. He always managed to make it clear that the lack of respect between them was mutual.

'What do you need from me today, Officer Parton?' Vivian smiled sweetly, knowing it killed him that she was the one with the power to do anything more than prevent someone getting on a plane.

Parton eyed the visitor chair opposite her desk, torn as always between the desire to sit down without waiting for an invitation that was never going to come and the need to tower over her. 'We got us a crazy woman. She set off the metal detector, an officer put her in the box to wait for a female assist. We were running a little slow on the box, you know how busy it gets this time of day.'

'I know,' Vivian said, wishing she didn't. Wishing this airport and all its internal workings were a mystery to her.

'Out of nowhere, she launches herself out of the box.' Parton sounded defensive, a man who expected to find himself in the wrong sooner or later. 'Officers go to intercept her but she's not ready to be stopped. Next thing is, I've got an officer down with a busted nose, blood everywhere and she's still going forward, yelling something that makes no sense to any of my guys.'

'She's not speaking English?'

Parton's mouth quirked to one side to show his distaste. 'She's English all right, but nobody can make out what she's yelling. So they taser her, like they're supposed to when they're met with violent resistance. She goes down but she gets right back up. Like a crazy person. So they zap her with a longer blast and this time she stays down till they cuff her. Lopez took her down to the interview room.'

Vivian felt a moment's relief. Lia Lopez might be Parton's

junior, but she had more sense than the rest of her shift put together. 'Good move,' she said.

'So that's when I get called in. And that's where it gets complicated.'

'Complicated how?'

'For a start, she's a smartass. Every time I ask her a question, she just harps on about whether she's legally obliged. Running me around in circles. And then she starts in about how her kid's been kidnapped. Now, we got no alert in the zone. Nobody saw any kid being abducted. The only unusual thing in my area this afternoon was this crazy-ass woman breaking out of the box. So I was disinclined to take her seriously. I thought she was trying to distract us from doing the search on her that we should be doing.' Now his chin was up, his self-righteousness to the fore.

'I can see why you might think that way.' *If you were an idiot.* 'So where are we up to now? You want me to talk to her? Get her to agree to a search?'

Parton folded his arms across his chest. 'It's gotten more complicated. Lopez got her name from her passport and checked with Immigration. Turns out she did have a kid with her when she arrived at the border earlier this afternoon.'

'And the kid is missing now?' Now he had Vivian's full attention. Whatever this was, it wasn't the run-of-the-mill that had ground her down.

Parton nodded. 'Looks like it.' His mouth did the wry twist again. 'And here's the thing. She's not the mother. She brought the kid in with British court documents giving her authority to travel with him. So who knows what the fuck is going on here.'

The sudden rush of adrenalin galvanised Vivian as nothing had for months. 'Jeez, Parton. We're going to have to call a Code Adam.' She reached for the phone, wondering who she should phone first when it came to closing down the world's busiest airport.

Shamefaced, Parton half-turned his head away. 'It's too late to go to lockdown. We didn't understand what was happening fast enough. They'll be long gone. You can check the footage if you don't believe me. You really don't want to call a Code Adam unless you're sure they're still on the premises.'

Vivian took his point. That would be a fast way to end her career. She gave a short, sharp sigh and hit the rarely used speed-dial button for the airport CCTV control centre. Parton, looking offended, started to speak but she held up a finger to silence him. 'Hey,' she said when the controller answered. 'This is Special Agent McKuras in the FBI office. I need you to send me the feed for the last hour from—'

'Security area two, terminal three.' Parton was eager now, sensing that Vivian's actions might get him off an awkward hook.

Vivian repeated the details and reminded the controller of her computer ID. She hung up and attacked her keyboard, fingers deft and fast. Strictly speaking, she should bring in one of her colleagues to watch the footage with her. But the two men she shared the airport posting with inhabited a cubbyhole office in the international terminal. She didn't want to wait for one of them to drag himself over. If there had been a kidnap, every minute counted, especially since they'd been too slow off the mark to call a Code Adam. Besides, she had a ready-made witness in the room, however low her opinion of him. She looked up at Parton. 'We'll have a better idea of what we're dealing with now. Why don't you bring the chair round where you can see my screen? Two pairs of eyes are better than one.'

Parton grabbed the chair and angled it by the corner of the desk so he could see the screen. He sat down, stretching his long legs out and folding his arms across his chest. A whiff of laundry detergent and fried meat caught her throat and without thinking she drew away from him. He caught her

20

movement and grunted, tucking his legs under the chair to take up less space. 'It's a great system,' he said. 'When it works.'

'Let's hope this is one of those days,' Vivian muttered, clicking her mouse button to open up a new window. She was offered a choice of three cameras that covered the security area. 'Which one?'

Parton leaned forward, a long bony finger extended. 'That one. The middle one.'

Vivian checked her watch. 'How long ago did this happen?'

'About twenty minutes ago.'

She pulled up the camera feed and scrolled back twenty-five minutes then set it running. They watched in silence for a couple of minutes. Then a woman and child walked into shot, filling the plastic trays on the far side of the metal detector. 'That's her,' Parton said.

'And that boy is definitely with her.' Vivian paused the recording and studied the pair. The woman looked taller than average. Around five nine, maybe. Mid-brown hair in an untidy jaw-length bob. Striking looks, with high cheekbones, a square chin, a wide mouth caught in a smile as she looked at the boy. She looked like she had that English-rose colouring, all pink and white. The kid had a thick mop of black hair, olive skin, cheeks like apricots. He was all arms and legs, wiry and clumsy like a foal in one of those sentimental race-horse movies. He didn't look like he'd sprung from her genes. And yet there was no denying it. 'They're together, Parton.'

'Shit.'

They watched the boy move through the metal detector and over to the far side of the X-ray machine where their possessions would reappear on the delivery belt. He looked over his shoulder towards the woman, who smiled and gave him the thumbs-up sign as she entered the box to wait for a female officer to pat her down. So far, so good. Vivian realised she was holding her breath, as if she was watching a thriller.

A few seconds passed. The boy shuffled from one foot to the other; the woman watched him. Then a man dressed in what appeared to be a TSA uniform shirt and black trousers appeared from the concourse and approached the boy. Just before he reached him, Vivian paused the video. 'What's wrong with this picture?'

'He's wearing a ball cap,' Parton said without hesitation. 'That's not uniform issue. We don't wear headgear.'

'And he's wearing the one kind of headgear guaranteed to obscure your face when you're dealing with overhead cameras.' Vivian set the video running again.

'He's not one of my team. No way.' Parton unfolded his arms and clenched his fists.

The man walked straight up to the boy and put a hand on his back. The boy looked up and nodded. The man in the TSA uniform picked up a backpack from one of the plastic boxes then ushered the boy away from the belt and towards the concourse. The effect on the woman was electrifying. As soon as the man put a hand on the boy, she started moving. They'd barely cleared the end of the scanner conveyor belt when she was out of the plastic box.

Vivian ignored the drama in the foreground and concentrated on the man and boy. They remained in sight for a few yards then, as the concourse curved round to the right, they cut sharply left. 'Shit,' Parton said again.

'That's an exit, isn't it?'

'Takes you landside,' Parton confirmed. 'You'd be kerbside inside a minute. Then you could be anywhere.'

Vivian paused the video again. 'Looks like the lady was telling the truth,' she said, her voice as bleak as her heart. A child had been snatched and the bureaucracy of airport security had handed the kidnapper a head start. 'Christ, Parton. How come nobody listened to this woman?' She was already reaching for the phone again.

'Nobody could understand her at first,' he said. 'I swear to God.'

'I'm sure that's going to cover your back when the lawsuits come down. But as of now, I need you to get me a list of everyone who was on duty this afternoon. We're going to have to interview them all. Find out who saw what.'

Parton didn't move. He seemed fascinated by the hand holding the phone. 'Parton,' Vivian said impatiently. 'Get me that list of names.'

His eyes met hers. He seemed dazed. 'He'll be OK, right? The kid? You'll find him, right?'

He didn't deserve the effort of lies. 'Alive? Probably not. Now go.' She watched him stumble over the chair on his way out. Then Vivian took a deep breath and composed herself. She pressed the speed-dial number for her boss. The number rang out, signalling the end of her autonomy on the case of the kidnapped child.

4

The urge to get up and pace was almost overwhelming. Stephanie had already tried to stand up, only to have Lopez insist sharply that she stay seated. 'Don't make me have to cuff you again,' she'd warned.

'Don't I get a phone call or something?' Stephanie asked. 'I thought you Americans made a big deal out of people's right to legal representation?'

Lopez gave a mirthless laugh. 'You never heard of Guantanamo Bay? We're not so keen on human rights when it comes to the kind of people who want to blow us off the planet.'

'But I'm not a terrorist. I'm obviously not a terrorist. I'm a woman whose child was kidnapped in front of her eyes and you're treating me like I'm the criminal. When is someone going to start taking me seriously?' In spite of her determination to stay calm, Stephanie couldn't help her voice rising. She felt nauseous and sweaty, sick with fear and worry. But she had to keep it together. For Jimmy's sake. For the sake of the promises she'd made.

They should never have come on this holiday. But she'd allowed herself to be seduced by the idea of California.

Beaches and surf, Disneyland and Universal Studios, sunshine and Yosemite. Ever since she'd heard that Joni Mitchell song, the city of swimming pools had held her imagination close. She wanted to know what the waves at Malibu sounded like. Jimmy needing a holiday had just been an excuse to indulge herself.

Stupid.

They should have gone to Spain. Taken the car on a ferry to Santander and driven across to the Costa Brava. Or dawdled up the French Atlantic Coast to Brittany. Something that didn't involve metal detectors and separation. Something that didn't hand Jimmy on a plate to whoever wanted to steal him away.

And who would do that anyway? Who would have the nerve and the brains to abduct him in the middle of a busy airport, under the watchful gaze of CCTV and some of the most stringent security arrangements on the planet? It was beyond belief.

It was hard to believe it was a random abduction, a spur-of-the-moment snatch. Someone had planned this. Obviously it hadn't been a real TSA officer who had walked off with Jimmy, otherwise Parton or Lopez would have known about it. That meant it was an impostor. But you couldn't just hang around indefinitely in a lookalike uniform without attracting attention from the real security people. It was hard to resist the conclusion that Jimmy had been a very specific target. And that meant a kidnapper who knew his tragic history. Not to mention their travel plans.

Please God, let him be OK. She couldn't bear the thought of Jimmy suffering any more. He'd already gone through more than any five-year-old should have to endure. Sometimes when he snuggled into her at bedtime, she imagined herself soaking up his pain, taking it up into her body like lymph nodes absorbing toxins, restoring him to some magical default state where he hadn't been hurt beyond bearing. What sort of bastard would be willing to add to that burden of pain and fear?

Stephanie pushed the thought away, refusing to acknowledge that she knew anyone who could contemplate such cruelty. But the rogue notion wouldn't be hushed.

She needed to do something that would shift her focus. 'Isn't there some sort of system for sending out an alarm about kidnapped children? I'm sure I saw a TV programme about it. You signal to drivers on the motorways or something?'

'You're thinking about the Amber Alert,' Lopez said. 'When there's a child abduction, they put messages up on the gantries on the highway. But it goes a lot wider than that. They broadcast it on the radio, they put a ticker on the TV news stations. A lot of people subscribe to SMS messages too. It's been real effective in a lot of cases.'

'They should be doing that for Jimmy.' Stephanie grabbed her hair on either side of her head and clung to it. 'They should be doing it now.'

'Officer Parton has the matter in hand.' Lopez didn't sound too convinced.

'You've got a radio there. Can't you find out what's going on? Please?'

Lopez looked embarrassed. 'There's nothing I can do. Believe me, the wheels are turning now.'

'But not fast enough,' Stephanie said savagely. 'There's a little boy out there who's growing more and more scared the longer he's away from me. I hope you can live with that, Officer Lopez. Because when I get out of here, yours will be one of the names in the headlines. I have media contacts that would make your eyes water. And I will be putting them to good use.'

'I don't think threats are the way to go right now, ma'am.'

'From my perspective, threats are the only way to go.

Because appealing to you people's humanity isn't working, is it? Maybe I need to start appealing to your self-interest. Do you want a future in this career, Officer Lopez? Or do you want to come out of this as one of the good guys?'

Lopez took a step towards her. Stephanie expected anger or fear, but what she got was something completely different. Lopez laid a hand on her shoulder. 'I'm going to pretend you never said any of that. You're scared. I get that. But my advice is to dial back on the threats till you get some place you can act on them. This organisation doesn't need much excuse to hold people incommunicado.'

On the surface, it sounded like gentle reason. To Stephanie, it seemed a more chilling threat than anything she could have come up with.

Vivian McKuras put the phone down gently, as if she didn't want to startle it into biting her. She'd expected her boss to rip the kidnapping case from her grasp and assign her to going through passenger lists or something equally mindless. Instead, she'd interrupted what sounded like a major alert. He'd gabbled – gabbled! – that they'd intercepted a credible suicide bomber threat to an imminent political rally featuring the First Family. Every available body – except hers, obviously – was out there trying to close down the risk before it spiralled beyond control. Normally, she'd have been unsettled by such a display from a man who had apparently adopted cool as his watchword in high school and hadn't veered from it since. But today, she welcomed it. Because today it meant she had control of her first major case. Twenty-seven years old and she had her own major case. Never mind that her boss had told her to bring in her airport colleagues to run things with her. She preferred to think of that as a suggestion rather than an instruction. This was her case. This was where she got the chance to turn things round for herself.

The first thing she had to do was to set up the Amber Alert. She needed a description of the child and a recent photograph. Luckily, all that was at her fingertips. Literally. Vivian opened her email and sent an urgent message to her opposite number at ICE HSI, the catchily named Immigration and Customs Enforcement and Homeland Security Investigations.

> Hi, Kevin. I'm inquiring about a minor child your team admitted this afternoon. No immigration issue, but it looks as if the boy may have been subsequently abducted. He came in from the UK accompanied by Stephanie Jane Harker, UK citizen. According to my info, she was carrying British court papers authorising her to travel with the child. We have to put an Amber Alert together, so I need copies of everything you've got asap – the child's name, DOB, description. If you've got a photo, either from the passport or the system, so much the better. We've got CCTV images, but they're never hi-res enough to do much with. Also, any notes you've got regarding the paperwork would be helpful. Thanks.

And because she was a belt-and-braces kind of woman, she sent Kevin a text message to alert him to her request.

Deep breath.

Until she had some information to work with, there was nothing more she could do to set the Amber Alert in motion. Time to talk to Stephanie Jane Harker.

When a woman walked into the room instead of Randall Parton, Stephanie felt irrationally relieved. Years of working in an industry where the women were as likely to put the shaft in as any man should have cured her of such gender-based optimism, but she couldn't help it. Especially where children were concerned, she still expected a smidgeon of solidarity from another woman.

This one looked as if she meant business. She glanced at Stephanie, then took Lopez to one side and bent her head to speak softly to the TSA officer. *How would I describe her if I was writing about her?* It was Stephanie's default position when she met anyone new. Her clothes were neat but anonymous – dark-grey trousers, navy blazer, dark-green shirt with only the top button undone. A flash of gold chain at the neck, plain gold studs in the ears. Short brown hair, feathered round the ears and forehead to emphasise looks that might have been elfin if it hadn't been for the square jaw. A lazy writer would have made something of the hint of Irish in the green eyes and faint dusting of freckles across nose and cheeks. But although Stephanie knew she was no great shakes as a writer, she'd never been quite that lazy. This was America, land of the melting pot. Not a place to make easy assumptions about roots.

Now the woman turned back to face her, flashing a perfunctory, formal smile. 'I'm Special Agent Vivian McKuras,' she said, pulling out the chair and sitting down. 'Federal Bureau of Investigation.'

'Thank God for that,' Stephanie said. 'A proper law-enforcement official at last. Presumably you know my legal rights?' She was pleased to see a flash of surprise in the agent's eyes.

'As far as I'm concerned, Ms Harker, you've made an allegation of a serious crime. That's my sole interest in you. I don't see why you would need a lawyer to make a crime report. At some point, my colleagues in the TSA will want to give you a pat-down, since you set off the metal detector at the security point, but I don't see why you'd need a lawyer for that either.' She flipped open a tablet computer and woke it from its hibernation. 'As far as I'm concerned, the most urgent thing right now is to track down a missing child.'

Stephanie felt her shoulders drop a fraction. At last, someone who was capable of talking sense. 'Thank you for clearing that up,' she said. 'So have you put out an alert for Jimmy?'

Vivian looked her straight in the eye. 'We're in the process of gathering the necessary information to do just that. I've examined the CCTV footage of what happened in the security area but unfortunately we can't see the face of the man who took your child.'

Stephanie swallowed hard. 'He's not actually my child.'

Vivian nodded. 'We are aware of that. And I'm going to be asking you some questions about that shortly. But right now, my priority is to get this alert out there. First, what's the boy's name?'

'Jimmy Joshu Higgins.' She watched as Vivian typed. 'That's Joshu, without an "a" on the end. After his father. He was a DJ.' Stephanie couldn't quite keep a note of contempt from her voice.

'You don't think much of his father?'

'No. I don't.' There was more to that story, but it would keep.

'OK. How tall is Jimmy, would you say?'

'He's about three foot six. Quite gangly and skinny. He's light for a five-year-old. He weighs just under three stone.' Seeing Vivian's frown, she added, 'Around forty pounds.'

'Thanks. We're going to need a description, to put out with a photograph of Jimmy.'

'He's got thick black hair, cut quite shaggy. Did you ever see *Jungle Book*?'

Vivian looked at her as if she was crazy. 'No. Is that a movie?'

'It's an animation. The kid in the cartoon, he's called Mowgli. Jimmy looks kind of like him. Same hairstyle, similar kind of cheeky face. I don't know how else to describe it. Google Mowgli, you'll see what I mean.' Frustrated by her inability to communicate an image of Jimmy, Stephanie thought for a moment. 'Don't you have his passport? It was in the same bin as mine.'

Vivian turned to Lopez. 'We got that, Lia?'

Lopez shook her head. 'No, ma'am. Only Ms Harker's passport. There was nothing in the bin for the boy. I'll check again, but ...' She crouched down and began searching the plastic boxes.

'What about his backpack?' Stephanie asked.

'The man he left with picked up the backpack. He must have grabbed the passport too.'

'Nothing here,' Lopez reported.

'Shit,' Stephanie said. Then she brightened. 'My phone. I took a couple of pictures of him at the park last week. Would that help? My phone's in the bin, right?'

Lopez stood up, waving the phone. 'Here it is.' She looked to Vivian for guidance. 'Is it OK to give her the phone?'

'Give it to me.' Vivian quickly brought up the photo store and tapped the last photograph. A man in a denim shirt was sitting on a high stool, bent over a National steel guitar. His hair obscured most of his face. Obviously not Jimmy Higgins.

'That's a friend of mine,' Stephanie said. 'Try going back a bit.'

Another shot of the guitarist, this time with his head thrown back, the tendons in his arms and neck standing out. Then a small boy grinning at the camera, arm thrown out in an expansive gesture towards a clutter of ducks milling nearby. 'That's him. We were feeding the ducks.' Her voice wobbled and tears pricked at her eyes. 'He's only little. You have to find him before something really bad happens to him. Please.'

5

Stephanie wasn't sure how the hierarchy ran between the FBI and the TSA, but now Vivian McKuras was on the case, things were definitely improving. Vivian had departed, promising she'd be back once the Amber Alert was in place. In exchange, Stephanie had volunteered to let Lopez pat her down in the approved TSA manner, which was definitely more like a minor sexual assault than a security procedure. Lopez tried hard to maintain her distance and her dignity, but it was a struggle.

'It's not so straightforward when you've got to know the person you're frisking, is it?' Stephanie said, trying not to flinch at the hand probing the inside of her waistband.

'It's for your own safety,' Lopez said. 'You'd be pretty unhappy if you got blown up in mid-air because I didn't do my job.'

'You strike me as far too smart to fall for that bullshit.'

'You want a cup of coffee?' Lopez said, stepping back and peeling off the blue nitrile gloves.

It was ridiculous to feel weepy in response to such a banal kindness. But the longer she was separated from Jimmy, the more vulnerable Stephanie felt. Before Jimmy, she'd never known the responsibility of another person depending totally on her. There had been times in the previous nine months when she'd felt overwhelmed by the weight of it, and times when she'd had sudden flashes of unexpected delight that had made her heart swell. The very burden of the duty made the joy all the more devastating. She would have sworn the sensation was physical. And now he was cast adrift in the unknown, she felt lost. How much worse it must be for him.

It was ironic, for a woman who had never had any desire for motherhood. But she had been so beguiled by her life with Jimmy, in spite of all its complications and difficulties, that it was hard to remember what life had been like without him. Her initial reluctance to take him on now seemed an incomprehensible memory. Helping him to rebuild his happiness in the face of so much loss had become her mission, and every step on his journey had made her rejoice. And all those hard-won steps might count for nothing now he had been ripped out of his reconstructed life.

'Coffee would be lovely,' she said. 'But aren't you afraid I'll take off if you leave?'

Lopez gave her an odd look. 'Why would you do that? Unless there's something you're not telling us about the man who walked off with your kid.' As her hand gripped the door handle, she turned her head and gave Stephanie a pitying look. 'Not to mention there's a guard on the other side of the door. The guy who already tasered you, if you really want to know.'

Talk about mixed messages, Stephanie thought. Lopez was a mash-up of Good Cop and Bad Cop, all in one package. She wondered whether that spilled over into her private life. Stephanie shivered. She'd had enough of relationships with men who hid their truth behind a mask of false benevolence. She thought of the man with the guitar and allowed herself a moment of warmth. She'd broken the habit with him, she was convinced.

But Stephanie was smart enough to know that didn't mean she was free of her history. And right now, the coldest fear in her heart was that Jimmy was the latest victim of her past.

The dregs of the coffee were stone cold by the time Vivian returned, and Stephanie's anxiety had soared to new levels. 'What's happening?' she demanded as soon as the FBI agent entered the room. 'You've been gone nearly an hour.'

'I had to pull together all the available information then speak to the Emergency Alert System people. I'm sorry it took so long, but I needed some information from Immigration before I could go ahead. We're also pulling in all the CCTV footage for the whole terminal. We need to backtrack the kidnapper's movements, to see if we can figure out where he came from. If he was dropped off kerbside or if he came in on public transit.'

'What about forensics? Surely there must be fingerprints or DNA or something?'

Vivian shook her head. 'There's nothing meaningful we can pick up from the security area. Too many people pass through there. And because we didn't realise right away what was going on, other people passed through after the abduction. I'm sorry, but that's a dead end.' She sat down and placed a digital voice recorder on the table between them. 'Now everything's running, it's time for you to fill in a few blanks for me. According to the documents you presented to the Immigration Service, Jimmy's not your actual son? But you're responsible for him?'

'That's right. I'm his legal guardian.'

'So what's the story there?'

Stephanie ran her fingers through her hair, leaving it in a chaotic cloud around her head. 'How long have you got?'

Vivian leaned back in her chair. 'We've got all night. There's nothing more we can do right now except try to figure out who's behind this. Unless this was a random thing, the chances are the reasons for this crime lie in the boy's background. And you're my only source for that. So unless you've got any bright ideas about the kidnapper's identity, you'd better start at the beginning.'

The air conditioning suddenly kicked into life, startling Stephanie. But the shiver that ran through her was nothing to do with the draught of chill air. She couldn't give voice to the suspicion gnawing at the back of her mind. That would give it too much solidity. She was crazy even to entertain the thought. She wrapped her arms around her slender frame and blinked hard. 'The first thing you need to know is who Jimmy is. And to understand that, you need to know who his mother was.'

PART 2

ghost

1

London. Five years and five months earlier

Sometimes random play of the music streaming on my computer seems to conspire against me. So far that morning, I'd had Janis Ian being miserable, Elvis Costello being miserable and The Blue Nile being miserable. Now Mathilde Santing was singing 'Blue Monday', which just about summed up my mood. My last project had been exhausting but it had been three weeks since I'd finished it. I'd been looking forward to spending more time with Pete – that's Pete Matthews, the man I'd been going out with for the past seven months. But the end of my undertaking had marked the start of a new assignment for him, and he'd been working crazy hours in the studio. I'd discovered some time earlier that there was nothing glamorous about being a sound engineer. Just unpredictable hours, late nights and the sour aftertaste of prima donnas with less talent than they believed or their fans knew.

I'll be honest. A little light romance would have suited me perfectly right then. I always become antsy when I'm between jobs. As soon as I've recovered from the exhaustion of meeting my deadline, I start to obsess over where the next contract's going to come from. What if that was it? What if I crashed and burned and didn't get any more work? How would I pay the mortgage? Would I have to sell up, abandon London and go back, God help me, to my parents in their poky little terraced house in Lincoln? I could handle a few days of reading and shopping, a couple of lunches with the girls, a movie matinee or two. But then I started chafing at the bit for a new challenge.

Pete always laughed at me when I talked about my fears. 'Listen to yourself,' he would tease. 'You go from nought to disaster in ten seconds. Look at your track record, girl. They know when they hire you, they get total commitment. You're their bitch from the minute the ink's dry till you've delivered the goods.'

It's not really how I see myself, but I took his point. I've never taken my projects lightly and in this business, people talk to each other about that kind of thing. I try to believe I have a good reputation. But sometimes it's hard to cling to that self-belief. Pete could point to his name on CDs. He had tangible validation. But the whole point of what I do is that I remain invisible. Sometimes I show up on the title page or in the acknowledgements, but mostly my clients want to maintain the illusion that they can string sentences together on the page. So when Pete and I were out with friends, there was almost nothing I could say about my work. It was like being a member of the mafia. Except they have the family around them for support. Me, I was just the insignificant one in the shadows.

I cut Mathilde Santing off mid-bar and retreated to the kitchen. I'd barely set the kettle on to boil when the phone rang. Before I could say anything, the voice on the other end had launched into conversation. 'Stephie, darling, I have such a *fabulous* assignment for you, wait till I tell you. But how *are* you, dearheart?' My agent, Maggie Silver. Irrepressible, irre-sistible and irreplaceable. And always italicised. Nobody does the business like Maggie. Well, nobody does it louder, at least. My spirits lifted at the very sound of her voice.

'Ready for a fabulous assignment,' I said. Even I could hear amusement in my tone.

'Perfect. Because I have *just* the thing. They asked for you. No messing about with beauty parades. The publisher is *convinced* you'll be the perfect fit.'

'Who is it?' Pop star? Actor? Politician? Sportsman? I've done them all. When people do find out what I do for a living they always ask who I've done and what category I like best. The truth is I have no favourites. There isn't much to choose between those who have been kissed by fame. Scrape away the superficial differences and the gilded pretensions are much the same. But revealing that to the public isn't my job. My only role in my subjects' lives is to make them interesting, loveable and desirable. They call me a ghost, but I think of myself as the good fairy, waving a magic wand over their lives to make a narrative that glows with achievement.

'You know *Goldfish Bowl*?'

I couldn't help myself. I groaned. Reality TV. Was this what it had come to? I'd just transformed a former Tory cabinet minister into a dashing, intellectually respectable hero. And my reward was some here-today-gone-tomorrow nobody from a boring market town who would be famous for fifteen minutes. A bestseller for a month, then straight to the remain-der table. 'Christ, Maggie,' was all I could manage.

'No, *listen*, darling, it's not what you think. *Truly*, there's a story to tell. It's Scarlett Higgins. You *must* have heard of her.'

Of course I'd heard of Scarlett Higgins. High Court judges and homeless people had heard of Scarlett Higgins. And even if I say so myself, I've got a knack for keeping my finger on the pulse of the zeitgeist. It's one of the reasons for my success. I totally get popular culture and how to plug into what people want from their celebrities. So yes, I knew the public face of Scarlett Higgins. The Scarlett Harlot, she'd been dubbed by the tabloids. Not because she was particularly promiscuous by tabloid standards. Mostly because it rhymes and they're lazy.

'What's to tell? Hasn't she already spilled everything to the tabloids and the slag mags?'

'She's having a *baby*, darling.'

'That's not news either, Maggie. The pregnancy is what saved her from a public lynching after the debacle of the second series.'

'Her agent has come up with the idea of doing an autobiography in the form of a *letter* to the baby. Where Scarlett reveals the *tragedy* of her own upbringing and the mistakes she's made. She went to Stellar Books, and they *love* the idea. And of course, they want you. Biba *loved* the Maya Gorecka book you did for them, and she's *absolutely convinced* Scarlett will love you.'

Sometimes listening to Maggie is like drowning in italics. 'I don't know,' I said. 'I can't get excited about someone who's already spilled so much about so little.'

'Sweetie, the money's *lovely*. And frankly, there's not a lot else around at the moment. The bottom's dropped out of footballers and WAGs, most of those ghastly rappers and Mercury Prize nominees have *no* crossover value for the mainstream readers, and *nobody's* interested in Tony Blair's sacked cabinet ministers. I've been beating the bushes for you, but at the moment Scarlett Higgins is the *only* show in town. If you want to hang fire, I'm sure something will trundle along in a few months, but I don't like to think of you sitting there twiddling your thumbs. You *know* how twitchy you get, darling.'

Annoyingly, she was right. Inactivity wasn't an option. If Pete had been free, we could have gone away, taken a holiday. But he wouldn't have liked it if I'd gone off without him. And to be honest, neither would I. It had taken me a long time to find a man I wanted to make a commitment to, and now I was with Pete, I didn't relish the solitary trips I'd always enjoyed in the past. These days, I wondered how much of that solo travelling had been me kidding myself. 'All the same,' I said weakly, not wanting to give in too easily.

'It can't hurt to *talk* to the girl,' Maggie said firmly. Wheedling is beneath her. She always prefers assertiveness to supplication. 'Who knows? You may find you *like* her. Stranger things have happened, Stephie. Stranger things *have* happened.'

2

Maggie hung up as soon as she'd extracted a promise that I would at least meet the Scarlett Harlot. She always maintained that one of the secrets of her success as a literary agent was getting out of the door before anyone could change their mind. 'People are generally too *embarrassed* to go back on their word,' she told me early on in our relationship. 'You might like to bear that in mind with the ghosting. Whenever a client produces a revelation *you* think they might regret, make your excuses and *leave*. Don't make a *fuss* about it, just act as if it's no big deal, time for you to trot off home now. *Much* easier that way.'

I've found Maggie's advice surprisingly effective. It hasn't made me immune to her tricks, however. 'Bloody Maggie,' I muttered at the phone as I replaced it. I finished brewing my pot of coffee and settled at the breakfast bar with my iPad. If I was going to sit down with Scarlett Higgins, I needed to be up to speed with her exploits. And since all the reality-show temporary celebs tend to blend into one amorphous blonde, I had to make sure I knew enough about Scarlett to distinguish her deplorable exploits from the others. There would be hell to pay and no forthcoming contract if I asked about the wrong boy-band lover or soap actor. Or even the wrong drug of choice. I couldn't help smiling as I recalled Whitney Houston's notorious interview with Diane Sawyer. All tears and confessional till Sawyer mentioned crack. Then, outraged, the diva bridled and stated sharply, 'First of all, let's get one thing straight. Crack is cheap. I make too much money to ever smoke crack. Let's get that straight. OK? We don't do crack.' OK, lady.

First things first. I wanted to remind myself of the format of *Goldfish Bowl*, the reality show that had catapulted Scarlett from Yorkshire oblivion into the nation's living rooms. Wikipedia would do for that.

Goldfish Bowl is an elimination-based reality TV show developed in the UK and first aired in 2005. It takes place on Foutra, a small Scottish island at the outer limits of the Firth of Forth. The island, about a mile from end to end and half a mile across at its widest point, is uninhabited except by the game contestants. The only building on the island prior to the show was a ruined gun battery dating from WWII. This has been renovated and provides the contestants with their only shelter. For the purposes of the game, rabbits and cows have been introduced to the island. There are also areas of cultivated land where the TV company has planted edible crops, if the contestants can find them.

The twelve contestants are deliberately chosen for their urban backgrounds and their lack of practical skills. They are taken to the island by boat and left to find shelter and food. Part of the entertainment value of the show has come from the haplessness of the city kids cast adrift on the land.

I groaned at the memory of that opening episode. The gob-struck panic of the contestants when they realised that their urban street savvy was completely redundant. Their disgust at the natural world. Their bewilderment at where food actually came from. It had been simultaneously comic and tragic. Their ignorance was toe-curling. They'd probably have made a better fist of being abandoned on Mars.

The first impression Scarlett had made on the viewers had been when she'd encountered one of the three highland cattle on the island. 'Fucking hell,' she'd exclaimed with a mixture of horror and admiration. 'Who knew cows were that big?' Well, Scarlett, most of us, actually.

As I skimmed the rest of the article, more memories crystallised. There had been only six narrow single beds in the barracks. So the first challenge had been to sort out the sleeping arrangements. It had also been the source of the first argument. The lad I'd mentally dubbed Captain Sensible had suggested a sleeping rota; since there were no windows in the underground sleeping quarters, there wouldn't be daylight to keep awake those whose sleeping shifts happened during daylight hours. The others had ridiculed him straight off the bat. The idea of sharing the beds had appealed until they actually tried it and discovered they were so small they kept falling out.

It had been Scarlett who had come up with a solution. Among the supplies they'd been given were bales of hay for the cattle. 'We can sleep on the hay,' she'd said. 'Like in that Christmas carol, 'the little lord Jesus, asleep on the hay'. They always do that in old films when they're on the run.'

'And what are the cows going to eat?' Captain Sensible objected triumphantly.

'Well, they're not going to eat it all at once, are they?' Scarlett said with a flounce of her thick blonde mane. 'And one of us gets the bullet every week. By the time we're running out of hay, there'll be enough beds to go around.' For someone who had seemed dangerously dim, it was a surprisingly convincing argument.

It had been a rare flash of brilliance from Scarlett, however. What had struck me most at the time about Scarlett in that first series of *Goldfish Bowl* had been her willingness to take on whatever task Big Fish – the voice that represented the controlling TV company – set the contestants, coupled with a shrewd eye for the weaknesses of others. Scarlett had been adept at appearing to offer support while actually undermining her fellow contenders. It was hard to believe this was a deliberate tactic because she seemed remarkably stupid most of the time. Her first attempt at putting together the contestants' shopping list within a budget demonstrated the literacy and numeracy of a six-year-old. Her grasp of current affairs was pitiful; she was convinced that Prime Minister Tony Blair was the son of dancer Lionel Blair, and that Bill Clinton was still President of the United States. ('Well, why do they call him President Clinton if he's not the president, then?') She demonstrated weepy sentimentality over children, kittens and puppies, while revealing terrifying ignorance about the care of any of them. She was unpopular with her fellow contestants in the Bowl because of her tendency to speak her mind. But the public grew to like her because she had the knack of hitting the nail on the head and saying what the viewers were thinking. They admired her brass neck. And she made people laugh, which is always a winner on reality shows.

She was overweight and nobody's idea of pretty, but she made the most of herself. She took the same care with her hair and make-up whether she was about to go in search of carrots to dig up or talk to Big Fish in the Aquarium – the glass-sided room at the heart of the complex where contestants were summoned for progress reports, debriefs and instructions.

The punters also gradually came to admire her refusal to give up. When the contestants were low on food, she made a virtue of the opportunity for weight loss. When Captain Sensible dropped their only fishing rod in the sea during the

'Larder of the Ocean' challenge, she beachcombed till she found a substitute. Even though she let her guard slip often enough to reveal herself as a foul-mouthed bigot, people warmed to Scarlett. She was nominated for elimination by her fellow contestants a record six times. Every time, the public chose to keep her and ditch the other candidate.

But they didn't quite love her enough. In the final vote of the series, she lost out to Darrell O'Donohue, an amiable lump of beefcake from Belfast. I reckon he won because there was absolutely nothing to object to about Darrell. He was good-looking, kind and hard-working. He appeared to have no strong views on any subject. And he'd made a fine job of Shania Twain's 'Man! I Feel Like a Woman!' in the karaoke challenge. Still, I'd have killed him within the hour if I'd been forced to spend an evening in his company. After the show was over, he had his five minutes of fame, then disappeared back to Northern Ireland, happy to be a C-list fish in a small pond.

Despite being the beaten finalist, it was Scarlett who went on to make the most of her success. I wanted to refresh my memory of her trajectory of fame, so I moved to Scarlett's own Wikipedia entry. As I read, I remembered how ballsy she'd seemed. Shedding her past in the sink estates of south Leeds, she'd headed straight for the celebrity circuit. She hooked up with an agent and within days she'd become a staple of the red-tops and the slag mags that celebrated drunken women falling into limos or gutters at three in the morning. Slimmed down and burnished by stylists, Scarlett seemed to become almost beautiful and it wasn't long before she'd landed a boyfriend with a foot on the celebrity ladder.

Scarlett hadn't quite built up enough superstar Brownie points to snag a Premier League footballer, but she managed the next best thing. Reno Jacuba was a striker with a Champion-ship side struggling in mid-table. He'd suffered from a couple of allegations of nasty sexual assaults, he shared the same agent as Scarlett and there was benefit to both of them in a link-up. So, linked they were – for a couple of magazine cycles. Once he was rehabilitated and her stock had risen a little, he ditched her. Or she ditched him, depending on which account you bought into.

Next up was a second division gangsta rapper whose principal claim to fame had been mooning on the MOBO red carpet. A few short months of nauseating lurve were followed by an acrimonious bust-up. Three nightclub fights ended on the front pages of the tabloids and he was history.

And then along came Joshu. A British Asian DJ, titan of the turntables, a strutting bantam of a boy who thought every word that dripped from his mouth was golden. King of the clubs, or so he thought. He never tired of publicly telling Scarlett she should be grateful to have him because he could have any woman he wanted. It was a claim he regularly put to the test. They rowed about it in nightclubs, in bars and in restaurants. They rowed about it on TV chat shows, in press interviews and in the street. The trouble was, it seemed the silly girl was in love with the idiot boy. She kept on coming back for more. Just reading about it made me want to shake some sense into her.

Having very public love affairs wasn't the only thing that Scarlett was good at. A bright TV producer had understood that she had the gift of communicating with a particular demographic. The chattering classes might sneer, all the papers from the *Daily Mail* upwards might scoff, but when it came to reaching out to empty-headed young women with enough disposable income to be interesting to advertisers, Scarlett had an unerring instinct. It seemed she knew when to be raunchy, when to be vulnerable, when to be sexy and when to be bloody rude. And because she was pictured out on the lash at least twice a week, her audience really got that she was one of them.

Scarlett was living proof of the dream for those young women. She validated their shallow ambition. They saw her hitting the high life, in spite of her terrible childhood, her poor education, her limited looks, and it helped them believe it could happen to them. And that was what got them through the shitty days.

So they devoured her late-night satellite-channel show. The programme charted her life. Scarlett provided beauty tips, fashion guidance and a window on a world slathered in product placement. There was talk of a signature fragrance, a line of clothes in a downmarket high street chain, a monthly magazine column. Thank God that didn't come off. I shuddered at the thought of the poor subeditor charged with rendering Scarlett's simplistic yet totally fucked-up world view into a form that would please the readers and satisfy the lawyers.

Still, I had to admit she'd been doing really well for herself, had Scarlett. Well, by her lights, anyway. She was living in a hideous hacienda-style villa on the edge of Epping Forest that had been built originally for some minor East End gangster, according to *Yes!* magazine. It looked like the house that taste forgot, with its mish-mash of styles and its job-lot furnishings. She'd bought a house for her mum and her sister, but she'd had the good sense to keep them firmly offstage, up north in Leeds. Not much detail had escaped about Scarlett's family. Which, in my experience, translated as 'scum'. From my perspective, that was a good thing. It promised piquancy at the very least. Skeletons clattering out of closets like flamenco dancers on speed at best.

So, there was Scarlett, bumping along nicely, comfortably above the bottom of the barrel of fame. When it came to casting the second season of *Goldfish Bowl*, the producers hit on the bright idea of bringing back two of the participants from the first series. They dressed it up as giving the contestants more of a chance because they'd have a couple of team members

who'd been through the experience before and would know
how to milk a cow and skin a rabbit. I figured it was more of
an insurance policy. Viewers loved them the first time so
they'd be more likely to tune in for a second series.

And of course, Scarlett was the first port of call. To tell you
the truth, I hadn't been paying much attention at the time –
I'd been in the final throes of my top Tory's tale, trying to
apply positive spin to some of his less attractive achievements.
And there were plenty of those to work with.

It had all gone well to begin with, but soon the contestants
realised that having previous contenders maybe wasn't such a
brilliant idea. There was discontent in the ranks at what they
felt was an unfair advantage. Until they realised that some of
the things Scarlett and Darrell thought they knew – such as
the locations of food sources – were no longer the case. And
then the worms turned, taking the piss out of the so-called
Island Experts.

It didn't take a psychologist to work out that the one thing
Scarlett couldn't deal with was having the piss taken out of
her. She'd learned the hard way that she was generally considered to be ignorant and stupid. Even the ignorant and
stupid can read a tabloid headline, after all. But she hated
being condescended to, and in her eyes, when anyone mocked
her, they were asking for trouble. And she was the one to
hand it out.

Things got fractious fast. They came to a head one evening
on the second week. The islanders had earned a case of wine,
thanks in part to Scarlett's willingness to immerse herself in
the freezing Firth of Forth to find crab pots hidden on the sea
bed just offshore. They attacked the wine with gusto over
dinner, and inhibitions began to vanish. Danny Williams, who
called himself a landscape gardener but was actually a labourer
for a garden design firm, started holding forth about why
Scarlett had got the location of the vegetable beds so wrong.

He was smart enough to make his sarcasm cut her, and she wasn't in the mood to take it.

'Fuck off back to bongo bongo land, you fat black arse-bandit,' she'd screamed at him. Cha-ching. It's hard to imagine a line that could cause more offence on prime-time TV. The media lit up like the main drag in Vegas. Jackpot time. And of course, somebody's tame monkey got up in the House of Commons and did the whole 'a nation is outraged' number. Scarlett's goose was well and truly cooked.

Goldfish Bowl pretended they were just as outraged as the country's moral guardians and that night Scarlett was summoned to the Aquarium. Big Fish did the whole 'more in sorrow than in anger' routine and made her apologise to Danny, the rest of the contestants, the country at large and, really, the entire solar system. He made it sound like she could win a reprieve by grovelling enough, but of course the viewers knew it was nothing but a ritual humiliation. Scarlett was going and everybody knew it except her.

I can still remember the shocked disbelief on her face when, after she'd shed her tears and abased herself, Big Fish told her to pack her bag and make her way down to the dock. Everything went on hold for a long moment. Then Scarlett jumped to her feet and stabbed her finger at the camera. 'You bastard,' she said. 'You were never going to let me stay, were you? Well, here's the truth. I'm not fucking sorry. Not one fucking bit. So stick that up your arse and spin on it.'

I have to admit, right then it was hard not to admire Scarlett.

3

As far as the watching world was concerned, that was it. Scarlett was whisked away from Foutra in shame. The press camped outside the hacienda were disappointed that she didn't turn up there next day. Nobody seemed to know where she'd gone. 'Where is the bitch?' the headlines screamed for a couple of days, then the circus moved on.

But Scarlett wasn't destined to stay out of the limelight for long. A week after her ignominy, readers of the *Sun* were greeted with a world exclusive. '"I'm pregnant," Scarlett reveals.' We were informed that disgraced reality TV star Scarlett Higgins had been so deranged by the hormones of pregnancy that she'd spoken words that never would have passed her lips in normal circumstances.

To his credit, like any good ghost, the journalist had put some fine sentiments in Scarlett's mouth. She was apparently devastated at the pain and embarrassment she'd caused Danny; the makers of *Goldfish Bowl*; her partner Joshu ('who is a person of colour too'); her unborn child; and every minority citizen of these islands. What she'd said was the opposite of everything she believed. She loved gay people and black people and especially gay black people (not that she could actually name one ...). Her own baby would be mixed race, she pointed out. And she was so ashamed that one day her child would discover her disgraceful past.

But the hormones ... Everybody knew pregnancy turned women into mental cases. Poor Scarlett hadn't realised she was pregnant, so what had happened had been even more bewildering to her. If she'd known she was pregnant, not a drop of alcohol would have passed her lips. Plus, everybody also knew that, when you were pregnant, you got drunk a lot more easily. So it was the wine too, not just the hormones.

And suddenly, Scarlett was the favourite daughter of a sizeable chunk of the British population again. They loved her for her fallibility. What had happened to her could have happened to any woman. The blokes totally got it, because they'd experienced women going off their chops about all sorts while they were pregnant. The women totally got it, because who hadn't had a guilt-inducing drink or smoked themselves silly before they knew they were expecting? The tabloids loved it because it gave them an excuse to print endless features about women going off the rails because of their hormones. Lurid tales of the violence, strange cravings and temper tantrums of pregnant women filled pages of magazines and newspapers. It almost began to feel as if pregnancy was synonymous with psychosis.

And now I was being dragged into the final step on the road to Scarlett's rehabilitation. The perfectly crafted final piece of the jigsaw would be her three-hundred page letter to her unborn child, a sanded-down and varnished version of her autobiography to resonate with her public and make sure the love-fest continued. I had a sneaking suspicion it would be a big ask. But I've never shied away from a professional challenge.

Of course, Maggie knew that.

*

The more dubious the grounds for an individual's celebrity, the more they need to be in control every step of the way. The ones who have genuinely achieved something or overcome true adversity are always happy to go along with my suggestions on how we manage the process. They understand that I'm the expert here, that experience has taught me the best way to do this. But when I'm dealing with the likes of Scarlett, the ones who are famous only for being famous, they're always full of demands thinly disguised as suggestions.

The first of what I knew would be many skirmishes came over the venue for the initial meeting where Scarlett would decide whether she liked me as much as her agent and publisher did. She wanted us to take a suite in a Mayfair hotel. I wanted to go to her place. We both had our reasons. She wanted a symbol of how important she was. I wanted the scent and taste of her. And Maggie never wants to spend an unnecessary penny, because everything that gets lavished on the client up front has to be paid for somewhere down the line. There is no such thing as a free publisher's lunch.

You don't get anywhere as a ghost by stamping your feet and insisting on doing things your way. You have to sidle past their defences and make them think it's all their idea. You know you've succeeded when you see them on daytime telly earnestly explaining to the host how they got up every morning two hours before the kids so they could find some peace to do their writing. By that stage, they really believe they did it themselves. That you were only there to put in the commas and check the spelling.

So Maggie called George, Scarlett's agent, and they did their ritual dance. Maggie's argument was that hotels leaked like sieves. That as soon as Scarlett showed her face in a five-star hotel, one of the staff would be on the phone to the press and they'd be full of Scarlett kiss'n'tell spoilers. I sat on the sofa in her office, admiring her greasing her way round Gorgeous

George, a notoriously difficult man to flatter or cajole. But as I'd seen before, even he was no match for Maggie. 'Darling,' she said. 'Let's *face* it. Once they find out Stephie's doing the book, she'll be the focus for *every* devious *hack* in town. They'll be going through her *bins*, chatting up her *cleaner*, tapping her *phone* for all I know. *Anything* to get the inside track.'

She stuck her tongue out at me then rolled her eyes and reached for the electronic cigarette she'd adopted since she'd given up smoking ahead of the workplace ban. She dragged on the tube and made a face. 'New flavour,' she muttered, hand over the phone mouthpiece. '*Supposed* to be Camels. More like camel *dung*.' A quick, artificial smile flashed across her face. 'Well, of *course*, Georgie. I'm *aware* that the press have been staking out Scarlett's house. But now the *Sun's* broken the story, they'll move on. In a day or two, it'll be business as usual. And of *course*, I'll make *sure* the car has blacked-out windows so any of the *parasites* who are still hanging around won't know it's Stephie.' There was more of the same. I tuned it out, confident of the outcome.

I was right. Two days later, a Mercedes with tinted windows whisked us past a couple of paparazzi. They'd been so bored for so long they barely got their cameras to their faces by the time we passed through the electric gates and up the herring-bone brick drive to the hacienda. One of the triple garages was standing open, ready for us to drive in. 'It was less hassle when I was doing a Spice Girl,' I said.

'You'll be fine,' Maggie said briskly as the rolling shutter descended behind us.

'It's not me I'm worried about.' It was always like this before the start of a new job. My stomach chewing itself into knots, convinced that this time I would be exposed for the fraud I was.

Pete had hardly been reassuring the night before. 'Why are you getting so worked up?' he'd said. 'She's just some scummy bimbo. I've had dogs with more about them than her. If somebody like that is capable of putting you on the back foot, maybe you should think about jacking it in.'

'Jacking it in? What would I do then?'

His eyebrows flickered. I loved his eyebrows; so straight and fine, not thick and coarse like most men's. I always thought they were surprisingly expressive. Beneath them, his brown eyes looked like they were weighing me up. I felt uncomfortable, as if I were being scrutinised and found wanting. 'You could be here when I get home,' he said. It was hard to tell from his voice whether he was serious.

'You want this to be your home?' We hadn't actually talked about living together before. Not in so many words.

'I'd like you to be waiting for me when I get back from work,' he said carefully, his face giving nothing away.

'When you're in the middle of something, I never see you,' I said. 'You work such weird hours, I never know when to call you. If I was supposed to be here when you get back from work, I'd never be able to leave the house, never mind do my job.' I tried to keep my voice light and teasing but the anxiety was running through me like a wire.

Pete shrugged. 'At least then I'd never be wondering where you've got to.' And then he turned and kissed me, which led straight to the sort of distraction that completely removed the conversation from the front of my mind. But now it was back again, feeding the niggle of apprehension about my encounter with Scarlett. Looking back, I realise how undermining Pete could be. Always was, really. But back then, I couldn't see it. Just felt the effects. So when Maggie and I got out of the car, my confidence wasn't at its peak.

We entered the hacienda through the kitchen. I expected brushed steel and granite, in keeping with the age and style of the house, but the first incongruity of the day was the cream and pine of a Cotswold cottage kitchen, complete with the enamelled range cooker. Behind closed doors, there would be a fridge, freezer and microwave. But you'd never guess which ones. Everything was spotless, immaculately arranged like the display in a kitchen showroom. The room smelled of citrus and herbs from one of those sprays that cost a small fortune in South Molton Street. 'Not a cook, then,' Maggie said drily.

A skinny young woman in jeans, high-heeled boots and a skinny-rib sweater clattered in through the door at the far end of the kitchen. 'Stephanie?' she said, looking at Maggie.

'I'm Stephanie,' I said. 'This is Maggie, my agent.'

Flustered, she nodded frantically. 'I'm Carla. I'm with George's agency.'

'Ah. New girl, eh?' Maggie smiled. 'You'll soon pick it up.'

Carla gave a frightened rabbit smile. 'Scarlett and George are waiting for you in the den.' She led us down a wide hallway that opened into a white cube with a sunken seating area arranged round a fire pit where gas-fuelled flames flickered. The room fragrance here was more floral but just as fake.

Scarlett and her agent were lounging on white leather sofas with cow-hide throws. The walls featured decorative displays of longhorn skulls, interspersed with sub-O'Keeffe Western landscapes. A long way sub. It felt much more Essex than Texas. If I'd been Scarlett, I'd have stripped it right out. All it did was draw attention from her, and that's never what minor celebrities are aiming for.

But Scarlett was what I was interested in, so I dragged my gaze from the décor to her. Her hair had been expertly coloured, highlights and lowlights coming together to produce a natural-seeming cascade of dark-blonde hair. To my surprise, she wasn't slathered in make-up – just a slash of dark-red lipstick and a coat of mascara to emphasise the blue of her eyes. The spray tan, which I assumed was top-to-toe, filled in the rest. She was wearing a red muscle T-shirt that showed off full breasts and the rise of her pregnant belly. Her legs were covered in loose grey sweatpants. Her feet were bare, but her toenails were painted the same shade as her lipstick. She didn't look like a reality TV show slapper. From somewhere, Scarlett had dredged up a whiff of sophistication.

George struggled to his feet as soon as we walked in, but Scarlett didn't budge, making us come to her. George ran through the introductions with his usual urbanity. Scarlett slipped warm, dry fingers into my hand and withdrew them almost as quickly. She didn't say anything, just tipping her head and squeezing out a meaningless smile. I think I'm pretty good at pulling something useful from first impressions, but with Scarlett, I got nothing to add to what I'd already gleaned from my research. I was intrigued, and that was enough to stifle my anxiety. Never mind the cat, curiosity's always killed my collywobbles.

'So, what we're here for is to iron out the fine print of our agreement,' George said once we were all settled in the enveloping sofas and Carla had been dispatched to produce coffee.

'Well, not quite, Georgie boy,' Scarlett said, the hard drawl of her Leeds accent noticeable even in those few words. 'The first thing we're here for is to see if I want to work with Stephanie. 'Cos if we don't hit it off, there's not gonna be no agreement.' She was much more assertive than I'd expected.

It was George's turn for the meaningless smile. 'Naturally, my dear. Stephanie, perhaps you could outline your working methods for Scarlett's benefit?'

'I've got a better idea,' Scarlett said. 'Me and Steph here, we need to get to know each other without you two breathing down our necks. Georgie, you and Maggie might as well go back to London and sort yourselves out there. I'll take care of Steph.' She stood up and made a shooing motion with her hands. 'Go on. Bugger off, the pair of you.' She turned to me and jerked her head towards the far end of the room. 'Come on. Let's get our kit off and get to know each other.' And off she walked, as if there was no need for further discussion.

4

It turned out a lot less scary than it sounded. Scarlett had a swimming pool. Well, of course she did. And a Jacuzzi, and a sauna and a gym. What every well-dressed Essex hacienda is wearing. I followed her to the back of the house and through a double door that acted as an airlock for the smell of pool chemicals. In a changing room heavily fragranced with cedar and vanilla, Scarlett flung open a locker to reveal a selection of identical black one-piece swimsuits on hangers. 'There's a full set of sizes from ten to twenty,' she said. 'Help yourself.'

With the complete lack of self-consciousness that comes from having been drunk and naked on the nation's TV screens, she stripped off and slipped into a turquoise and blue suit. She looked surprisingly toned and fit, which made the gentle swell of her four-month pregnancy seem incongruous. I'd been right about the all-over spray tan, though.

I didn't share Scarlett's ease at public nakedness so I stepped into a curtained cubicle to undress. By the time I emerged, she was ploughing up and down the ten-metre pool in a ragged but effective crawl. I sat on the edge and dangled my legs in the water. I reckoned it wouldn't hurt to give Scarlett the initiative and see where it took us. There would come a point where I would need to draw my own lines. If she couldn't stick to that, it was as well to find out now, while I could still walk away.

I could see her checking me out every time she headed back down towards me. I think she expected me to crack and slide into the water. To go head to head with her in an attempt to show who was boss. But I wasn't playing that particular game. After a dozen lengths, she'd had enough. She glided to a halt alongside me and looked up. The swim had sleeked her hair back against her head but her waterproof mascara was still holding fast. Her lips were pulled back against her teeth as she caught her breath, and I could see the dental work that had transformed her smile after that first series in the *Goldfish Bowl*. Sometimes the cosmetic dentistry goes too far, giving people a glow-in-the-dark smile never found in nature. But Scarlett's dentist had done a good job. If you'd never seen the 'before', you wouldn't have thought it was an 'after'. Just the smile of someone blessed with good dental genes.

'D'you not swim, then?' she asked. Straightforward curiosity or aggression; I could have read her tone either way.

It was time to give her a little bit of me. 'I like swimming. But I don't like pools much. I prefer the sea. So I don't swim very often because it's too bloody cold in this country.'

She folded her forearms on the edge of the pool and looked up at me with a grin. 'Fair enough. What happened to your leg? It's not like you limp or owt. I didn't know there was anything wrong with you till you took your trousers off.'

I looked down at the long scar that runs from my left knee almost to my ankle. 'I was in a car crash. A drunk drove into my friend's car. We hit a tree and my leg got trapped by the car door. I've got a metal plate and a handful of screws holding my leg together. They did a good job and I did what the physio told me, and that's why I don't have a limp.'

'That must have hurt like a bitch,' Scarlett said. She pushed herself out of the water and scrambled to her feet.

'It did. But it doesn't now. Only when I do too much walking. Then it aches a bit.' I lifted my legs out of the water and stood up. I was a good three inches taller than her; I could see the roots of her hair would soon need touching up. 'Would you like me to tell you how I go about helping people tell their story?'

Scarlett dragged her hair back from her face and gave a little snort of laughter. 'You never call a spade a spade, you lot.'

'What lot?'

'Journalists. Writers. Interviewers. All you lot that take me and twist me into summat for your readers to feed off of.'

'Is that what you think this is all about? Because if that's what you genuinely believe, there's not much point in us carrying on this conversation.' I walked across to a table that held a stack of clean towels and picked one up.

'What are you here for then?' Scarlett challenged me. 'Come on, get in the Jacuzzi and tell me there.' Again, there was no backward glance. I wasn't ready to give up on her yet, so I followed.

She fiddled with the controls and the deep pool began to rumble and bubble. I don't like Jacuzzis much. They're too hot for my taste. I always come out feeling over-heated and sweaty and in need of a shower. But this was work, so I simply settled myself down at right angles to her. People argue less that way than when they sit opposite each other. I gave her the full-on reassuring smile. 'What you've done is not ordinary,' I began. It's a shtick I've honed over the years. 'That means you're not ordinary any more either. Other people, the ordinary ones, they're desperate to know your story. They want to find out how you became extraordinary. They want to share your secret. My job is to help you to tell them. It's simple.'

She frowns. 'How is that different from all them journalists that wrote all that crap about me when I fucked up in the *Goldfish Bowl*? And the other times, when I've said one thing and it's come out totally different?'

'Because I'm not working for a newspaper or a magazine. I'm working for you and for your publisher.'

'But you want to sell books. The more books you sell, the more money you make. So it stands to reason you'll do whatever it takes to sell the most books.' There was a stubborn set to Scarlett's mouth, coupled with an uncertainty in her eyes. I'd seen it before with people who had grown up with good reasons not to trust.

'If we do this, we make a deal, Scarlett.' It was the first time I'd used her name and yes, it was calculated. The same way you stroke a strange dog you think might be getting used to you. 'As far as I'm concerned, the best story isn't necessarily the one with the most shocking revelations. It's the one that speaks loudest to the readers. What I promise you is that I will tell your story the way you want your story to be told. If you tell me something that I think you would come to regret, I will leave it out and I'll tell you why. I won't tell your publisher though. Because you're right. If I do, they will want to keep it in the book for the sake of making a few extra grand selling it to the *Daily Mail*.'

'Why would you do that? I don't believe this bleeding heart shit about protecting me from myself. Why would you leave out the really juicy bits? Are you soft, or what?'

It was another of those surprising flashes of intelligence. Or maybe it was just a hard-won shrewdness born of being exploited once too often in the past. I shook my head, laughing. 'I'm the opposite of soft, Scarlett. I do it for one very good reason and it's called the second bite of the cherry. I've helped a lot of extraordinary people bring their story to an audience. And I've learned that those people mostly don't go back to being ordinary. They carry on doing stuff that makes amazing stories. Now, if I write your story with my eye on how much I can score off you, it's not going to be me you talk to next time, is it?'

There's no motive clearer to a minor celebrity than self-interest. Scarlett perked up. 'So if you don't fuck me over, you can come back for more when I get to be even more famous?'

'That's right. When I look at you, Scarlett, I don't just see the story you're going to lay out for your baby to read when they're old enough. I can see you've come a long way. And I believe you've still got a long way to go. And I want to be the person who tells all those stories still to come. That's my vested interest in doing the right thing by you.'

She gave me a grudging nod. 'That makes sense. I couldn't figure out why you would be on my side. But I get it now. You don't just want my story because it'll make us all a load of dosh now. You think I can be a cash cow down the line.'

Brutal, but not so different from the way Maggie would have put it. 'I think of it more as a long-term partnership,' I said wryly.

'I want to see what you write before it's turned into a book.' Scarlett wiped the sweat from her upper lip with the back of her hand.

'Of course you do. How else will you know I'm not putting the shaft in? You'll be the first person who reads it. You get it before my agent, before your agent, before the publisher. After you've read it, we sit down together and go through anything you're not happy with. But there shouldn't be any problem. Because this is your story, after all. I'm just the person who knocks the sentences into shape and gets the spelling sorted.' It never ceases to amaze me how my subjects always swallow this. They're completely comfortable with the idea that there's no skill in what I do. They genuinely believe all I'm there for is getting the commas in the right place. Because I'm such a good ventriloquist, what they hear is their own voice. They have no idea how much craft has gone into shaping what are often little more than inchoate ramblings.

Scarlett had taken the bait, though. And that was the main thing. 'Sound as a pound,' she said. 'I like you, Steph. You talk sense. You don't try and blind me with science. So how do we go about this?'

'You talk, I tape. I'm told you want this to be in the form of a letter to your unborn baby? Is that what you've got in mind?'

Scarlett's chin jutted up. 'There's nothing wrong with that, is there?'

It's interesting to me that it's always the women I write about who see criticism in the most straightforward of questions. The men – even the ones who are abuse survivors – are seldom assailed by any flicker of self-doubt. Deep down, they believe they have a right to be heard. Even when they've been mired in sexual and financial scandal, like another politician I did a few years ago, they're still convinced that their story should be told exactly as they perceive it.

'Quite the opposite. I think it's a good idea. It always helps to have a theme that pulls the book together. How did you see it taking shape?'

'I know it sounds back-to-front, but I want to start where I am now, pregnant and getting over being in disgrace. But how my baby's saved me from myself. About Joshu and how loving him's changed everything. And then go back to the beginning and talk about my crappy childhood and my shitty family and how I got out alive.' Scarlett dipped her head and gave me the up-and-under look that Princess Diana added to the armoury of generations of women. 'Without sounding like a twat, obviously.'

I gave her a twist of a smile. 'I think we can just about manage that. It would be good if I could talk to Joshu too.'

She looked uncertain. 'I suppose. He's not one for sitting around talking, Joshu.'

'It wouldn't have to be a long chat. Does he actually live here with you?'

Now Scarlett was positively shifty. 'He's supposed to. Only, when he's DJing club nights and shit, it gets late and he crashes with his mates in town instead. So sometimes he's here and sometimes he's not. I used to go out on the town with him, but obviously now I'm pregnant I can't be doing that kind of shit. Not with the paps round every bloody corner.'

I do try not to be judgemental. Mostly because it makes the job easier. But sometimes there's a little voice at the back of my head that gibbers things like, 'Never mind the paparazzi, what about the fucking baby?' And I struggle to keep my face on straight and my voice even. 'That's fine. I'm sure he'll turn up sometime when we're doing the interviews and I can slot in a chat with him. And if that doesn't work out, we'll set something up.'

'So we do this talk and tape here, do we?'

'Not actually in the Jacuzzi. We need to be somewhere quiet. But yes, here at your place would be the easiest.'

The wary look was back. 'Would you stay here, like?'

'No, I'd go home at the end of the day. Back to London.'

She nodded. 'Yeah, you wouldn't want to be round here when Joshu starts playing his music. Some nights, bands come back here and all sorts.' Her mouth curled in an indulgent sneer. 'You wouldn't like the kind of stuff they get up to, a nice respectable lady like you.'

I laughed. 'I've not been called a lady for a very long time. Or respectable, come to that.'

Scarlett's eyes clouded over. 'Compared to my life, chuck, you're Mother Teresa. And while we're on the subject, I don't want you shooting up to Leeds for a cosy little chat with my mam and my sister. You keep them well the fuck out of it. I'll tell you all you need to know about them and then you'll understand why I don't want you listening to their poisonous crap. We clear on that?'

I eased myself up till I was sitting on the lip of the Jacuzzi. 'You're the boss. But it would make good reading if we could meet up with somebody who does know you from those early days. Just to make the comparison more powerful.'

Scarlett scowled. 'I'll have a think. Trouble is, they're all drunken slags and junkie wankers. You wouldn't want to be in the same room.'

'I'm sure you can come up with—'

'What have we here?' An amused voice cut across mine. 'Scarlett, my girl, my woman, what's on your mind? You bringing your girlfriends round to have fun with us now? You got a nice little threesome in mind?'

I swung round to see a young Asian man in familiar uniform – baseball cap set at an angle, athletic letter jacket two sizes too big shrugged on over a dark polo shirt, low-slung baggy trousers falling in folds on over-sized trainers.

But it wasn't the outfit that caught my attention. It was the gleaming chrome handgun cradled in his hands.

5

Stephanie stopped in her tracks, clearly reliving the shock of that moment. As a trained FBI operative, Vivian McKuras had faced danger and loaded guns and taken them in her adrenalin-fuelled stride, but even she was taken aback by Stephanie's revelation. Till then, the woman's story had seemed a pedestrian tale of low-level fame gilded with the rosy glow of Vivian's idea of British life mainly garnered from Mystery Theatre. But it had been starkly transformed by the introduction of a big shiny handgun.

'He was toting a gun?' She wanted to be clear about this before she put out an APB on this British DJ.

'With the emphasis very much on toting,' Stephanie said. 'The thing about Joshu is that he was always a complete tosser.' Seeing Vivian's frown, she clarified. 'A wanker. A jerk-off. All mouth and trousers.'

'Even so. He was carrying a gun the first time you met him. That must have been pretty scary. As I understand it, that's not exactly commonplace in the UK.'

Stephanie stared at a patch of wall over Vivian's shoulder. 'There was a moment when I couldn't make sense of what I was looking at. This shiny thing in his hands. He was almost cradling it. Then it dawned on me that it was an actual gun. And yes, I was scared. And yes, I showed it. And he just stood there giggling.' She shook her head and dragged her eyes down to meet Vivian's. 'He was high, of course. Which made it considerably scarier.'

'What did Scarlett do?'

'She rolled her eyes and said, "For fuck's sake, I told you not to walk around with that. Some five-oh is gonna see that and take you down." Then she told me to chillax because it was only a replica. Which, as it turned out, was very Joshu.' She sighed. 'He was always on the fringe of the action. Never a serious player. He knew the big-time dealers and gangstas, charmed his way into their circle and skated close to the edge, but he wasn't one of them. And assuming he was in a position to do anything about his son, this business with Jimmy would be nothing to do with him. Scarlett and Joshu were married and divorced before the kid was a year old.'

'That doesn't change the fact that Joshu is his father. These emotions run deep. They've got a way of coming back at you. If it's not him, it could be a family member acting on his behalf or on their own initiative.' Vivian reached for her computer and started tapping the keys.

'You're not getting it. Jimmy doesn't exist for the Patels. Joshu's family hated Scarlett. They blamed her for everything that went wrong for their precious son. They didn't come to the wedding, they never came to the house and Scarlett never crossed their front door. As far as I'm aware, they've never set eyes on their grandson outside the pages of a tabloid.'

Vivian shook her head. 'All the same. It's the strongest lead you've given me so far. What's his surname, this Joshu?'

'It's Patel. But—'

'Joshu Patel.'

'Actually, it's Jishnu, that's his given name. He left that behind when he became a DJ.'

'OK. Jishnu Patel, then. Do you have an address for him? Date of birth? Family details? Anything that would help us track him down?'

'I can tell you exactly where Joshu is right now,' Stephanie said wearily. 'Believe me, this is nothing to do with him.'

6

When I think back to that first encounter with Joshu, I can't help seeing the final act foreshadowed in every aspect. That need always to look like a big man. The way he filled the gap between his reality and his fantasy with drugs. His failure ever to step up to the plate and be a man.

But I'm running ahead of myself. Once I'd realised Scarlett was telling the truth and I didn't need to be scared witless of the pillock with the pistol, I could see Joshu for what he was. As far as I was concerned, right then he was nothing more than an irritating distraction. I'd started to build a rapport with Scarlett then he'd slouched in and broken the mood. I knew I couldn't creep any further into Scarlett's confidence with him there. It was obvious even in those few moments. She only had eyes for him and he only had eyes for himself. My sole function in this triangle was to big Joshu up, and I didn't need to bother with that just yet. I wanted to hear from him, but not before I had a clearer idea of how he might be useful to making Scarlett's story work. The only thing I could do now was lay down a timetable.

'Let's sort out when we can meet,' I said, setting off for the changing room. Scarlett followed and so, disconcertingly, did Joshu. I closed the curtain on the cubicle firmly and tried to ignore his attempts to turn the situation into a sexual encounter. 'Not now, babe,' Scarlett kept saying amid the scuffles and moans.

When I emerged he had her against the wall, his hand between her legs. 'Have you got your diary handy?' I said briskly.

He cast a dirty look over his shoulder. 'Listen to you. "Have you got your diary handy?"'

'You need to work on your impressions, innit,' I said, dropping into his patois.

Scarlett giggled and ducked out from under his arm. 'I got it in the kitchen,' she said, grabbing a luxurious towelling robe from a hook on the wall as she passed Joshu, flirting a little wave at him. 'Why don't you go upstairs? I'll be there in a minute.'

Joshu's scowl lifted and he slouched after her, turning back to target me with a self-satisfied sneer. As I followed Scarlett down the hall, he peeled off and disappeared up a shallow flight of stairs.

We settled on three blocks of three days' interviewing time, built around Scarlett's schedule of public appearances, product promotions and meetings with TV executives and brand managers. She'd certainly learned how to turn racism and homophobia to her advantage.

'Before we meet again, there's one thing I need you to think about,' I said.

'What's that, then?'

'How do you want to be presented? What do you want them to think of you? What impression of you should they take away? You need to be clear about that before we start, so I can focus the direction of our conversations.'

'You mean, like, I want them to think I'm an ordinary Northern lass? Or, like, I'm lucky and it could be them next? That sort of thing?'

I nodded. 'Yes. Because although I'm just presenting what you tell me, the way I present it can make a huge difference. In a way, I have to think of you like a character in a book. So I need to make the feel of the book consistent. As if it was a novel. That's why I need to know how you want the world to feel about you after they've read it.'

She grinned. 'You're a very smart lady, Stephanie. What are we going to call this book, then?'

We. I liked that. In spite of Joshu, we'd made real progress. Scarlett considered me on her side, in her camp. That was half the battle. 'Did you have any ideas?'

I wasn't expecting much. 'What about "Scarlett: My Story",' she said. I'd been right.

Time for a touch of tact and diplomacy. 'Well, it's not going to breach the Trade Descriptions Act. But I think we can do a bit better than that. "Scarlett: My Story" will attract your fans. No doubt about it. But I want to get people picking it up who really don't know much about you. So we need to intrigue them. I was thinking, maybe something like "Fishing for Gold"? How does that sound?'

She looked dubious. 'But how will they know it's about me?'

I grinned. 'Your face'll be all over the cover, love. There won't be any room for doubt whose story it is.'

Scarlett still wasn't convinced. 'I'm gonna have to sleep on it.'

'No problem. So, are we solid, you and me? You think you can stand having me around long enough to get this done? There's no going back once we've started, you know. We'll be tied by a contract.'

'I think so.' She laid a hand over her stomach, as if she was swearing on her baby's life, then cocked her head to one side. 'You won't let me down, will you, Steph?'

If I'd had any inkling of what I was committing myself to, I would never have said what I did. 'The people I write about become my friends, Scarlett. And I don't let my friends down.'

7

There was no sign of Joshu when I pitched up at the hacienda four days later. Maggie and George had nailed each other to the wall over the contracts, Biba from Stellar Books was shouting about the deal all over the trade press and the tabloids were already sniffing around the serialisation. In my world, it doesn't get much better than that.

This time, I drove myself to darkest Essex. Clearly my car was low status; the duty paps didn't even stir as I pulled up to the gate. Scarlett buzzed me in and I parked in the same garage slot we'd used on my first visit. The red Mazda convertible I'd noticed before was still sitting in the far bay. It didn't look as though it had moved. Scarlett was riding high; she only had to drive herself if she wanted to.

I found Scarlett in the kitchen, leaning on the range with a mug cradled against the top of her belly. This time, the joggers were black, the muscle T-shirt white. When I walked in, she was yawning luxuriously, unselfconsciously revealing the glitter of gold-crowned molars. Clearly she'd always lived in a world where nobody ever covered their mouth. 'Hiya,' she said through the end of her yawn. 'Fuck, I stayed up so late last night.'

'Were you partying with Joshu?' I said. Not that I was interested. But part of my job is making conversation, bridging the gaps between me and the clients.

She snorted scornfully. 'He's up in Birmingham. Some new club opening. Needed the king of cool to scratch and scribble and stutter for them.' She giggled. 'It sounds like somebody's granddad, doesn't it? Like some old fart that's lost his marbles. Scratching and stuttering. No, there was a *Wife Swap* marathon on and I got sucked in, watching all them hopeless pillocks trying to fit into somebody else's life.'

'It's the bitching and the niggling we watch for.' I have to admit, I've got a soft spot for *Wife Swap* too. 'It's car-crash telly. I'm holding out for the night somebody's kid slaps the invader.'

Scarlett giggled again. I could imagine how much that was going to irritate me over nine days of interviews. Sometimes the clients have incredibly irritating verbal tics or physical twitches that drive me crazy. The only way I can deal with it is to keep an hourly tally and set little mental bets with myself.

'If it was me, I'd totally turn them on their heads,' she said, pushing off from the cooker and heading for the kettle. 'Brew?'

'I'd love a coffee. What do you mean, you'd turn them on their heads?'

'I'd wait till they were all out at work or at school. Then I'd hire in a cleaning service and caterers. They'd come back home and think I was amazing. And they'd be totally pissed off with their real wife.'

'I take it you're not much of a housewife, then?'

She pulled a face. 'I can clean if I have to, but these days I don't have to. As for cooking – beans on toast, scrambled eggs on toast. Toast on toast. And that's your lot. That's what takeaways are for, right? So we don't have to waste our time in the kitchen. You're not one of them Nigellas are you? Domestic fucking goddesses?' She couldn't have got much more scathing contempt into three words.

'I don't do any of that fancy shit, but I like to make a proper roast dinner at the weekend.' More Nigel Slater than Nigella Lawson in the kitchen, that's me.

'That's cool, a proper roast,' she conceded. 'But I bet you're one of them that likes proper coffee.'

I grinned. 'You got me bang to rights. Have you got some?'

'Yeah, that Carla turned up with a box of them metal pods for the coffee machine when she drove Georgie up the other day.' The cupboard she opened contained a giant box of teabags and a plastic bag filled with a mixture of coloured metal capsules. 'We only drink tea,' she said. 'We're total plebs, me and Joshu. Well, he pretends to be. He's not really. His dad teaches at a university and his mum's a doctor. He's a big disappointment to them, is Joshu.' She dumped the bag by a coffee machine that looked like it'd had more design input than the space shuttle. 'I hope you know how to work it.' She turned and gave me that hundred-watt smile again, the one that made her whole face come to life. 'Or I'll have to give Carla a bell and tell her to get her arse out here to show us what to do.'

'How hard can it be? George Clooney seems to manage it, and he's a bloke.' It didn't take much figuring out, but Scarlett was impressed when I managed to fix myself a decent coffee in a matter of minutes.

'You want to work in here?' Scarlett asked, eyeing my shoulder bag. ''Cos there's a table so you can take notes easily.'

'I don't need a table. I'll be taping our conversation. I make the occasional note, but I just lean my notebook on my knee. We're going to be sitting around for hours. It's better if we're somewhere comfortable. What about the living room, with the sofas?'

'You don't think that's too much like, just hanging out?'

'Trust me, just hanging out is good. The more you relax, the more natural you're going to sound.' She still looked dubious, but she led the way through. 'Did you get a chance to sort out those photos?' I asked before she settled in.

'I had a look,' she said. 'There's not much. Hang on a minute.' Scarlett disappeared down the hall, and I heard the soft shuffle of her feet on the stairs. I'd asked her to show me her life in photographs, going all the way back to childhood. I'd found that photos often jogged memories. But they also made the clients drop their barriers as they were drawn back by the image into a sense of place and time, a vivid recapturing of smells and sights and sounds that could often unlock a whole stream of recollection.

As Scarlett handed over the meagre bundle, I knew this wasn't exactly going to be a fertile field for us. Like most people, I spent my teens thinking my parents were pretty useless – out of touch, out of time, out of ideas. But at least they understood that when you have a kid, you're supposed to pay attention to them. My life in pictures would have been a thick bundle of holiday snaps, school photos, moments of pride captured by the camera and a record of family celebrations. My cousin's wedding, my grandparents' golden wedding, my nephew's christening. All faithfully preserved for posterity.

It hadn't been like that for Scarlett. Whatever her parents had been doing, it hadn't included demonstrating their pride in their offspring by capturing her every endearing moment. 'Like I said, there's not much.' She shrugged and fell backwards into the sofa, her lips turned down in a pout.

Top of the pile was, predictably, the hospital shot. The new mum propped on pillows, holding the new baby close to her chest and giving the camera an exhausted smile. Chrissie Higgins looked more raddled than radiant. She must have been about the same age her daughter was now, but you wouldn't have guessed it. Her face was puffy, her skin looked rough and there were dark smudges under her eyes. It could have been the toll of a hard labour, but more likely it had been a hard life. Nevertheless, I could see the resemblance to her daughter.

'I wasn't much to look at,' Scarlett said without glancing at the photo. 'I look like a hundred-year-old monkey.'

She wasn't far wrong. 'All babies look like that,' I said. 'But we're programmed to love our own so we don't notice.'

Scarlett snorted. 'Programmed to love our own? I don't fucking think so! My mum couldn't wait to get out of the hospital and have a drink. She was down the pub before I was a week old.'

'Did she take you with her?'

'Sometimes. Mostly she left me with her mum. She was already an alcoholic. And my dad was in between stretches and she didn't want to lose him, which meant she had to go out on the town with him. She didn't want some other slapper catching his eye and snagging him.' That blistering contempt again. 'Like anyone would think he was a catch, for fuck's sake.' She folded her arms tight against her chest and sighed. 'Is this what we're going to do, then? Look at old photos so I can have a good bitch about how crap my life's been?'

I smiled. I had to defuse her defensiveness. 'Well, the readers have to learn how crap it was. That's the only way they'll understand the scale of the journey you've made,' I said mildly. 'We'll come back to the pictures another time, once I have a clearer sense of where they fit in. What I want to talk about today is when you were a kid. We can't just ignore it, pretend it never happened. Not if you're going to explain your life properly to your own child. I can see it wasn't a great time for you, which is all the more reason to get it out of the way. Then it's not hanging over you.'

She considered what I'd said, then nodded. 'You're right. OK. What do you want to know?'

Standard procedure, step one. 'What's your earliest memory?'

Like they all do, she thought for a moment. 'At the funfair,' she said slowly. 'With my dad.'

I softened and lowered my voice. 'What I want you to do now is close your eyes and picture that memory. I want you to sink back into it, like you were sinking into the most comfortable bed. Let everything go and picture that little girl at the funfair. Let the years float away and flow backwards in time to that trip to the funfair.'

Scarlett burst out laughing. 'What is this? You trying to hypnotise me, or what?'

'Not exactly. I'm trying to get you to relax, that's all. A strong memory's a good place to start.'

'You're not going to get me under the influence and make me do all sorts?'

From what I'd seen of Scarlett on TV, it didn't take much to achieve that. But it wouldn't have been helpful to point that out. 'No. I'm just trying to get the ball rolling. If you don't want to start with that memory, we'll move on to something else. But I'm warning you now, I'll want to come back here. So we might as well deal with it now.'

'Why not? It's not like there's a problem with it or owt. It was only a trip to the fair.' She rolled her eyes then leaned back, resting her head against a cowhide-covered cushion and closing her eyes. I waited and, after a pause, her breathing slowed. When she spoke again, her voice was slower and more measured. 'I'm at the funfair. It tastes of hot dogs and onions and diesel and candy floss. The air smells hot. I'm up in the sky . . .'

'Are you on a ride?' I spoke softly, not wanting to break the moment.

'I'm on my dad's shoulders. I'm up above everybody's heads. It's dark, 'cos it's night time. There's coloured lights everywhere, it's like I'm inside a rainbow or summat. My hand's in my dad's hair, it's really thick and wiry and if I grab on too tight he shouts at me to leave off.'

'Is your mum there too?'

'I can see the top of her head if I look down. They've both got cans, I can smell they're drinking beer. But they're laughing and joking and it's like we're just like everybody else.' She opened her eyes and sat up abruptly. 'That's why I remember it. For once, I didn't feel scummy. Like everybody was looking down on us.' She shook her head with a grim smile. 'We were the neighbours from hell. Nobody wanted us living next door.'

'But you still managed to have a good time together. At the fair.'

'Why do you think I remember it?' Scarlett leans forward, apparently animated by genuine curiosity.

'Because it was fun, I suppose?'

'Because it was a complete bloody one-off,' she said bitterly. 'I hardly have any memories of my dad. I was only six when he died and he spent most of those six years inside. Apart from the fair, all I remember is him and my mum drunk and fighting. Shouting and slapping each other. The kind of thing that makes you want to hide under the bed and lie in your own piss when you're little.'

There wasn't much I could say that didn't sound patronising or dismissive. 'Do you ask people about him? People who knew him?'

'Of course I do. You want to know shit like that, don't you?'

'Of course you do. And you want to pass that knowledge on to your kid. So tell me what you know about him. What other people have told you.'

It was a depressing tale. Alan Higgins was one of seven kids who had run wild from childhood thanks to an alcoholic father and a tranked-up mother. His older brothers had introduced him to burglary, car theft and a wide range of scams at an early age and he'd taken to crime with gusto. Unfortunately his enthusiasm wasn't matched by his skill, his intelligence or his luck. By the time he'd met Chrissie, he'd been in detention twice as a juvenile and once as an adult. Last time, he'd discovered the delights of heroin and from then on, his life became a tired treadmill of stealing to feed his habit, getting caught, going to jail and coming out to start the cycle all over again. He managed to stay out long enough to impregnate Chrissie with Scarlett and Jade, her older sister, but he was seldom around for the day-to-day.

'Everybody that knew him says he wasn't a bad lad,' Scarlett said wearily. 'He was just weak. And lazy. If you're rich and you're weak and lazy, somebody makes sure you end up with a job and shit. But if you're poor, you end up like my dad.' It was another of those startling insights. And as soon as she'd spoken, Scarlett looked as if she wanted to snatch the words back.

I didn't want to make an issue of it. I was beginning to suspect there might be more to the Scarlett Harlot than met the eye, and I didn't want to make her wary of me. 'How did he die?' I said, moving the conversation along. I thought I knew the answer, but I wanted to hear it from her. To see how honest she was going to be.

'You know how he died. You've not come here without googling me. It's on the Internet. You tell me.' Arms folded again, she stared me down.

'Of course I googled you. I checked you out before I agreed to meet you in the first place. If I hadn't been interested by what I read, you'd never have heard my name. But that doesn't mean I believe everything online. I'd be pretty crap at my job if I did. I know what I read about your dad. You probably know what I read. What I'm asking is for you to tell me the truth.' We were barely an hour into the day and already I was feeling worn out. Scarlett was harder to calm down than a cat in a vet's waiting room. Most minor celebs were so thrilled to have an audience and so convinced that every aspect of their lives was fascinating, the problem was shutting them up. But Scarlett was making me work for a living. It had been a while, and I was no longer certain I was going to enjoy this project.

She glared at me for a little longer, then relented. 'It's true. What it says online. He died from AIDS. He must have got it off a dirty needle. In jail, they all shared needles all the time. They didn't have a choice. There's no fucking needle exchanges in the nick. So, yeah, a dirty needle.' Her mouth twisted in a harsh line. 'Or else whatever he had to do to get smack when he was inside. I'm not stupid, I know what goes on.'

'That must have been hard for your mum.'

'No kidding. All the finger-pointing, the name-calling. I was too young to get it at the time, but believe me, it went on for years. Until I was well able to understand. Ignorant bastards that thought because he had AIDS, so did she. And so did me and Jade. At school, in the street, lads would point and jeer, "There goes the AIDS sisters," and shit like that. We had to toughen up early, me and Jade.'

'Was he back home when he died?'

'No, thank God. That would have made it even worse. He died in jail. My mum went mental at them, said he should be allowed out on compassionate grounds, but her heart wasn't in it. She likes a battle for its own sake. Having him home would have done her head in. It would have been me and Jade looking after him, not her.'

'But you were only six. And Jade was, what, eight?'

Scarlett's wry smile reappeared. 'You've led a sheltered life, haven't you? When your dad's a junkie and your mother's an alkie, you grow up fast. Or you don't grow up at all. I looked at them and I knew one way or another I wasn't gonna end up like them. Like Jade turned out.' She locked eyes with me. 'I didn't just fall into the *Goldfish Bowl*. I had a plan.' She pushed her hair back from her face and thrust her chest out in a parody of seduction. 'But we don't have to tell them that, do we?'

8

I don't know which of us was more taken aback by Scarlett's moment of revelation. She backtracked almost immediately. 'Listen to me,' she laughed. 'Bigging myself up. Like I've got brains enough to plan any further ahead than my next shag.'

But I knew better. I knew I'd seen a glimpse of something that didn't fit with her public image. Thick but well-meaning, that was how the world saw Scarlett. And that was the story I was being well paid to reproduce. I could do that standing on my head. What would make it much more interesting would be if there was another layer hidden beneath that surface. A layer I could never use in my 'autobiography'. But writers waste nothing. Scarlett's secret interior life might possibly be the springboard for the fiction I'd always nursed a desire to write.

For the rest of the day, she played to her image so thoroughly I almost believed I'd been mistaken. But when I went home and started transcribing the recording of our session, I could hear that spark firing like an artillery piece among the dull thudding of Scarlett's narrative. I'd garnered a lot of material for Scarlett's early days – and a lot I would leave on the cutting-room floor, for everyone's sake – but more importantly

I'd found a reason to be excited about this project. I was just sorry that Pete was working so I couldn't share my enthusiasm with him. Disappointed, I settled for texting him. But he was obviously too busy to respond. At least there was a reply waiting when I got up – he'd eventually got back to me at 3.17 a.m. Of course, I'd been fast asleep by then.

I was eager to get back to Scarlett. I had no idea what I might tease out of her but I had a feeling that what lay beneath might animate the superficial story itself, making it a better read.

This time, when I pulled into the hacienda there was no room in the garage. The convertible had been joined by a jacked-up black Golf with a full body kit, gold trim and tinted windows. It had to be Joshu's wheels. Anybody else would have been too embarrassed to be seen behind that bling on wheels. Next to it was a discreet silver BMW 5-series.

I didn't have to wonder about the Beemer's owner for long. When I walked into the kitchen, Scarlett, Joshu and George were standing at three points of a triangle, every one of them posturing like an illustration for a kinesics seminar. Scarlett had her arms folded tight across her chest in a defiant statement I was growing all too familiar with; Joshu, charmless in bed hair, boxers and an Arsenal T-shirt, had his head thrust forward and his hands on his hips; while George leaned languid against the range, right hand cupping his left elbow, left hand tickling the air.

They barely glanced at me as I entered. 'It makes sense whichever way you look at it,' George said. 'Surely you must see that?'

'Not the way I look at it,' Joshu muttered mutinously. 'What about my image, man?'

'You're already spoken for, in the eyes of your public, Joshu,' George said. 'It's not as if your relationship with Scarlett is a state secret.' He dipped his head towards me and, without breaking stride, added, 'Good morning, Stephanie. How lovely to see you.'

'Just because everybody knows she is my woman doesn't mean I is not my own man, like. And what you is proposin' is like a shackle to me.'

In spite of Joshu's mangling of the English language, a little sense was starting to emerge. I gave George my best Lady Bracknell. 'You're suggesting they get married?'

'Call me old-fashioned, but she is having his baby.' George unfolded his arms and made for the coffee machine. Scarlett opened the cupboard and threw the bag of capsules down in front of him. Dangerously close to 'at' him.

'We're having a baby together,' Scarlett corrected him. 'And I don't see any need to be married for that to happen.'

'Yeah. We don't need a piece of paper from the man.' Joshu scratched his balls. I think he was going for nonchalant.

'I appreciate that.' George turned to me. 'Coffee, Stephanie?'

'Please. I think I had the purple one yesterday.'

'Good choice. Joshu, I'm not suggesting for a moment that you need a marriage licence to legitimise your relationship with Scarlett. The paparazzi seem to have obviated that necessity, frankly. What I am suggesting is that a wedding would be a marvellously profitable enterprise in the not too distant future.'

'Say again?' Joshu cleaned his ear with his fingernail then chewed off the residue.

'What he's saying is we can turn it into a nice little earner,' Scarlett said. 'Am I right, Georgie?'

He smiled. 'In a nutshell, my dear. Think of it as a business proposition. We'll make a TV documentary, get some designer to do the clothes and some hotel to do the catering. We'll flog the exclusive to *Yes!* and we'll bring out a new fragrance for the ceremony. Stephanie, remind me, when's the book due to be published?'

'A month before the baby's due.'

'Perfect. Then that's when we'll do it.' George beamed around the room as he handed me my coffee. 'It'll put thousands on the book sale.'

'What? So I can look like a bloody beached whale in my wedding photos?' Indignation had brought a flush to Scarlett's cheeks.

'Darling, we'll get the best designer to do the frock,' George said. 'You'll look bloody gorgeous – nobody will notice your bump.'

Joshu sniggered. 'It's not a designer you're gonna need, it's a brick wall for her to stand behind.'

'Shut it, you,' Scarlett snarled. 'If it wasn't for me, nobody would be interested in buying up your wedding.'

'If it wasn't for you, nobody would be talking about me having a fucking wedding except my aunties.'

The conversation was depressing the hell out of me. It's not that I'm a great believer in the institution of marriage. But one thing I do believe is that love should have something to do with it. For as long as I'd been in the room, nobody had mentioned love or affection. They'd only talked about the baby as a cog in the business wheel. You didn't have to be clairvoyant to know that, if this marriage happened, they'd be lucky to make their paper anniversary.

'Think of it as the final public rehabilitation,' George said. 'Nobody can accuse you of being racist if you're marrying Joshu.'

'Oh, so I is the token black man in my own marriage, is that it?'

For once, I was with Joshu.

'Shut up,' Scarlett said again. 'I got nothing to prove on that score, Georgie. If I do marry this twat, it won't be to save my skin from the bleating lefties. What you said about making a big deal out of it – you think that'll work? You think we'll get it all paid for, and an earner too?'

'I'm absolutely certain,' George said. 'I've sounded out a couple of people already and believe me, the market is definitely there. Stephanie, tell her how getting the headlines can impact on a book's sales.'

I gave George a quick glance that should have told him how little I appreciated being dragged into this sordid arrangement. 'He's right,' I admitted. 'Being in the news will take the sales to a different level. It reminds people of who you are and why they should be interested in you. It's like doubling or trebling your advertising budget.'

'See, Joshu?' Scarlett crossed the room and put her arms round him. 'We should do it. We're not going to be headlines forever, babe—'

'You speak for yourself,' he grumbled.

She pulled away. 'OK, then. *I'm* not going to be headlines forever, so I need to make my pile while I can. And don't be kidding yourself, Joshu. This isn't the wedding I was dreaming of. A little bit of romance would have been nice. But I gotta take my chances when they come up. If we can really make ourselves some serious cash here, we should do it. It's not going to change anything between us.'

'And you can have a pre-nup drawn up, if you're worried about losing out should things not go the way you hope,' George chimed in. 'Really, Joshu, there's no downside to this.'

'Not for you, maybe. But my family's never going to speak to me again.'

'You hate your family,' Scarlett said. She leaned into him and rubbed the tip of her nose against his. 'And who else would have you, anyway?'

'I could have my pick,' he said. But his heart wasn't in it. He grabbed her buttocks and hauled her close. 'Aw, fuck it, why not? OK, George, we'll do it. Sort out all the arrangements, but you better make sure we got an A-list guest list and all the expenses covered. I don't want to be shelling out for no wedding.'

George beamed. 'I knew you'd see sense.'

I tried not to gag. 'There's just one thing,' I said. They all looked at me expectantly. 'You need to come up with a romantic proposal story for the media. Because it's supposed to be the groom who makes the proposal, not your agent.'

For the first time, they were all lost for words.

Trust is the keystone of being an effective ghost. You've got a very small window of opportunity to build a bridge. I've heard some ghosts say it doesn't matter whether the clients like you, it's whether they think you can deliver. But I don't agree. I think you need to make them think you're friends.

I take pride in my work. I want to write the best book possible. Don't get me wrong, I've worked with individuals I didn't gel with and I knocked myself out to keep that lack of rapport from the readers. But if you want them to open up, to share the things they've never spoken of before, to admit you to the story behind the story, you need trust.

Damage takes people different ways. Sometimes it leaves them frantic to believe in someone. Anyone, really. Even someone who's paid to smile and tell them they're extraordinary. Others swing to the opposite pole. It's as if their receptors have been permanently degraded so they can't let themselves rely on another. I thought at first Scarlett was one of those. That no matter how hard I tried to build a connection with her, it wouldn't ever be more than superficial. It was a frustrating thought, because those glimpses behind the mask had intrigued me personally as well as professionally.

But I was wrong about Scarlett. By the end of our nine days together, it felt like we'd taken the first steps towards an unlikely friendship. I'd started in my usual position of being prepared to put aside what I thought of her in the interests of making a book. By the end, I found that I actually liked her. That liking didn't alter the facts of Scarlett – she was ignorant, she was brash, she was adrift from any kind of roots. But honestly, what else could she have been, given the hand she'd been dealt?

The thing about Scarlett was that she was a lot smarter than she let on when the cameras were on her. She knew the unpalatable facts about herself and in private, when nobody was looking, she was trying to change that. I caught her watching a history channel on the TV one morning when I arrived earlier than expected. Once when she was out of the room, I flicked on her iPad and found she was reading a book about Michelle and Barack Obama. One evening when there had been a mix-up over car bookings, I drove her up to Stansted airport and when I went to change the station from Radio 4, she told me to leave it on, casual as you like. It wasn't exactly *Pygmalion*, but it was interesting.

I admired her for that. I also respected the way she hadn't been destroyed by her background. It seemed that everyone she'd grown up around was addicted or behind bars. Or both. Drink, drugs and violence were the chains that shackled her family and her neighbours. Somehow, Scarlett had found the bloody-minded strength to choose a different path. Even Joshu wasn't quite the skank he appeared to be – I had a shrewd feeling the nice middle-class upbringing would surface when he'd finished playing with the bad boys. I'm pretty good at walking in other people's shoes, but I could not imagine what it had taken for Scarlett to reach escape velocity from the grinding awfulness of her life in Leeds.

Scarlett had made a difference in her own life. It was up to me to help her show the world – and the kid this book was for – just how much steel there was beneath the brass.

9

Vivian McKuras looked unimpressed with Stephanie's description of Scarlett Higgins. But before she could pass judgement, her phone beeped. 'I'll be back,' she said, heading for the door without a backward glance.

'Abbott,' she said once she was clear of the interview room. 'Thanks for touching base.'

She'd kept her message to her two colleagues as low key as she could. They were both technically senior to her, but she was determined not to back down from the lead role in this investigation. The ambitious part of her had almost hoped neither would get back to her, but the decent humane part knew she'd need help with the nuts and bolts. Of the two agents stationed at the international terminal, Don Abbott had been the one she'd hoped would respond to her message about the abducted child. He was smart and keen, but most of all, he treated Vivian exactly the same as his male colleagues. 'What do you need?' he asked. 'You got the Amber Alert up and running, I see. You got any leads that need chasing down?'

'It's not straightforward.' It wasn't easy for her to admit that, but at least Abbott wouldn't use it against her in front of colleagues later. 'They're British. I've been interviewing the woman who was with the kid – she's in the process of adopting him. And so far, she's not given me anything you could call a motive.'

Abbott made a growling noise in his throat. 'Pain in the ass. Your note says the kid's birth mother was a reality TV star. What about good old-fashioned kidnap for ransom?'

'It could be, but that's a waiting game and we've heard nothing so far.'

'Sounds like you need to get back in the interview room. See if you can get something more solid from this woman. In the meantime, do you want me to check out the CCTV footage? See if I can maybe pinpoint them leaving the terminal?'

'That would be great. The control room are pulling it together for us, but I'd be a lot happier to have your eyes across it than theirs. The other thing I haven't had a chance to check out – this guy must have followed them airside somehow. The easiest way is for him to have had a boarding pass for a flight going out of here sometime today. But obviously, he didn't get on a plane. So some airline has a no-show that must be our guy.'

'I get you. Someone who checked in and cleared security but didn't show up at the gate. There's always a few of those every day. Leave it with me, Vivian. I'll see what I can chase up.'

'Thanks, Don.'

'No problem. When it's a kid at stake, we all gotta run the extra mile.'

She remembered he had a child of his own. A daughter, a couple of years older than Jimmy Higgins. She imagined that made the abduction of a child the most powerful spur to action. 'Whatever it takes,' she said. 'Let's meet later and see what we got.'

'Sure. Call me when you're done with the interview.'

God knew when that would be, she thought. Stephanie

Harker's story was complicated, and the woman seemed determined to share every detail. Probably talking about her history with the kid made her feel like she was doing something useful towards his rescue. Vivian couldn't blame her for that, but the fact remained that she had a job to do where time generally played a significant role. As soon as her butt hit the seat again, she was back in interrogative mode. 'So what about Scarlett's family?'

'Hang on a minute,' Stephanie protested. 'What's happening? That call? Was it about Jimmy? Have you any news?' Her anxiety surfaced again, breaking through the careful containment she'd been building.

Vivian stifled an impatient sigh. 'No news. I was just briefing a colleague who's following another line of inquiry.'

'What line of inquiry? Has anyone come forward? Have they seen Jimmy?' Stephanie's eyes sparkled with tears and she rubbed them impatiently with the back of her hand.

'Nothing like that. My colleague is going to review the CCTV, to see if we can establish the movements of the kidnapper ahead of the kidnap itself. And if we can find out where and how they left the airport precincts. There's a lot of practical ground to cover. For example, the kidnapper must have produced either valid ID or a damn good fake to get a boarding pass and slip through security ahead of or alongside you guys.'

Stephanie frowned, her emotions checked by the immediacy of seeing a practical problem. 'Not necessarily,' she said.

Vivian was startled. 'What do you mean? Security here is tight as a drum. You can't talk your way past the TSA without the proper paperwork.'

'If the kidnapper knew our schedule, he wouldn't have had to follow us. There's more than one way to get airside in this terminal,' Stephanie insisted. 'I noticed it last year when I came back from visiting a friend in Madison. It struck me because in the UK we're really strict about segregating arrivals and departures. But here, if you arrive on a domestic flight, you're just spilled out into the main concourse, so arriving passengers mix with the departing ones. The kidnapper could have flown in from anywhere served by this terminal then changed in the toilet.'

She was on the money, Vivian thought. Why had she jumped to the wrong conclusion so quickly? Why had something they knew perfectly well not occurred to her or Abbott? The obvious answer was that their concerns were always with possible breaches of security from outside. Once you were inside, you were, by definition, secure. You'd been verified, screened and deemed acceptable. Why would there be any further cause for concern? But Stephanie Harker had looked at the system with the eyes of an outsider and she'd seen something they'd missed. Maybe the interview room was the place where this would be resolved after all. 'I need to make a call,' she said, pushing her chair back and dialling Abbott's number on her way back out to the hallway.

'We got sidetracked by the idea of somebody following the kid. We forgot about incoming passengers,' she said as soon as he answered. 'They come from all over the US and they walk straight out into the main concourse. You can't tell who's an arrival and who's a departure. Our guy could have flown in from anywhere.'

'Shit,' Abbott said.

'We're going to have to backtrack the CCTV to see if we can figure out where the fuck he came from,' Vivian said. 'If he came off a flight, he could have been wearing anything. But he had to change somewhere. He must have used a bathroom, right?'

Abbott sighed. 'We need more bodies.'

'Check with security in the camera room. This takes priority. A kid's life could be on the line here. I'm going back in to the interview now.'

'OK. Good call, Vivian.'

When she sat down this time, Vivian eyed Stephanie with more respect. 'It's in hand,' she said. 'Thanks for that insight. Now, can we get back to Scarlett Higgins' family? I'm wondering whether they might be behind all this. Were they not pissed that you ended up with the kid? And presumably the money too? I'm guessing Scarlett left her money to you? For Jimmy?'

'Ha,' Stephanie said. 'I wish. They were pissed off at first. When they thought there was some money. But you couldn't see them for dust once they realised Scarlett had left all her money to the charitable trust she set up after she discovered she had cancer. I got the kid. Not the money.'

'Jimmy didn't inherit? Surely she left you something to take care of him? Just to pay the bills.'

Stephanie shook her head. 'Not a bean.' Her smile was wry.

'That's totally bizarre.'

'Tell me about it. Her rationale is that she started out with nothing and that's what spurred her on to make something of herself. She didn't think throwing money at kids was good for them.'

Vivian couldn't decide whether she was impressed or appalled. 'So her family really weren't interested in the boy?'

Stephanie sighed. 'Her mother's a drunk and her sister's a junkie who's already had one kid taken into care. Even if they'd known Jimmy – which they didn't – no judge in his right mind was going to let them anywhere near him.'

Vivian shook her head. 'That doesn't mean they didn't want him. Blood's thicker than water, after all.'

'In the Higgins family, money's thicker than water. And if there was no money in it for them, they couldn't have cared less about Jimmy.'

'How come you ended up with the boy? Are you trying to tell me the best friend she had in the world was her ghost writer?' Vivian tried to keep the incredulity from her face as well as her voice, but it wasn't easy. It was hard to imagine an emotional life so impoverished that the nearest thing you had to a bgf was the woman who'd been hired to portray you to the world in the most flattering light.

Stephanie shrugged. 'That's one way of putting it. The other way would be that we fell into friendship five years ago when I wrote Scarlett's first book. Neither of us expected it. But it happened and it persisted. There was a lot more to her than met the eye. I'm not proud of the fact that the woman I portrayed to the world was not the woman I knew, but for all sorts of reasons, most of them economic, that was what worked for both of us. And when she knew she was dying, I was the person she knew she could trust with her boy.' Stephanie blinked away more tears. 'Looks like she couldn't have been more wrong.'

'It wasn't your fault,' Vivian said.

Suddenly Stephanie snapped into anger. 'Of course it was my bloody fault. He was in my care. And now he's not. Scarlett trusted me. Jimmy trusted me. I've let everybody down. If anything happens to that boy, if he doesn't come back to me alive and well . . . ' The muscles in her face went slack as the prospect sank in.

'We'll find him,' Vivian said, hating herself for the false hope. But she had to do what she could to keep Stephanie on her side. She had to keep teasing away at the details of their history in the hope she could find a reason for what had happened. 'I accept what you're saying about your friendship. Even though, frankly, it looks unlikely from where I'm sitting. But how was it that you got so close that she felt you were the one to entrust with Jimmy?

10

A ghost is a professional hypocrite. We're constantly editing the person we've discovered into the person they want the world to see. We are the cosmetic surgeons of the image. We become experts in what should be left out. I generally ask clients if they would be comfortable with their mother or their child reading particular episodes that I consider to be prurient or predatory. And when I'm writing about sexual abuse, for example, I'm always conscious that there are creeps out there who look for this sort of memoir only because it turns them on. So I'm careful not to include any explicit descriptions or much detail about the process of grooming children for sexual exploitation. I'm not in the business of writing a primer for paedophiles.

Even with all the practice I'd had at creating a central fiction to form the spine of my 'autobiographies', *Fishing for Gold* turned out to be one of my more challenging enterprises. I think the issue was that Scarlett had given me a problem I'd never faced before. Usually, what I'm editing out is the material that paints the subject in a less than flattering light. For example, when I was ghosting a champion snooker player who had successfully battled cancer, the heart of the book was the strength he'd found in his loving marriage. It didn't need any intervention from me for the player and his agent to be clear that they did not want the public to read about the prostitutes and the drugs that had been the reality of his backstage life.

I've become an adept at treading the narrow line between providing just enough revelation to justify newspaper serialisation but not so much that the client becomes a pariah in their own life. And while it was true that what I was hiding about Scarlett would make her life uncomfortable, it wasn't because the secrets were dirty and damaging. Apart from Joshu, who was her one blind spot, the truth about Scarlett was that she was smarter, shrewder and much more sensitive than any TV viewer or tabloid reader would have thought possible. I'd found it hard to believe myself at first, but I'd gradually had to accept the creeping suspicion that the Scarlett the world had been privy to was mostly as artificial a creation as Michael Jackson's face.

I couldn't believe she'd got away with it for so long. It was on the seventh or eighth day of our interviews that I broached the subject. 'You're a lot smarter than you let on,' I said.

We were lounging on the leather sofas in the late afternoon. We'd been talking about the ill-fated second series, and Scarlett had clearly been bored by my insistence that we had to talk about the horrible thing she'd said to Danny Williams. 'Look, it happened,' she said, struggling upright and glaring at me. 'You don't need me to go through it all again. It's there on YouTube for ever.'

'YouTube doesn't tell me what was going through your mind.'

She looked away. 'What do you want me to say? It was like I lost my mind? Like I totally didn't know what I was saying?' She pushed herself upright, impatient. 'Look, I said something that I don't even believe. I'd been out of sorts for days. All kinds of crap just came bubbling up. I know now it was because I was pregnant and my hormones were all over the place, but at the time, nobody was more gobsmacked than me at what came out of my mouth.' She sniffed. 'Will that do?'

And that was when I broke all the rules and stepped across the line of tacit agreement between ghost and client. I'm not an investigative journalist. It's not my job to challenge what my client tells me. Unless what they're saying is completely at odds with all the known facts in the public domain, I'm supposed to swallow it whole. Sometimes I feel like a python confronted with a double-decker bus, but you'd be amazed what the punters will accept as gospel. On the rare occasions when I've had to point out very gently that my client's version of events does not quite tally with what the rest of the world remembers, I've felt like I was skating on thin ice. The ghost-writing equivalent of ripping a hole in the space-time continuum. Because once you confront them with one lie, it's hard to stop the whole thing unravelling.

But with Scarlett, I couldn't help myself. I'd grown to like her a lot over the three weeks we'd been talking. I generally manage to stay on good terms with the people I write about, but this time I suspected we might actually form a genuine friendship. If that was going to happen, we both needed to stop pretending. I'd never write the truth, obviously. I just needed to know it.

So, 'You're a lot smarter than you let on,' I said. 'There was nothing spontaneous or hormonal about any of that, was there?'

Scarlett's slow smile said it all. 'I don't know what you mean,' she said, pointing to my little digital recorder.

But I knew what she meant. I don't like going off the record. It can put you into all sorts of awkward places. I remember the middle-aged man who had survived a child-hood of hideous abuse at the hands of the Christian Brothers who asked me to turn off the tape, whereupon he confessed that his marriage was an empty shell and he was having a sexual relationship with their parish priest. The same parish priest who was leading a campaign to name and shame the members of his church who had sexually abused children. That was one of those times when I wished I had a time machine that would take me back to the place where I didn't know that.

So it was a big step of trust for me to turn off the machine. But sooner or later I was going to have to step outside the box if I was going to attempt to make proper friends with Scarlett.

I turned it off.

We both sat in silence for a moment, staring at the recorder. Then Scarlett cleared her throat. 'You're right. I planned it. I knew I was pregnant when I went back to Foutra. Plus I knew the second series was my chance to take myself to the next level. I figured I'd only get one chance to make a splash with the news about the baby, so I better go for broke.' She gave me a sly look. 'I think I did a pretty good job of it.'

I laughed. 'You hooked me. And I'm the best. That's how good a job you did. Has it all been planned, Scarlett? From the off?'

'Right from the off.' She fell back against the sofa in an exaggerated pose of relief. 'Steph, it's bloody great to share it at last. I've had to keep my gob shut for so long, it's been killing me.'

And out it poured. The strange, twisted plan of a woman who had no prospects, no qualifications and no obvious escape from a dead-end life she adamantly did not want. 'I remember when *Big Brother* started. I was way too young to get on it, but I could see how something like that might be the way out for somebody like me. Somebody with a totally shit life.'

'And a brain,' I said. 'That's what made you different, isn't it?'

'Well, I think so,' she said. 'I was never any good at school, mostly because they wrote me off before I even got my feet under the table. But I reckoned if I could get on one of those shows, I could play a good enough part to make something of myself. I studied them like it was maths or history or summat. I could have gone on *Mastermind* with reality TV shows as my specialist subject.' She chuckled. 'Mind, the general knowledge would have been a bit of a disaster.'

She'd auditioned three times before she finally got her slot on *Goldfish Bowl.* 'I had to keep dumbing down.' She rolled her eyes. 'You would not believe how fucking dim most of the people who get on these shows are. They haven't got a clue. No wonder the TV companies love shows like *Goldfish Bowl.* They can exploit the living daylights out of the contestants and the poor sods don't even notice.'

'So it was all a con job?'

'Start to finish. Remember that night on the first series when I got drunk and danced naked on the table?'

I shuddered. It had been unforgettable, for all the wrong reasons. 'Oh, yes.'

Scarlett rocked with laughter. 'I know, it's excruciating to watch. But it didn't half grab the headlines. I wasn't drunk at all, you know. I made it look like I was drinking a lot more than I did. And I was totally stone-cold sober. I played them all for suckers, Steph. And look at me now. I've got my own house and money in the bank. You're going to make me a bestseller. And my baby's going to have a daddy.'

'What about Joshu? Is he part of the game?'

She looked outraged. 'Of course not. I wouldn't be that cruel. I wouldn't play with somebody's emotions like that. I love Joshu, and he loves me.'

I wasn't entirely sure about the second half of that sentence. Especially if Joshu ever realised that the woman in his life was about seven times smarter than him. 'As long as you're happy, that's what counts. But I have to congratulate you, Scarlett.

You've done a terrific job. When I was just another punter, I had no idea that you were anything other than a nice-but-dim bimbo.'

Scarlett scooted forward to high-five me. 'Props to you, Steph. You're the only one who's ever worked it out. All the hacks, the TV producers, the business people that make my brands – they think I'm thick so they patronise the arse off me then funnel everything through Georgie. And bless him, Georgie's like most people. He made up his mind about me before he even met me. He thinks he knows my limits and he plays to them. He never actually looks at me or listens to me. He only pays attention to the surface. It's one of the reasons why I chose him. That and his reputation for being honest. Let's face it, if you're supposed to be thick, you need to be bloody sure you pick an agent who's going to take care of you and not rip you off.'

I had to admit she'd made a good job of it. 'Don't you get fed up, though? Always pretending?'

'I do sometimes. Being pregnant's done me a big favour. I was getting knackered with having to be out on the lash three or four nights a week. But now I'm supposed to set a good example and stop at home. Early nights, no smoking or drinking. Because you know there's a whole world of media out there who would give their right arms to catch me being a shit mum-to-be. You've no idea what it's like. Every time I leave the house, they're on my tail. I go to the supermarket, they're snapping my groceries. I go to lunch and talk to the parking attendant, they're all over him, asking what I said. I have no fucking privacy unless I'm in here, behind these walls. They're all waiting for me to end up on my arse outside some nightclub six months pregnant. And that's not a headline I could come back from. So I have to pull the tragedy face for poor Joshu and tell him I can't come and watch him doing his pumping rideouts all over town.'

'"Pumping rideouts?"'

She snorted. 'DJ wankspeak for a set. He takes it all seriously, bless him. He's got a little studio out the back, he spends days in there putting stuff together in the right sequence. He's doing really well, you know. He's starting to get some top gigs.'

'Which might have something to do with being your boyfriend.'

Scarlett gave me a dark look. 'That might have raised his profile, but he is actually good, you know.'

'Even when he's off his face?' A small test of our incipient friendship.

'What do you mean?' Now the old belligerent Scarlett came leaping out of the cave.

'About half of the times I've seen Joshu, he's been high. You've spent too much time round people who abuse drink and drugs not to see that for yourself.'

'So he uses. That doesn't make him a junkie. He likes to have fun. That doesn't mean he's hooked.'

This wasn't the time or the place to point out to Scarlett that I wouldn't have Joshu anywhere near any child of mine, with his drugs and fake guns. But I had made my point. If we were going to be mates, it was as well that I'd got my reservations out in the open sooner rather than later. At least Scarlett knew now that she could rely on me to be honest with her, even when she didn't like what I had to say.

We turned a corner that day. I only wish I'd had a clearer view of the road ahead.

11

Once I've finished the interviews, I generally don't see anything of my clients until I've completed the first draft. When I have queries, I email or phone them. It was different with Scarlett. Five days after we were done talking, she texted me to say she was in town, could she come round to mine?

I never let clients into my life. They don't know my address, they don't come to my home. They are professional acquaintances and they stay in my professional sphere. But Scarlett had blown a hole in her barriers to let me in. The least I could do was to return the favour. So I texted the address back and put a bottle of mineral water in the freezer to chill.

She turned up in the red Mazda sports car. My house is the end one of a grimy yellow-brick terrace in what barely scrapes by as Hackney. The car stuck out like a pickled onion on a cream cake, but Scarlett had the good sense to stuff her hair in a snood and cover her eyes with a pair of tinted glasses. Not big, outrageous 'look at me' sunglasses but understated specs that made her face look different. She made it up the path without dragging anyone's attention away from the car.

Once inside, she made no secret of the fact that she was curious. While I made tea, she poked around downstairs, checking out the CD collection, the books and the pictures on the walls. 'Nice,' she offered in final judgement as she wandered back to the scrubbed pine table that occupies the dining-room end of the open-plan space I live in, trailing a miasma of Scarlett Smile, the sweet floral signature fragrance the perfumiers had created for her.

'A bit different from yours.' I poured boiling water into the mugs and stirred the bags around.

'Tell you the truth, I didn't have a bloody clue when I moved into mine. Half the décor I inherited from the bankrupt geezer I bought it off. The other half, Georgie organised.' She gave a half-laugh. 'Nobody I knew ever had "interior décor".' She used her fingers to signal quotation marks in the air. 'You just slapped a bit of paint on the walls. Or picked up some wallpaper off the market. So I'm learning as I go along. This here—' She gestured at my lemon walls, stripped boards with their blue-and-white striped jute rugs and pale wooden cupboards and shelves. 'I like this. I could live with something like this. I like coming into people's houses and seeing what they've chosen. I'm learning all the time, Steph. I'm getting the hang of stuff that people like you take for granted.'

I'd never really stopped and considered how much people in Scarlett's shoes missed out on. It's not that I'm posh. My dad works for an insurance company, my mum's a primary school secretary. But Scarlett was one of Thatcher's illegitimate kids, the workless underclass. The rest of us, we're too busy taking the piss or patronising or judging to stop and wonder why people suddenly thrust into the spotlight have such crap taste. When you did bother asking, the answer was uncomfortable.

Scarlett broke the seriousness of the mood. 'Got any biscuits? I'm starving.'

I found the remains of a packet of chocolate digestives that Pete had been working his way through the previous evening.

'You're in luck. I don't usually keep biscuits in the house. It's too tempting when I'm working at home.'

'Where do you work, then?' She looked around vaguely, as if she'd missed something.

'I had the loft converted about five years ago. I've got an office up there.'

Scarlett took the offered cup of tea and sat down, stretching out her legs under the table as if she belonged. 'You live here all by yourself, then?'

'Pretty much. My bloke often stays over but we don't live together.'

'Why not?' She stirred sugar into her tea and smiled to soften the question.

I sighed. 'I'm not sure, to be honest.' I thought about it. 'I like my own space too much, I think. I've lived on my own for a long time and I don't want to give that up.'

'Sounds like you don't love him,' Scarlett said.

I laughed awkwardly. 'That's what he says. But it's not true. You can love someone without wanting to spend every minute of your life with them. Like Joshu with you. He loves you, but being free to do his own thing matters to him too. I'm a bit like that, I suppose. But my bloke, Pete, he'd like us to live together and for me to give up work so I can devote myself to him. Which I definitely don't want to do.'

Scarlett pulled a face. 'Too right. I see what you mean, about having your own space. And I suppose if Joshu was around twenty-four seven, I'd get stir crazy. It's going to be weird enough when the baby comes along.'

'How are you feeling about that?'

'Pretty cool. You know? It's like I spent all my life watching people fuck up with their kids. I'm the greatest living expert on what not to do to your kids. I'm gonna be a good mum. I'm gonna bring this kid up proper. And nothing's going to stop me.' And I believed her.

She delved into her shoulder bag, pulled out a scrunched-up bundle of pages torn out of various brochures and catalogues, and spread them out on the table. 'This is the cot I'm having,' she said, flattening a brightly coloured photograph and pushing it towards me. As she went through her purchases, it dawned on me that she probably didn't have anyone else she could do this with. The girls she went out on the razz with didn't have the attention span; Joshu didn't seem bothered about the practical details of their life as parents; and she had no matriarchal family figure to turn to. I was the nearest thing she had to an auntie or a big sister. I couldn't help feeling that, if I was the answer, Scarlett was definitely asking the wrong question, since I've never felt I had a maternal bone in my body.

Still, watching her enthusiasm was infectious, and in spite of myself I began to engage with the debate over buggies and car seats. We were flicking back and forth between cot mobiles when the alarm on her phone went off. Startled, Scarlett began to gather her papers together. 'Ah, shit,' she said. 'I've got to go. I'm modelling maternity wear at some charity do up Knightsbridge. Scummy mummy meets yummy mummies.' She shoved the papers in her bag. 'This has been great. I've had a fucking fantastic time.' She stood up, hand in the small of her back, groaning. 'Bloody back. This doesn't get any easier.' She gave me a hug. 'Can I come again?'

I returned the embrace. 'Of course you can.'

We were halfway down the hall, nattering about when we'd see each other again, when the front door opened. Pete took a step inside then stopped dead. His face gave nothing away. That was never a good sign. Scarlett stepped back and somehow in the narrow hallway I managed the introductions. Pete grunted in response, but Scarlett either didn't notice or didn't care. 'You got a good one there, mate,' she told him as she squeezed past him to the door. 'You want to take care of that one. See you, Steph.' And she was gone, leaving only a whiff of Scarlett Smile in the air behind her.

It would be fair to say that Pete wasn't best pleased by my new best friend. He seemed affronted that I would want to be pals with someone I'd come to know through ghosting them. No, that's not quite true. If it had been a politician or someone else with status and power, he'd have been happy to include them in our circle. But all he could see was the Scarlett Harlot and all that went with that image.

'People make judgements about us by the company we keep,' he said patiently, as if he was explaining to a child. 'I don't want them misjudging you because you're choosing to be with her. Everybody knows she's racist and homophobic and thick as a brick—'

'And they're wrong. That's not who she is. It's who she's chosen to portray.'

He waved a hand dismissively. 'It doesn't matter whether they're right or wrong. What matters is how people view her. They think she's a contemptible slapper. And that should be enough to keep you away from her. You've got nothing in common with her, Stephanie.'

'I like her.'

'I like Reginald D. Hunter, but I don't want him in my kitchen.'

'Who's the racist now?' I tried to sound light-hearted, but Pete didn't see the funny side.

'Don't try to be clever,' he said, going to the fridge and taking out a bottle of beer. 'I'm only thinking of you.'

I knew that was a big fat lie. He was only thinking of himself. Concerned that people would judge him because of the company I kept. But I didn't want to make a big deal of it. It would only end with bad feeling and I hated to see the hurt in his eyes when he was upset. 'I'll make sure your paths don't cross in future,' I said.

Evidently I hadn't managed to sound conciliatory enough. 'The easiest way to make sure our paths don't cross is not to invite her here again,' he grumbled, walking past me and settling down on the sofa, remote in hand. 'What's for dinner?'

'I didn't know you were coming over,' I said. 'I'll make some spaghetti carbonara.'

He grunted. 'That'll have to do then. Come here and give me a cuddle before you get stuck in. It's been a long and weary road, getting this mix right.' And that was that. Looking back, I wonder whether he thought I'd agreed to dump Scarlett. It never occurred to me that he'd read me so wrong.

12

While I was working on the first draft, Scarlett and I met up once or twice a week. Mostly we got together for lunch in town, but she did come back to the house a couple more times. By now, we both knew we were going to be pals. But there was business to be done too. The plans for the wedding were rattling on, including the selling of the exclusive stories. In spite of Georgie's entirely reasonable protestations that I wasn't a journalist, Scarlett had insisted I was the only writer she would talk to. So as well as sorting out the book, I had to write a big magazine piece and a newspaper special about the bloody wedding.

It was like wrestling cats. Neither Scarlett nor Joshu seemed to have the slightest interest in talking about their love, their wedding or married life and parenthood. In the end, I drove out to the hacienda when I knew they'd both be home and corralled them in the Western-themed living room, where I forced them to give me enough quotes to cobble something together.

While I played at being a journalist, Scarlett was reading the first draft of the book. We were up against it now, since Stellar Books wanted simultaneous publication with the wedding.

Thankfully, Scarlett liked what I'd done, only asking for a few minor changes where I'd misunderstood what she'd been trying to say in her Scarlett Harlot persona. By the week of the wedding, the book was at the printer and the articles were with their respective publications. I had fulfilled my end of the professional bargain.

That only left the personal stuff. My invitation had been for both Pete and me. I'd dithered over whether I should even tell him about it. He'd probably be working. And he wouldn't want to come anyway. In the end, I decided not to mention it. I realise I was taking the coward's way out, but I just wanted to enjoy the day without feeling crap about myself. I knew there would be lots of photos in the press, but I reckoned I could stay out of the front line. Nobody would be interested in me when there was a whole raft of C-list slebs to choose from.

The happy couple were dressed to the nines. Scarlett's dress was a miracle of designer finesse. Although she was almost eight months gone, so artfully was the ivory silk dress cut and styled, the pregnancy barely showed. A froth of lace and gold thread surrounded her head in an extravagant halo, turning her into a *Yes!* magazine madonna. Joshu had cleaned up nicely too. His morning suit fitted perfectly, his hair was neatly barbered and he appeared to be drug-free. I wished for his sake that his family had been there to see how beautifully turned out he was. Mind you, given his adamantine conviction that his mother would not be happy till she saw Scarlett stoned in the street, it was probably as well they'd stayed away.

The ceremony itself was surprisingly dignified. They'd opted for a non-denominational service with a spiritual dimension. The readings were genuinely moving, the music had not been mixed or juggled by Joshu, and because they held it in the morning, before most of the guests had started drinking, nobody disgraced themselves in public. I was amazed; the media were disappointed.

By the end of the evening, the hotel ballroom wasn't trashed, though the majority of the guests were. The groom included. Scarlett had spent most of the wedding reception sprawled on a banquette with a cushion rammed into the small of her back. She'd held court, graciously air-kissing everyone who wanted to stop by and be snapped with her. But I could see that she was starting to wilt.

I found Joshu in the bar with a gaggle of his buddies. His tie dangled from his collar, his coat was slung over a chair and his hair was plastered to his forehead with sweat. He was the very picture of ruined debauchery. It was clear there was no prospect of calling on him to rescue his wife from her hangers-on. I left him to it, wondering if this would end up being the impetus for the first of many marital rows. At least he wouldn't ruin the honeymoon.

There wasn't going to be one.

Well, not for a while anyway. Scarlett's pregnancy was so advanced no airline would touch her as a passenger. And neither Scarlett nor Joshu could conceive of a honeymoon that didn't involve intercontinental air travel. The plan was that they'd have a quiet couple of days at home. The honeymoon would have to wait until the baby was old enough to make it to the Maldives. So it wasn't like Joshu was strictly necessary for this part of the proceedings.

My next best option was George. But he was nowhere to be found. I did eventually stumble on Carla, his assistant. She was fawning drunkenly over a minor soap star but she unpeeled herself long enough to reveal that George had left hours ago. She did, however, have the details of the car service that had been detailed to take the newlyweds home.

I called the driver and told him to be outside in five minutes. I sidled along the banquette next to Scarlett and leaned over to mutter in her ear. 'I think you're about to turn into a pumpkin. I've ordered the car.'

She turned and kissed my cheek. 'I love you, Steph,' she said. 'Come on then. Since my husband's neither use nor ornament, you'd better keep me company.'

'I wasn't planning . . .'

'Aw, come on, Steph, it's my wedding night and I can't even get pissed. The least you can do is come home and have a laugh with me.' She pulled a pitiful face and whimpered like a puppy.

And so Scarlett ended up sneaking out of her own wedding reception with her ghost. We giggled all the way back to Essex, cheerfully ripping into the wedding guests, their outfits and the more outlandish bits of behaviour on display. But by the time we got back to the hacienda, Scarlett was definitely running out of steam. She could barely get out of the back of the limo, and under the security lights she looked drawn and frail. She threw her arm round my waist for support and together we hobbled inside. I tried to get her to go straight to bed, but she just groaned and subsided on to one of the sofas. 'I need to get out of this bloody frock,' she complained. 'But I can't be arsed.'

I went off to the kitchen to make tea. When I returned, she'd crawled out of the confines of her dress and was half-sitting, half-lying on the sofa in a sheer silk slip, the kettle drum of her belly tight against the material. 'What a day,' she sighed. She held her left hand up to the light and admired the big chunk of gold on her ring finger. 'Mrs Patel.' She sniggered. 'They'd love that back in Holbeck.'

'Holbeck?'

'Leeds' answer to the Lost Continent. Where I grew up. Where half the population are British Asian and the other half think the BNP are too bloody left-wing. You know what, I think I'm going to stick to my own name.'

'Did you miss your family?'

'Nope,' she said. 'Did I tell you, my mum tried to get in touch? The publicity must have penetrated her drunken haze. Either that or my sister put her up to it. Thinking there was maybe an earner in it for them. Luckily, the only number she's got for me is Georgie. When push comes to shove, there's nothing like having the posh gits on your side. They totally know how to put the fear of God up the lower orders. He menaced the living shit out of her. Told her he'd set the five-oh on her and all sorts. So she backed off. And I'm not sorry. I'd have spent the whole bloody day wondering when it was all going to go off.'

I yawned. 'Fair enough.' I stood up. 'And now I'm heading for home.'

'Aw no, Steph,' Scarlett protested, pushing herself upright. 'You can't leave me all alone on my wedding night. That would be so wrong.'

I laughed. 'Can you imagine what the red-tops would make of that? "Scarlett Harlot spends wedding night with ghost." No, I'd better get back.'

'No, seriously, Steph. I don't want to be alone in the house tonight.' All at once, the frivolity had dissipated. Scarlett was deadly serious. 'I feel like shit and I don't want to be alone.'

I could see she wasn't joking. I didn't want to be stranded out in the wilds of Essex, but I didn't want to let her down either. Typical of that useless wanker Joshu, leaving her on her tod on her wedding night because he was too busy playing the big-time DJ with his mates. 'I'll tell the car to go, then,' I said with as good grace as I could muster.

We parted for the night almost as soon as I returned, Scarlett plodding wearily up the stairs while I headed down the hall to the guest rooms by the pool area. The room I chose was already made up, as immaculate and impersonal as a hotel room, save for the large fluffy chimpanzee perched on the pillow. I wondered if that was Scarlett's inspired choice or something that had been left behind by the previous owner. In the chest of drawers, as promised, there was a folded stack of unisex nightshirts. The bathroom cabinet held sealed packets of toothbrushes, disposable razors and condoms. Expensive toiletries lined the shelf in the shower cubicle. Given the paucity of Scarlett's experience, I suspected George had given instructions to Carla or the cleaning service.

I barely had the energy to undress and clean my teeth. Next day, I had the wedding chapter to write. The very thought of it was enough to drain the last drops of energy from my weary body. I swear I was asleep before I closed my eyes.

13

It was the sudden bright light that woke me from the depths of sleep. Blinking, I cried out as I pushed myself upright. 'Sorry,' Scarlett gasped. 'But I think the baby's coming.' She was leaning in the doorway clutching her bump and sweating like a field hand in high summer. 'I woke up all wet,' she said. 'My waters broke. And I keep getting these contractions.'

I jumped up and ran to her. I put my shoulder under her arm and guided her to the bed. 'Lie down,' I said. All I knew about giving birth was what I'd learned from film and TV over the years. Right then, it did not feel anywhere near enough. 'How often are you having the contractions?'

'I don't fucking know,' she yelled, doubling over in pain and groaning through clenched teeth. It seemed to last for ever, but according to my watch it was only about twenty seconds. After it passed, she visibly relaxed and wiped her mouth with the back of her hand. She looked up at me, piteous as a frightened child. 'It fucking hurts, Steph.'

'How long has this been going on?' I asked.

'When we were at the hotel, my tummy started to feel a bit crampy. Like when you've got trapped wind, you know? I thought it was because I'd eaten too much crap. I've had indigestion for about six weeks. I thought it was the same kind of thing. But this isn't wind, Steph.' She breathed heavily.

'Are you booked in at a local hospital?' I asked.

'Course not. I'm booked into St Mary's, Paddington. Where Princess Diana had her boys.'

I couldn't help giggling. 'You are such a pro, Scarlett. Always an eye on the headlines.'

'What? You think I did this because it's what brainless bimbos do? Think again.' She groaned. 'I figure they wouldn't have let Diana go anywhere except the best. That's why I chose it. Because if anything goes wrong, that's where I want to be.'

'So who do I call?'

'There's a Louis Vuitton holdall in the bottom of the walk-in wardrobe in my bedroom. Bring it down, would you? There's a folder in it with all the details. Arrgh!' This time she yelled like a wounded pirate. According to my watch, it had been a fraction under three minutes since the previous contraction. That didn't sound good to me.

Fifteen minutes later, I was reversing out of the garage in Joshu's ridiculous Golf. When I'd explained the situation to the duty midwife, she'd told me to bring Scarlett in straight away. I tried to get a limo, but the company Scarlett used had nobody available for at least an hour. I didn't want to call a cab because that would have been like direct-dialling the red-tops. I tried Joshu, but his phone went straight to voicemail. So it was down to me. Three in the morning, there wouldn't be much traffic. And I'd stopped drinking around six hours earlier. I'd probably be OK. But there was no way Scarlett would be OK in the little bucket seat of her car.

I wasn't paying much attention to the speed limit, which was pretty dim, given what I was driving. I'd barely hit the A13 when my rearview mirror lit up with flashing blue lights. To tell you the truth, I was actually quite relieved. Scarlett's contractions seemed to be coming closer together and with more intensity. I was starting to feel a bit worried.

The traffic cop who swaggered up to my driver's window looked visibly shaken at the sight of a woman in her thirties behind the wheel of the pimpmobile. He was even more disconcerted when Scarlett started shouting from the back seat. 'Give us a fucking escort,' she yelled.

'She's in labour,' I said. Pretty needlessly, I thought.

'Is that—'

'Yes,' I said impatiently. 'And if we don't get her to hospital soon, you might find yourself in the headlines for making a roadside delivery.'

I could see the cogs turning. 'OK. Follow me.' He turned and headed back for his car.

'Wait,' I yelled. 'You don't know where we're going.'

He turned, laughing. 'You're going to the nearest hospital. She's in no condition to wait.'

He'd get no argument from me, though Scarlett was swearing like it was an Olympic sport. I wasn't sure if it was because of the pain or because her carefully orchestrated plans had all gone tits-up.

By the time we got to the hospital, Scarlett was mostly howling like a wolf or whimpering like a chained-up puppy. Sod compassion. All I wanted was for it to stop. I got my wish soon enough. The moment we arrived, Scarlett was whisked away on a trolley and I was directed to the reception desk to book her in. I thanked the cop, who was already preening himself at the desk. 'I called ahead,' he said. 'That's why they were waiting for her.'

'I know she'll appreciate it when she comes out the other side of this,' I said.

'Are you her PA, then?'

'No, I'm her friend.' I caught his sceptical look and checked myself out. A pair of Scarlett's joggers, about four inches too short for my longer legs. A sagging T-shirt sized for her bosom rather than mine. It had been that or my best frock, which didn't seem quite the thing for a hospital dash in the middle of the night. I looked more like a cleaner than any PA I'd ever met, apart from the fuck-me party shoes. But I wasn't about to explain myself to a cop. Instead, I made a point of getting a piece of paper from the receptionist and taking down his details. George could send him a bottle of Scotch later.

When it came to booking Scarlett in, I was impressed by how much detail I had at my fingertips. Date of birth, full name, address. I even knew where her GP's surgery was because I'd picked up a prescription one afternoon on my way out to her place. At least it made me look credible in the eyes of the receptionist. I really knew her. I wasn't just some passing stalker.

Up on the ward, I felt like I'd stepped into a no man's land between two irreconcilable states. On the one hand, the calm and capable midwives. On the other, the women crazed with pain, fear and discomfort. I found Scarlett in a small side room, squatting on the floor in a hospital gown. 'Are you OK?' I said. 'Sorry, that's a really stupid question. What have they said?'

'Nothing much.' She groaned. 'Somebody's coming to examine me properly in a minute.'

'I'm going to go and try to get hold of Joshu again,' I said.

'No,' she yelled, reaching out and grabbing my wrist like a vice. 'Stay here with me. I don't want that useless twat. It's our wedding night and where is he?' Another contraction gripped her and she subsided on to the floor, holding her bump and rocking from side to side. I was pretty sure this wasn't the best idea.

I didn't have to make the call, luckily. A strapping Scottish midwife strode in and got Scarlett on to the bed apparently by magic. 'Doctor will be along in a minute,' she said. 'Are you the birth partner?' I said no, Scarlett said yes. The midwife gave a prim little smile. 'That'll be a yes, then. Now we've got her on her side, you can rub her back.' Then she was gone.

'This is not a good idea,' I said. 'I've no bloody idea what to expect.'

'A baby. That's what I'm expecting.' Scarlett gave a feeble chuckle. 'I'm the one doing all the work, Steph. You just have to be here.'

And so I was. Because I hadn't a clue what was going on, it's hard to describe what happened over the next four hours. I know they gave her an epidural almost as soon as the doctor examined her. Between that and the gas and air she was sucking on, Scarlett wasn't making much sense about anything. 'They zone out in the second stage,' the midwife said, as if that was an explanation. She might as well have said, 'Cabbages dance on the moons of Jupiter,' for all the sense it made to me. I kept stroking her back and her head and her hands and mumbling platitudes. And trying not to pay too close attention to the business end of things.

The professionals didn't appear worried. It all seemed to be going calmly and smoothly. Until it wasn't. The medical team didn't flap or raise their voices. But all of a sudden there was a flurry of activity. There were more people in the room and they looked more serious, as if something had happened to make them stop coasting and pay particular attention. Scarlett seemed oblivious; she was sweating and swearing and panting and proving remarkably obedient to the midwife's instructions.

'What's happening?' I chose my words carefully. I wanted to ask what was wrong but I didn't want to frighten Scarlett.

'The baby's got a big head,' the doctor said. 'It's stuck in the birth canal.'

'That's not what's supposed to happen, right?'

She gave me an impatient glance. 'No. We're going to take Scarlett through to another room, where we can carry out procedures more easily.' As she spoke, the nurses were raising the sides of the bed and freeing the wheels from their brakes.

'Procedures? What procedures?'

'We're going to try something called a ventouse,' she said. By now, we were both following the bed down the hall.

'What's that?'

'Think sink plunger. Only kinder. Have you done *any* preparation for this?' she said as I trotted after her into a large room kitted out like a set from *Casualty*.

'I wasn't expecting to be doing this,' I said with some asperity. 'She's got a husband.'

The doctor tipped her head towards me and smiled. 'You're doing OK for a first reserve. Now keep out of our way.'

In a few moments, everything had changed. Now I was in the thick of a medical process. Scarlett wasn't an individual any more; she was a patient. A body to be worked on. A problem to be solved. It wasn't that anyone was unkind or careless of her. It was simply that kindness wasn't a factor in what was happening now. There was a sense of urgency in the room that hadn't been there before. Fear had taken up residence in the back of my throat and I felt on the verge of tears.

A few minutes in, a passing nurse said over her shoulder, 'Things will move fast now. We have to make sure the baby's getting enough oxygen.'

She was right. I was at the heart of a whirlwind of action. Apparently the ventouse wasn't working. The baby was stuck fast. All at once we were on the move again. A clipboard appeared out of nowhere with a pen tied to it. The doctor put the pen in Scarlett's hand as we headed back out into the corridor. 'You need to give your consent,' she said, sounding much more relaxed than anybody looked.

'Consent for what?' How could this be consent? Scarlett was off her head on pain relief and pain itself.

'We need to do an emergency C-section,' the doctor said.

She looked around and snagged one of the nurses. 'You, help Stephanie here. She needs to get gowned up and into theatre.'

'Me?' I yelped. 'Surely you don't expect—'

'Just do it. Please,' the doctor said as they all disappeared round a corner.

I let myself be led away. The nurse opened a cupboard and gave me a quick assessing look before yanking out a set of green scrubs. 'What's going on?' I said.

'You need to get changed. Hurry,' she said, leading me to a cubicle. 'They can't get the baby out. It's stuck. They're going to have to do an emergency section so they can pull the baby back up the birth canal. And they have to move fast in case his oxygen supply is compromised.'

'She's not going to like that,' I said, shrugging out of Scarlett's clothes and into the scrubs, which fitted me much better. 'She's already been complaining about the stretch marks. She'll be really pissed off about a scar.' I emerged and saw the nurse's face. 'I'm only joking. She's not that shallow and superficial, you know.'

My memory of what happened next is like one of those Roman mosaic pavements they excavate on *Time Team*. Fragments of a picture with gaps in between whose content you can only deduce or imagine.

A group of people in green or blue scrubs all focused on the operating table. A green fabric screen placed across Scarlett's chest so I wouldn't see the blood. A voice with an edge of desperation saying, 'There's a lot of blood here and I can't see where it's coming from.' Terror gripping my chest like the claws of a predatory bird. I imagined breaking the news to Joshu that his wedding day had ended here on a bloody operating table.

Then a midwife scurried across the room with a bloody bundle and disappeared into an anteroom. The next thing I heard was the thin cry of a baby. One of the gowned figures put a hand on my shoulder and said, 'It's a boy. They're just checking him out, don't worry.'

'What about Scarlett?'

It was hard to read him. All I could see were his eyes and eyebrows. 'They're doing their best. But we're a good team. You need to focus on the baby now.'

And then the midwife put him in my arms, swaddled in a blue cellular blanket. His thick dark hair was plastered randomly over his forehead, his nose was squashed like a boxer's and there were still traces of bloody mucus round his ears. But he was smiling. He was smiling and his eyes were open and they looked straight into mine and I was lost.

14

S cientists tell us that babies are genetically programmed to smile when they're born. It's a mechanism designed to save their lives. They smile, we fall in love. Because we are also programmed to be captivated by that smile. It's nothing to do with biology. You'll fall equally hard for the child of a complete stranger as you will for the fruit of your own loins. Think about it. It's estimated that a quarter of all children are not the offspring of the man who thinks they're his. And yet those fathers who persist in ignorance love their children as completely as biological parents. And it's not only fathers. Think of those stories where children are accidentally swapped at birth and the mothers love the substitutes every bit as much as their other kids.

Which is a roundabout way of saying I bonded with Jimmy Joshu Higgins minutes after he was born. They hustled us out of the operating theatre and back into the side ward where we'd been earlier. They sat me in a chair, provided me with a bottle of formula milk and showed me how to feed him. I thought nothing of it at the time. I assumed it was standard operating procedure.

I learned differently a couple of years later, when I was telling the tale as a lure to a prospective client who had done pioneering work in treating infertility. She looked aghast. 'Really? They got you to give him a bottle of formula?'

Baffled, I said, 'Yes. They said he'd had a bit of a struggle being born, he'd be hungry. And he was. He polished off the whole feed.'

She gave a wry little laugh. 'And the mum's OK?'

'She's fine. Still moans about her scar, but other than that, she's completely OK. Why?'

'Well, it sounds like they thought they were losing her.'

'You mean . . . as in, dying?'

She nodded. 'That's why they got you out of there so quickly. They didn't want you in the room if she died on the table. And that's why they got you to feed him.'

'I don't understand.'

'They're obsessed with breastfeeding these days. The reason they got you to give him a bottle was because they were afraid she wasn't going to make it. And the kid has to bond with someone.' I must have looked as appalled as I felt, for she burst out laughing. 'They were setting you up as the foster mum.'

Which is all the more ironic, given where we've ended up. But at the time, I just thought, yeah, of course the kid's hungry. And within the hour, Scarlett was back in the room. On a morphine drip and looking like she'd gone fifteen rounds with a brick wall, but indisputably there, smiling radiantly at the tiny bundle in her arms. 'He's beautiful,' she kept saying. Frankly, I lost interest fairly quickly. Even though I did agree with her.

'I'm going to let you two enjoy your lovefest,' I said. 'My work here is done now.'

Scarlett barely looked up. 'Thanks,' she said. 'You've been a total star.'

'What friends are for. I'm going to take Joshu's car back to yours. Can I borrow your car to get me home? You can't drive for six weeks anyway.'

'You what?' Now I had her attention.

'You've had a caesarean. You're not allowed to drive for six weeks. You're not supposed to lift anything heavier than a kettle. Joshu's going to have to wait on you hand, foot and finger.'

'You're joking?'

'No. Listen, I'll try to get hold of Joshu again when I get out of here. And I'll also call Georgie. He'll want to sort out the media deals. And I need to get some sleep.'

'Thanks. See you later.' I leaned over and kissed Jimmy on the forehead. 'He's gorgeous.'

Scarlett gave me an odd look, as if something had just occurred to her. 'Would you be his godmother?'

'Me? I know nothing about kids.'

'Time you learned, then.'

'I'd be crap at it.'

'No, you wouldn't. You wouldn't let yourself. Go on. For his sake. He needs somebody in his life that isn't mental.'

I don't know why I agreed, but I did. And that's how it started between me and Jimmy.

I tried to call Joshu from the hospital, but my phone had died. He'd probably have appreciated a little advance warning since he was fast asleep and stark naked on one of the leather sofas when I walked in. It wasn't a pretty sight. I grabbed one of the cow hides and threw it over him. He grunted and stirred then his eyes snapped open. The sight of me in Scarlett's clothes provoked a look of total bewilderment.

'Wassup?' he grunted, then gave a massive yawn that sent a blast of undigested alcohol my way. Belatedly, he noticed I was alone. 'Where's the wife?' he added with a sly grin. 'I saw you girls had taken off in my wheels.' He dragged himself upright and yawned again. 'Fuck, my head hurts. I need some drugs.'

'You need tea,' I said. 'Because you need to go and check out your wife and son.' I turned on my heel and marched off to the kitchen. I didn't trust myself to speak to the shiftless, feckless, heedless little shit.

I'd barely got the kettle on when he staggered in, the cow hide wrapped round his waist like a bizarre kilt. 'Did you say "son"?'

'While you were spending your wedding night out on the razz with your homies, your wife was giving birth, Joshu,' I snapped. 'Wondering, in between contractions, where your sorry ass was hiding.'

Water off a duck's back. 'I've got a son?' He shook his head, incredulous. 'Am I hallucinating this? I mean, who knows what I took last night, but it was a serious head-fuck. Is this for real? I've got a son?'

'Six pounds two ounces. His name is Jimmy.'

'But she's not due for another ... what? Six weeks?'

'She got her dates wrong. She's probably a couple of weeks early, but no more than that.' I popped a pod into the coffee machine for myself.

He laughed affectionately. 'Silly bitch can't count. Well, shit me a rainbow. I'm a dad.' He rubbed a hand over his hair and lurched towards the breakfast bar where he'd apparently left the contents of his pockets. He grabbed for his cigarettes and lit up. 'It's supposed to be a cigar, but this'll have to do for now. You might have bought me a cigar on the way home, Stephanie.'

'Funny, it never crossed my mind. You better get yourself cleaned up and over there. Oddly enough, she's not best pleased with you.' I plonked a cup of tea in front of him. 'Get that down you.'

'Was you there, like, with her?'

'I was. It was really scary. They had to do an emergency section.'

'A what?'

In my head, I sounded like my mother. *What do they teach them in school these days?* 'The baby got stuck coming out. So they had to cut her belly open and get him out in a hurry.'

He took a tentative sip of his tea, then swigged the whole cup back in one. He shuddered, then straightened up. 'What? They cut her belly open? That's horrible. She gonna have a scar and that?'

'Christ, Joshu. She lost more than half of her blood. They thought they were going to have to give her a blood transfusion. I think a scar was the least of her worries, frankly.'

He gave me a placatory nod. 'Well, I suppose that means she'll be OK down there. Like, still tight and that.'

I closed my eyes for a moment, wondering whether I should just throw my coffee over his head. I reminded myself that he was Jimmy's father and Scarlett's husband and better that he went to hospital as a visitor than as a patient. 'You won't have the chance to find that out for a while, you selfish bastard. She's had major abdominal surgery, Joshu. You're going to have to run around after her for months.'

He gave a nervous laugh. 'I don't think so. Georgie can sort somebody out to take care of her and the kid, yeah? That's what we fucking pay him for, innit.' He grinned again, and I caught a glimpse of the roguish charm that had captivated Scarlett. 'I've got a son.' Then he frowned. 'Wait a minute. Did you say she's called him Jimmy?'

'That's right.'

'No, that's all wrong. Jimmy Patel? What kind of name is that?'

Actually, it was going to be Jimmy Higgins. But I thought I'd leave that revelation for Scarlett. 'It's the one she wants. And since you weren't around when he popped out, I reckon you've forfeited the right to have a say.'

'Fucking Jimmy,' he said, turning away and stubbing out his

cigarette. 'I'll have something to say about that. I'm going for a shower, then I'm going over to see my son. And he's not going to be Jimmy for much longer, you can count on that.' And off he went, chest puffed out like a bantam cock.

The coffee was bitter and dense in my mouth. I was too tired to taste properly. I knew it was crazy to drive back to Hackney, only to return in a few hours to visit Scarlett and Jimmy. Joshu was about to go out. And there was a perfectly good guest room down the hall. The temptation was irresistible.

15

Hearing Stephanie describe Joshu's reaction to his son's birth, Vivian found it hard to resist the notion that he regarded the boy as his property. A man with that attitude would be the natural suspect in a case like this. The overwhelming majority of abducted children were stolen by or on behalf of the parent who didn't have custody. In a case like this, where the person who had charge of the boy wasn't even a relative, the father was the obvious person of interest.

'You said you know where Joshu is,' Vivian said. 'I have to tell you, it sounds like he's the person with the strongest interest in taking Jimmy away from you. Are you so sure he's where you think he is, and not here in the US?'

Stephanie looked amused. 'He's definitely not in the US. He—'

'Maybe not. But does he have the resources to hire people to kidnap Jimmy and bring the boy to him.'

'No. If you'd just let me finish what I was about to say ... Unless I've been burgled since we left for the airport, Joshu is exactly where I last saw him. Sitting in an urn on my mantelpiece. Joshu's dead, Agent McKuras. His and Scarlett's ashes sit in my living room like bookends above the fireplace.

Jimmy says good morning and good night to them every day.'

Vivian felt ambushed. The blood rose in her cheeks and she drummed her fingers on the desk. She wanted to yell at Stephanie, but that wasn't an option while the woman still might be the repository of information about the kidnap. 'What happened to him?'

'Like everything else connected to Scarlett and Jimmy, it's a long story.'

This time, Vivian was not about to be seduced by narrative. Stephanie Harker was a terrific raconteur, so good that Vivian risked losing sight of the importance of time in tracking down a missing child. And maybe – just maybe – there was a deliberate point to Stephanie's meandering stories. After all, who knew better than she that she'd be stopped by security? Who was better placed to set this up? She'd been left in charge of a rich woman's brat with no money to pay for it. Maybe she'd decided to extort some cash from the charitable foundation she'd mentioned earlier. 'These long stories aren't taking me any nearer a valid suspect,' she said, her voice cold. 'Tell me, Stephanie. If you got a ransom demand for Jimmy, who would pay?'

Stephanie looked startled. 'I . . . I don't know. I never even thought about it.' She spread her hands in a gesture of openness. 'I don't have that kind of money.'

'What kind of money?'

She looked puzzled. 'Well, when you hear about ransoms, it's usually seven figures and upwards. I'm not a rich woman. I make a decent living, but I'm not a millionaire. I'd do my best to raise the money, but I don't have much.'

'Couldn't you approach his mother's charitable foundation?'

'No chance,' Stephanie said. 'It was set up to benefit an orphanage in a remote part of Romania. Scarlett went there in

2007 as part of *Caring for Kids* – that's a big charity telethon in the UK – and she was completely bowled over by the children. A lot of them have AIDS, and that's how her dad died. She was appalled by the conditions there. So she set up the trust to take care of them. The orphanage is the sole beneficiary and there's no way round it. I've got a friend who's a trust lawyer and I asked her to check out whether I could claim anything for Jimmy's education or maintenance. She said the trust was watertight. Unless we can transform Jimmy into a Romanian orphan, I'm all he's got.'

'What about his father's estate?'

Stephanie snorted her ridicule. 'What estate? Joshu spent money like water. Faster than he could earn it, latterly. He was too fond of drugs and fast cars and stupid women. The only thing he left Jimmy was his music, which is all boxed up in a storage unit. It might make a few grand if I sold it off on eBay, but not enough to pay a ransom. No, if somebody's taken Jimmy for money, they've made a serious error of judgement.' She ran a hand through her hair. 'But at least they've got a vested interest in keeping him alive. Which is better than the alternative.'

'Which means we're back to square one.' Vivian couldn't help showing her impatience. 'If you can't take me closer to a viable suspect, who can?'

Stephanie gave her a nervous glance. Not for the first time, Vivian felt there was something lurking between them. Something Stephanie didn't want to give up. Something she didn't even want to contemplate. She looked down, studying her neatly manicured nails. 'There is someone it might be helpful for you to talk to. He's a detective with Scotland Yard. Detective Sergeant Nick Nicolaides.'

Vivian was taken aback. Out of nowhere, two hours into this interview, Stephanie Harker was introducing a cop who had something to bring to the party. 'Who the hell is

Sergeant Nick Nicolaides? And what does he have to do with this?'

'When Joshu died he was the officer who did all the interviews. He was really sympathetic but he seemed to be thorough too. Anyway, when I had some problems of my own this past year, I rang him because he was the only cop I knew. So he knows Jimmy and he knows the background too.' She raised her eyes and met Vivian's incredulous stare.

'And I'm only hearing about him now?'

'I'm sorry.' The talkative Stephanie seemed to have run out of steam. She rubbed her eyes, her face a grimace of pain. 'None of this is easy, you know. I'll give you his number, shall I?' She recited it from memory and Vivian keyed it into her phone.

'Wait here,' she said grimly. 'I need to see what this Nicolaides guy has to say.'

16

With every passing day the soundproofed room seemed to grow more oppressive. Detective Sergeant Nick Nicolaides knew the personal scents of the other five occupants so well he could have picked them out of an identity parade blindfolded. He knew their physical tics; the tapping of a pen against teeth, the soft percussion of fingertips on desktop, the sucking of air through the front teeth, the scratching of fingernails on designer stubble, the endless fiddling with the bridge of the reading glasses. He knew who would crack which kind of joke over the contents of the emails they were working through. He knew who was tweeting his mistress instead of working, who was texting his bookie and who was ordering groceries online from Tesco. And of course, he knew more about the professional and personal lives of News International journalists than any adult human should have to.

When he'd been seconded to the team investigating the allegations of News International's phone hacking and corrupting of public officials, Nick had been excited. It was a headline-grabbing case, and its potential repercussions for the media and the Met were thrilling. Though not in a good way.

But the glitz had worn thin pretty quickly. News International had handed over three hundred million emails. Three hundred million. Nick suspected they'd dumped everything they could find on to the inquiry in the hope that the trees would get lost in the wood. It wasn't humanly possible to read every one. He remembered reading about a project to classify every galaxy in the universe according to shape. The astronomers involved had asked members of the public to log on to their website and take part in the process. It was the only way to get enough bodies on the case. Even then, it would take years. But that wasn't an option here because it was a criminal investigation.

So what they had was a computer program that was gradually working its way through all of the three hundred million, primed with key words and phrases that should, in theory, mean that all the dodgy emails would be spat out into the inboxes of the people grafting away in rooms like this all over the old Wapping printworks. Every team was a mix of the company's own watchdogs and police officers. Embedded, that was what they called what he was doing. And embedded was what it bloody felt like. Embedded up to the neck in other people's shit.

Now, instead of actually working real cases and catching real criminals, Nick was locked in a bunker looking for evidence which, even if he found it, probably would never see the light of courtroom day. A few months ago, his career had seemed to be on an upward trajectory. But this was the backwater to end all backwaters.

He clicked on the next email in his queue. It had been flagged up because it contained the word 'credit'. One of the ways journalists paid backhanders to sources was to list their associates in the credits book. If you wanted to pay DCI XXX for giving you an exclusive tip, you put a payment through to his girlfriend or his mum or his best mate. So every time a journalist or an executive mentioned, 'taking the credit', or 'credit where it's due', Nick would have to read the innocuous message. Just in case.

This time, it was from an editorial executive complaining that his company credit card had been refused at the petrol station that morning. Nick sighed and sent it to the 'checked' folder and clicked on the next one. The ringing of his phone felt like a stay of execution. A glance at the screen revealed an unfamiliar number. But it was an American number. And there was a good reason to answer a call from America this morning.

'Hello?' he said, always wary of giving too much away.

'Have I reached Detective Sergeant Nick Nicolaides?' An American voice. Not what he expected at all. A twitch of anxiety in his chest.

'You have. Who am I speaking to?'

'This is Special Agent Vivian McKuras of the Federal Bureau of Investigation. I'm based at the O'Hare Airport office.'

'Has something happened to Stephanie?' He couldn't help himself.

'Sergeant, I need to confirm your ID before I can say anything further. Can you give me a landline number for the police office where you are based so I can do that?'

Now he was seriously worried. What on earth had Stephanie got herself into? He rattled off the number for the major incident team he was nominally attached to. 'You'll have to call me back on the mobile, I'm based out of the office at the moment.' The line went dead.

Nick jumped to his feet and hustled out of the door. There was a shout of protest behind him. He wasn't supposed to leave the civilians unattended. But he needed to be moving. His long legs ate up the corridors and the wind of his passage whipped his shaggy hair back from his face. Out in the car park, he paced, heedless of the misty rain drifting around him. Wiry and restless, he looked almost feral in his black jeans and untucked denim shirt. Without a guitar in his hands, he didn't know what to do with himself.

When the phone rang again, he squatted in a corner of two walls and hunched over it. 'So tell me, Agent McKuras. What's up that you need me?'

'I believe you're acquainted with Stephanie Harker?'

'That's right. What's she supposed to have done?'

'It interests me that you jump to the conclusion that she's the doer rather than the done to, officer.'

Nick cursed himself for his impetuosity. 'It was a light-hearted figure of speech, that's all. Stephanie's not a criminal. Can we please rewind and you tell me why you're making this phone call?' He was so much better at the face-to-face. What charms he had never seemed to survive the phone.

'I'm calling you as part of our investigation into the apparent kidnap of Jimmy Higgins—'

'Jimmy's been kidnapped? Where? How? What happened?' It made no sense. Not in America.

'They were separated in the security area so Ms Harker could undergo a pat-down. A man approached Jimmy and walked away with him. By the time the authorities realised what had happened, they had disappeared.'

It didn't sound anything like the whole story. But Nick knew better than to push for more right now. If all else failed, he would get Stephanie's version soon enough. 'Disappeared? In one of the most heavily surveilled places around? How can that be?'

'We're still investigating,' she said repressively. 'However, because Jimmy and Ms Harker are both UK residents, we're having some difficulty in developing any credible suspects or leads over here. Now, she seems to think that you might be able to assist us in that regard, since you are already acquainted with the boy.'

Nick's mind was racing. There was one obvious answer to that question. What he couldn't work out was why Stephanie hadn't reported it herself. The only reason he could imagine was that even after everything she'd gone through, she still wanted to think the best of Pete Matthews. While it made him furious that she could waste a shred of positive emotion on that piece of shit, he had to admit it spoke well of her loyalty. But still. She should have coughed about Matthews herself, not left it to him. Clearly the bastard had done her more damage than Nick had realised. 'I do know Jimmy's history, it's true. You've not heard anything from the kidnappers?'

'Nothing as yet. There's nothing to point specifically to a kidnap for ransom. Can you think of anyone who might have a motive for stealing the child? I wondered about family, on either side.'

'I can't see it,' Nick said slowly. 'His dad's family disowned Joshu when he married Scarlett. As far as I'm aware, they've never set eyes on the boy, never mind wanted anything to do with him.'

'Do they have other grandchildren?'

'I have no idea. What are you getting at?' If she was going to push him down this line of inquiry, let her be the one who laid it out.

He heard Vivian sigh. 'I'm thinking cultural imperatives here,' she said slowly. 'Some cultures place a high value on descent through the male line. If circumstances have dictated that Jimmy is the only male heir, that could change their view.'

Nick exhaled hard. 'I'll check it out, if you think it's a line of investigation that needs attention. However, I think we can discount Scarlett's family. They don't have the money or the brains to mount what sounds like a very well-organised operation. Even if they wanted Jimmy. Which they don't, unless he comes with a pocketful of cash.'

'That's pretty much what Stephanie said. So much for where we shouldn't be looking. What about where we should?'

'There was an obsessive fan who kept pestering Scarlett during her final illness. She was convinced that God had told her to become Jimmy's mother if Scarlett didn't survive. I ran across her during the investigation into Joshu's death. We warned her off, but she wouldn't stay away. In the end, she lost it in the hospice day room. Ended up being sectioned. I doubt she's got the wherewithal to pull off something like this, but I will make inquiries.'

'That definitely sounds more promising. Is that it? I have a feeling you've got more to tell me, Sergeant.'

She was good, this one. Nick pushed himself upright and began pacing again. 'Stephanie used to have a boyfriend called Pete Matthews. He was one of those insidious bullies. The kind who make out it's all for your own good, that they're just pointing out your shortcomings so you can improve yourself. I'm sure you've come across the type? In your professional life, I mean?'

'I know the sort of thing you're talking about. Go on, Sergeant. This is interesting to me.'

'To cut a long story short, when Steph dumped him, he turned into a stalker. She had to take out a restraining order. She ended up selling her house and more or less going into hiding for a while. It worked, in the sense that it seemed to shake him off. But because of the publicity around Scarlett's death and Stephanie taking over caring for Jimmy, she's been scared that he might be able to track her down again. It's a long shot, but this is the kind of cruelty he might perpetrate.'

Vivian sighed. Nick pictured a woman with a pissed-off look

about the mouth. 'Any idea why Ms Harker didn't volunteer this information to us herself? Right away? Instead of taking me the scenic route?'

His instinct was to leap to Stephanie's defence, but the caution his job had taught him battened down the urge. He didn't want this FBI agent thinking the pair of them were hand in glove in a bad way. It would poison any possibility of him helping to recover the boy Stephanie loved so much. And that would not help their relationship to flourish. 'You'll have to ask her that. But if I had to hazard a guess, I'd say it might be something to do with the shame women in abusive relationships often feel. In her shoes, I probably wouldn't want to own up to Pete Matthews.' Or to Nick's role in getting him off her back.

'Do you know where this Pete Matthews can be found?'

'He shouldn't be too hard to find. There'll be a last known address on the computer, I imagine. He's a sound engineer, and he's got a good professional rep. He's generally in work. Do you want me to follow that up too?' He stopped pacing outside the main door and leaned his forehead against the glass. Its chill made him feel feverish in spite of the rain soaking his hair.

'It would be helpful.'

'You'll have to put a formal request in to my boss, then,' he said. 'You need to get me seconded to your inquiry if you want my help.' Realising he sounded brusque, he added, 'I'm in the thick of a major long-term investigation right now. I can't squeeze other stuff in around it. Call that number I gave you and clear it with DCI Broadbent.'

'I'll do that. One more thing. You understand, I have to ask this. Because nobody is better placed than Stephanie to set up something as delicately poised as this kidnap. Have you any reason to suspect that, for whatever motive, she could be behind this abduction?'

Careful, he told himself. 'No,' he said. 'She's always seemed like a decent person to me. Nobody made her take the kid on. Social services have been all over her – even though Scarlett left instructions in her will, nobody's going to hand a kid over to someone who's not a family member without pretty stringent investigations. So if there was anything dodgy going on, they'd have picked up on it.'

'I guess.' Vivian drew the words out, as if she was reluctant to accept what he was saying.

'Listen, get Broadbent to release me from what I'm doing and I'll get on to this like a shot.' He paused for a moment, remembering how hard it was for Jimmy to trust anyone after what he'd already lost. 'He's a good kid,' he said. 'I hate to think of him being among strangers, scared. All that. I'll do everything I can to help.'

'OK. I'll put in a call to your boss.'

'Thanks. And ...' His voice tailed off. He wanted to let Stephanie know he was there for her, but using an FBI agent as conduit probably wasn't the best way to do it.

'Yeah?'

'Will you be releasing Stephanie any time soon?'

'We're not holding her in any formal sense. She's a cooperative witness, that's all. A case like this, we try to get as much background info as we can. I imagine we'll be talking for a while yet. Why?'

It was a question that didn't have an easy answer. 'If she wants to talk to somebody – somebody that knows Jimmy, I mean – tell her she can give me a call any time.'

'Sure. I'll talk to you soon, Sergeant Nicolaides.'

And the line went dead. Nick strode back to the office to pick up his jacket. He was confident enough of Broadbent to believe he wouldn't be back at Wapping for as long as it took to sort out whatever had happened in America. Already he was making a 'to do' list in his head.

The only problem was that the most important item on the list was the one he could do nothing about right now. 'Talk to Stephanie' was going to have to wait till Special Agent McKuras had finished raking through her past. Nick couldn't resist a wry smile.

Given how much past there was, it could take a while.

17

Vivian had gone back to her own office to call DCI Broadbent. She'd wanted privacy, a chance to pick up a latte at
Starbucks and access to her computer in case Sergeant
Nicolaides' boss wanted the request in writing. He turned out
to be remarkably cooperative but yes, he wanted an email to
confirm her request. She sipped her coffee and hammered out
what she wanted from the English cops. She was glad
Broadbent hadn't made a big deal out of it. If she'd had to run
it through her boss, God alone knew how long it would have
taken today. But then, it wasn't like she was asking for much.
Just a few hours of a detective's time. It was amazing how a
child's life on the line could cut straight through red tape.

She leaned back in her chair and considered what she had
learned. Either Stephanie Harker was as decent as Nicolaides
believed or else she'd comprehensively fooled him over some
time. Not knowing him, it was hard to tell. For the time being,
she was inclined to believe Stephanie. Her reactions thus far
seemed credible to Vivian. She'd have behaved in much the
same way, she reckoned. But teasing out what lay beneath
those reactions was not quite so straightforward.

The ping of her email inbox derailed her thoughts.

Broadbent had confirmed his agreement to her request for help. She forwarded it to her boss in the Chicago office, just to cover all the bases. While she was waiting for Abbott and Nicolaides to fill in some of the blanks, she'd see what else Stephanie Harker was willing to tell her.

When she returned to the interview room, Stephanie eyed her coffee greedily. 'Any chance I could get one of those?' she said. 'I've been up for a long time and I'm pretty much running on empty.' It was hard to argue against; she looked frayed and frazzled. They always did when they went into adrenalin deficit.

Vivian dug into her pocket for a twenty and gave it to Lopez. 'Get one for yourself, Lia. You want a latte, Stephanie?'

'Could I have a mocha? I need sugar as well as caffeine. And maybe a muffin or something?'

Vivian nodded to Lopez. 'Get me a receipt, please.' She took a sip of her own coffee. 'Tell me about Pete Matthews,' she said. 'And before you say it, I know it's a long story. But until we have some positive leads to chase, we may as well use the time.'

What with one thing and another, it was a couple of days before I made it back home. I'd barely had time to put the kettle on when Pete turned up with a face like a poisoned pup. 'About bloody time you got back,' he grouched as soon as I opened the door.

'And it's lovely to see you too.' I was trying to tease him out of it, not to be sarcastic. But when he was in that kind of mood there was no point in anything other than total capitulation. 'I did text you yesterday. Didn't you get it?'

'I should have a key for this house,' he said, stomping down the hall into the kitchen. 'I was frantic with worry when I didn't hear from you for two bloody days. I tried to ring you, I tried to text you. But nothing.'

'I told you. My phone was dead, and there was no Nokia charger at Scarlett's. I didn't manage to get another one till yesterday.' I followed him through and carried on making a pot of coffee.

'I came round the house to check on you. To make sure nothing had happened.'

I burst out laughing. 'What was going to happen? I'm not an invalid, Pete. I'm a healthy woman who can take care of herself.'

'Anything could have happened. You could have slipped in the bath and hit your head. You could have fallen downstairs. You could have been attacked by a burglar.'

I shook my head, my back to him as I pressed down the plunger in the cafetière. 'It's being so cheerful that keeps you going.'

Suddenly he gripped my upper arms and whirled me round. Then he clamped his hands tight round my biceps and shook me. 'You silly bloody woman. I was worried about you.' The anger in his face was frightening. I knew it was rooted in fear and concern, but that didn't make it any less scary.

'Let go, Pete, you're hurting me,' I yelped.

My words seemed to break the spell of his rage. Abruptly he let go and turned away. When he spoke, his voice sounded choked. 'You have no idea how upset you made me,' he said. 'And over what? That bloody slapper Scarlett Higgins.'

'She's not a slapper,' I said, rubbing my arms. I'd have bruises later, I knew it. 'I happened to be with her when she went into labour. And then there were things that needed sorting out.'

He turned back and poured himself a cup of coffee. 'And why's that your responsibility? You're her bloody ghost writer, not her mother.'

'Because she hasn't got anybody else. Joshu's as much use as a cardboard hammer, most of her mates are only interested

145

in clothes, clubbing and copping off, and she doesn't have anything to do with her family.'

'She's got an agent, hasn't she? I still don't see why it's down to you.' He opened the fridge and peered suspiciously at the milk.

'Because we're friends, Pete.'

He snorted and sniffed the milk. 'This is off. That's what happens when you're busy chasing after the Scarlett Harlot. You don't look after yourself or the people who really care about you.'

'Don't call her that. It's horrible. And she's not. I'm sorry about the milk but there's a carton of cream in there that hasn't been opened. That should be fine.' I reached past him and handed him the cream. 'Have a bit of luxury for once.' I was determined not to give in to his bad mood.

'It's not the same,' he grumbled, tipping cream into his coffee with a mistrustful look on his face.

'So, how's things with you? How were the Northumbrian pipers?'

'They were good,' he said, brightening a little. 'Very professional. They turned up on time, they got what we wanted straight off and they delivered. It was only the one track we needed them for, but they were a dream to work with.' His mouth turned down again. 'I wish I could say the same about the bloody band. Sam changes his mind more often than he changes his socks.'

Getting him off the subject of Scarlett changed the atmosphere between us, and we prepared dinner together, arguing with the radio and laughing at each other's smartarsed remarks. Later, when we were sitting at the table, finishing off the wine, Pete suggested going out to a gig the following evening. Some indie band he'd mixed a couple of tracks for were playing down the road in Hoxton and he'd been invited.

'As long as it's not too early,' I said. 'I promised I'd pop in tomorrow at evening visiting to see Scarlett and Jimmy.'

Pete groaned. 'Oh Christ, Stephanie. Is this how it's going to be from now on? You running around after Scarlett and her bloody sprog? You need to back off.'

'Pete, she had a really rough time giving birth. It's going to take her a while to recover, so yes, I'll be helping out for a few weeks. That's all. Once she's back on her feet, things will go back to normal.'

He tipped the last of his wine down his throat. 'You're being taken for a mug, Stephanie. And I don't like it one little bit.'

'It's not like that, Pete. I keep telling you. We're friends. Mates. We get along.' I squeezed his hand. 'You do things for your mates all the time. And that's a good thing.'

'Yeah, and they do me favours in return. It's not a one-way street like you and Scarlett.'

'That's not fair.'

'No? Well, what's she done for you lately?'

'Friendship's not a balance sheet, Pete. It's not about keeping score. Scarlett's my mate. You ask what she's done for me lately? She's brightened my day more times than anybody else I know. And she's asked me to be Jimmy's godmother.'

He spluttered with laughter. 'You think that's her doing something for you? You don't even like kids. Stephanie, that's just another way of getting her claws into you.'

I felt sad for him that he couldn't understand the compliment. 'No, Pete. It's a gift. Inviting someone into your child's life is a gift.'

'Yeah, and you'll be giving gifts for life in return,' he said cynically. 'I'll meet you at the gig, then. If you get back in time.'

'You could come with me?' I cleared the plates and glasses from the table.

'I don't think so,' he said, his derision obvious.

And that was how it went on. Pete expected me to be available when his irregular hours gave him free time. He'd always grumbled when my work took me away, but when I wasn't actually doing interviews, I managed to be fairly flexible to suit him. But it wasn't always easy to accommodate the timetable of a new mother and a young baby, and Pete grew increasingly irritable if I was too busy with Scarlett and Jimmy to devote myself wholly to him. To be honest, it began to feel quite stifling. It was as if he was jealous of the time I spent with Scarlett and Jimmy.

As with all bullies, his constant niggling was at its most effective when it echoed my own misgivings. Because it was true that Scarlett needed a lot of support after Jimmy's birth. When she came out of hospital, she wasn't in great shape. A C-section is major abdominal surgery and that means taking things easy. She didn't like the restrictions on her movements and activities, but she had no choice. It's hard enough to get over major surgery; it's an even bigger ask when your life's been transformed by the arrival of a baby. Nothing runs the way it used to. It wouldn't have been so bad if she'd had a supportive husband or family members around to pile in and give her a hand. But Joshu gave a whole new meaning to part-time parenthood. He would breeze in with flowers and soft toys, cuddle his son for ten minutes, then phone for a takeaway. He'd stick around long enough to share his food with Scarlett, then he'd be off again, working or clubbing. His life hadn't changed at all. Drugs, drinking, DJing were still at the heart of his agenda. Women too, I suspected.

I dropped in almost every other day, running the gauntlet of media hacks who seemed to be practically living outside the gates. I began to understand how oppressed Scarlett felt by their constant presence. She certainly wasn't in any mood to feed their hunger.

That brought its own problems. After she'd been home for

four or five days, I called George. 'You're going to have to sort out some live-in help for Scarlett,' I said. 'She's not coping. The house is a tip, the washing's piling up and somebody needs to do a major shop.'

'Can't you give her a hand, Stephanie?'

Posh men. They pretend to be feminists, but really, they don't have a bloody clue. To my horror, I found myself echoing Pete. 'I'm her ghost, Georgie, not her mother. Sort it, would you?'

And so Marina turned up. A buxom brunette in her late twenties, Marina was from Romania but she spoke better English than most of the bimbos Scarlett hung out with when she was in her public persona. She had a sardonic sense of humour but in spite of a figure like a fifties Hollywood starlet and a face to match, she was a grafter. I liked her; more importantly, so did Scarlett. And best of all, she was entirely immune to Joshu's charms. She made it plain that she thought he was a tosser, without ever saying or doing anything that crossed the line.

She was very clear where she drew the lines, was Marina. She was there to work, not to be Scarlett's confidante. Whenever we tried to draw her into our circle, she'd always withdraw politely. She kept the house clean and tidy, she did the shopping and cooked the meals, she took care of Jimmy for two hours in the afternoon and that was that. In the evenings, she retreated to her room where she had a TV and a cheap laptop, or else she got on her bike and cycled to the nearest village where there was a pub and, apparently, a couple of other Romanian workers.

After that little drama, Scarlett and I fell into a more regular pattern. We would do a bit of work on magazine profiles when Marina had Jimmy in the afternoons. We generally spent our evenings with a bottle of wine and a DVD of *The West Wing* or *Footballers' Wives*. Then we'd talk about books we were reading and the parlous state of the country under New Labour. I had to explain why Margaret Thatcher had been A Bad Thing and how her regime had created a new underclass and smashed the old alliances within the working class. The deaths of Betty Friedan and Linda Smith gave me the chance to hold forth with a brief history of feminism, which intrigued Scarlett. I kept forgetting how much she didn't know. Sharing without patronising became one of my constant goals. But now she had discovered the wider world of politics and society, she was like a sponge, soaking up information and figuring out what it meant in her world.

Just as I was getting grief from Pete about the time I spent with her, she was getting a hard time from Joshu. Whenever our paths crossed, he was always trying to enlist me in his cause. His complaints cycled round the same basic poles. He wasn't getting enough sex and Scarlett never wanted to go out on the town with him any more.

I couldn't do anything about the sex, but I did try to encourage her to go out with him, if only to keep the peace. I offered to babysit, to stay over if need be. But she wasn't keen. 'I can't be arsed,' she'd say. 'There's no fun in it. I don't want to get off my face and stagger around a dance floor with a bunch of airheads and dickheads. I don't want to be where the music's too loud to think, never mind talk. Plus I'm up half the night with Jimmy more often than not. Why would I want to be up half the night from choice? I tell you, Steph, these days my idea of a good time would be eight straight hours of sleep.'

Scarlett's attitude didn't help Joshu's relationship with his son either. He ascribed the change in Scarlett's behaviour to motherhood, not understanding that motherhood was her excuse to cover the fact that she was finally behaving as the woman she was, not the woman he believed her to be. I can see how it must have been confusing for him; emotional intelligence wasn't his strong suit. Not that he was any better when it came to the other varieties.

And even if he'd had the nous to suspect the truth, it wouldn't have been that easy to figure it out. Because the public Scarlett was still very much in evidence. And I have to take my share of responsibility for that. I was the only writer she could trust, so I was the one who got all the assignments from the slag mags and the red-tops.

Despite George having made it clear that the only autho-rised interviews would be written by me, and the only photographs would be supplied by a snapper employed by his agency, the media camp at the gates never seemed to diminish. There was a hardcore of half a dozen who were there every day. Scarlett couldn't take the baby out for a walk; the long lenses could pick her up two fields away.

Out of sheer frustration – and, probably, a nagging picture desk – one of the notorious paps, a favourite of the red-tops, actually climbed over the wall and got inside the compound. Scarlett raised her head at the end of a length of the pool to see him banging off a clutch of shots through the window. She had the good sense not to attack him, calling the local police instead, followed in short order by a local contractor who spent the next week coating the top of the perimeter wall with glass shards.

Maggie was in seventh heaven. Nothing sells on the news-stands like a cute baby and a celebrity mum, especially with a bit of aggravation on the side. Me and Scarlett, we ran the gamut from A is for antenatal to Z is for Z'baby designer clothes. The popular version of Scarlett was constantly re-inforced by endless photo spreads bolstered up by my image-making. I look back at it now, and I'm not proud of myself.

However much I might wish otherwise, there's no denying that I played a role in how things went so very badly wrong.

18

The afternoon Leanne turned up, Scarlett and I were supposed to be working on a feature about getting back into exercise after a C-section. It was early summer and she'd sent Marina off with Jimmy for a walk in the woods. 'He needs fresh air,' she'd insisted in the teeth of Marina's mutinous glare. 'If you walk through the woods for about twenty minutes, there's a pond with ducks. Take some bread, feed the ducks.'

'He is seven months old,' Marina said. 'He's not interested in ducks.'

'Of course he is. All babies like feeding the ducks. Go on, off you go.'

About ten minutes after they'd left, I understood why Scarlett had been so eager to get rid of Marina. I was in the kitchen brewing up when I saw a taxi pull up at the gate. The intercom buzzed and I picked it up. 'Yes?' I said, glancing at the video screen.

I nearly dropped the handset. I could have sworn it was a brunette version of Scarlett squinting up at the camera from the back of the cab. 'Is that you, Scarlett?' she said, northern vowels flat as a toasted teacake.

'Who is this?'

'Tell her it's Leanne. Her cousin Leanne. She's expecting me.'

'Hang on a minute.'

I put the handset down and shouted down the hallway. 'Scarlett? There's someone at the gate says she's your cousin.'

She ran down the hallway, a wicked grin on her face. 'This is going to crack you up, Steph. Swear to God, crack you up.'

She grabbed the handset and howled gleefully. 'Leanne, you bugger! Get your arse in here.' And buzzed her in.

'You never mentioned a cousin,' I said, following Scarlett back down the hall to the front door. 'I wanted to talk to family for the book, you know that. You said they were all wasters and wankers.'

She gave a wicked grin. 'You've seen Chrissie and Jade. You can't argue with that.'

'So who's this Leanne?'

She stopped and looked me square in the face. 'Maybe I just wanted to keep control, Steph.' She carried on walking, talking over her shoulder. 'Leanne grew up on the same estate as me. Our dads were brothers but her mum's Irish. After she split up with Leanne's dad, she moved back to Dublin with Leanne. When we were kids, everybody said we were like sisters. I wanted to see if it was still true.' Scarlett opened the door as the cab drew up. She turned and winked at me. 'I have got such an evil plan, Steph.'

Looking at them side by side as they played catch-up in the kitchen, I could see the differences between them. Leanne's face was longer, her nose a little more snub. Her ears were quite different in shape, but if her hair had been blonde and hanging loose, the resemblance would have been quite eerie. Her voice was different too – a little higher in pitch, a bit less Northern in its inflexions. I was beginning to have some very uncomfortable suspicions.

After they'd got up to speed with each other's gossip, and Leanne had made the appropriate noises over the latest photos of Jimmy, Scarlett took her off to one of the guest rooms down by the pool to unpack and have a shower.

'You're up to something,' I said as soon as Scarlett returned.

She grinned. 'And how. There was this totally weird old movie on the other night, *Dead Ringers* it was called. It was about these twins—'

'I've seen it,' I said hastily. One of my pet hates is when people try to explain the plot of something they've seen or read. I suppose it's because they're never succinct or clear, and I get enough of that at work.

'Right. So you see where I'm going with this?'

'You're going to pimp your cousin to Joshu?'

As I saw the look of shock and hurt on her face, I realised I'd underestimated Scarlett yet again. 'I'm joking,' I said hastily, trying to cover myself.

She looked uncertain for a moment, but went with it. 'You have a weird sense of humour sometimes, Steph. I love him, you know that. Even if he is neither use nor ornament most of the time. No, what I'm thinking is Leanne could be, like, my body double. Like they have in the movies.' She opened the cupboard and took out a tall glass pitcher. 'You remember when Brad Pitt made that movie, *Troy*?'

Wondering where this was going, I nodded. 'Bloody awful film.'

'Never mind the film. He worked out like crazy to bulk up for it, but he ended up all out of proportion. Great shoulders and chest and six pack, but he still had skinny legs. So he had a leg double.' Scarlett emptied a tray of ice cubes into the jug and added a terrifying slug of Bacardi.

'Are you kidding?'

'No, I'm dead serious. The reason I know is that they used a lad who was a student at Leeds Uni. He was Brad Pitt's leg double. And see, I thought Leanne could be my clubbing double. Have you seen the pina colada mix?'

Luckily, her head was in the fridge so she couldn't see my face. Words failed me. I simply stared, incredulous.

'Think about it, Steph.' She emerged from the fridge, waving the plastic bottle of cocktail mix. 'Got it. Here's the thing. Most people who see me out and about in the clubs, they don't know me. They've only ever seen me on the TV. And everybody knows people look kind of different in real life.' Scarlett poured the ready-made mixture over the rum and ice, then stirred it with a wooden spoon. 'And Leanne sounds more like me than me. She's totally into all that *Yes!* magazine crap. She walks the walk and talks the talk. She could be me for public consumption, out on the razz, giving the gossip columns and the paps all they need to keep them happy. That way, Joshu gets somebody to play with and show off out on the town, and I get to not go out clubbing.' She plonked a glass of pina colada in front of me and looked pensive. 'And if we're not fighting all the time about me not wanting to go out, maybe I'll feel more like shagging him. Which is worth a try, right?'

I took a big drink. I had a feeling it was going to take a fair bit of pina colada, even at Scarlett's industrial strength, to make this sound like a good idea. 'And she's up for this?'

'I haven't exactly gone into the details. I didn't want her blabbing to her Irish mates. All I said was that there might be a job for her on my staff.' She poured herself a drink and chinked her glass against mine. 'Here's to my body double.'

I snorted. 'Your staff? What have you told her?'

Scarlett looked offended. 'There's Marina. And there's Georgie.'

Somehow, I didn't think that was how George pictured himself. But I let it go. 'You really think you need a body double?'

She sighed, deep and heartfelt. 'I need something. I feel

haunted by those fucking jackals at the gate. Every place I go, they're on my shoulder. Unless you've been there, you've got no idea how stressful it is. Sometimes the thought of going outside the gates makes me feel ill. Like I'm going to throw up. I realise people think it's cheeky to complain when publicity's what I live by. I mean, I know it's getting my face all over the papers that pays the bills. But surely that doesn't mean I've got no right to a private life? What about Jimmy? Does he not have a right to grow up without some fucking hack on his tail? I tell you, Steph, it's dragging me down. And I thought maybe Leanne could take the heat off a bit.'

I could see her point. And my heart did go out to her. Even the most avid publicity hound needed to pull the drawbridge up sometimes. 'Could Leanne hold her nerve? Has she got the bottle?'

Scarlett nodded. 'I think so. The thing is, Steph, I need to keep my profile nice and high. I've been offered a TV series. It's daytime, but it's a chance at something with a bit more oomph to it. It's going to be a kind of chat show – sort of, Where are they now? Every week we'll be looking at a couple of reality TV show stars and seeing what's happened to them. Some that've gone on to make something of themselves, some that have ended up on their beam ends.'

'Sort of, triumph or tragedy,' I muttered.

Scarlett, with no sense of irony, pounced on my words. 'That's not a bad title,' she said. 'Triumph or tragedy. I'll run it past the producer.'

'And you're thinking Leanne can be Scarlett by night and you can be Scarlett by day? Are you sure you can trust her not to drop you in it?'

Scarlett sipped her drink and considered. 'She's always been loyal, our Leanne. She's a year younger than me. Always looked up to me. I don't think she'd grass me up, not even if there was an earner in it.'

'An earner in what?' Leanne walked back into the kitchen. With her hair swathed in a towel, the resemblance was quite unsettling. She sat down at the breakfast bar and Scarlett fixed her a drink.

'Just a little something I've got in mind.'

Leanne made a dent in her drink and smacked her lips. 'Ooh, that's bloody lovely, our Scarlett. Nice room, too. I've never had an en suite before, except in a bed and breakfast. I could get used to this.'

'I'm glad to hear it. I could get used to having you around.'

'So what's this job you've been hinting at? You know I've got no secretarial skills or owt. All I've ever done is work in the nail bar. And you don't need to bring me over from Dublin just to keep your manicure up to scratch.'

Scarlett flashed me a quick look. 'You know how people used to mistake us for each other when we were kids?'

Leanne giggled. It was identical to Scarlett's irritating cackle. 'Eeeh, do you remember when Miss Evans thought I was you and dragged me along to the head for your bollocking?'

Scarlett gave me an 'I told you so' smile. 'I reckon if you dyed your hair, we could still get away with it. What do you think?'

Leanne eyed her critically. 'I'd need to do my eyebrows a bit different. But if it wasn't your nearest and dearest, I reckon I could pull it off. Why? Are you making some porno flick where you don't want to show your scar?'

'Fuck off. Of course I'm not doing porn. I might be a slapper but I've got standards, Leanne Higgins.' Scarlett dug me in the ribs. 'You tell her.'

'Me? Why me?'

'Because that's what you're good at. Explaining stuff so it sounds normal.'

It was, I suppose, one way of describing my job. So I outlined Scarlett's suggestion to Leanne, emphasising the secrecy of the project at every stage. At first, she looked sceptical. But as I outlined what Scarlett wanted, she started to look more interested. By the end, she was grinning.

'And that's all you want me to do? Go out on the razz three or four times a week and pretend I'm you? You want to hire me to do your bad behaviour for you? That's mental, that is,' Leanne said, shaking her head and chuckling.

'That's all there is to it. You'd be staying here. Obviously you couldn't go out when I'm out. I can't be in two places at once. But it's not like you'd be a prisoner here. You can go out shopping and shit when I'm home with Jimmy.'

Leanne drained her drink and waved the glass at her cousin. 'Gimme another one of them. If I'm going to pretend to be you, I need to get into training. And what about Joshu? What does he think about all this?'

'He doesn't know about it yet.'

Now Leanne looked anxious. 'But he is going to know about it, right? Because there's limits to how far I'm prepared to go with this. And sleeping with him is definitely off limits. I mean, what you do is your business, but I wouldn't sleep with a Paki.'

'Jesus, Leanne, you can't go round saying shit like that. That's how I got in trouble in the first place.'

Leanne shrugged. 'I'm not going round saying it, am I? This is just us, in your kitchen. I'm not stupid. I wouldn't say that where anybody else could hear me. But it's true, all the same. I'm not shagging him.'

Exasperated, Scarlett slammed her glass down on the counter. 'Of course you're not bloody sleeping with him. He's my husband. I love him. I don't want him catching something off the likes of you.'

I thought war was going to break out. But I clearly understood nothing of the history between these two women. Instead of a catfight, they burst out laughing and playfully punched each other's shoulders. 'What are you like,' Scarlett said.

'Mental,' Leanne replied immediately, as if it was their own personal comedy routine rather than a straight lift from a *Catherine Tate Show* sketch. 'What are you like?'

'Mental.'

And that was that. The whole arrangement had taken about twenty minutes to set up. A smarter woman than me would have picked up the clue phone and learned something about Scarlett that afternoon. But I was slow, and it took me a lot longer.

19

Maggie had fixed me up with a new project ghosting for teenage twins who had rowed the Atlantic, so I didn't see much of Leanne and Scarlett over the next couple of months. Well, I didn't see them in the flesh, but it was hard to pick up a red-top without being aware of 'Scarlett'. Between the teasers for the new TV show and paparazzi shots of her staggering out of clubs in the small hours, often with Joshu, the coverage must have plastered a smile all over George's face.

When I finally resurfaced from the Atlantic, I met Scarlett for lunch near the production offices for her new show, *Real Life TV*. We settled into a corner booth with a bottle of Prosecco and a couple of bowls of pasta and she passed me a bundle of photos. There was a clutch of recent shots of Jimmy, who looked cuter with every passing month. I'd surprised myself by how attached I'd grown to him. I'd missed his cuddles and giggles while I'd been locked down with someone else's book. 'He's started pulling himself up on the furniture,' Scarlett said fondly. 'He's into everything. I tell you, Steph, it's been a real bonus having Leanne around. She's really good with him. Now Jimmy's on the move, it's great having an extra pair of hands on deck.' She chopped her spaghetti up with the side of her fork and began spooning it in while I studied the photos.

As well as the pics of Jimmy, there were several shots of Leanne looking weirdly similar to Scarlett. I could only tell the difference because I was looking for it. 'It doesn't confuse him? With her looking so much like you? Because I have to tell you, Scarlett, the resemblance is uncanny.'

She swallowed a mouthful of pasta, shaking her head. 'Doesn't seem to. If we're both in the room he heads for me. I read somewhere that they go by smell as much as by sight. Obviously I smell different from Leanne.' She grinned. 'That'll be the smelly Irish tinker in her.' She held her hands up defensively when she saw the look on my face. 'I'm only winding you up,' she said. 'You're so easy, Steph.'

'And you're so bad. It's great that Jimmy's OK with Leanne. What about Joshu?'

'He seems pretty chilled about it all. It means he gets to go out with a woman on his arm when he's not actually working. And because we're not arguing all the time, things between us got a bit sweeter. Which means it's good all round. All I got to do is make sure nobody susses it out.'

'How long are you planning on keeping this up?'

Scarlett frowned at her food, poking it with her spoon as if she expected it to develop independent life. 'Obviously, not for ever.'

'Obviously. But do you have some sort of timescale in mind? Is there a master plan?'

She gave me a sharp look. 'Are you taking the piss?'

'No, no way. If I've learned one thing about you, it's your capacity to wrong-foot me. The predictable thing here would be for you to be clueless about the endgame. But I've spent enough time with you now to know that you wouldn't have set the ball rolling without having a pretty good idea where you want it to end up. I shouldn't have said, "Is there a master plan?" I should have said, "What's the master plan?"'

Scarlett ate another mouthful of pasta. Then another. 'Sort of,' she said eventually.

'Do you want to share it? Or is it going to be another one of your bloody surprises?'

'I want to get my TV show established. It's time to show people the truth. That there's more to me than they think. And when that begins to dawn on them, I'll get Leanne to start tapering off the night life.' She gave me the familiar piratical grin. 'Then you can write a load of articles about how I'm a new woman, a reformed character. How motherhood transformed me. I'll be so boring the paps might just decide to leave me alone.'

'And what's going to happen to Leanne?'

'I've bought her a nice place in Spain, up in the mountains. There's a big expat community up there. The property's got a pool house, she can set up a nail boutique there. Her own little business. Obviously, she'll have to go back to being brunette, maybe cut her hair short.' She shrugged.

There was a ruthlessness to Scarlett's planning that I almost admired. But not quite. I pushed my plate away. 'And you think she'll settle for that?'

'Why not? A haircut and a dye job? It's not much of a price to pay for being well set up at her age.'

'I meant, giving up the party life. From what I've seen of Leanne, it's meat and drink to her. She's found her calling, Scarlett. Being out on the tiles at somebody else's expense is her vocation. Why would she cheerfully give up all that fun for the expats up in the mountains in Spain?'

Scarlett's surly expression wouldn't have been out of place on a teenager. 'Because that's the deal. She knew when she took it on that it was only temporary. And she's OK with that.'

'I'll take your word for it,' I said, not meaning it.

As it turned out, I was right about Leanne creating problems. Only they weren't the problems I'd expected.

Three weeks later, I turned up at the hacienda without phoning ahead. I'd been up in Suffolk, being interviewed by a comedienne looking for someone to write her memoir of fifty years in the laughter game (her pitch, not mine ...) and we'd wrapped up earlier than I'd anticipated. Mostly because I'd loathed the woman within five minutes of meeting her and I couldn't be bothered to push for the job. Scarlett's memoir was still selling well in the paperback charts and the rowing book was due out soon, so cashflow wasn't an issue. And Maggie had tipped me the wink about a retail entrepreneur who wanted to write a book about leadership which sounded a lot more interesting.

So I'd escaped early from the suffocating knick-knack heaven inhabited by the comedienne. Rather than head straight home, I decided to call on Jimmy and his harem. I was out of luck, however. Marina had taken him to a toddler playgroup for the afternoon, and Scarlett was having a final wardrobe fitting for *Real Life TV*. Joshu was somewhere. Leanne had no idea where except that it wasn't there. She was home alone and I was surprised by the effusiveness of her greeting. Don't get me wrong, we'd always got on fine. But today she seemed both relieved and pleased that she had me to herself.

Leanne made coffee and raked in the cupboard for biscuits. 'I'm glad you stopped in,' she said. She produced a box of organic wholemeal biscuits in the shape of gingerbread men. 'Do you want one of these? Jimmy loves them.' She looked dubious.

'I'm OK,' I said. 'How's things?'

'Well, that's just it,' she said, settling in with the air of a woman who has much to impart and generations of imparting behind her. 'On the face of it, everything's hunky-dory. I'm getting my face in the papers, Scarlett's getting her beauty sleep and nobody suspects a thing.'

'But . . . ? I'm hearing a "but" in there.'

Leanne fiddled with the handle of her mug. 'Can we go outside? I'm gagging for a fag and Scarlett doesn't like us smoking in the house. With Jimmy, you know?'

I followed her out into the garden. Weak sunlight made us both look anaemic and there was no heat in it. But it was better than being shut indoors with Leanne's cigarette smoke. We hunkered down on a couple of curved wooden benches that looked across a pond where bored goldfish pottered around among the water lilies. I wondered whether it should be fenced off now Jimmy was mobile.

'Not that Joshu pays any attention,' Leanne continued. 'He smokes whatever he likes, wherever he likes. And Scarlett lets him get away with it. She spoils Joshu more than she spoils Jimmy.'

'Maybe that's because Jimmy's still young enough to learn.'

Leanne squinted through the smoke at me. 'You're not that keen on Joshu, are you?'

I shrugged. 'He wouldn't be my choice of a life partner. But Scarlett obviously sees something in him that I'm missing.'

Leanne sipped at her cigarette like she didn't really mean it. 'That's kind of my problem,' she said.

'Has he been coming on to you?' It wasn't much of a reach.

'No. He wouldn't dare. I made that totally clear right from the off. When Scarlett first came up with the idea, we all sat down and thrashed it out. We have to, like, hold hands and have the odd kiss for the cameras. But I told him, any more than that, any tongues, any hands where they shouldn't be and I'd cut his cock off. And Scarlett said she'd have his balls for earrings. When she does put her foot down, she can be well scary.'

'So he's been a good boy?'

'With me, yeah.' She dropped her half-smoked cigarette and ground it out. 'Trouble is, I'm not the only woman out there, if you get my drift?'

I closed my eyes momentarily. I got her drift, in spades. What I wanted to know was how bad things were. 'Tell me what you know. And then we'll figure out what's the best way to go,' I said.

Leanne's face crumpled in relief. She might look spookily like her cousin, but she had none of the iron in the soul that had lifted Scarlett out of the shit and into the glitz. What she wanted was to hand off responsibility for what she knew, and I was the lucky patsy. 'When we're out, we're always in the VIP areas, yeah? You see a lot of the same faces. A lot of them are total slappers on the make. Once or twice, I noticed women starting to come over to Joshu then noticing me and backing off. I reckoned it was because they saw I was with him and realised he was spoken for. Then it dawned on me that they couldn't not know he was spoken for, if you get my meaning?'

I nodded. Women like that read the red-tops and the slag mags as religiously as a nun reads her missal. It's their guide to who's in and who's out, who's single and who's taken, who's irredeemably fucked up and who's still worth a go. They'd have read all about the wedding and the baby and the game of happy families being played out at the hacienda. They'd know Joshu was off limits.

Unless of course they had reason to know otherwise.

'That must have made you wonder.'

'You could say that. It made me start watching him a lot more closely. I cut back my drinking a bit, you know? Just to stay more alert, like. Tried to fade into the background. And I started to think that some of those slags were a bit too touchy-feely with him, if you catch my drift? Too much flirting. Too much touching. It's hard to explain. Hard to pin down. But it's the way you are with somebody you've slept with, as opposed to somebody you just fancy. Or somebody you're pals with. Do you know what I mean?'

'I think I do.' I've seen it at publishers' parties sometimes. People stand a bit too close to each other. They contrive to touch in apparently innocuous ways. Except they do it a lot more than friends or colleagues do. It's hard to pinpoint anything you could confront them with, but it's there if you're looking. I even remember watching one series of *Masterchef* where I was convinced two of the contenders were having a fling based purely on the way they touched in passing. Maybe I'm living on fantasy island, but I don't think so. I'm good at reading people. It's part of the reason I'm successful at my job. 'I don't think you're imagining things.'

Leanne pulled a scornful face. 'I know I'm not. I thought I was, to begin with. But now I know I'm not. A couple of nights ago, I had a bit of an upset tummy. I was in the bathroom for about ten minutes. In this club, right, you come down the hall to the main VIP area and there's like a lobby off to the side before the main area. And there was a lass there who hadn't been around when I left. Anyway, she didn't see me come back and neither did Joshu. And they were going at it hammer and tongs, out there away from the main room. She was telling him he couldn't just pick her up and drop her like she was a packet of fags. That she was fed up of hearing about other women he'd shagged, fed up of hearing him bullshitting about leaving his wife, fed up of him being Mr Unreliable.' She stopped, visibly shaken at the memory, and lit another cigarette.

'What did you do?'

'I wanted to rip the bitch's hair out, for our Scarlett's sake. But I knew if I did that, it would turn into a major ruck and it'd end up all over the papers. And our Scarlett doesn't deserve that. If anybody deserves to be humiliated, it's that little shit Joshu, not her. So I sneaked back down the hall to the loo then made loads of noise coming back. I pretended I was shouting back at somebody in the bathroom. And when I got to the lobby, they were gone. She was in the VIP area, but I think Joshu must have gone down into the main part of the club because he turned up on the decks about twenty minutes later. Did a guest rideout, all scratching and scribbling and generally showing off like the prize pillock he is.'

Elbows on her knees, Leanne sighed and stared gloomily across the pond. 'I can't stand that he's making a fool out of her.'

'You're going to have to tell her.'

She gave me an 'are you crazy?' look then shook her head vigorously. 'No way. She wouldn't believe me. She'd think I was after him for myself or some muppet thing like that.'

'You have to tell her because if there's a loose cannon bitch out there, it's going to come out in the press. It's going to come at her out of the blue. It's going to be sensationalised and exaggerated and she's going to be utterly humiliated. That would be so much worse. Not to mention the fact that she's going to realise you must have known about it. She'll end up feeling stupid and humiliated and betrayed twice over – by Joshu and by you. And you'll come off worse, because he might be a twat but she loves him.'

Leanne muttered, 'Fuck's sake,' under her breath.

'I don't see that you have any alternative. And you need to do it sooner rather than later. Because that bitch is out there and she's not going away.'

20

I really tried to get out of holding Leanne's hand while she told Scarlett the tacky truth about her husband. But gradually I realised that if I wasn't there to lend moral support, Leanne was going to bottle it. I can't say I blamed her. The news she had to deliver was the sort of thing nobody wants to hear. When Marina came back from the toddler group, I dug into my wallet and paid her extra to take Jimmy up to his nursery for the evening.

It was almost seven when the studio car brought Scarlett home. She was on a high after an afternoon of being pinned and tacked into a succession of sexy dresses. My presence was a bonus, she said, heading straight for the fridge and opening a bottle of Prosecco. She poured three glasses in spite of my protestations and gave me a kiss on the forehead as she handed mine to me. 'Chill, sister,' she said. 'You can always stay over if you want to have a drink with me and Leanne. Right, Lee?'

There was no point in holding back. This was not a conversation that would improve with keeping. 'You might not want either of us in the house when you hear what we've got to say,' I said.

Scarlett stopped in her tracks and frowned. 'That doesn't sound good.' She looked from me to Leanne and back again. A flare of panic lit her eyes. 'It's not Jimmy, is it? I mean, I'm assuming he's gone down for the night, yeah?'

'No, Jimmy's fine. Marina's got him up in the nursery. We didn't want him to see you upset.'

'That only leaves Joshu.' She sat down heavily, her mouth a hard line. 'Spill it, then. Has he wrapped that stupid bloody car round a tree?'

'No, nothing like that.' I looked at Leanne. 'Though you might wish he had by the time we're done.'

'Spit it out, then. Jeez, Steph, it's not like you to beat around the bush.'

'OK.' I took a deep breath. Like that ever made anything easier. 'It looks like Joshu's been putting it about a bit.'

Scarlett didn't move a muscle. She sat, frozen, staring straight ahead, not even blinking for what felt like an impossible length of time. I could only imagine the hurt. She'd been serially let down by every adult who owed her care and love. And still she persisted in loving. I found it impossible not to admire that.

At last, she looked away, delicately wiping her mouth clean of lipstick with her index finger. It was a curious gesture, as if she was removing the very taste of him. 'Tell me what you know,' she said, hard-edged Yorkshire to the core.

So Leanne told Scarlett what she'd already told me. Halting and nervous, she got through her story. Scarlett sat stony-faced throughout, sipping metronomically from her glass. At the end, Scarlett's face twitched once, a momentary lapse of control. Then she was back in charge. 'Do you know who she was, this slag?'

'I think I heard somebody call her Tiffany. But I couldn't swear to it.'

'Ha!' Scarlett's cry was bitter. 'Not Tiffany – Toffany. Stupid fucking made-up name. Toffany Banks. She's always wanted him. Well, she's welcome to him. Come on, girls. We've got work to do.'

That night, Scarlett confirmed what I'd believed for some time. She was not a woman to mess with. First, cool as a cucumber, she called Joshu. 'Hey, babe,' she said. 'Are you working tonight?'

When she came off the phone, she said, 'He's running the decks at Stagga. Then he's going on to a party in Fulham. So the night is ours.'

Next she called a local van-hire firm that Joshu had an account with. 'He uses their vans for festivals and private gigs,' she explained. She arranged for them to drop off a Transit at the hacienda on Joshu's account. Then we headed upstairs to the bedroom with a roll of black bin liners. Scarlett threw Joshu's clothes out of wardrobes and drawers and we filled the bags. As soon as the bags were full, she'd tip in a bottle of cologne or aftershave lotion or one of the other expensive toiletries that colonised Joshu's half of the bathroom. 'He always likes to smell nice,' she said with grim satisfaction as we carried the reeking bags down to the garage.

When the van arrived, we loaded up all the equipment from his studio, his boxes of CDs and vinyl and the bags of clothes. It took us till gone one in the morning, but we'd been through the entire house and cleared it of every trace of the two-timing little shit. 'Where to now?' I asked, wiping my hair out of my eyes.

'It's on his account,' Scarlett said. 'I think we should drive it down to Stagga and leave the keys with one of the lads on the door. What do you think, Steph?'

'Sounds good to me. You drive the van, I'll follow in your car and bring you back here.'

'I'll go in the van with you,' Leanne said. 'Keep you company.'

We both gave her an incredulous stare. 'I don't think so,' Scarlett said. 'We don't want the doormen thinking they're seeing double.'

Leanne slapped herself on the forehead and burst out laughing. 'Shit, I forgot. What am I like?'

'Mental,' Scarlett giggled. 'Come on then, Steph. Let's get going.'

It went without a hitch. Scarlett parked the van on double yellows outside the club and spoke to the gorillas on the door. 'Joshu asked me to drop his gear off,' she said. 'Can you give him the keys?' She gestured at her joggers and muscle vest. 'I'm not dressed for it. I don't want to ruin my reputation.'

Scarlett didn't say much on the way back. 'I left him a note propped up on the steering wheel,' she said. 'Told him to fuck off to Toffany's if he wanted a bed for the night and not to bother coming back.'

'You'll have to talk to him about access to Jimmy,' I said.

'That's what lawyers are for,' she said. 'He's been no kind of father to Jimmy while he's been under the same roof. He can see his son, but he's not having no fifty-fifty deal. Nor nothing like.'

A few traffic lights went by. 'He'll try and screw you on the money too.'

'Let him try. My accountant's got most of my assets where he can't get his hands on them. Plus we did a pre-nup. He keeps what's his and I won't come after him for maintenance.' She shook her head. 'I can't believe he did that to me. Toffany fucking Banks. That's really insulting, you know that? She hasn't got the brains God gave a goldfish. She makes me look like Jeremy bloody Paxman.' Then her face crumpled and she began to cry. Great howling sobs and shuddering moans ripped through her, filling the car with terrible noise.

I didn't know what to do so I just kept driving. After a few minutes, Scarlett began to run out of steam. Her face was a mess of tears and snot. She rubbed her eyes with her fists and sniffed, then wiped her nose with the back of her hand. 'That's it,' she said. 'That's all the bastard gets from me.'

It was a wildly over-optimistic assertion, but I suspect it made her feel a bit better in the moment. Over the months that followed, Scarlett shed plenty of tears for Joshu. In spite of everything, she had loved him and it had cut the ground from under her feet to be so thoroughly betrayed by him. But that night she was determined to hold firm.

'Will you stop with us for a few days?' she said. 'He'll be round, he won't take it lying down. And then there'll be the media. I could do with a bit of back-up.'

I couldn't refuse her. In Scarlett's shoes, I'd have wanted one of my mates in my corner. I didn't realise that supporting her would put me just there. In her shoes.

21

We didn't have long to wait. Joshu turned up shouting the odds about an hour after we got back to the hacienda. He had to shout because Scarlett had changed the access code on the electric gate and turned off the intercom. We were sitting in the kitchen drinking tea, too wired for bed, when we heard the van draw up. 'Here comes trouble,' Leanne said.

The sound of the van's horn blasted through the dawn. 'Neighbours won't like that,' Scarlett said. She sniffed. 'Fuck 'em if they can't take a joke.'

'I think you should talk to him,' I said. 'Even if it's just to tell him you're done.'

Scarlett gazed out of the window at the garden with a hundred-yard stare. 'I really can't be arsed,' she said. But she slid off her stool and headed for the door. She turned and summoned us with a jerk of the head. 'Come on. I need witnesses. So I don't cave in at the sight of his pretty face.'

Leanne and I exchanged glances. She looked about as thrilled as I felt. Getting between a warring couple is never a good place to be. I had a feeling this was going to be like a Michael Douglas and Kathleen Turner film, but without the laughs. So we followed along, Leanne automatically twisting her hair into a ponytail and shoving it through the back of a baseball cap. A minimal disguise, but it had proved effective enough.

At first glance, the scene was mildly laughable. Whoever Joshu had talked into driving him out here had parked the nose of the van bang up against the gates and Joshu had clambered on to the sloping bonnet. He was leaning on the gate, his wrists between the metal spikes that adorned its top edge. 'About time, bitch,' he shouted, weaving slightly from side to side. He sounded stoned. Probably because he was. True to form, he'd been drinking and ingesting assorted substances for hours. The only positive aspect of the whole scenario was that it was the middle of the night and the long-lens jackals were all in their lairs, asleep.

'You think that's the way to sort this out?' she yelled back at him. 'Coming round here off your tits and calling me names?'

'What the fuck is this all about?' he demanded, all injured innocence.

'It's about you sticking your dick where it doesn't belong. I'm through with it. I thought becoming a dad had changed your ways, but that's not what I'm hearing. You dirty bastard. Shagging that cow Toffany then coming home to me? Now I'm going to have to get tested for every bloody sexually transmitted lurgy under the sun. You are a complete and utter prick.'

Joshu kept trying to get a word in, but it wasn't happening. Scarlett was off and running and she wasn't giving him a chance to change her mind. 'I packed up your stuff and now you can sling your hook. I'm not having you back here – I want a divorce. I want nothing to do with your skanky arse ever again.'

'You can't do this,' he finally howled when she paused for breath.

'I already have, dickhead.'

They glared at each other. 'It's a lie, what Toffany said,' he tried.

'You are pitiful,' Scarlett countered. 'You think I'm going to fall for the oldest line in the book? You think I'm stupid?'

'You can't throw me out. What about the boy? I'm his dad.'

'His dad? You can barely bring yourself to call him by his name because you didn't get to choose it. You think I haven't noticed how he's always, "my boy" or "the kid" or "junior"? His name's Jimmy, dickhead. And he won't even notice you've gone. He misses Steph if she's not around for a few days. Or Leanne. But he doesn't ever miss you.'

'Oh yeah, he misses Steph.' His lip curled in a sneer, his voice mocking her. 'Your fucking lezza girlfriend Steph.'

My mouth fell open. It did. Literally. I couldn't have been more taken aback.

Scarlett roared with laughter. 'You are so pathetic and so predictable. You're all the bloody same. The only possible reason there could be for us not fancying a he-man like you is that we're big old lezzas. That's what you have to tell yourself, because you can't face the truth. Well, here's the truth, little big man. I don't fancy you because you're always drunk, or fucked up on drugs, or you stink of sweat and fags. It's because you're disgusting that I don't fancy you, not because you're a man. It's because you're not enough of a man, as it happens.'

His eyes widened in hurt. She'd got through his addled state and scored a bull's eye on his self-esteem. 'But I love you,' he said, his pitch cracking like a teenage boy.

'And I don't love you.' Scarlett spoke in a low, choked voice. 'You killed it, Joshu. You killed it.'

'You can't do this, Scarlett.' Now his eyes were wet. I almost felt sorry for him, then I remembered how much I disliked him.

'I have to. Being with you, it's one big recipe for misery.

And I won't put Jimmy through that. He's better without a dad than stuck with a deadbeat like you.'

He gripped the top of the gate. 'You bitch. You think you can lay down the law to me? You've got another think coming.' It was striking how, under stress, the affectation of street speak had fallen away, leaving Joshu sounding exactly what he was – a well-educated middle-class lad.

'You don't scare me, Joshu. I'm not the same woman who fell in love with you.'

Now it was his turn for scorn. 'Listen to you. You've got no idea. You need to remember who knows your secrets. How do you think your precious fans will like it when they find out you've been taking them for a ride this past year? You and your airhead cousin – you won't last five minutes when I tell my story.'

From where I was standing, I could see Scarlett stiffen. For a moment, I thought he'd trumped her ace. But yet again, I'd misjudged her. She took a couple of steps closer to the gate and tipped her head back to look Joshu in the face. 'You think? It's me the public loves, not you. They'll totally get that I had to deal with your scumbag behaviour. You'll be the one who gets savaged for being a pig. And don't forget, your hands are as dirty as mine. You're the one who's been touting Leanne all round town as your missus. Either you were in on the whole thing, in which case you're as bad as me. Or you're too fucking dim to know the woman you're out on the razz with isn't your wife. So don't you dare threaten me, you worthless piece of shit.'

He tried to launch himself at her over the gate. But the sloping bonnet of the Transit was too much for him and he slid out of sight, swearing. There was a clatter and a crash and a yelp then more swearing. 'I'm not done with you, bitch,' he yelled from the other side of the gate. The van door slammed, the engine raced and the tyres screamed on the road. Within seconds, the usual early morning sounds of birdsong and the distant hum of traffic were the only soundtrack.

Scarlett kicked out savagely at the gate. 'Bastard,' she spat. She turned back to face us and gave a crooked smile. 'First blood to the bimbo, I think.'

First blood, but not the last.

22

The first thing Detective Sergeant Nick Nicolaides did when he got to his car was to make a list. He liked lists. They almost made him believe the world was tractable.

- Talk to Charlie
- Track down Pete Matthews
- Check whether Megan the Stalker is still under lock and key
- Double check Scarlett's mum and sister are where they should be
- Is Leanne still in Spain? Ask Steph about her relationship with Jimmy
- Check out Joshu's family

The first item on the list was the one he didn't want to do from the office. Dr Charlie Flint was a psychiatrist and former offender profiler who had only recently been reinstated after a controversial suspension. The whole process had turned Charlie into a pariah as far as the police were concerned. Which was why he didn't want to make the call where Broadbent could overhear it. But Nick and Charlie went back a long way. Back when he'd been studying psychology at university and running a lucrative drug-dealing business on the side, Charlie had stepped in and given him a harsh ultimatum. Stop it or she would shop him to the police. Her intervention had saved Nick from his adolescent arrogance and he knew he owed this life he loved to her. 'It's not that I liked you,' she had later told him. 'I just hated to see a good mind wasted.'

She'd been teasing him, of course. In spite of – or perhaps because of – his complicated past, they'd become friends. Not that he was short of friends. Few of them were cops, but there were plenty of musicians, both professional and amateur. But Charlie was the only person in his circle these days who knew how close he'd come to a very different life from the one he lived now. When things got tough, it made a difference to have someone completely trustworthy in his corner. And this was exactly the kind of case where Charlie might have useful insights.

As he summoned her number and waited for it to connect, he admitted to himself that he might not have bothered Charlie if this had been a routine case. He was fired up about this because the person sitting in the FBI office freaking out about little Jimmy Higgins was Stephanie.

It had been a couple of years since they'd first met, and he'd been attracted from the beginning. But there hadn't been any opportunity to make something of it. Besides, he'd always felt awkward about the idea of mixing business and pleasure. His wasn't a line of work where your first encounters generally provoked happy memories. Cops were there for the bad things in life, and that wasn't likely to get a relationship off on the right foot. The power balance was all wrong, for starters. He wanted a relationship based on equality, not on him as hero, her as vulnerable damsel in distress.

Then she'd called him out of the blue. Admittedly for

professional reasons. But she could have picked up the phone and spoken to her local CID. That she'd considered him a sympathetic figure definitely buffed his ego. And once the matter had been sorted out, he'd dropped by and made it delicately clear that he'd like to see her when she felt up to having a date. Because there was no getting away from the way she made him feel. In spite of his determination to stay away from women with complicated lives, he couldn't resist Stephanie.

They'd taken it easy to begin with. They'd gone to lunch, seen a movie, had dinner three times and taken Jimmy to the Tower of London. They'd talked on the phone late at night, they'd used the message channels on Facebook and Twitter. And it had been a couple of months before they slept together, which these days felt unusual. It hadn't been lack of desire, at least not on Nick's part. It was hard for him to articulate precisely what it was, but he thought it had something to do with the fact that this felt serious. And something to do with the kid. You didn't take chances when a kid was part of the picture.

Charlie answered her phone on the second ring. 'Hi, Nick. What a nice surprise. How's tricks?'

'Been better, Charlie. What about you? Is this a good time?'

'Sure. Maria's doing something sensational in the kitchen so I've got nothing to occupy me but this glass of wine. What's bothering you?'

'I told you about Stephanie, right?'

'When we had breakfast in that lovely little café in Paddington, yes. Has something gone wrong?'

Even across the distance from Manchester to London there was no mistaking the concern in Charlie's voice. 'Yes, but not between me and her,' he said. 'It's much worse than that, Charlie. And I need your help.'

'Anything I can do. You know that.'

'The boy's been kidnapped. Jimmy, Scarlett Higgins' son. Stephanie took him on holiday to the US and he was snatched when they were changing planes.'

Charlie drew her breath in sharply. 'Over there? He was kidnapped over there?'

'Yes. The FBI are talking to Stephanie. Taking a history. They've drafted me in to help develop leads. But there's bugger all to grab on to, Charlie.'

'Which of course is why you're talking to me,' she said wryly. 'And that's as it should be, Nick. Why don't you take me through everything you know about the abduction?'

So he did, wondering not for the first time what it was about Charlie that made the act of confiding in her a relief in itself. Nick concentrated on recalling everything Vivian McKuras had said and relaying it to Charlie without putting his own spin on it. When he'd finished, she grunted. 'Interesting.'

'Well, yeah. I knew that already, Charlie,' Nick grumbled.

'I'm just buying time, Nick. Just buying time.'

'Do you want to call me back when you've had time to think it through?'

'One or two thoughts for now. First and foremost, Jimmy knew the person he walked away with. The kidnapper didn't have time to talk Jimmy into leaving with him. Even with figures of authority like cops, kids of that age will show reluctance or opposition. The overwhelming probability is that it would have been somebody he already knew.'

'Shit,' Nick said. 'So we really should be looking on this side of the Atlantic. At people who know Jimmy and Stephanie.'

Charlie spoke slowly, considering her words. 'It's interesting that Stephanie didn't recognise him. If it was someone she knew well, she might have recognised his build, his gait, his gestures, whether she saw his face or not. So maybe not someone she knows.'

181

'They'd have to know something about Stephanie, though. They'd have to know about her leg always setting off the metal detectors. And their holiday plans.'

'That's true. But whoever took Jimmy, he's had friendly contact with him and probably recently. The boy's at school now, isn't he? You might want to check out classroom assistants, teachers, caretakers. Anyone who could have built a relationship of trust with Jimmy.'

Nick scribbled a note to remind himself of the line of inquiry. 'But if it's someone like that, why wait till the kid's in America? Why not do it over here, where it would presumably be easier? This was an audacious kidnap, Charlie. A lot could have gone wrong.'

'I know. That was my other point. Whoever did this has got planning skills and a lot of nerve. But to go back to what you said – why America? It's a good question.' She gave a short, sharp sigh. 'I don't know the answer, but maybe it's something quite simple. The kidnapper might only be acting as an agent for the person who really wants Jimmy. And maybe that person is in America.'

As usual, talking to Charlie opened all sorts of possibilities. 'So I should start with anyone who could have got alongside Jimmy recently?'

'Either that or someone who has a long-standing relationship with the kid. Family?'

'I don't think there are connections there. Not from what Stephanie's said. Both parents are dead. His paternal grandparents want nothing to do with him, though I need to check out whether that's still the case. Cultural sensitivities and shit, you know?'

'That can be a bitch,' Charlie said. 'And not very susceptible to reason. What about his mother's family?'

'Scarlett made a fetish of not letting them have anything to do with Jimmy. Granny's a drunk and auntie's a junkie.

According to Stephanie, they got lawyered up when Scarlett died because they thought there was money attached to Jimmy. As soon as they found out Scarlett had left her entire estate to charity and that Jimmy was, in financial terms, nothing but a burden, you couldn't see them for dust. They haven't got the financial or the intellectual resources to mount something like this, even if they wanted the kid. There's another auntie, Leanne, but she lives in Spain and Stephanie's not seen her or heard from her since Scarlett died. She's made no attempt to stay in touch with the kid.'

'So you're ruling out the mother's family. And the father's family are long shots. What about staff?'

'What do you mean, "staff"? Stephanie doesn't have staff. She's a writer, not a movie star.' Nick couldn't help a spurt of amusement rising in him in spite of the situation.

'I know it sounds mad, but I don't have another word for what I mean. Cleaner. Childminder. Little man who does stuff. People who come to the house or people whose house Jimmy goes to.'

Nick made another note. 'He doesn't have a childminder. Stephanie picks him up from school. She's changed her working habits to accommodate him. She says he's had so much upheaval in his life, he deserves some stability. Now when she's doing the interviews for a book she only makes herself available from ten till two.' He smiled in affectionate memory. 'She says she wishes she'd thought of it years ago.'

'OK. What about a cleaner?'

Nick pulled a face. 'I know she's got one, but I think she comes when Jimmy's at school.'

'Babysitter?'

'Emily. She's Stephanie's agent's daughter. I really don't think she's someone we should be worried about.'

'Probably not. You said the boy's five?'

'That's right.'

'Was there anybody who consistently took care of him when Scarlett was still alive? Because he'd probably still have a strong enough memory of her to trust her.'

Nick thought back to when he'd been introduced to what had struck him at the time as a chaotic household. He'd gradually realised it was anything but. 'The person who held everything together was Marina. She was housekeeper, child-minder, cook. Without her, everything would have fallen apart. But she's well out of the picture.'

'Why do you say that?'

'Scarlett left all her money to a charitable foundation that supports an orphanage in Romania. According to Stephanie, when she knew she was dying, Scarlett sent Marina back to Romania, where she's from, to be the foundation's representative at the orphanage. Basically, to run the place properly. Scarlett wanted somebody who knew how things work over there, but who wasn't dependent on keeping in with the locals for her wages.'

'And you know she's still there?' Charlie asked.

Nick made yet another note. His list was starting to look horrible. 'I can check. But why would she get involved with something like this?'

'Maybe she misses Jimmy. If she took care of him for the first four years of his life, it would have been a wrench to leave him. Maybe she didn't have a high opinion of Stephanie's childcare skills. You need to look at her, Nick. She's someone that Jimmy would trust unquestioningly. If she could have found a way to get alongside him, she could have introduced him to the man who took him. It would have been easy for her to groom him.'

'It seems a bit far-fetched,' he complained.

'This whole scenario is far-fetched,' Charlie said. 'It's so public. Too many things could have gone wrong. It's very bold.'

'That's why I was leaning towards Pete Matthews before I spoke to you,' Nick said. 'He's a bully, he's a stalker, he's a control freak. He's organised and he's plausible.'

'How well did he know Jimmy?'

'I'm not sure. I think the boy was pretty young when Stephanie dumped Pete. But the guy's a stalker, he might have found a way to get to know him.'

'That's true. I wouldn't rule him out. But don't lose sight of the other possibilities.'

Nick sighed. 'If this is what you come up with off the top of your head, I'm not sure I've got the strength for a more considered response.'

Charlie chuckled. 'Don't hold your breath. There may not be much more.'

'Before you go – what do you think this kidnap's all about? Is it someone who wants Jimmy for himself, or is it going to come down to ransom?'

The line went silent. He knew she was thinking and he endured what felt like a long pause. 'I don't think this is about money. Because there is no money. There's an intelligence at work here, and if a big payday was what they were after, there are a lot more promising targets than Jimmy. And that's a good thing.'

'Why do you say that? If it's Jimmy they're after, he might be gone for good.'

'I appreciate that. But the chances are he'll be kept alive. And that's better than the alternative, don't you think?'

23

Nothing was pleasant or easy when it came to dealing with Joshu. Every encounter with him or his lawyers was bruising and tiresome. I don't know how Scarlett would have got through it without Leanne and me. We were the punchbags, the sounding boards, the support system. Marina did the practical stuff, but for everything else, Scarlett turned to the pair of us. We were her safety valve. On the days when she was off recording the TV show, she used up every ounce of energy maintaining Public Scarlett. Often when she came home, all she wanted to do was cuddle up on the sofa with a slumbering Jimmy, watch crap TV and drink Prosecco. But there were other times when she wanted to rant, and that was OK with us too. Leanne occasionally went out on the town. 'Brave Scarlett', she was these days, which was a definite improvement on the Scarlett Harlot.

'He did you a favour, you know,' I said one evening. I felt I was taking my life in my hands. She still wasn't over him, not by a long way. But sooner or later, I was going to have to start saying what I really believed.

'Oh yeah. Breaking my heart. That's been really good for

me,' she slurred. 'Like I totally needed something to push me into the family tradition of drinking like a fish.'

I squared my shoulders and looked her in the eye. 'That's your choice. And it's a pretty spineless reaction, if you ask me. I think you're better than that. Stronger than that. You prove it every day when you walk on that set stone-cold sober. This drinking at home, it's nothing but self-indulgence.'

'I thought you were supposed to be my friend.' Her sulky mouth pouted even further.

'Who else is going to tell you the truth? Joshu did you a favour. There's the superficial thing of making you the victim in the eyes of the media, which is a whole lot better than them treating you like a villain.' I waited for her to acknowledge I had a point.

Realising I was waiting in vain, I ploughed on. 'He treated you like shit, Scarlett. You deserve better than that. But better wasn't going to come along while Joshu was around, strutting his stuff. You've said yourself a thousand times, he was a crap dad. Well, the truth is, he was an even worse husband. You keep telling me about the grand plan. About making something of yourself. Face it, Scarlett, that was never going to happen while Joshu was still around. He's on a downward spiral. You want to keep moving up, you're better off without him.'

'That's easy for you to say.' Her tone was surly, but she put the bottle back in the fridge without refilling her glass.

'I know. That doesn't make it any less true. You're better off without him.'

The uncomfortable aspect to the whole business was that the more I dished out advice to Scarlett, the less I seemed able to apply it to my own life.

To me, it didn't make much practical difference whether I was out at the hacienda or in my own home. Apart from the interviewing aspect of my job, I could work anywhere with a door I could close on the outside world. Now Joshu's sound equipment was gone, the glorified shed he'd used in the back garden was free. So on the mornings when I woke up in Scarlett's spare room, I would take my laptop out there and plug my earphones in to transcribe my interviews. If Scarlett was filming, I'd head back to my own house after lunch and stay there for a day or two. It was all pretty random, and I soon realised that, however much it might suit me, it didn't suit Pete.

It started with him picking holes in everything I did. The vegetables I'd bought were past their best, the meat wasn't good enough quality, the wine was a lousy year. The house was too warm or too cold. Then it got more personal. Apparently I needed a haircut or a pedicure or a whole new wardrobe. In bed, I was too demanding, too passive or too critical of his performance. Never mind walking on eggshells. I felt as if I was encased in them from head to toe. I felt anxious and apprehensive all the time I was with him. And of course, when someone you love constantly finds fault, it's hard not to feel at fault.

Looking back at it now, I can see it was all about power and control. Pete could only see my friendship with Scarlett in terms of himself. Every evening I spent with her was, in his eyes, undermining our relationship. Why would I rather be with someone he despised when I could be sitting alone at home waiting for him to possibly show up? But at the time, I was bending over backwards to see his point of view. He worked hard and when he had free time, he wanted to spend it with me. That was an advance on a lot of the men I'd tried to have relationships with over the years. And he was still capable of moments of tenderness and humour, moments that transcended the unpleasantness and convinced me that yes, it was all my fault.

But once I'd established a work routine out at Scarlett's,

Pete's aggression began to escalate. If I wasn't around when he was free and wanted to be with me, he would send snotty texts. I'd told him he was welcome at the hacienda, but he sneered at the idea. 'Why would I want to spend my nights in a witches' coven?' was one of his responses. 'You witches did your voodoo on Joshu. I'm not giving you the chance to do it on me.'

All of that I could put up with. I actually felt sorry for him. There must be a reason why someone who could be so loving it was almost smothering could also be that harsh. And the only reason I could think of was damage. Which meant I forgave him, time and time again. In my head I scolded myself for being so lacking in compassion.

It's what abused women – and children – do all the time. They find a mechanism to blame themselves, partly because they're innately kind and partly because that's what the abuser inculcates in them as the appropriate response. I blamed myself for Pete's anger.

But when he started shouting at me every time I didn't match up to his impossible standards, I came to my senses. I'm a lucky woman, you see. I was brought up in a house where the adults respected each other. And they brought me up to respect myself. And I knew that Pete had crossed a line. Whatever history he was working out here had taken him too far. I tried to explain this to him, but he wouldn't listen. He just kept on yelling. I belonged to him and I was going to have to learn how to behave. I was going to stop hanging around with those lesbian bitches. I was going to have to toe the line. Or else. It was scary. I really thought he was going to hit me. I'd never felt like that in my adult life.

I walked out. I walked out of my own house and got in my car and drove away. Of course I went to the hacienda. It was the easiest option. I'd already complained to Scarlett and Leanne about Pete's unreasonable behaviour. If I'd gone to any of my other friends, I'd have had to explain the whole story, and I didn't have the energy for that. One night, I thought. I'll stay for one night and I'll go back in the morning. I knew Pete was due in the studio the next day. Even if he stayed all night, he'd have to be gone by ten at the latest.

Scarlett was depressingly unsurprised to see me. 'I could see this coming,' she said. 'He's a bully, that one. Surly bastard, and all. I remember that time I dropped you off and he was waiting on the doorstep. Face like a slapped arse.'

'Are you finishing with him?' Leanne asked, putting the kettle on. We were trying to wean Scarlett – and ourselves – off the Prosecco and back on to the great Northern panacea of Yorkshire tea.

I could feel tears welling up. 'I don't want to. But I can't put up with this.'

'It's like he wants you behind bars, waiting for him to come home and free you,' Scarlett said.

'Prisoner of love,' Leanne intoned. 'You could sell your story to a magazine.'

'I don't want to *have* a story.' I like being a ghost. Insubstantial. Transparent. Anonymous.

'Not like me, then,' Scarlett said with a chuckle. 'Fuck him, Steph. You're worth a dozen of him. Just like you're always telling me. You won't find Mr Right with Mr Totally Fucking Wrong blocking the light.'

I wasn't scared about going back the next morning. I thought Pete would have come to his senses and calmed down. But Scarlett was concerned. 'You've led a sheltered life, you have,' she said. 'Where I grew up, toerags like Pete were ten a penny. Think they own you. Think you were put on the planet for their benefit. Tossers like him, they don't let go easily. You've got to be prepared for it to get worse before it gets better.'

I wasn't paying much attention. I thought I knew best. But when it came to men behaving badly, I had no idea.

24

The first shock was that Pete was still there. His car was parked outside my house and the bedroom curtains were still closed at half past ten. 'That doesn't look good,' Scarlett said. 'I thought you said he was supposed to be at work this morning?'

'That's what he said.' But it looked as though he'd changed his mind. Or I'd changed it for him.

'Do you want me to come in with you?'

To be honest, I wasn't sure that I wanted to go in at all. Pete's rage had unsettled me as well as frightened me. That he was still there indicated I'd been wrong about him getting over his tantrum. I didn't want to confront that anger again. Ever. I'd never been more certain of anything in my life. In my head, I was finished with him. No amount of contrition could undo those moments of unchained fury and the promise of violence they held. 'Let's wait a bit,' I said.

'OK.' Scarlett reclined the seat and closed her eyes. Since Jimmy's birth, she'd developed the enviable habit of being able to catnap anywhere, at any time. I might be on tenterhooks. But Scarlett was asleep within a couple of minutes. I listened to the radio and her soft snores, trying to slow my own breathing to her rhythm.

It was almost eleven when the front door swung open and Pete emerged. Even from a distance, he looked wild-eyed and unshaven. As shocking as his appearance was the fact that he left the front door wide open behind him as he hustled down the path and into his car. The tyres screeched as he shot away, rousing Scarlett from her slumber.

'Wassup,' she grumbled. 'Wassit?'

'Bastard,' I said, already halfway out of the car.

She caught me up on my doorstep. 'He left the door open?'

'Obviously hoping for some passing burglar,' I said bitterly over my shoulder as I walked in. Then stopped short. The hallway looked like the burglary had already happened. And a pretty spiteful one at that. Pictures had been stripped from the walls and dropped to the floor. Broken glass and fragments of frames were trodden into the carpet. A couple of the prints themselves were torn where a foot had gone through them.

'Oh, shit,' Scarlett said from behind me. I was beyond speech.

I didn't want to go any further for fear of what I would find. A heady brew of smells was enough of a clue to what lay ahead of me. But uncertainty was worse than anxiety. I walked into what had been my beautiful open-plan ground floor living space and staggered as my knees lost the power to hold me straight. Scarlett grabbed me, saving me from collapsing amid the ruins of my kitchen. Now I knew what Pete had been doing all night.

It looked as if he'd opened every cupboard and drawer and swept the contents to the floor. Broken crockery, jars and bottles lay in random heaps linked by piles and pools of flour, rice, jam, pasta, ketchup, olives, oil, melted ice cream and alcohol. In the living space beyond, books and CDs were strewn all over the floor, more broken pictures and frames scattered over them. I thought I was going to throw up.

'I'm going to fucking kill him,' Scarlett said. 'I swear to God.'

She picked up an overturned chair and lowered me into it. 'But first I'm going to call the cops.'

'No,' I said. 'Don't do that. He'll twist his way out of it.'

'How can he? We saw him leave.'

'I saw him leave. You were still asleep.'

'So? He doesn't know that. I'll tell the five-oh I saw him walk away and leave the door open.'

'He'll only lie about when he left. He's got mates that'll lie for him. It's what they do, men like him. They gang up on us. And he'll drag you into it. He'll get his version out there. Hysterical men-hating women, that's what we'll be.' I dropped my head into my hands.

'You can't let him get away with this,' Scarlett protested. 'Bastards like him, we need to stand up to them.'

'Let somebody else do it,' I said, on the verge of tears. 'I haven't got it in me, Scarlett. He'll win and then I'll wind up feeling worse. If that's possible.'

She looked mutinous, but she backed off. 'You're coming back to mine, then,' she said decisively. 'I'm going upstairs to pack a bag for you. No arguments.'

I sat there, stunned. The wreckage of my home felt like a dark stain inside me, spreading like dirty oil over a warehouse floor, tainting everything in its path. I loved this house and what I'd made of it. And he'd trashed it without a care, all because I'd wounded his precious male pride. How could I have missed this coiled rage lurking inside him? How could I have loved someone with this darkness at his heart?

Eventually, Scarlett reappeared, looking shaken. 'I sorted out some clothes, and packed up your laptop and all the papers on your desk. Let's go.'

Numb, I followed her out to the car, pointlessly locking the door behind me. I let Scarlett drive. Traumatised as I was, I still wanted to survive and I knew I wasn't safe behind the wheel in that state.

Back at the hacienda, she dosed me up with tea and Valium and packed me off to bed. I slept on and off for the best part of twenty hours, and when I re-emerged into consciousness, I felt almost human.

I found Leanne and Scarlett in the kitchen, diaries open on the worktop as they went through their plans for the week. Scarlett leapt up and swept me into her arms. 'How're you doing, babe?'

'Crap. But I'll live,' I said, disentangling myself and heading for the coffee machine. 'I think I need to get a locksmith over there to change the locks. The bastard didn't have keys before but he might have helped himself to my spares.'

'No need,' Leanne said briskly. 'It's all sorted.'

'What do you mean?'

'I got a locksmith out there soon as we got back yesterday,' Scarlett said. 'And a professional cleaning crew. You won't have to look at the state he left your place in again.'

That's when I finally did cry over what Pete the bastard had done. Looking back at it now, I do take solace from the fact that it was kindness rather than malice that provoked that response.

Pete had done everything in his power to make me doubt the reality of Scarlett's friendship. If I'd harboured any doubts, they died that morning. I knew Scarlett and I had the kind of bond that makes women friends for life.

I only wish we'd had longer to enjoy it.

25

Vivian wasn't much of a homemaker, but even so, she understood the violation Pete Matthews had inflicted on Stephanie. It sounded as if this was a man with a serious axe to grind. The only question was whether he could bear a grudge for four years. 'I get why you maybe thought going to the police was pointless. But you must have wanted to make him pay for what he did to you?' she said.

Stephanie sighed. 'To be honest, what I wanted was to have him gone from my life. I didn't want to do anything that would prolong my connection to him. It was everybody else that wanted to avenge what he'd done to me. Scarlett, Leanne, Maggie, my other friends. My pal Mike wanted to get a bunch of the lads together and go round to Pete's. Trash the place and beat the shit out of him. But I put the blocks on that.' She shook her head. 'It wouldn't have made me feel any better. I was determined not to be dragged down to his level. Can you understand that?'

Vivian wasn't sure whether any law enforcement officer would have felt kinship with Stephanie on that one. 'I strive for justice in my job,' she said. 'I don't think people who do bad things should walk away scot free.'

'But shouldn't the victims have some say in outcomes? I wanted to draw a line under what he did to me. I didn't want to think about him for one second more than I had to. Any connection to him would have been a bad deal for me. That was my thinking at the time. As it turned out, I probably made the wrong decision. But it was the choice I needed to make then and there for the sake of my own well-being.'

'I take it that wasn't the last you heard from Pete?' Now Vivian could explore what interested her – whether Pete Matthews was the kind of man who would cling to his sense of being wronged down the years.

Stephanie shook her head ruefully. 'Far from it. I thought he'd vented his feelings and I'd never hear from him again. But he apparently thought we still had unfinished business. After I'd been at Scarlett's for a couple of days, he started texting me. It was as if nothing had happened. He was talking about work, when he'd be finished for the day, and where should we meet for dinner?'

'That's very weird.'

'You think so?'

Vivian wondered if Stephanie was quite as balanced as she appeared. Not to think Pete Matthews' follow-up was weird seemed perverse to her. 'You don't?'

'Stop and think for a moment. He didn't know I'd seen him leave the house with the door standing open. For all he knew, I hadn't been back there. I assumed he was fishing to see whether I was aware my house had been wrecked and, if so, whether I held him responsible. I mean, he had to be at least a little bit worried that I was going to report him to the police.'

Again, Stephanie had caught her on the back foot. This was one seriously smart woman, Vivian thought. Her stories might be long-winded, but along the way, a lot of useful points got made. 'That makes sense,' she acknowledged. 'What did you do about these texts?'

'I ignored them. I didn't read most of them. At first I deleted them, but Scarlett pointed out that if I did have to go to the police, they would be evidence of him hassling me. So I kept them on my phone but I didn't pay attention to them. Then he started emailing me as well. These hurt, bewildered emails, acting like he didn't know why I was ignoring him when his only crime was to love me.' She rolled her eyes and groaned. 'I'm sure you've seen the kind of thing.'

Vivian nodded. She didn't think it would be helpful to remark that generally she'd viewed them in the aftermath of violent death. 'I get the picture. And did you call the cops?'

'I didn't think there would be any point. On the face of it, there was nothing threatening about his texts and emails. Apart from the sheer volume of them, I suppose. Scarlett said I should talk to the police, but I thought they wouldn't take me seriously. Because there was no apparent threat.'

'Did that change?'

'After he vandalised my home, I stayed at Scarlett's for four or five days. To be honest, I was dreading going back home. My recollection of what he'd done was too vivid. I couldn't see a cleaning company doing much to erase that image. But I was wrong. Scarlett hadn't only got them to clean the place up. One day when I thought she was at the TV studios she'd done a commando raid on John Lewis and Waitrose. Obviously, she hadn't been able to replicate what I'd lost, but she'd done a bloody good job of finding acceptable replacements. You know that theory the quantum physicists have about multiple universes? Well, when I finally walked back through my front door, it was as if I'd walked into a parallel version of my house. It felt the same, but there were lots of subtle differences. It was very weird. It was only when I went upstairs that I really noticed big differences, because of course Scarlett had never been up there. Her guesswork wasn't bad, though. Even when she'd gone for something very different from what had been there, she'd chosen things I liked. I was so touched.'

There was no arguing with what Scarlett had done. And Vivian imagined that if Pete had found out, it would have driven him crazy. 'Did Pete know what she'd done?'

'I don't know if he realised it was down to Scarlett, but he was obviously keeping tabs on the place. His emails said things like, "You can try to erase the traces of me from the house, but you can't erase me from your heart. You know you love me, there's no escape from that. You can put different paintings on the wall, but I'll still be the face you see when you close your eyes at night."' She closed her eyes momentarily and Vivian could see the strain in her face.

'You read that one way and it's incredibly romantic,' Vivian said. 'Read it another way and it's oppressive and threatening. I understand why you felt it might be hard to have people take you seriously. Did you pluck up the courage to move back into your house?'

Stephanie picked at the lip of her cardboard cup. 'I did. And for a couple of weeks, it was OK. I wasn't going out much because I was transcribing interviews. When I'm in that phase, I'm very focused on what I'm doing. I sit with my headphones on, oblivious to the outside world. I have my groceries delivered so I don't have to leave the cocoon of the client's voice. It's total immersion.' Her face relaxed into a smile and Vivian caught a glimpse of how Stephanie must seem when her life was not infested with fear and anxiety. 'It makes it easier to catch the flavour of their voices when I come to write the book itself. During that period, Pete could have been sitting on my garden wall for hours at a time and I would have been blissfully unaware, sitting up in my little office under the eaves.'

'Do you think he was?'

The stressed and worried woman was back. 'Probably,' she

sighed. 'Well, maybe not sitting on the wall, but certainly driving past several times a day, parking where he could see my house, walking up and down the street. Because those were the things he was doing when I became more aware of my surroundings after I'd finished doing the transcripts. It seemed as though every time I looked out of the window, he was there. Or his car was parked outside the house. I tried hard not to let him stop me going about my normal business. But it was almost impossible. When I left the house, he would fall into step beside me and speak to me. I ignored him but he wouldn't give up. If I caught the bus or the tube, he was there across the aisle or strap-hanging further down the carriage. One time he even tried to get into a cab with me. I practically had to slam the door shut on his fingers to get him to back off. But that wasn't the worst. There was one other occasion that really freaked me out.'

'What happened?'

Stephanie shuddered. 'You're going to read more into it than there was. It was me he was trying to get to, not Jimmy.'

'What happened, Stephanie?' Now Vivian was warm, slipping effortlessly into woman-to-woman mode to extract more from Stephanie.

'Scarlett had brought Jimmy into town with her. They'd been to the Natural History Museum to see the dinosaurs, then I met up with them in Regent's Park. Jimmy was letting off steam in the kids' playground while we sat on a bench chatting. We had half an eye on Jimmy, the way you do. And we both realised at the same moment that there was a man over by the slide who was having much too much to do with Jimmy. I'd kind of registered the guy and thought he was with a couple of other boys, so I hadn't really paid attention. But then he turned round and I recognised Pete. With his hair cut short. Looking really different. But clearly Pete.'

'That must have been horrible. What did you do?'

'We took off like raging banshees, me and Scarlett. But he only smiled and walked away. Briskly, but nothing that would look suspicious to anyone else. It was as if he'd flicked us the bird. Saying, "I can find you wherever and whenever I want." It really unnerved me.'

'Was Jimmy bothered?'

She shook her head. 'Not in the least. He looked bewildered for a minute when we came running across the playground. Scarlett scooped him up and we took off in the opposite direction. But that was the last straw for me. First I googled stalking to see what remedies I might have. There's a law, the Protection from Harassment Act, that sounds like it should do the trick. Stalkers, in theory, can face criminal charges or you can take civil proceedings against them. Injunctions and the like. I felt quite cheerful about it. I made an appointment to speak to a police officer at my local station. She was really sympathetic, but the problem was that Pete had been very careful about the content of his texts and emails. He hadn't done anything in the street that could have been construed as an assault or a threat. At least, not in terms of the criminal law. There was nothing she could do.'

'Not even a quiet word?'

Stephanie's mouth twisted in a wry smile. 'That's the irony. If the police spoke to Pete without good legal reason, they'd be the ones doing the harassing. It's crazy, isn't it?'

Not for the first time, Vivian felt the frustration of due process. But this wasn't the time or the place to get into that. 'So there was nothing?'

'She suggested I talk to a lawyer. The civil courts have a lower standard of proof, you see. So I made an appointment with a lawyer who specialises in this kind of case and it turned out that, even with a lower standard of proof, I didn't have enough against Pete to take out an injunction. It would have been different if I'd reported the criminal damage to my house when it happened. But her advice was to go away and keep a log of everything he said and did. Then come and see her again for another expensive appointment in three months' time.' Stephanie shook her head, wondering. 'Obviously, she didn't mention the expense. That was just my cynical take on it. The bottom line was, you're on your own, sister. The law was not on my side.'

'I take it he persisted.'

'He persisted, all right.'

26

Scarlett was waiting for me in the car after I'd seen the lawyer. I told her the verdict and she swore like a football hooligan then said, 'That is just so wrong. He can do what the fuck he likes. Get in your face as much as he wants. And there's fuck-all you can do? He needs sorting out, he does. I tell you, Steph, I still know some lads in Leeds who'd be happy to come down and do him over.'

'No, I told you. That's not the way to go. Apart from anything else, what happens if one of your old mates makes a secret recording of you putting the word out then sells it to the papers? All your hard work over the past year goes straight down the tubes. Not to mention you get arrested for conspiracy to have somebody beaten up.' I rolled my eyes. 'We've got to find another way to get him.'

Scarlett pouted. 'And so far you've come up with zilch.'

'Yeah, well. I've been giving this some thought. And I've decided that I'm going to sell the house. No estate agent's board, no details in their window. Just a very discreet word of mouth to the people on their books. Then one day Pete the Bastard will turn up to follow me to the bus stop and it won't be me who walks out of the front door.'

Scarlett looked dumbstruck. 'Can you do that?'

'It won't be easy, but yeah, I think so. Every time there's going to be a viewing, I'll make sure I act as a decoy. I'll trail him all over town on a jolly while the agent's showing the property to prospective buyers. The day before the move, I'll let him follow me to the Eurostar and we'll toddle off to Paris for a couple of days.'

Scarlett laughed with delight. 'You are one clever bitch, Steph. And where are you going to live then?'

'I thought I might come and crash with you for a few months. What do you say?'

She did a little shoulder-and-hand jive in the seat. 'Cool, cool, very fucking cool,' she said. 'We'll have a right laugh.' She frowned. 'You never told him about Leanne, did you?'

I shook my head. 'No way. That was our secret. He knows nothing that can damage you, believe me. I've always been very discreet. That's how I protect my investment.' I gave her a friendly punch on the arm. 'Are you OK with me moving in for a bit?'

'Stay as long as you want. I like having you around.'

'I like being around. But I'll be honest, the big advantage for me in staying with you over any of my other mates is that I've got a proper place to work. Somewhere that's not in the way, so I don't feel like I'm imposing,' I added hastily, in case she thought a workroom of my own was the only reason I preferred her place.

'Not to mention the high wall and the security gates,' Scarlett said. 'He could sit out there for bloody days and never get so much as a glimpse of you.'

'He doesn't even know where it is. Just the general area.'

She snorted. 'He'll find out. All he has to do is ask around the pubs. It might cost him twenty quid, but there's plenty ready to shop me. For all the good it'll do him. Like I said, he's not going to be able to pester you behind my walls. Not now we've got the broken glass.' She pretended to wince.

'Thanks, Scarlett. I appreciate it.'

'And I mean it. Stay as long as you want.' She shrugged. 'Make it permanent, if you want.'

'That's kind. And no disrespect, but I like having a place of my own. I just need to think about where I want to be then find a house that fits the bill. If I can get a bit of breathing space at yours, I won't be rushing into the wrong choice, making it too easy for him to find me.'

We set off through the afternoon traffic, hoping to make it back to Essex before the roads grew too congested. Scarlett's offer was kind, but if I'm honest, I couldn't stomach the idea of living in the fake-tan belt permanently. Not to mention the fact that I'd never see any of my other friends, for whom Essex loomed large in the imagination as a wasteland devoid of culture, cuisine and conversation. I hadn't made my mind up where I was going to settle, except that I knew it would be outside London. And not Essex.

'You need to get a new phone as well,' Scarlett said. 'And a new email address. Just for your mates and for Maggie. You don't want to be dealing with his shit on a day-to-day basis, but you do need to keep a record of it.'

What she said made sense. And I'd deal with it in the morning. I'd hoped for a different outcome from the day. I'd hoped it would end with Pete in a police interview room or about to be served with court papers for an injunction hearing. But it wasn't the end of the world. One way or another, I was determined not to have my life defined by one twisted inadequate.

Realising I wasn't the only one being stalked by a twisted inadequate probably shouldn't have made me feel better, but it did. Within days of me setting up base camp at Scarlett's, Leanne came back from a night on the town bursting with indignation. It soon became clear that her anger was covering a much deeper seam of unease.

She was sitting at the kitchen table, defiantly smoking, scowling into a mug of tea. She didn't look up as I brewed a coffee and sat down opposite her.

'Rough night?' I said.

'You have no idea.'

'What happened? A few too many cocktails?'

'Huh. I wish. No, I got monstered by this mad fucking stalker chick who thinks Scarlett is her best mate because she donated a few signed boxes of Scarlett Smile to some fucking charity fundraiser. I'd barely walked in the place when she started hovering, doing that, "Don't you remember me, babe?" thing. It's always a bit dodgy when they pull that because I've got no idea whether they really know Scarlett or not, you know? So I have to busk it. Like, pretend I've got a shit memory for faces. Anyway, I thought I saw her off OK. Only I hadn't.'

'That must have been uncomfortable.'

'It was more than uncomfortable. It was fucking spooky. It was like she was glued on. I couldn't shake her off. And because she was acting like we was best mates, I couldn't just tell her to fuck off, not in front of everybody. Because that's the kind of thing that goes straight into the morning papers and on to the Internet. "Foul-mouthed Scarlett devastates charity supporter." You know what they're like.'

'How did you handle it then?'

Leanne suddenly looked shifty. She stubbed out her forbidden cigarette on the underside of the table, a move that Scarlett would have raged at her for. 'I'd had enough. I couldn't get a minute's peace. She kept going on about how she wanted me to come back to her place for a party. Wouldn't take no for an answer. So I went off to the VIP loo, knowing she'd follow me. Only, I didn't go into the loo. I went out on the fire escape. And she came after me. I pretended I'd gone out for a fag, and once I'd lit up, I stubbed it out on her neck. Then I kicked her down the fire escape.'

I was shocked and I must have shown it.

'Well, what else was I going to do?' Leanne demanded. 'She wasn't going to back off. She was doing my head in. And I got rid of her in a way that won't blow up in Scarlett's face. She should be grateful. That's one less mad stalker bitch on her tail.'

Of course I'd known that Scarlett and Leanne had come up as street fighters. But this was the first time I'd seen such stark evidence of how unpleasant things could get if you pushed one of the Higgins girls too far. I knew how scary obsessed fans could get, no denying that.

But I really didn't warm to Leanne's way of dealing with it.

27

'And did your plan work?' Vivian asked, tapping the keys of her computer to bring up an urgent message from the Chicago office. 'Did you manage to escape from Pete Matthews?'

'Amazingly, it did. He turned up at Scarlett's place a couple of times, but we didn't answer the intercom and he never caught sight of me, as far as I know. Various friends called to say he'd been looking for me, but nobody grassed me up. I stayed with Scarlett for about six months altogether, while my house was being sold and I was figuring out where to move to. Eventually I—'

Vivian held up one finger. 'Could you bear with me a moment? I need to deal with this message.'

The email was from her boss.

Vivian:

I've had a message from our colleagues at State. The Embassy in London has been inundated with media inquiries about your Amber Alert kid. They've been told he's the child of a reality TV star who died last year and they need an update. I've told them the circumstances, but I need a here-and-now from you.

I understand from your brief that Jimmy Higgins' guardian is a writer? Is there any possibility that this could be a publicity stunt? Abbott says she inherited the kid but no money. Could there be a book in the works that she's trying to build up a profile for?

I shouldn't have to remind you that I need you to stay on top of this. The timing couldn't be worse from an agency point of view. I can't spare someone to come out there and hold your hand. Let's get a good result on this one.

Succinct and to the point. Demanding the sort of response she really didn't have. And throwing a spanner into the works of her witness interview. First things first. How could she dress up this scenario to make it look as if she had some kind of a clue what had happened to Jimmy Higgins? She bit her lip and considered how best to say nothing at all.

We're pursuing all avenues to trace the movements of Jimmy Higgins and his abductor, who was dressed in a replica TSA uniform and is believed to have left the precincts of the airport. We are also working with Scotland Yard detectives to develop leads on both sides of the Atlantic. Jimmy's guardian, Stephanie Harker, is giving her full cooperation as we all work to bring Jimmy safely home. Anyone with any information should contact blah blah blah.

That's really all we have at present. This is not a straightforward Kidnap for Ransom. As yet, we are not clear what the motive might be, but it does seem likely that the child was taken by someone who has a personal connection. I'll let you know as and when I have anything substantive to report.

It looked woefully thin and it wasn't going to win her any friends in high places, but better that than to promise what she couldn't deliver. She read it through again and removed the word 'replica' because it was pointlessly speculative.

The second paragraph posed a more thorny question and one she couldn't really answer except to say her gut instinct was that Stephanie Harker was not a con artist, nor the agent of this crisis. When men claimed gut instinct, it was taken seriously. But still women were condemned to 'feminine intuition', as if that were somehow inferior. In Vivian's experience, the women were on the money more than men, if only because girls were conditioned to listen and pay attention much more than boys were.

Harker's concern and fear for the boy seems genuine. Her reaction when he was taken was extreme; nobody volunteers for a second blast of the taser. Also, Harker is not the kind of writer who has ever courted publicity. The nature of her work as a ghost writer is the opposite of seeking publicity. If she was trying to make a big splash to win publicity for a book about inheriting the boy, surely she would be better off making herself look like the good mother? The one who foils the kidnap rather than lets it happen? Furthermore, she has volunteered extensive information including direct contact with a Scotland Yard detective who has personal knowledge of both her and the boy. For all those reasons, I don't think this is a stunt, nor that she has any part in the abduction.

Then she sent it, hoping it would pacify her boss. Really, he should be too busy with threats against the President to be unduly concerned with her investigation. Or to question her instincts about Stephanie Harker.

Vivian retuned her attention to Stephanie, who was visibly

tiring now. 'Your media has got their claws into the story, I'm afraid.'

Stephanie groaned. 'Can I have my phone back? There are probably a hundred texts and voicemails on it already. Not just from the press, but from my friends and family. They'll be scared and worried. I need to talk to people.'

'I appreciate that. And it's not my intention to keep you from talking to anyone. But first and foremost, for Jimmy's sake, I need you to keep talking to me. I need to make sure we've gone down every possible road that might lead us to the person who took Jimmy this afternoon. Besides, it's getting late back in the UK. I'm sure people won't expect you to call tonight. They'll understand what's going on.'

Stephanie looked doubtful. 'You've clearly never met my agent. Not to mention my mother. Please, what harm can it do to let me make a couple of calls? I only want to reassure my mother and my literary agent. Who's also my best friend. The rest can wait. You can listen in if you want. I've no secrets.'

Vivian pondered. It wasn't exactly protocol, but nothing about this case fit the usual parameters – no violence, no ransom demands, no obvious motives. And Stephanie was a witness, not a suspect. It was hard to justify keeping her in purdah. And even if she was somehow tangentially involved in the abduction, it didn't seem likely that her mother or her agent would be involved. Besides, she felt sure Stephanie had more of relevance to tell her. Vivian needed to keep her on side. A couple of phone calls couldn't hurt. And it was possible the conversations might remind Stephanie of something she'd forgotten. The final argument for allowing the calls was that it would answer her boss's fears about collusion. If this was a set-up to sell books, surely a conversation with her agent would provide a clue? These were not professional criminals, after all.

Vivian checked out the phone on the desk. Yes, it had speakerphone capability. She gave Stephanie a long, level look. 'I'm not obliged to facilitate any personal communications you want to make. Not in the middle of an investigation as serious as this. But I'm willing to let you make the two phone calls you asked for. I'm going to put you on speakerphone so I can hear the conversation and if you stray into an area I consider to be inappropriate, then I will intervene. Is that clear?'

Stephanie looked relieved. 'You mean, if I call Randy Parton an authoritarian twat, you'll shut me up?'

Vivian couldn't repress a smile. 'More like, "Here's what the FBI are doing." Who do you want to call first?'

'My parents. Now the news is out, my mother will be in a state.'

'You'll need to hit nine for an outside line.' Vivian pushed the phone towards her and watched her key in the number. They both listened as the phone rang out. Once, twice, then the tinny emptiness of a transatlantic speakerphone line. 'Hello?' It was the voice of an older woman – hesitant, light, insubstantial.

'Hi, Mum. It's Stephanie.'

'Thank God! Robert, it's Stephanie. We've been so worried, we saw on the ten o'clock news that Jimmy's been kidnapped. We couldn't believe it. You don't expect things like that to happen to people you know.' She sounded affronted, as if the abduction were a personal insult.

'It's all been a bit of a shock,' Stephanie said.

'Well, it's been a shock for us too. You must be in a terrible state. How did it happen? You take your eyes off them for a moment . . .'

'I was in a cubicle waiting to be patted down. I set the metal detector off. My leg, you know? And a man walked off with him.'

'Well, I never. That's America for you. You wouldn't have something like that happening over here, would you?'

Stephanie made an apologetic face at Vivian, who smiled and shrugged. 'It could have happened anywhere, Mum.'

'And what about you, you poor thing? Are you all right?'

'I'm fine. I'm helping the FBI put together a picture of our life.'

'The FBI? Oh, Robert, she's with the FBI. I never thought a child of mine would end up in the hands of the FBI. Oh, Stephanie, you must be worried sick. I hope they're treating you properly. You hear all sorts—'

'Don't worry about me, Mum. I'm fine. It's Jimmy you should be worrying about.'

The sound of a dismissive sniff travelled the best part of four thousand miles. 'I knew it would be nothing but trouble, you taking on that boy.'

Stephanie pinched the bridge of her nose between her thumb and index finger. This was the last thing she needed. 'Let's not go over this again. The point is that somebody has abducted Jimmy and yes, I am worried sick about him. He's only five, Mum. Try and remember what that's like. I've got to go now. I just wanted to let you know there's no reason to worry about me. I'll call you when I've any news.'

Without waiting to hear any more, Stephanie pressed the button to disconnect the call. She exhaled heavily, staring at the table. 'My mother thinks I should have handed Jimmy over to social services,' she said, her voice heavy and dull. 'She's led a pretty narrow life.'

Vivian often wished her own mother's life had been a little narrower. She'd been a major in Army Intelligence and made no secret of the fact that she thought the FBI was a poor second to her own world. Maybe if her mother had been like Mrs Harker, Vivian wouldn't have felt quite the same urge constantly to prove herself. 'Mothers,' she said. 'We're never the daughters they hoped for.'

Stephanie lifted her head in surprise and gave Vivian a tiny nod of acknowledgement. 'My agent?'

Vivian extended a hand. 'Be my guest.'

This time, there was no hesitancy in the voice that answered. 'Maggie Silver,' came the confident greeting.

'Maggie,' Stephanie said. 'I thought I'd better give you a call.'

'*Darling*,' Maggie drawled, her excitement obvious. 'I'm *so* pleased to hear your *dear* voice. I left a voicemail when I heard the *news*. I couldn't *believe* it. How absolutely *awful* for you. And that *poor*, dear boy. It's all *over* Twitter, you know. Not to mention the rolling news. *Do* tell me they've *found* him safe and well.'

'I wish I could. But there's no trace of him yet.' Stephanie looked as if she might burst into tears. 'It's really scary, Maggie. One minute he was there, the next he was gone.'

'I simply don't understand how this could *happen*. Was no one paying *attention* to Jimmy while you were *off* being searched?'

'Apparently not.'

'How simply *frightful*. But there's no point in *blame*, not now. The important thing is getting Jimmy back safely. Do they want *money*? Or is it one of these *mad* political groups looking for *publicity*?'

'We don't know. We've heard nothing. I'm talking to the FBI, telling them everything I can about Jimmy's history. And mine.'

'You'll be there all *night*, then, darling.' Maggie said tartly. 'I hope you've got a nice dishy *profiler* like William Petersen in *Manhunter*.' The women's eyes met and they both smiled. 'Now, look, the papers are going to be *all over* this.' Maggie's tone turned businesslike. 'I'm going to need copy from you whenever you can sit down and collect yourself. It's too late for tomorrow's papers, but I'm sure I can get you a *nice show* in the *Mail* or the *Mirror*. How soon can you let me have an "I" piece?'

'I've no idea. It's the last thing on my mind, to be honest.'

'Sweetie, it'll be good for you to order your thoughts rather than sitting *brooding*. Trust me, Maggie knows best. Call me in the morning, we'll take it from there. And look *after* yourself, darling. Get some sleep, OK?'

'I'll try. I'll talk to you tomorrow.'

And that was that. There was no doubt that Maggie Silver saw Jimmy Higgins' disappearance as a potential source of income. But it seemed as much of a shock to her as it had to Stephanie herself.

As if Stephanie were reading her mind, she said, 'So now you've experienced the lovely Maggie. You have to admit, if I was planning this as a publicity stunt, she's the agent you'd want to have in your corner. Let me set your mind at rest. I won't be writing anything for the *Daily Mail* tomorrow. Or any other day, if it's up to me. All I want is to have Jimmy back in my arms. Besides that, everything else pales into insignificance.'

Vivian nodded, believing her. 'Sure. Now, can we get back to Pete Matthews? I need to ask you: Do you think he's capable of nursing his grudge against you for all these years? Do you think he would abduct Jimmy simply to get back at you?'

Stephanie frowned. 'That's too much of a straight line. If Pete did this, his motive would be different. Somehow, he'd have convinced himself that this was the way not to get back at me but to get me back.'

28

Talking to my female friends about Pete, it was sometimes hard to gct through to them how scary he'd become. When I talked about his constant messages and emails, the flowers he sent to Maggie's office for me, the way he'd followed me in the street, one or two of them were incredulous. 'And you keep knocking him back?' one said. 'I'd love to have a man that devoted to me.'

Because he never openly menaced me, it wasn't easy to explain how threatening I found his behaviour. Scarlett totally got it, though. Because of her own experiences with the media, she understood my terror of being turned into what Leanne had jokingly called a 'prisoner of love'. It made her shudder with horror, and it was one of the many reasons why living at the hacienda was a very easy option.

But I couldn't stay there for ever. After a lot of thought, I'd decided to move to Brighton. I'd always liked the seaside, in spite of dispiriting childhood holidays in the teeth of easterly gales at Cleethorpes and Skegness. Parts of Brighton reminded me of the bits of Lincoln I'd liked – the narrow twisting streets of the Lanes, the less grand terraced streets, the green spaces at the heart of the town. There was a cultural life and easy access to London. But perhaps most importantly of all, I'd never mentioned Brighton to Pete. Not even casually, in passing. I'd never said, 'I fancy a day out in Brighton,' or 'One of my favourite authors is doing the Brighton Festival, let's go down and make a weekend of it.' There was no reason on earth why he should come looking for me there.

I eventually found a sweet little Victorian terraced house ten minutes from the sea. There were local shops, a couple of bustling pubs where easy acquaintance seemed to be on offer, a neat little park where I could take the air when I needed to have a pause for thought. The house was tall and narrow, with a converted attic that served me well as an office. The master bedroom revealed a sliver of sea between the houses opposite, and the previous owners had installed a generous conservatory that caught the morning sun. It was perfect, tucked away in a quiet street with parking for residents only. I felt safe.

I didn't see much of Scarlett while I was settling into the new house. I was painting walls and choosing curtain fabric, having sofas reupholstered and scouring the Lanes for bits and pieces to replace items that Pete had broken during his malicious spree. She came down a couple of times with Jimmy, who loved the beach. He could sit for ages sifting through the chunky pebbles, picking his favourites and building little piles around his chubby legs. But there was too much going on in her other life for Scarlett to have much free time.

Her reinvention was coming along apace. Her show focusing on reality TV stars had developed a cult following. It had become a favourite with the student audience, who apparently enjoyed it in a post-modern ironic way. It had also won an audience among the older viewers, the staple of daytime TV. Between the two groups, the show had earned significant ratings. Advertisers loved it and the punters loved Scarlett. Now she was in talks to front a late-night chat show on a popular digital channel. Every now and again I'd stumble on a piece in one of the broadsheets exploring her apparently inexorable rise with a slightly bemused air. But she hadn't let go of her core fan base. There were still the features in *Yes!* magazine and the occasional Leanne appearance in the gossip columns. Scarlett even guest-presented a celebrity special of the reality makeover show *Ladette to Lady*. She was well on the way to becoming a cultural icon.

There was a downside to her success, however. I had a rare opportunity to see it at first hand when she persuaded me to come to a book signing in an Oxford Street department store. Of course, the person who'd actually written *Jimmy's Testament* wouldn't be the one doing the signing, but that was fine with me. I've never had a hankering for the limelight.

We were smuggled in via the delivery entrance to avoid the crowds I'd clocked as we'd crossed Oxford Street in the Mercedes with the tinted windows. The queue stretched out of the brass-bound double doors and round the corner. 'Good turnout,' I said as we swept past.

'Yeah, they always do well for me here.' Scarlett allowed herself to preen a little, then gave me a cheeky smile. 'People love the book, Steph. You did a great job helping me knock it into shape.'

It was always good to hear a morsel of praise. And of course, a morsel was all I generally got from my clients. Scarlett was more generous than most, but even so, it felt like scant acknowledgement of the work.

Still, the champagne and canapés that were waiting for us were a welcome acknowledgement. The signing was a joint event between our publisher and the perfumier who produced Scarlett Smile. They'd provided special pens that would write on the high-gloss finish of the perfume's packaging; the store had provided a handler who would make sure Scarlett always had the correct writing implement to hand. I would have grumbled at the condescension but she didn't seem to mind being treated like an idiot.

Once she'd been coached in how to sign books and perfume boxes, we were led through to the event space, an area in the cosmetics department that had been cleared of product islands for the occasion. All the available space was crammed with fans – mostly young women – who broke out in whoops and cheers and screeches of delight when they caught sight of her. The store had tried to corral them into a queue via metal pillars and webbing, but the system broke down within minutes.

Cameras were flashing, punters shouting and bodies pressing forward against the table separating Scarlett from the hordes. To me, it seemed both terrifying and precarious, as if Scarlett could be overwhelmed at any moment by the sheer weight of numbers. The noise was insistent, beating against my ears in brutal waves. I wanted to turn and run. God knows what it was like for her.

Just when the hysteria approached the tipping point, the store security guards finally moved in. Firmly but gently, they moved the front line a few inches backwards, putting a little distance between Scarlett and her public. At least now there was some semblance of order at the front of the mob. And Scarlett was able to begin signing.

After an hour, it seemed she'd barely made a dent in the crowd. But when I peeled away from her minders and circled round the back of the mob, I could see it was beginning to ease up. On the fringes, I clocked three fans with cameras, relentlessly shooting pictures of Scarlett. They were obviously not paparazzi – neither their cameras nor their clothes were expensive enough. But they were not going anywhere. Towards the end of the signing, when only a few customers remained, all three – a woman and two men – made their way to the signing table and, instead of books, produced folders of glossy photographs downloaded from the Internet that they wanted Scarlett to autograph. None of them looked wholesome. I imagined them back in their lonely bedsits, printing out their photos, searching for the image that would make them feel they'd finally captured Scarlett.

I reckoned capture was what they wanted. It creeped me out to think of those strange obsessives following her round the country, convincing themselves they were her friends. The truly scary thing was that Scarlett knew them. She bestowed her smile on them, even though I could readily see it was a low-wattage version of the real thing. But you couldn't fault its sincerity.

In one sense, her career was carefully choreographed by Scarlett herself. But it only worked because there was nothing cynical about what she was doing. The real Scarlett was the one she was gradually releasing into the wild, and at bottom, the person she was revealing was a good-hearted person. She was well aware of how far she had come and how lucky she had been to make her escape, and unlike so many who have made that journey, she was willing to reach out a helping hand to others who shared her determination to change their futures.

It was that willingness that opened the door for her greatest act of generosity. Back when Jimmy was nearly three, she was invited to take part in the *Caring for Kids* telethon. The initial idea was for an upbeat piece where Scarlett would visit Romania and reveal how the orphanages that had shocked the world after the downfall of the Ceauşescu regime had been transformed. And there was a lot of truth in that version of events. Money raised in the UK had helped to change the lives of thousands of children and disabled people who had been condemned to conditions that gave most of us nightmares to think of. The word coming out of Romania was that the hellhole institutions were a thing of the past, and that's what Scarlett was supposed to go and celebrate. To show the viewers how their donations worked at ground level.

But then a BBC investigative journalist heard that things weren't quite as hunky-dory as the Romanian authorities would have us believe. He went in undercover and found that although most of the worst cases had been closed down, there were still isolated pockets of the country where conditions would have had their bosses tried for crimes against humanity if they'd been in war zones.

Before his report was aired, Scarlett was invited to come in for a screening. She told me later it was the most harrowing thing she'd ever seen. 'One room, there must have been twenty disabled teenagers tied to cots, lying in their own piss and shit, skinny as skeletons. It turned my stomach, Steph. And the little kids, playing in the snow with stones and sticks because they didn't have a toy to their names. Their clothes in rags. Filthy dirty, some of them with open sores. All of them, abandoned by their parents. A lot of them with AIDS.' She was welling up, talking about it.

'And I thought about my dad, and how I could have been one of those babies born with AIDS. But I've got this lovely life, with Jimmy, and my nice house and my career, and money in the bank. And I thought, fuck it, Steph, I've got to do something about this.'

So she insisted that, instead of painting a rosy picture of how there had been a successful transformation in the lives of thousands, she would go back with the journalist and confront the terrible reality that hundreds of people continued to endure. Never mind what had been achieved – Scarlett wanted to ram home the message of how much more was left to be done. Somebody else could deliver the happy-clappy message. She was going straight to the sharp end.

It was an astonishing move. The woman who had been dismissed as a brainless bigot had undergone the ultimate makeover. She wasn't just making caring noises. She was prepared to stand up and be counted. And so she went to

Timonescu orphanage in the Transylvanian mountains and confronted the horrors head on. She spoke to camera with tears running down her face and swore that she was going to do everything in her power to make a difference. 'I want my son to grow up proud of his mum. Not for being on the telly, but for helping to transform the lives of these children,' she said, a catch in her voice.

When it was screened as part of the *Caring for Kids* telethon, it created a sensation. Because the shock value of having a segment like this presented by someone like Scarlett was almost as great as the footage itself. I was at the hacienda with her and Leanne that night, and she was so proud of herself. 'I'm going to set up a charity to support Timonescu,' she said. 'I've been talking about it with George and he's getting all the paperwork done. I'm going to donate a tenth of all my income, and I'm going to get somebody to organise fundraisers. All them women out there doing their exercise classes – I'm going to get them to donate a week's exercise expenditure to making a difference in some kid's life.'

Even I was gobsmacked, and I already knew Scarlett was a very different proposition from the person the world thought they knew. As for the media, they were reeling in shock. Scarlett's stock had never been higher. There were profiles of her everywhere, her troubled past being recast as youthful misdemeanours. Amazingly, given the tendency of the British media to take delight in chopping down to size anyone who dares to rise above the herd, there wasn't a single bit of dirt-digging from any of the red-tops.

I said as much to George as we sipped champagne and nibbled canapés at the launch of TOmorrow, the charitable trust Scarlett had founded to support Timonescu Orphanage. 'It's not for want of trying,' he said. 'The thing is, Scarlett's made such a fine job of cutting herself off from her past that her mother and her sister really have no possible revelations. That part of her history they know about is what's covered most thoroughly in your excellent book.' He chinked his glass against mine. 'You gave the world just enough sordidness to make it interesting, and also to declaw Scarlett's family. The tabloids can't go with the "heartless bitch" line because she bought them a perfectly decent house to live in. And she still pays the council tax and the utility bills. She's covered herself very cleverly.'

'There's always Joshu,' I said. 'Doesn't he worry you?'

George sniffed. 'With his drug habit? I rather think Scarlett has enough insurance to keep Joshu quiet.'

I hoped so. It would be a cruel person who wished Scarlett ill now she was riding the crest of a wave for all the right reasons. But as things turned out, I'd been looking for disaster in all the wrong places.

29

Nick had learned early on in his police career that nobody appreciated a copper on the doorstep late at night unless it really was a matter of life or death. He suspected that as far as Joshu's parents were concerned, he'd be unwelcome at any time. They were under no obligation to talk to him, and he reckoned they would exercise their freedom of choice, not least because his was the face they would associate with the investigation into their only son's death.

But there were other sources for information about the Patel family's circumstances. During the inquiry into Joshu's death, Nick had also spoken to both of the dead man's sisters. Unlike their brother, Asmita and Ambar had fulfilled their parents' ambitions. Asmita was an accountant with an international consultancy; Ambar had been on the point of qualifying as a barrister specialising in tax affairs. Dismayed but not surprised by her brother's death, Ambar spoke about him with a world-weariness depressing in one so young and privileged, suggesting he had been a tragedy waiting to happen. 'We washed our hands of him years ago,' she'd said. 'He made it clear he despised all of us, and frankly, I'd had enough of it. When he took up with that vile woman, that was the last straw. I never even told my friends we were related.' It was a depressing epitaph for a young man who had been, in Nick's view, essentially harmless. A waste of space, perhaps. But not a bad man. Not by the standards Nick was familiar with.

Asmita had been more upset. 'I keep remembering what a funny little boy he was,' she said. 'My sweet little brother. I wish my parents hadn't cut him out of our lives. We should have been there for him.' Her regret was eating her up, that much had been clear. What depressed Nick more than her sister's cynicism was that this grown woman hadn't been able to find the courage to defy her parents and maintain contact with the brother she'd clearly still cared about. He wasn't sentimental; he didn't think Asmita could have saved Joshu from his burning drive towards self-destruction. But he didn't think Joshu had deserved such an almighty fall from grace and he thought he'd let Asmita see that. If anyone in the Patel family was going to talk to him, it would be her.

This time of night wasn't ideal, but child abduction changed all the rules. He hoped Asmita would appreciate that. She was still living at the same address, according to the council tax roll. As he drew near to her address, Adrian Legg's polyphonic guitar blasting from his speakers, Nick's memories of Asmita's flat took shape. The building where she lived had been a primary school, built in the year of Queen Victoria's Diamond Jubilee, which probably explained the extravagance of the architecture. It looked more like a church with cathedral aspirations than an education factory for the children of the London poor. Nick pulled into the car park that had started life as the girls' playground and found a guest slot in the furthest corner.

Asmita's apartment was housed in the former infant

department, occupying the upper floor of what would have been the nave if it really had been a church. He remembered high arched windows, a ribbed wooden ceiling like an upturned boat and wood everywhere – stripped floors, panelled walls, furniture in sympathetic shades. He pressed the intercom and waited. The voice that answered him was firm and slightly peevish. 'Yes? Who is it?'

'Ms Patel? It's Detective Sergeant Nicolaides from the Met Police. I spoke to you after your brother died. I'm sorry to bother you at this time of night, but I do need to talk to you.'

'Can't it keep till tomorrow? Don't you know what time it is?'

Nick tried for the right mix of apology and insistence. 'I'm afraid it's urgent. I wouldn't be here this late in the evening if it wasn't.'

The only response was the loud buzz of the door release. It was so abrupt that he almost didn't catch it in time. Lights came on in the stairwell as he climbed the flight of stairs that led up to the interior door of the flat. The walls were painted in broad stripes of warm earth colours, a statement of welcome as well as taste.

Asmita was standing in the doorway waiting for him. She was wearing a long kaftan with a hood. Nick had seen Arab men wearing something similar but he didn't know what it was called. The material was a blend of shades – saffron, cinnamon, chocolate – with gold threads running through it that caught the light when she moved. Her hair was caught up in a scrunchy on top of her head, making the resemblance to her late brother more obvious than when it was loose. Her eyes looked tired, her skin drawn. Her face was scrubbed of make-up, ready for bed. 'Come in,' she said. It sounded more like, *sod off.*

He followed her into the main living space. Squashy sofas focused on a giant plasma-screen TV. Behind them a long table was set against the wall, clearly functioning as a desk. Neat piles of papers flanked an ultra-thin laptop. Two small speakers sat on the desk, playing quiet, minimalist piano music. The sort of audio wallpaper Nick despised with all of his musical soul.

Asmita stood by the sofas, one hand on her hip, lips pursed. It didn't look as though she was going to invite him to sit down. Maybe he hadn't done as good a job last time as he'd thought. 'Why are you here?' she asked.

'I'm working on an investigation that—' He shrugged and spread his hands. 'This is an incredibly long shot, but we're short on leads, so here I am.' Nick tried his best puppy-dog look, one he'd been reliably informed was a bit of a heart-melter.

Asmita was not moved. 'I don't understand.'

'I'll cut to the chase,' Nick said. 'Your nephew has been abducted.'

Her eyes widened and her mouth opened. 'Rabinder?' Her hands flew to her face, pressing against her cheeks. 'Oh my God, what's happened to Rabinder?'

Nick was taken aback. 'Who's Rabinder?'

'What do you mean, who's Rabinder? He's my nephew.' She frowned, bewildered. 'You said he's been abducted. How can you not know his name?'

'It's not Rabinder,' Nick said hastily. 'Can we just back up here? We're at cross purposes. I'm talking about Jimmy. Joshu's boy. I don't know who Rabinder is.'

Panic visibly drained away from Asmita, leaving anger behind. 'You really freaked me out there. I can't believe you did that.'

'I'm sorry,' Nick said. 'I genuinely had no idea you have another nephew. Has Ambar had a baby?'

Asmita turned away, shaking her head. 'Who trains you people? You come barging into my home at this time of night, scaring the living daylights out of me because you haven't bothered to brief yourself properly, then you start chatting away like it's a social call. Your people skills are in the negative numbers.'

'Like I said, I'm sorry.'

She faced him again, back in complete control of herself. 'Ambar got married about six months after Jishnu died.' Nick had to think for a moment who she meant, then remembered Joshu hadn't always been called Joshu. To his family, he would always be Jishnu. 'Rabinder was born about a year later. He's seven months old now.' Asmita couldn't resist a smile. 'We all adore him. That's why I was so freaked out. He's the only person I think of as my nephew.'

'But Jimmy is too, whether you like it or not.'

'But I don't know him. He's never been part of my life. And I do regret that, but I have to respect my parents' wishes. And they wished to have nothing to do with him. My mother is adamant that Jimmy isn't even Jishnu's child.' This time her smile was apologetic. 'She has a very low opinion of Scarlett Higgins and her personal morality.'

'So you're saying your family really don't consider Jimmy to be one of you?'

Asmita folded her arms across her chest. 'Biologically, he might be. But he's not part of our family in any meaningful sense. He's not part of our culture, our family traditions. He doesn't belong.'

'He looks like one of you,' Nick said. 'He looks more like a Patel than a Higgins.'

'Maybe. But looks are only skin deep.' She cleared her throat. 'You say he's been abducted? How did that happen?'

'His guardian took him on holiday to America. While she was waiting for a security pat-down, a man walked away with Jimmy. It was very well orchestrated. By the time anyone realised what was happening, they were gone.'

There was a long silence. Asmita crossed to one of the tall windows that looked out towards the glittering skyscrapers of the City. 'What has this to do with me and my family?'

Not a question that would be easy to answer without treading on cultural sensibilities. 'Like I said, it was a long shot. And you kind of answered my question when you told me about Rabinder.'

She swung back to glare at him. 'I get it.' She shook her head in disbelief. 'You think we're some primitive hill tribe who need a male heir to preserve the family line. Do you have any idea how insulting that is?'

'It wasn't meant to be an insult. Quite the opposite,' Nick said. 'I was trying to be sensitive to what might seem important to someone from a different cultural perspective. I'm not an expert in these nuances, I'm a detective trying to do my job. And that job is all about trying to rescue a small boy who has been snatched from the person he loves and the life he knows. If I've trod on your toes, I'm sorry. But that's not my number one priority at the moment.' He started to head towards the door.

'Wait,' Asmita said. 'I think we both got off on the wrong foot here. I'm sorry to hear about Jimmy, but only in the way I'd be sorry about any other stranger's kid being abducted. I can't pretend to feel an emotional connection that doesn't exist.'

'I understand,' Nick said. He couldn't help thinking that if she spent so much as an afternoon in Jimmy's company she'd be singing from a different song sheet.

'But you're right to think a male heir is important to my father. Although he couldn't admit it, he was devastated by Jishnu's death. And Rabinder's birth was an obvious relief to him. It eased the pain of his loss and it gave him hope. But even before that, Jimmy wasn't the answer. You have to believe me on that.'

It sounded like the truth. And Nick had no reason to disbelieve her. He wasn't sorry that nothing had come of his idea. It simply strengthened his belief that Pete Matthews was the most credible suspect. Now all he had to do was find the bastard.

30

It's a terribly irony, but it was thanks to her celebrity that Scarlett's breast cancer diagnosis was so prompt. One of the daytime lifestyle shows asked her to front a piece about breast cancer awareness for younger women. We'd taken to meeting up for afternoon tea in one of the smart London hotels once a month, and she'd been excited to tell me about the latest assignment. 'It's like they're really starting to take me seriously,' she'd said. 'I'm not just doing beauty tips and stuff about how to pull a bloke when you're a mum. This is proper presenting.' She was proud of herself and nobody with a heart would have rained on her parade by pointing out that choosing her might have had something to do with her perfectly splendid and completely natural bosom.

Scarlett's job as presenter was to point out that, although the numbers were relatively small, young women were also susceptible to breast cancer. She'd be working with a specialist to demonstrate how to examine her breasts. They'd talk about the signs to look out for – not just a lump, but a change in texture or weight. And then they'd run through the tests that a woman would have to go through if anything anomalous was discovered. Scarlett had been swotting up on the subject, and our dainty sandwiches and scones were accompanied by a detailed description of mammograms, ultrasound and biopsy. As far as she was concerned, she had all the bases covered.

All the bases except the one that mattered, as it turned out. They had barely begun filming at some private clinic when things started to go awry. The specialist nurse who was showing Scarlett how to examine her breasts stopped abruptly in mid-sentence, a stricken look on her face. At first, Scarlett thought it was a wind-up – that the nurse was in cahoots with the crew, who were having a practical joke at her expense. It's the sort of black humour that happens all the time in factual programming, or so I've heard.

Scarlett giggled. Of course she did, it was her default response to things she didn't quite get. And she did genuinely think this was a joke. But in mid-giggle, it dawned on her that she was the only one laughing. The nurse looked shocked, the crew were simply silent, puzzled. Only the director spoke. 'What's the problem?' he said, pushing past the camera and checking out the scene.

The nurse looked around wildly, as if she didn't know the protocol for the situation. Then she got a grip and said, 'Can we clear the room, please?'

The director was slower on the uptake than the rest of the crew who obediently started to shuffle out of the door. 'We're in the middle of filming – surely whatever it is can wait till we've got these shots?'

The nurse was tougher than him. Which, according to Scarlett, wasn't hard. 'You too, please,' she said firmly, advancing on him.

'This has all been agreed,' he protested. 'We've got this room all morning.' She kept coming at him. He had no choice but to back up to the door. 'I'm going to speak to the clinic director,' he blustered on his way out. 'You're supposed to be cooperating with us.'

Through all this, Scarlett had been trying not to panic. 'Soon as I realised it wasn't a wind-up, I knew it was bad,' she told me later. 'The look on that nurse's face and the way she was hustling the rest of them out of there, it wasn't so she could get an autograph.'

As soon as the door closed behind the director, the nurse was back by Scarlett's side, totally focused. 'I didn't mean to alarm you,' she said. 'But something's not right here.' She delicately palpated the underside of Scarlett's left breast. 'The skin texture feels wrong, and when I press a bit harder, I'm feeling a series of tiny hard lumps.'

'Have I got cancer?' Never one to beat about the bush.

'I can't say. But we need to do more investigation.' The nurse patted Scarlett gently on the shoulder. 'It's turned out to be the best thing you could have done, this TV show.'

Since Scarlett was already in the right place, she was instantly subjected to a full battery of tests. Mammogram, ultrasound, MRI, needle biopsy – the works. The worst of it was that she was in such a state of shock that she agreed to have them film the whole bloody lot. They sent her home in a studio car still reeling. The first I knew about it was when Leanne rang me in a state of rage.

Two hours later, I felt like I'd been travelling in a time machine. Just like the worst days of Scarlett's notoriety, the media pack was baying at the gates. Satellite TV vans, photographers with long lenses, reporters with thrusting mics – they were all there, thronged round the entrance. Nothing travels faster than bad news in the twenty-first century.

I thought I was actually going to have to mow a couple of them down in order to get through the gate, but they backed off at the last minute. Most of them didn't have a clue who I was but they snapped me and my car and my snarl anyway, on the off-chance I might turn out to be somebody important.

I found the girls in the nursery. Scarlett was playing pirates with Jimmy, steering his pirate ship across the ocean of the carpet to the harbour of the walk-in wardrobe where he was defending his Viking castle against her forces with the full force of his lungs. Leanne was lying face down on the bed, hanging over the edge and lobbing plastic cannonballs at both of them. When I walked in, Scarlett flashed me a look of exquisite pain but managed somehow to continue her assault on the castle. As she crashed the ship into the castle walls, she pretended to run aground and capsize. 'That's me done for, Jimmy. You win.' She crabbed across the floor and scooped him up, covering him in kisses as he wriggled and giggled. 'Time for your bath now, my sweet poppet.'

'No,' he yelled in protest. 'One more time. I want to be the pirate.'

She tickled his tummy and carried him towards the bathroom. 'You can be a pirate in the bath, mister.'

He giggled and squirmed, face pink, shouting, 'Dead man's chest, dead man's chest.'

'I'll see you downstairs in a bit,' Scarlett said over her shoulder.

I followed Leanne to the kitchen. This wasn't a Prosecco night. We went straight for the brandy. 'What exactly have they said to her?' I asked.

'They won't say for sure till they've got the test results back. But from the way they took it all dead serious, it's not looking great.'

'You don't think they might have exaggerated a bit because it was being filmed?'

'Not from what Scarlett said.'

We went out on to the patio so Leanne could smoke. Scarlett found us there a little later, huddled over our drinks in the twilight. She helped herself to a cigarette and hunkered down with us.

233

'You don't smoke,' I said mildly.

'I used to.'

'Like a chimney,' Leanne added helpfully.

'I gave up before I auditioned for *Goldfish Bowl*. I knew it was going to be hard enough without craving a fag all the time.' She inhaled with all the panache of a serious smoker who had never been away. 'If I've got cancer already, I might as well have a fucking smoke.'

'It's not the recommended method for fighting it,' I said.

'I know that,' she snapped. 'Have you forgotten I'm not fucking stupid?' She closed her eyes and breathed heavily through her nose. 'I'm sorry. I'm not planning on taking it up again.' She gave me a lopsided smile. 'Not unless the diagnosis is terminal. Then I'm planning on devoting myself to everything that's bad for me.' She took another deep drag. 'I just want to smoke tonight. Don't get on my case, Steph. Not tonight.'

She leaned into me, head on my shoulder. I stroked her hair back from her face, feeling the damp of her tears on her cheek. 'What are we going to do, Scarlett?' I asked.

'I don't know about you, Steph, but I'm going to fucking fight every inch of the way.'

And fight was exactly what she did. The diagnosis was horrible – invasive lobular breast cancer. Something I'd never heard of before. I soon learned more about it than I ever wanted to know about any disease because of course there was going to be a book in Scarlett's 'battle for survival'. The presumption was that she would win, of course. But I knew that as far as the publisher was concerned, the outcome wasn't the important thing. It was the tear-jerking quality of the story. Which of course would be written as a second epistle to Jimmy.

Naturally I had to be by her side every step of the way. I like to think she'd have wanted me there anyway, but I'm not sure

I would have chosen such an intimate relationship with the process of her treatment.

My journey started at her first appointment with the specialist who would accompany her every step of the way. Simon Graham was the antithesis of the stereotypical consultant. No Savile Row suits, no expensive cologne, no golf bag in the boot. That day, he wore black jeans with a pink-and-white striped shirt, no tie. On his feet, beautifully tooled black leather cowboy boots. You could always hear Simon coming from a long way off.

He didn't look old enough to be a consultant either. He had those perennially boyish looks that leave some men apparently stranded in their twenties for decades. Men like Alan Bennett, who look like overgrown children into their sixties and seventies. Men you have to get close to before you can see the fine lines and the silvering at the temples that reveal they're not quite what they seem. Simon had thick dark hair whose style was apparently modelled on the early Beatles, when it was still reasonably short and mildly unruly. He had serious blue eyes behind the kind of steel-rimmed glasses that science teachers wear in 1950s American films. His mouth seemed always to be on the verge of a smile. When he gave in, he revealed a single dimple in his left cheek. He was a doctor made for reality TV. I wondered if he'd been chosen to supervise Scarlett's case when a TV documentary had still been on the cards.

Oh yes. George had indeed tried to talk Scarlett into having a camera crew do a fly-on-the-wall film of her treatment. Now, you might say I didn't have a moral leg to stand on, given how much money I stood to make out of telling Scarlett's story, but even I baulked at that. The difference, as I pointed out to Scarlett, was that she'd have control over what appeared in the book. Whereas she'd be entirely at the mercy of the TV company when it came to what appeared on the screen.

I was far too tactful to point out that, if she didn't make it, what went into the book would be up to me, not her. But she was smart enough to work that out for herself if she stopped to think about it.

George tried to persuade Scarlett that doing the documentary could be another way to raise funds for TOmorrow, but she wasn't having it. 'I don't want to go through this treatment wondering about what people will think of me. If I need to cry or swear or howl like a fucking werewolf, I want to be able to let rip. I'm not having some poor sod break bad news to me three different ways because the crew missed it the first time. No way. I want to be in control of what happens and how it happens. Not the director, with his mind on the ratings rather than my health.'

I really hoped they hadn't chosen Simon because he was photogenic. I hoped they'd picked him because he was the very best in his field. It was what Scarlett deserved.

That morning, he sat us down in his minimalist consulting room and introduced himself. 'The first thing I want to do today is to explain the diagnosis we've arrived at and what that means for you. None of this will be easy, and I want you to know that my team are committed to helping you make a full recovery. Anything you want from us, any time of the day or night, you can speak to one of us.' He pushed a card across the low coffee table. 'There's a dedicated mobile number there. There is always one of the team on the end of that phone. And my personal direct number is there too.'

Scarlett picked it up and tucked it in her pocket without glancing at it. 'That's what we're paying for, right? Five-star treatment?'

Simon's eyes crinkled at the corners when he smiled, as if he was squinting into the sun. 'I promise. Whatever we can do for you, we will do for you.'

He was very good. I certainly felt reassured. But I wasn't the one in the hard place.

'Fine,' Scarlett said. 'Taken as read. So what actually is wrong with me?'

'I won't beat about the bush, Scarlett. Our tests indicate that you've got invasive lobular breast cancer.'

'And what's that when it's at home?' Scarlett crossed her legs and folded her hands over the upper knee. It was as if she was folding herself tightly together, physically preventing herself from coming apart.

'You've got glands in your breasts that produce milk.' He smiled. 'You probably remember after you had your son, when your breasts were full of milk they felt quite lumpy?'

She nodded. 'I used to think they felt like bags of pasta salad.'

'That's actually a very good way to put it,' Simon said, managing to stay on the right side of patronising. 'This cancer forms in those glands and it makes the structure of the breast swell up in patches. It can make the skin texture seem a bit peculiar as well. What you said about pasta? Most breast cancer takes the form of lump. It's like a meatball in among the pasta, you can feel it quite easily. But this kind of cancer, it's like a spoonful of bolognaise sauce stirred in. The lumps are small, they're hard to pin down. Scarlett, if you hadn't come in here to do the breast exam feature, you might not have discovered there was a problem until it had grown much more serious.' He leaned forward earnestly, elbows on knees, hands clasped. 'This is an unusual cancer, particularly in someone as young as you. It only accounts for about five per cent of all breast cancers. I've only seen it a few times, and in all of those cases, it was much more advanced. It's my opinion that because we've made this diagnosis early, you have an excellent chance of a full recovery.'

'What does that mean? "An excellent chance of a full recovery"?' She sounded belligerent but I knew it was because she was afraid. I hoped he was experienced enough to understand that too.

'OK. I'll lay out the numbers for you. Five years after diagnosis, eighty-five per cent of women with this form of cancer are still alive.' He paused, waiting for her response.

Scarlett didn't look particularly delighted by the news. 'That means fifteen per cent of them are dead,' she said.

'True. But you've got what's classified as a Stage Two cancer. That puts you somewhere in the middle of the spectrum when we're talking about seriousness.'

'What are you going to do to me?'

Simon reached across the table and covered her clasped hands with his. 'We're going to work out a course of treatment that will give you the best possible chance to see your son grow up.'

That was when we both cried, me and Scarlett.

31

The kid was driving him crazy. Patience wasn't Pete Matthews' strong suit and he'd run out of road with the kid within a very short time of picking him up. In the car, he'd been a pain in the ass. Singing tunelessly along with Pete's favourite road music. Whining that he needed to go to the bathroom. Complaining he was hungry. Crying because he was thirsty. How many demands could one kid have?

He'd never been happier to get back to the row house in Corktown. He'd shut the kid in the attic bedroom with a sandwich and a bottle of water and turned the TV on to keep him amused. With luck, he'd shut the fuck up and go to sleep. Pete hated the way the kid looked at him; that mixture of adoration and fear made him feel uncomfortable.

Pete was a man who was accustomed to getting his own way. In his working life, he'd developed all sorts of subtle mechanisms to make sure the final sound mix ended up the way he thought it should. Mostly, the artists he worked with believed all the best ideas were theirs, but he knew that a significant element of the production that listeners enjoyed had come from his input, his individual mix of skill, experience and imagination. Here in Detroit, he worked a lot with experienced session men who'd been around since before the artists they were working with had been born. Those musicians knew they were in the hands of a true pro and they responded to Pete with enthusiasm. They never gave him any trouble.

It was the young bloods who thought they knew best, and sometimes it took a while for Pete to drag them round to his way of thinking. If they didn't agree with him, he went ahead and did it his way and pretended it was what they'd asked for. Most of them were too ignorant of the finer points of production to know any better. It simply took time and persistence.

He grabbed a beer from the fridge and fixed himself a sandwich. He loved American food. Wafer-thin ham, egg salad and Cheez Whiz on rye toast. Beautiful. Before he sat down at the table to eat, he stepped into the hallway and listened. He could hear the distant chatter of the TV, but that was all. The kid wasn't crying, which was what counted. The last thing he wanted was the neighbours calling the cops to complain about a screaming child.

He went back to his beer and sandwich and contemplated his options. He had another week's work here in Detroit, then he was due to fly back to the UK. He had unfinished business with Stephanie and he wanted it sorted out sooner rather than later.

Pete had been at a loss for some time over Stephanie. He couldn't work out why she hadn't come back to him. She belonged with him. He was devoted to her. Nobody could love her the way he did. He'd offered her everything a woman could want and still she denied herself. But now the kid was in the picture, he was sure she'd see things differently. You needed two people to take proper care of a kid. She must realise that now.

OK, he'd resented Jimmy when he'd first been born, but that was because Stephanie was spending so much time and energy on that slapper Scarlett and her bastard. Time she should have been devoting to him and their relationship. All his mates agreed. Her place was in her own home, not out in that bloody plastic palace in the middle of Essex, helping out with a kid whose own father was too busy with his parasite DJ career to be bothered taking responsibility. Early on, he'd driven out there to take a look at it. Just out of curiosity. It wasn't hard to find, and it was every bit as ugly as he'd expected. He couldn't understand how a woman with as much taste as Stephanie could abide being there.

But things were different now. OK, it wouldn't be the same as having his own son. That would come later, once they were settled down as a ready-made family. But he could bring Jimmy up properly. Show him what it was to be a man. The kid had been over-indulged from birth. He'd been cuddled and soothed instead of disciplined. And what was the result? He was a spoilt cry-baby. But Pete would soon change that. Teach him to be a little man. Strong and resilient. Stephanie would be proud when she saw how he could take responsibility for giving a boy manly guidance. He could see them in years to come, the boy knowing his place and showing he knew the way to behave.

He'd taken the first step by building a connection with Jimmy that was based on discipline and doing as he was told. Back when the Scarlett Harlot had still been alive, Pete had volunteered at the kid's nursery school. They'd been delighted by this charming man who turned up once a week with various musicians dedicated to working with the children. The kids made noise on a variety of instruments, which Pete painstakingly recorded then engineered into something approximating music. He posted the end results on YouTube, where adoring parents could indulge in the fantasy that little Orlando and Keira were fast-tracking towards the Young Musician of the Year.

And the teacher's pet was little Jimmy Higgins. Actually, he did seem to have a bit more of an idea than most of the kids. Probably because he'd been exposed to loud rhythmic music from an early age, thanks to his useless waster father. Pete fed that green shoot and made Jimmy push himself to try harder. It had been gratifying to watch the kid learn about carrot and stick. Maybe, once he'd got Stephanie sorted out, he could make something of the kid as a musician.

His fantasy was shattered by a faint, thin wail from above. Pete slapped his palm hard on the table then took off up the stairs. His hand was itching to deliver a hard slap. The kid had to learn, after all.

32

First there was the surgery. What Simon called 'a wide local excision', it was designed to leave Scarlett with as much breast tissue as possible. Because of the early diagnosis, he was confident they could cut away the cancerous tissue and clean margins around it, leaving the disease without a foothold in her body. As well as the cancer, they took the lymph node nearest that part of the breast. 'We call this a sentinel node biopsy because it's like an outpost for your immune system. If it's clear, the chances are the rest of your body's clear,' he explained.

Scarlett coped well with the surgery. Her high level of physical fitness helped. Even after Jimmy's birth, she'd continued to swim every day. She'd bought a cross trainer too, and ran five kilometres three or four times a week. Simon said apart from the cancer she was in great shape and encouraged her to get back on her regime as soon as possible.

But that wasn't enough to keep the pain and fear at bay. She wasn't on morphine for long, and I could see she was suffering. 'You don't have to put up with the pain,' I said. 'They'll give you something to ease it. There's no advantage in hurting.'

She grimaced. 'The painkillers send me sky high. I don't like drugs. Don't like the way they make me feel. Never have. It's bearable, Steph, trust me. Because I know I'm getting better, I can stand it. It won't last long.' She puffed out a breath. 'And Simon says the surgery was successful. Now I just have to go through the chemo and watch my hair fall out.'

Which it did, in handfuls. After the first dose of chemo, a grim day when Scarlett endured an intravenous infusion of toxic drugs and felt increasingly lousy as the hours passed, her hair started to thin. By the time she'd undergone three sessions, there were clumps missing. It looked like she'd been in a particularly aggressive catfight.

Back at the hacienda that evening, she decided to take the bold step of shaving her head. But first she had to find a hat. Nothing in her wardrobe fitted the bill, so she dispatched Leanne down the A13 to the late-night shopping possibilities of Lakeside shopping centre.

By the time Leanne returned with bulging carrier bags, we had trimmed Scarlett's hair to stubble. She held the heavy swatch in her hand, her eyes glistening with tears. 'What do you think, Steph? Should I keep it? Tie it up in a ribbon to remind myself what I've lost?'

'It's up to you. But it'll grow back, you know. With some people, their hair actually comes back thicker than before.'

She made a face. 'You're right.' She crossed to the kitchen bin but just before she dumped the hair inside, she stopped herself. 'What am I thinking?' she said. 'You need a picture of this. There's a piece in this for somebody's women's page.' Scarlett shook her head in disbelief. 'Bloody hell, Steph, we're losing our touch. Get the camera out.'

And so I did what I was told. I shot her stubbled head from every side, I shot her looking regretfully at the severed tail of hair in her hands, I shot her gleaming head after the electric razor had stripped it bare and finally I shot her trying on the array of hats Leanne had brought back.

'I like this best,' Scarlett announced, turning her head this way and that in front of her dressing-room mirror. It was a sage-green cloche with an upturned brim made from a light fleece. It suited her, especially when she smiled.

'Good pick,' Leanne said. 'They do it in three or four different fabrics and about ten colours. I can go back tomorrow and do a total commando raid. You'll have hats for all weather and all your different outfits.'

Scarlett caught my eye. 'It'll be a whole new me,' she said, not quite managing to hide her sadness. 'I'll be like the queen, never seen out of the house without a hat.'

'You'll be a style icon,' I said, trying to reassure her.

'Maybe. But right now, this style icon needs to go to bed.' She pulled the hat off, yawning. 'Poor Jimmy's going to freak out in the morning when he sees me.'

But he didn't. He barely registered the change. I was taken aback. Like Scarlett, I'd expected him to be scared or upset or, at the very least, bewildered. I asked Simon about it when I saw him at the next chemo appointment. 'You'd be surprised,' he said. 'Kids respond to the person, not the appearance. I've seen cases where the parents were terrified of letting the child see the patient because they thought it would be a nightmarish experience. But that's not how it works. Even when the cancer or the treatment causes quite serious disfigurement, the patient's children seem not to be frightened or revolted. It's an interesting demonstration of their ability to understand that what makes us who we are is what's on the inside, not the outside.' He gave a sad little smile. 'One of the traits I wish we could hang on to into adulthood.'

Scarlett had clearly taken Simon's point on board. We were driving back to Essex when she brought the conversation up again. 'I'm glad Jimmy isn't scared of my new look,' she said.

'He knows who you are. And he knows he loves you.'

'He's always known who I am. Not like the punters who've been fooled by Leanne all these years.'

'People see what they expect to see,' I said. 'It's why eye-witness evidence is notoriously unreliable in court. Our eyes see a glimpse of something and our brain fills in the rest of the picture based on what we remember and what we know. Punters in a club or at a fashion show or backstage at a gig expect to see Scarlett, so that's what their brain tells them. You might have run into trouble if Joshu had started running off at the mouth and people started looking for incongruities. Because then they would have found them. But luckily that never came up.'

'You wouldn't need Joshu mouthing off now, though. Look at me. I've put weight on, my face looks like the full moon, and I've got no hair. I can't have Leanne walking around look-ing like the old me, can I?'

I suppose I hadn't really considered the question till Scarlett brought it up. 'You mean it's time for her to go back to being a brunette?'

Scarlett sighed. 'For starters. Yeah. She needs a different haircut too. Short, something that makes the shape of her face look different. More than that, though. I think it might be time for her to bugger off to Spain.'

I was shocked by her casual delivery. Leanne had lived with her for a couple of years by that point. She'd picked up the pieces when Scarlett's marriage collapsed. She'd played a cru-cial role in bringing up Jimmy. She'd supported her through the cancer diagnosis, not to mention the exhaustion and depression that came with the chemo. And now Scarlett was talking about sending her cousin into exile with as much emo-tion as she'd shown when she'd changed window cleaners the year before.

'You don't think you're going to need her help getting through the rest of the treatment? She's been a real rock.'

Scarlett reached into her bag and pulled out her water bottle. She took a long drink, then smacked her lips in satisfaction. 'It's not been as bad as I thought it was going to be,' she said. 'Yeah, I feel like shit after I've had a session, but I can cope with it. I've got Marina looking after the cooking and taking care of Jimmy and running the cleaners.' She reached over and patted my thigh. 'And you've been fantastic. I couldn't have got through this without you, Steph. But the last thing I need at the moment is for somebody to see Leanne out and about in Tesco looking like a healthy version of me. All it takes is one happy snapper to post a pic on Twitter or a few seconds of video on YouTube and suddenly the red-tops'll be asking all the wrong questions.' She pulled her hat off and scratched her head. 'I'm not up to handling that,' she said. 'No way.'

She had a point. And it wasn't as if Leanne had any grounds for complaint. She'd done what was asked of her, no question about it. Even when she'd had a drink, even in the small hours when the freelances were pretending to be her friend, even in the ladies' rooms in the VIP areas when the Colombian marching powder was on offer, she'd kept her mouth shut and never so much as hinted that there was a dark secret lurking in the closet.

But on the other side of the equation, she'd lived a life she could only have dreamed of when she was scraping along the bottom on a scummy Dublin satellite housing estate. She'd been housed and fed, she had money in her pocket for clothes and make-up and spa treatments. She'd been to every cool party and hip club that she fancied and, unlike most of the bimbos on the circuit, she hadn't had to shag anyone to earn that access. The upside of the childcare she'd provided had been the chance to spend time with Jimmy, a kid who was generally more rewarding to be with than most toddlers.

And it wasn't as if Scarlett was planning to cast her adrift without a bean. Leanne had already visited the villa in the

Spanish hills that Scarlett had bought for her. Scarlett had organised the conversion of the pool house into a nail bar where she could do manicures, pedicures and reflexology. Leanne would walk into a home of her own with a ready-made business literally at her fingertips. Really, she could have no grounds for complaint.

And yet. And yet . . . I couldn't help thinking it wasn't going to be smooth sailing. But Scarlett clearly shared none of my misgivings.

'Yeah,' she said. 'I think I'll give it a couple of weeks then tell her it's time to start making plans.'

A lot can happen in a couple of weeks. By the time Scarlett's notional deadline rolled around, getting rid of Leanne was the last thing on her mind.

33

Stephanie paused to drink from her water bottle. Vivian glanced at her watch. She'd missed lunch and it looked like dinner was going the same way. 'You weren't lying when you said it was a long story.'

'I'm sorry. But you did say you wanted to know everything that might have a bearing on Jimmy's disappearance.'

'It certainly sounds like he's had an exceptional run of experiences.' *And will spend most of his adult life in therapy.* 'I think we need to—' Her attempt to suggest a break for food was sabotaged by a knock at the door. Vivian nodded to Lia Lopez, who opened up to reveal Abbott looking pissed off.

'Sorry to interrupt,' he said. 'But I need to speak with Agent McKuras.'

Vivian was on her feet before he'd finished talking. She took his arm and steered him back into the corridor. 'Sorry, but I need to eat,' she said, leading the way down the hallway towards the concourse. 'I can't concentrate for five more minutes unless I get some food in me.'

'OK,' Abbott said, trailing in her wake. He was a married man; he knew better than to argue when a woman displayed all the signs of low blood sugar. Vivian strode through the crowds of passengers, making straight for the Burger King on the food court. Once she had two cheeseburgers and a large coffee in front of her, he decided it was safe to speak.

'We've tracked the boy and his kidnapper from the security area. They took the first available exit and emerged on to the landside concourse. They didn't go near baggage reclaim. Instead they made straight for the parking garage across the way from the arrivals hall. Interestingly, the guy didn't go to the payment machines. He didn't seem to have a parking ticket to validate. He just walked straight in with the kid and they got into an elevator. And that's where it gets interesting. They don't show up on any of the footage of the elevator exits.'

Vivian frowned but couldn't say anything through a mouthful of food.

'Ask me how that could possibly be. I know you're dying of curiosity,' Abbott said.

Vivian swallowed and humoured him. 'How could that possibly be?' He was doing the scut work on the case, after all. He deserved a little slack.

'At twelve fifty-seven, somebody sprayed black paint over the lens of the camera that covers the elevators on the thirteenth level. There weren't many vehicles up there, so there wasn't anyone around to witness what happened. Or if there was, they didn't give a shit about somebody knocking out a CCTV camera.'

'What images are there before twelve fifty-seven?'

'Not much. There's no sign of anyone approaching, which means they likely came up on the camera from behind and sprayed it kind of up and under. The control room noticed the camera was out of action about forty minutes later and reported it for routine maintenance. It was only when I started asking questions that they checked it out and discovered it hadn't simply malfunctioned – it had been vandalised.'

'To stop us seeing them emerging from the elevator,' Vivian said. 'Judging by the look on your face, we're not about to cut to the good news.'

'There is no good news. Not at this point. We don't know what happened after they left the elevator. The presumption would be that they got into a vehicle. But which vehicle? We have no idea when they left the parking garage. They could have sat there for half-hour in the back of a panel van, for crying out loud. We have no way of knowing.'

'What about the exit footage? Whatever vehicle they were in, they had to leave at some point.'

'It's a waste of time, Vivian. We don't know what the guy looks like. It's starting to look like he has an accomplice but there's no telling whether that's a male or a female. We are totally pissing into the wind.'

Vivian suddenly lost her appetite. With every lead that frittered away to nothing, the chances of recovering Jimmy alive grew smaller. It had been over five hours since he'd disappeared. The shrinking window of opportunity for his recovery left a bitter taste in her mouth that no amount of fast food could take away. She pushed her second burger away, then, on second thoughts, she picked it up. If she'd been starving, Stephanie would be too. 'Thanks, Don. I appreciate you chasing this.' She stood up. 'I need to get back to the witness.'

'Sure. The control room's got a whole bunch of staff tracking back through the concourse cameras to try and get a fix on where he came from. I'll let you know as soon as I have anything. None of the no-shows matched our guy, by the way. An elderly Hassidic Jew, a middle-aged black woman and a female student from Northwestern. So your witness was on the money with her suggestion.' He followed her back down the concourse. As they grew close to the interview room, he put a hand on her arm. 'Don't take this too personally, Vivian.'

'If you'd sat listening to that woman for as long as I have, you'd be taking it personally too, Don. Sometimes that's the only acceptable route to go down.' She shook off his hand. 'I know you're working your ass off on this,' she added, softening her tone not because she was bothered about hurting his feelings but because she was happy to do whatever it took not to jeopardise Jimmy's chances. 'And I totally trust you not to leave a CCTV pixel unturned.' She delivered her best smile but her head was already back with Stephanie, ready for the next instalment.

34

After our conversation about Leanne, I didn't see Scarlett for the best part of a week. I was interviewing a TV presenter for her new motivational guide to rebuilding your life after divorce. Given how very publicly her marriage had collapsed, there was plenty of scope for the restoration project. I didn't much like the woman, mostly because she's one of those who never accepts any share of responsibility for what's gone wrong in her life. A bit like blokes who hit their wives then complain the women provoked them by daring to be more verbally agile. Still, she had a smart mouth and she was good at coming up with catchy lines for chapter headings.

Next time I saw Scarlett, she seemed much more cheerful. It turned out that in my absence, Simon had sat with her during her last bout of chemo and his conversation had lifted her to a more positive frame of mind. 'He says the right things,' she said. 'I don't know how he manages it, but he's got an instinct for putting his finger on what's scaring me or what's bothering me. And then he comes up with some story or statistic or whatever that just makes me feel better.'

I was relieved that she'd had someone there to keep her spirits up. I felt bad about missing a treatment, but Scarlett was insistent that I couldn't turn my back on my career for her sake. 'I'm glad you had good company,' I said.

'It turned out a real bonus,' she said. 'You'll never guess who turned up at the clinic.' Her lip curled in disgust. I could think of only one person who provoked that response in her.

'Not Joshu?'

She nodded. 'Got it in one. Bloody Joshu.'

My heart sank. Joshu was the ultimate bad penny. Whenever he turned up, trouble followed. He could still provoke Scarlett into a fight faster than I could credit. All her self-control went up in flames when he started on one of his riffs about her unfairness, her lousy parenting and her selfishness in respect of contact. It didn't help that his dependency on drugs seemed to have grown incrementally since they'd split up. That was one more piece of blame he would lay at her door. Every imperfection in his life could be laid at Scarlett's door. I felt sick at the thought of him showing up during her treatment. 'How did he know where you were? And when you were having treatment?'

She shrugged. 'It's not exactly a state secret. The clinic's been named in the papers. And you know how good Joshu is at wheedling shit out of women. He'll have chatted up some nurse or secretary and found out when I was due in.'

'How bad was he?'

She looked more pleased with herself than I expected. 'He burst into the room and started going on about how I needed to make a will signing Jimmy over to him since I was going to pop my clogs any minute.'

'What a complete and utter bastard he is. How dare he come storming in like that when you're fighting for your life? Doesn't he understand what's at stake for you?' I was outraged, but Scarlett wasn't joining in.

'The thing is, he was totally off his face. He was flapping his hands like a chicken. It should have been distressing but it wasn't. It was funny. I was holding in my laughter, because I knew that would only make him wilder. But before I knew it, Simon was on his feet and hustling Joshu out the door. Literally. He had him by the hoodie, frogmarching him off the premises.' She giggled. 'My hero.'

'Bloody hell,' I said. 'We should have had Simon on the team when Joshu kept trying to storm the gates after you dumped him.'

'Don't I know it. He was like a dog with its hackles up. Totally outraged that a gobshite like Joshu should disrupt his precious clinic and his patients.'

'He has a point,' I reminded her. 'Nobody visits that clinic for fun. They've got more on their mind than the self-indulgent ranting of a spoilt brat like Joshu.'

'Well, Simon sorted him out good style and in no time flat.'

'This is a new angle, though. "I should have Jimmy because you're dying."'

Scarlett grew serious. 'It's a horrible angle. When you strip away all Joshu's carry on, it's not a pretty thought. What if Simon's wrong and I don't make it? Joshu is Jimmy's dad, after all. It's not like he's estranged from the boy. They do have a relationship. They love each other, I've never denied that or tried to put a stop to it. But Joshu's an irresponsible twat who can't look after himself, never mind take care of a kid as well. Simon says not to worry, it'll never happen. And that's what I'm trying to hang on to.' She gave me one of the old Scarlett's smiles, that simple uncomplicated radiance that used to light up her face regularly before cancer complicated it.

'But now that Joshu's planted the seed, the idea's there and it won't go away.' I was talking to myself mostly, but Scarlett picked up on what I'd said.

'It won't happen,' she said. 'You're Jimmy's godmother and, if it comes to it, you're the one who should take care of him.

He's as close to you as he is to his dad and you'd take proper care of him.'

I was so flabbergasted I couldn't think of a thing to say. The idea of taking Jimmy on if anything happened to Scarlett had never crossed my mind. I suppose I'd imagined that Joshu's parents would step up to the plate when they were confronted with the reality of their own flesh and blood deprived of a parent. Or that Leanne would assume responsibility for a boy who was, after all, her cousin. It hadn't occurred to me that Scarlett would expect me to become Jimmy's surrogate mother if she died.

'You would, you know. You'd be better than you think,' she said firmly.

'Me? But I've got no experience, no maternal instincts. Christ, Scarlett, Joshu would be a better option.'

She laughed. 'Your face is a picture. You look like you've caught your tit in a mangle. It's OK, Steph. I'm not going to die on you. Simon says I'll make it, and he should know.'

That was pretty cold comfort. There was a reason I was childless, and it wasn't merely my failure to sustain a long-term relationship. I was childless from choice. I'd never wanted to be a mum, never felt the ticking of the biological clock, never considered my life unfulfilled in the absence of a child. Yes, I was good with Jimmy. But that didn't mean I wanted to be his mum.

Nevertheless, I didn't want Joshu to be Jimmy's fallback position if anything happened to Scarlett. 'He'd be better off with Leanne,' I protested. 'She's great with him. And she's family.'

Scarlett shook her head. 'She'll be off to Spain soon. I'm not having my lad brought up among a load of foreigners, not when he can stop here, where he belongs.'

'She can always come back from Spain if need be. She loves him, Scarlett.'

'It's not just about love,' she said, implacable as granite. 'It's about ambition. And aspiration. And desire. I dragged myself up this far in spite of a lousy start with a crap family who wanted to drag me down into the dirt beside them. And although Leanne's a decent enough lass, that's still her mind-set. She's always going to settle for what's easy, not push for the highest ground. She's a fighter all right. But she doesn't understand what goals are worth fighting for. What I want for Jimmy, what I dream of for my son, is for him to be amazing. For him to do amazing things. And he'll never do that if Leanne's in charge of his life. He'll learn to settle. To do the least he can get away with. But you? You're a different kettle of fish, Steph. Plus you'll never let him forget what I achieved. How far I came.'

Her words made me uneasy and uncomfortable. I knew Joshu would be outraged at the very thought. Leanne would be insulted and hurt. And God alone knew what Jimmy would make of it, should it ever come to pass.

But Simon had said it wouldn't. Simon had said I was safe from Scarlett's mad machinations. Unfortunately, Simon wasn't a clairvoyant. And by the end of the week, Scarlett's fallback plan had come one degree closer.

35

Joshu was dead. I heard it on the radio. It was a shocking way to start the day. I'd known about the drugs from the first time I met him, but it never occurred to me that they would kill him. Yet here it was on the morning news. DJ Joshu, star of the London club scene, ex-husband of TV star Scarlett Higgins, dead of a suspected overdose.

And yes, to be frank, I did feel put out to get that particular piece of news at the same time as the rest of the world. Scarlett called me most days. She called about all sorts of trivial stuff, but now something major had happened and I was hearing it on an early morning news bulletin. I know I should have been thinking about Scarlett first and foremost, but I held on to my chagrin for a few minutes before I put my own ego to one side and considered what effect this news would have had on my friend.

The life he'd chosen had changed the man that Scarlett had initially fallen for. Too many drugs, too much adulation, too many late nights and too much indulgence stripped away his better qualities. He'd grown increasingly petulant, self-righteous and abrasive. Lately, he'd become somebody I would have called the cops on if he'd shown up at my front door. But none of that erased the history between them. Scarlett had truly loved him for a long time. He was the father of her child and she'd never failed to acknowledge his right to a role in Jimmy's life. This news would have been crushing. The more I thought about it, the more I realised how badly she must have taken it for her pain to have overridden her instinct to get on the phone and share.

So I got on the road and headed north. As soon as I got on the main road, I called Scarlett's mobile. It was Leanne who answered. 'Hiya, Steph. You heard the news?'

'On the radio,' I said. 'How is she?'

'In bits,' Leanne said. 'She's in the shower right now.'

'When did you hear?'

'The cops came round a couple of hours ago and broke the news. I thought it was pretty good of them. I mean, technically she's not his next of kin any more. But obviously, they knew who he was.'

'Somebody with an eye for public relations didn't want the *Daily Mail* splashing tomorrow with "HEARTLESS COPS LET ME FIND OUT ABOUT JOSHU'S DEATH ON MORNING TV".' Cynical, I know, but probably close to the truth.

'Whatever. The main thing is they didn't let her find out through rumours and gossip.'

'How did she take it?'

'She looked like she'd been slapped. They didn't stick around long. I made her a cup of tea and got her to drink a brandy. She didn't say much. Didn't cry either. My guess is she's still in shock. It was about time for Jimmy to get up, so I told her to go and get in the shower, I'd see to him. He's eating his cereal in front of the telly and she still hasn't come out of the shower. I'm glad you rang, Steph. I was going to call you. You're better at dealing with her when she's in a state than I am.'

'I'm on my way now. Take care of her, Leanne. Get Marina

259

to take Jimmy out for the day. And tell her to make sure the press don't follow them. The last thing we need is "TRAGIC JOSHU'S SON PLAYS UNAWARE" in the red-tops. And talk to George, too.' I had no doubt there would be deals to be done when the initial shock wore off. I didn't relish writing the copy, but I already knew Scarlett would be in an 'only Steph will do' mood.

There was a familiar paparazzi camp outside the gates of the hacienda, reporters and photographers surrounding me and baying like crazy people. I refused to meet their eyes and concentrated on remaining stony-faced till I was inside. To my surprise, I wasn't the only new arrival. When I walked into the kitchen, Dr Simon Graham was nursing a cup of coffee at the breakfast bar. He looked more rumpled than usual, his hair tousled and a shadow of stubble on cheeks and chin. His shirt didn't look like this morning's model. I nursed a momentary bad thought before he greeted me with, 'I came as soon as the police were done with me.'

'The police? What were the police doing with you?' I headed for the coffee machine. I'd already been up for more than two hours without a caffeine fix and I needed to put that right before I had to deal with Scarlett.

He sighed. 'It looks like the drugs Joshu overdosed on were stolen from my clinic.'

That stopped me in my tracks. 'From your clinic? How did that happen?'

'He turned up last week when Scarlett was having her chemo. I had to throw him out.'

'I heard. Well done.' I slotted a capsule into the machine and set a cup in place.

'I was worried he might do it again. And I'll be honest. I was concerned that one of the clinic staff had fed him the details of her treatment. So I rearranged her remaining appointments but I didn't change them in the clinic diary.'

I took my coffee. 'You've dealt with celebs before, haven't you?' I said, weary at the thought of the hoops decent people like Simon had to go through to protect their patients.

'And the people who pursue them,' he said, looking depressed at the memory. 'Anyway, as I'd feared, Joshu turned up yesterday at the time Scarlett was originally supposed to attend the clinic. He barged into a treatment room where I was sitting with a patient. He was very irate that Scarlett wasn't there. He didn't make a fuss about leaving the room, but he wouldn't leave the clinic. He stormed into my office and wouldn't budge.' Simon sighed and ran a hand through his tousled hair. 'I know I did a stupid thing. I left him in my office while I went to get security. I should have called them from my office. But I didn't want to wind him up any more. I thought calling security might have sent him over the edge. There was a real sense of desperation and violence coming from him.'

'He could be very unnerving,' I said, remembering our first encounter and the replica gun.

'Unnerving, yes.' Simon seized on the word like it was the Christmas present he'd always wanted. 'So I left him alone while I fetched security.'

'Did he put up much of a fight?'

Simon frowned, perplexed. 'No. That was the funny thing. As soon as the two security guards appeared, he went off with them like a lamb. I thought at the time he must be one of those types who are all sound and no substance.' He lowered his eyes and stared into his coffee. 'Turned out I was wrong. The reason Joshu wasn't making a fuss was because he'd broken into my briefcase and pocketed all the morphine I carry for emergencies.'

I suspected 'emergencies' was a term that covered a multitude of contingencies, including helping people on their way whose quality of life had diminished to vanishing point. 'Ah,'

I said. 'I can see why he'd go quietly. When did you realise what he'd done?'

'When the police got me out of bed at half past three this morning. They'd been called out by the manager of the club where he died, and they found an empty box with my name on it.'

'That must have been a nasty moment for you.' I drained my coffee and slotted another capsule in the machine. The first one had hit the spot but reminded me that I was still in caffeine deficit.

He pulled a face. 'I could see they didn't believe me at first when I said I had no idea how Joshu got the drugs. But when we looked at my briefcase, it was obvious the locks had been forced. I just hadn't noticed earlier. I'm always so bloody tired at the end of the day, it's not something I would check.' He sighed. 'I think I convinced them I was the victim, not the drug dealer.'

'Not a great way to start the day, though.' I sipped the second coffee, appreciating the flavour more this time.

'No. But much worse for Scarlett.'

'Where is she, by the way?'

'Leanne said she was swimming.' He looked painfully confused at the idea. It didn't surprise me. I could see the attraction of doing something physical to stave off the moment when she had to face the fact that Joshu was dead and she had no formal role in what happened next. 'She's supposed to have chemo today. I thought I could drive her in. But maybe we should postpone it.'

'No, take her with you. The more distraction she has, the better.'

As I spoke, Scarlett walked in, bringing a whiff of chlorine with her. There was a hollow emptiness to her eyes that I'd never seen before. She threw her arms round me and clung on like Jimmy does now when he hasn't seen me all day. I could feel her breath shuddering in her chest. 'Steph,' she choked out. 'He's gone. My beautiful boy. He's gone.'

I patted her back and held her close. I knew there was nothing to be said. I just had to wait it out. At last, she drew away from our embrace with a juddering sigh. 'Leanne said you were here, Simon,' she said. 'I wasn't expecting you.'

He stood up and moved to her, taking both her hands in his. 'I'm so sorry, Scarlett. This has been a terrible shock for you.'

She gave a bitter half-laugh. 'I always thought he'd come to a bad end. But not like this. I thought it would be his mouth got him into trouble, dissing some gun-toting gangsta. Or his dick. Shagging the wrong tart. I never thought it would be the drugs.' She let go Simon's hands and slumped into a chair. 'You come to make sure I turn up for my chemo, Simon? You worried I'll go into a decline and give up over Joshu?'

He smiled. 'I know you better than that, Scarlett. I know you're not a quitter. And yes, I will drive you in for your chemo appointment as soon as you're ready. But I have something to tell you and I didn't want you to hear it secondhand.'

She raised her eyebrows. 'I don't think I'm up for any more bad news today, Simon.'

But he told her anyway. Her face seemed to slacken as his words sank in. When he'd finished, there was a terrible cold silence before she finally spoke. 'The stupid little fucker,' she said, shaking her head. 'He always thought he knew best.' I put a hand on her shoulder and she reached up to grab it tight. 'What the fuck am I going to tell Jimmy?' She looked up at me, a naked plea in her eyes.

'I'll stay with you,' I said. 'We'll tell him together.'

'Would you? Ah, Steph, where would I be without you?' She blinked a tear away and pushed herself to her feet, looking weary beyond words. 'Come on then, Simon. We'd better get a move on.'

'Do you want me to come?' I said.

She puffed out her cheeks and considered. 'Could you stay here and hold the fort? George is going to want to talk to you. Because we're going to have to respond to this and I don't want to be talking to strangers. Then when I get back, we can tell Jimmy.'

'You're not going to feel like telling Jimmy after you've had a round of chemo,' I said. Sensibly, I thought.

'I know that,' she lashed back at me, the stress taking over the driving seat momentarily. She pressed her eyes closed and shook her head. 'I'm sorry, Steph. Yeah, I am going to feel like shit. But I can't put it off till I'm feeling up to it. He's got to be told. Apart from anything else, he's a sensitive little lad. He's going to notice we're all walking round like a wet Wednesday in Wetherby. He needs to know there's a good reason for it.'

And I believed she was capable of it. She'd come this far on guts and gumption. There was no reason why they should fail her now. Except that none of the old certainties seemed to be holding fast.

36

I spoke to Maggie as soon as Scarlett and Simon left in his gleaming Audi TT convertible. They took most of the paparazzi with them, which made life easier for everyone else. Maggie knew how I felt about Joshu, so she didn't bother with condolences. *'Darling,'* she said, 'I've already *spoken* to Georgie. The *Mail* wants seven hundred and fifty *exclusive* words by half past four, *Yes!* needs five hundred words by *Thursday*. I'm still *negotiating* the *funeral* exclusives, but this will be a *lovely* little earner for us. And of course it keeps the *interest* lively for the *cancer* book.' Maggie only bothered with tact and diplomacy when there were strangers around. With me, she could be as blunt as she liked.

These days, I knew Scarlett well enough to knock out a *Daily Mail* feature on her grief without actually having to speak to her. I could tug at the heart-strings without tipping over into saccharine sweetness, I could convey the tragedy of a love that had died and the sorrow that there could be no attempt at reconciliation now. I was almost moved myself by the words I put in Scarlett's mouth.

I'd finished the first draft and given it to Leanne to look over when my mobile rang. I didn't recognise the number but I answered it anyway. 'Hello?'

'Is that Stephanie Harker?'

I didn't recognise the voice but I liked the sound of it. Northern, deep, warm. 'Yes. Who is this?'

'Detective Sergeant Nick Nicolaides of the Met Police. I'd like to talk to you about the death of Jishnu Patel.'

I hadn't heard Joshu's real name since the wedding and it gave me a jolt. 'Joshu? Me? Why me? I don't know anything about it.'

'George Lyall gave me your name,' he said. Bloody Gorgeous George. What was he playing at? 'I'm outside Ms Higgins' house now,' he continued. 'Your intercom doesn't appear to be working.'

'It's working fine. They turn it off when the media won't leave them alone,' I said sharply. 'On days like this.'

'Can you let me in? Since I'm here? And I want to talk to you?'

I didn't want to talk to him but I didn't think I had a lot of choice. I ended the call and opened the gate.

'Who's that?' Leanne looked up from the screen.

'A copper. He wants to talk to me about Joshu.'

She pulled a surprised face. 'Why you?'

'We'll soon find out. Is that piece OK?'

'It's great. You'll have them sobbing in the streets of Beeston,' she said cynically. 'I'll make myself scarce, then.' She grabbed her cigarettes and practically ran out of the room. Leanne had never learned to be comfortable around authority. I think she was always waiting for the other shoe to drop.

I opened the back door as a lanky man in black jeans and a thigh-length leather jacket was unfolding himself from the driver's seat of a weary-looking Vauxhall. His dark hair was shaggy, framing a lean and bony face with deep-set eyes and a nose like a narrow blade. I met his eyes and I felt a spark of danger. I know it's a cliché, but I've always thought of Nick Nicolaides as a handsome pirate. The Johnny Depp kind of pirate, not the ones who kidnap innocent holiday sailors in the Indian Ocean. To be honest, at that moment, I'd have answered pretty much anything he asked me.

I brought him into the kitchen and sat him down at the breakfast bar. I offered him coffee; he asked for espresso then sat in silence while I prepared it. I sometimes think espresso has become the twenty-first century equivalent of the vindaloo. You're not a real man unless you can take it full strength.

I put the cup in front of him and noticed the nails of his right hand were long and well-shaped with the gloss of acrylic varnish, while the left-hand nails were trimmed short and neat. He saw me notice and moved his right hand out of sight.

'You're a guitarist,' I said.

He looked uncomfortable. 'I play a bit,' he said. 'It's a good way to unwind.'

'What kind of stuff do you play?'

'Acoustic. Finger-picking. A little bit of jazz.' He shifted in his seat. 'Does it come with the territory, asking the questions?'

'You mean, because I'm a ghost writer?'

He nodded. 'Is it something you can't help?'

There's so much in our lives that we never question. I had to think for a moment before I could formulate an answer that wasn't a glib throwaway. Somehow, I didn't want to palm him off with that. 'It's a bit of a chicken and an egg question,' I said. 'I'm not sure whether I've developed the habit of asking questions because I'm determined to do my job as well as I can, or if I ended up going down this route because I like drawing answers out of people.' I smiled. 'I suppose I like being the one in the know. The one with the inside track.'

Nick nodded, looking pleased with himself. 'That's what

George Lyall said. "Stephanie notices things. And she knows how to ask questions that get answers."'

'I still don't understand why you want to talk to me. I don't know anything about what happened to Joshu.'

'According to Mr Lyall you know all the people at the heart of this tragedy. You knew Joshu. You're probably Scarlett's best friend. You know Dr Graham and you've been to the clinic with Scarlett while she's been undergoing treatment. I'm trying to form a picture of what happened here. And I often find it helpful to talk to someone like you. Someone not directly concerned with what happened but who has a good understanding of the individuals and the relationships involved.' His smile was dead sexy. I know it was wildly inappropriate to be thinking like that with Joshu barely cold, but I couldn't help it. Since the debacle with Pete, I hadn't met a man who'd provoked the slightest reaction in me.

'You don't sound very like a cop,' I said.

'Maybe it's your idea of cops that's out of date?'

I think I blushed. 'Well, ask your questions and we'll see, shall we?'

'Were you surprised to hear Joshu had died from an overdose?'

Straight to the point. No small talk to warm me up. I understood the gambit. I'd used the ambush technique myself more than once. 'He's been into drugs for as long as I've known him. Which is just over three years. So in that sense, no, it wasn't a surprise. But I was quite shocked because he always struck me as someone who knew what he was doing.' I sighed. 'It's hard to explain, but I never quite believed Joshu was as out of control as he wanted people to think. I always thought there was something quite calculated about his behaviour. I never saw him as a candidate for an overdose. But that's the thing about drugs. People think they're in charge of their abuse when actually they're not. Joshu might have believed he was managing his drug use when the truth was he didn't know what the hell he was doing.'

Nick gave me a shrewd look. 'I can't argue with that analysis.' It was a lot later when I discovered why he spoke with such feeling. 'Did he always seem to have plenty of money?'

'He was always flash. He earned a lot, I know that. But from what Scarlett said when they were divorcing, he spent it as fast as he made it.' My smile this time was wry. 'Scarlett said he'd found out the hard way how expensive cheap women were. I think he kept his head above water, but I don't know whether he had much in the way of assets. He didn't have a house, for example. He had a lock-up for all his work gear, but he used to crash with friends or shack up with whoever he was dating.'

'He didn't have any money worries that you knew of?'

I shook my head. 'He could always earn good money. When he came round to pick Jimmy up, he always seemed flush.'

'In that case, why would he steal drugs? It's not like he was some junkie on his uppers, from what you're saying.'

'I think you're asking the wrong question.' I realised I was talking to Nick the way I would to someone I knew. Someone I trusted. But it felt natural, so I didn't rein myself in. 'It's not why he would *steal* drugs but who he was taking the drugs from. Joshu was jealous of anyone who had Scarlett's attention. He was jealous of his own son, for heaven's sake. In his eyes, Simon Graham was no more than another competitor for Scarlett's attention. Stealing from him would be like a dog peeing on a lamppost. I think Joshu was staking out his territory. Showing Simon who was boss. It's heartbreaking, really. A bit of macho posturing, and this is how it ends up.' My stomach suddenly rumbled like car tyres on a cattle grid. That's what you get when you go all day without eating. I pushed my hair back and stood up. 'Do you want something to eat? I just realised I'm starving. I'm going to make a sandwich – do you want one?'

Taken aback, he scratched his head. 'Yeah, why not?'

I raked around in the fridge, all the while answering apparently pointless questions about Joshu and Scarlett. I ended up with two chicken salad wraps with Caesar dressing which I plonked on plates in front of us. 'Not very exciting, I'm afraid. This is not the home of haute cuisine.'

He chuckled. 'I imagine not.'

'We have a very fine collection of home-delivery menus, however.'

'Did you think Joshu and Scarlett would ever get back together?' he asked through a mouthful of sandwich.

'No chance,' I said. 'She loved him, but she knew she was better off without him. Getting cancer reset the zeros for her. She reordered her priorities and bad relationships was number one on the list of stuff she wasn't going to do any more. She hasn't so much as had a date with anyone since the divorce, never mind her diagnosis.'

He raised his eyebrows in a polite expression of dubiety. 'Not according to the tabloids,' he said.

I felt the sudden clench of horror in my chest. I'd let my guard slip and said something deeply, deeply stupid. It hadn't been Scarlett in the papers. It had been Leanne putting on a show, of course. Was I so pathetic that a kind and attractive man could dismantle my careful barricades as if they were made of paper? 'Not everything that's in the tabloids is true,' I said hastily. 'It's part of her job, to keep her name in the tabloids.'

He looked mildly scornful. 'I suppose.'

I tried not to show my relief at having apparently got away with it. And it seemed Nick had run out of questions. So I took my chance. 'How did you get to be a cop?'

'I did a psychology degree. And I didn't want to be any of the things people usually do with a psychology degree. The idea of being a detective interested me but I didn't know if I could hack the journey to get there. I signed up without really knowing if I could cut it.' He grinned and shrugged. 'So far, so good.' He finished his sandwich and stood up. 'Thanks for feeding me. And thanks for filling in the background.'

'It was an accident, wasn't it? You don't think it was deliberate?'

'It's not for me to say. I just present the information to my boss.'

'Not even a hint?'

His eyes flicked from side to side. 'Not even a hint. I'm sorry. I hope the kid's OK. It's hard to lose a parent that young.'

I was touched by his concern. But as he drove away, I found myself wishing Joshu's death wasn't quite so open and shut. I know it was a shitty thought, but I really wished I had an excuse to see Nick Nicolaides again.

37

Nick lingered outside Asmita Patel's flat, leaning against his car in the chilly night air. There was a whiff of curry spices from a nearby restaurant on the breeze and the constant hum of London traffic. He thought about getting something to eat, but he was too antsy for food. He could go home and pick up a guitar and play till his fingers tired. But that wasn't going to help Stephanie or Jimmy. Maybe if he went back to the office, he could find something useful to do.

The overhead lights were turned off in the squad room but a couple of pools of illumination revealed where colleagues were working late. As Nick made for his desk, a lone voice called out to him. 'Jammy bastard, how did you get out of the bloody bunker?' Davy the Fat Boy Brown had been assigned to the phone hacking and police corruption inquiry at the same time as Nick and he was even less suited to being stuck indoors with a bunch of suits.

'I found a shittier stick to get hold of,' Nick said, dropping into his chair and waking his computer from its hibernation. 'Running errands for the FBI. As glamorous as Dagenham on a Sunday morning.'

Davy lumbered across to Nick's desk. 'You got a cup?' He

produced a bottle of Scotch with a couple of inches remaining.

'You keep it,' Nick said. 'I'm too bloody tired already. If I have a drink, I'll fall off my perch.'

Davy shambled off, grumbling. 'I thought you Manchester lads were supposed to like partying?'

'True, Davy. But you don't have the right kind of tables for dancing on.' He clicked on his message queue to see what was waiting for him. He scanned the list of incoming mail, ignoring anything related to the task he'd been temporarily spared. There were three others that promised relevance to what he cared more about. The first was from Cambridgeshire Police. The woman Nick had dubbed Megan the Stalker had ended up in a secure mental hospital in their force area so they'd been his first port of call. The email was short and to the point. Megan Owen had been sectioned under the Mental Health Act but she had been released six weeks previously. She was currently living in a supported hostel, where she had been abiding by the terms of her release. At eight o'clock that evening she had been in the common room watching a TV soap with three other residents. She definitely was not in Chicago kidnapping Jimmy Higgins.

That was a relief. It was never good news when nutters got their hands on small children. One down, a couple to go. According to West Yorkshire Police, Chrissie and Jade Higgins were both at home in the house Scarlett had bought for them. Neither woman seemed to be particularly bothered by the news of Jimmy's abduction.

The other pertinent message was from the local nick in Peckham, which he'd asked to check on Pete Matthews' whereabouts. Again, the message didn't waste words. Pete Matthews was not at home. He was working away, according to a neighbour, who said he'd been gone for about six weeks. The neighbour had no idea where he was but said he knew

Matthews had worked in the US, the Caribbean and South Africa in the past couple of years.

Nick felt the hairs on the back of his neck rising. Child abduction generally had three motivations. A parent who felt unjustly deprived of their child; ransom; and something deeply twisted. Pete Matthews definitely had a deeply twisted possible motive – he wanted to hurt Stephanie and he wanted to show her who was boss. He'd already stalked her, demonstrating that his take on what was reasonable behaviour was deeply skewed. And Nick didn't know where he was tonight.

He thought back to his previous run-in with Pete Matthews. He'd had trouble tracking him down then as well, mostly because the man kept irregular hours and didn't have a set place of work. He'd ended up making a list of recording studios and patiently working his way through the list till he found the one where Matthews had been currently working. If he checked back through his pocket books, that might give him a place to start.

Nick headed for his locker, where he kept his completed pocket books, the records of his daily tasks and accomplishments that would be his aide memoire when cases came to court. He tracked back to the relevant one and sat down then and there to flip through the pages, not caring about the dank smells of stale bodies and questionable drains that permeated the room. The Matthews notes were towards the end of the book, but they were perfectly clear. At the time Nick had confronted him about stalking Stephanie, he'd been mixing a trip-hop album at a place called Phat Phi D up in Archway. Wherever Pete was tonight, it wasn't there. But they might know where he was.

He replaced his notebook and headed back to his car feeling unreasonably cheerful. He knew from his own occasional session work that record studios did not keep nine to five hours. The chances of finding someone still working close to

midnight at Phat Phi D were better than evens, Nick reckoned.

It was nice to be proved right. A percussionist and a keyboard player were working on a backing track for some female
singer songwriter, and the producer and the engineer were
happy enough to let Nick in to ask a few questions to break
the tedium. The studio was small and sweaty, but the equipment looked the business. 'These kids need that many takes,
I'm about dying in here,' the producer moaned. 'You said
you're looking for Pete Matthews?'

'Yeah,' Nick said, lounging against the back wall as the
musicians went again.

'You seen Pete lately?' the producer asked the engineer.

'Not for months. Last I heard, he was going to Detroit to
work with the Style Boys.'

Nick's heart leapt in his chest. His American geography
wasn't brilliant. But he was pretty sure that, in the scale of
things on that giant continent, Detroit wasn't too far from
Chicago. In the dimness of the booth, he struggled not to let
his excitement show.

'The Style Boys? The ones that didn't win *X-Factor*?'

'That's them. Sound like they're channelling sixties
Motown. Temptations, Isley Brothers, that kind of sound.'

'They've got the money to go to Detroit and record?' The
producer sounded incredulous.

'It's crazy, I know. But some shit-for-brains twat who thinks
he's going to be the next Simon Cowell loved their sound and
decided to bankroll them. More money than sense, if you ask
me.'

'And he chose Pete? To engineer a sixties soundalike
album?'

The engineer laughed. 'Which proves the shit-for-brains
bit.' He turned to Nick. 'Don't get me wrong, Pete's a good
engineer. But this is way out of his zone.'

The producer hit the talkback button. 'One more time, guys. Travis, I need you to be spot-on with the beat, you're still drifting in the middle bars.' He rolled his eyes at Nick.

'How can I find out where Pete's working in Detroit?'

The producer shrugged. 'Fucked if I know.'

The engineer pulled out his phone. 'If you want to know, ask an engineer.' His thumbs danced over the screen. 'Paul Owen at the Bowes Festival will know, he's got the Style Boys headlining for them.'

They leaned back in their seats and listened to another rendition that Nick could tell wasn't quite on the money. 'I'm going to fucking kill myself,' the producer said. 'Do you get days like that in your job?'

'All the time.'

'What are you after Pete for? I wouldn't have had him down as the criminal type,' the engineer said. 'Pretty straight guy, Pete. Well, what passes for straight in this game.'

'I need to ask him a few questions. Something that happened in his neighbourhood he might have witnessed. But if he's been gone for the last couple of months, chances are he's out of the frame altogether.'

The engineer's phone shimmied across the sound desk, signalling an incoming text. He picked it up and glanced at it, before holding it out to Nick. 'There you go, mate.'

'Style Boys @ South Detroit Sounds till end of week. Early mix sounds better than expected,' he read. Nick smiled. 'Thanks, lads. Hope your drummer finds his beat.'

All the resources of the FBI were chasing Jimmy Higgins. But the way things were looking, it was all going to come down to a single London copper with a feel for the music scene. Nick smiled. If he could bring Jimmy Higgins home, he'd be a happy man.

And more importantly, Stephanie would be a very happy woman.

38

When Scarlett came back from the chemo session, she was wrecked. The drugs had ripped the energy out of her, leaving her a pale husk. But it wasn't the chemo or the bereavement itself that had broken her. According to Simon, who had brought her back, she'd had a text from Joshu's sister Ambar on the way home. Ambar had stated categorically that neither Scarlett nor Jimmy would be welcome at her brother's funeral. 'If you have any respect for my family, please stay away. You have no place at a Hindu funeral.'

'Fucking bitch,' Scarlett said weakly once we'd got her to bed. 'Fucking, fucking bitch.' She gripped my hand so tight I could almost feel the bruises forming. She spoke in broken fragments of sentences. 'I'm going to show her. Tomorrow, Steph. We'll get started. We're going. To organise a memorial service. For all the people. That knew the real Joshu. Not this fake. Perfect son his family are trying to create.'

'That's a great idea,' I said. 'We'll give him a proper send-off. You're right, his friends should have the chance to say good-bye. But in the meantime you need to rest.'

She let go of my hand. I could see the fight draining out of her. 'Sleep now,' she said. 'Everything hurts, Steph. My body and my heart. Everything.'

I stayed with her till she fell asleep, which took less than five minutes. She looked so frail, so pale, the dark circles under her eyes a new addition since the start of the chemo. She looked closer to death than Joshu ever had.

When I left Scarlett, Leanne was carrying Jimmy downstairs. He was grizzling softly, repeating, 'I want my mummy,' in a low monotone.

'We're going for a little swim before bedtime,' she said, looking worn out. 'Do you want to come too?' She sounded almost desperate.

Obviously we weren't going to tell Jimmy anything that night. But he clearly sensed there was something bad going on. I didn't feel much like swimming, but I reckoned opportunities for relaxation would be in short supply over the coming days. And the kid needed a bit of love and attention. In spite of my gloom, I enjoyed frolicking in the water with Jimmy, who perked up as soon as we all started playing. When Leanne finally took him off to bed, too tired to miss his mother, I stayed in the water, swimming lazy laps and thinking about Nick Nicolaides, wondering whether I'd ever see him again.

The next few days were chaotic. Breaking the news to Jimmy was more harrowing for Scarlett than for her son, who was too young to understand the import of what she was telling him. He cried because she was crying, but we all knew he hadn't grasped the reality that his dad wouldn't be coming back. 'He's going to keep asking about Joshu, and I'm going to have to keep explaining it again and again,' Scarlett said afterwards. 'And then one day it'll sink in and his little heart will be devastated.'

What none of us wanted to think about was how it would be for Jimmy when the day came that he understood how his father had died. With luck, he would be secure and happy enough in his own skin not to be thrown completely off course by the information. But it would be hard to assimilate, however well adjusted he turned out.

But telling Jimmy was only a small part of what we had to get through in the days after Joshu's death. Scarlett was determined that the memorial service for Joshu should be held as soon as possible. I think she saw it as a spoiler for whatever his parents had planned. 'They didn't give a stuff about him when he was alive. They don't have the right to own him now he's dead,' she said. The morning after we heard the news, she dragged herself out of bed and into the kitchen in spite of our protestations. 'I've got a to-do list,' she said. 'Then I'll go back to bed.'

I really didn't have the time for sorting out Joshu's memorial. I had work of my own and deadlines to meet. But friendship trumps work in my world. 'Give me the list,' I said. 'We'll sort it out, won't we, Leanne?'

Leanne looked less than thrilled, but she nodded agreement. She gestured to the low table and chair where Jimmy was singing to himself and eating cereal with his Power Rangers posable figures. 'I'll take Jimmy to nursery, then I'll muck in.'

'No,' Scarlett said, mutiny on her face. 'I loved him. This is the last thing I can do for him and I want to do it myself.'

It was a fine sentiment, but it wasn't practical. 'I know you do. And it says a lot for you that you still feel like that in spite of the way he treated you. But the most important thing you can do for him now is stand tall and proud at his memorial service. You have to be strong for Jimmy as well as yourself. Leave the nuts and bolts to us. What you need to do is nothing. You need to be amazing at his send-off. You need to show the world you're winning your personal fight.' I pulled her into a tight hug.

279

'Yeah, you're Kate Winslet in *Titanic*,' Leanne said. 'You gotta show them, Scarlett. Joshu's gone, but you go on.'

I stifled an embarrassed snort of laughter at the image Leanne had conjured up. 'Show the world that you're a survivor, Scarlett. And in years to come, Jimmy will take strength from that. An amazing memorial for his dad, with you at the heart of it.'

To be honest, she didn't take much persuading to head back to bed. She squatted down beside Jimmy and played Power Rangers with him for a few minutes, then hugged him tight. They walked into the cloakroom hand in hand, where she zipped him into his coat, handed him off to Leanne then staggered back down the hall and up the stairs, refusing my arm and muttering under her breath.

Organising the memorial wasn't the easiest task I've ever taken on. Obviously, anywhere with formal religious associations was out of the question. Scarlett had no particular Christian affiliation and Joshu was as lapsed as it was possible to be, in spite of his parents' determination to give him a proper Hindu funeral. Leanne and I sat at the breakfast bar scratching our heads, trying to figure out what to do. Outdoors was too dodgy – you can never rely on British weather. The last thing Scarlett needed was for the heavens to open and for the memorial to descend into muddy farce.

It was Leanne who suggested a club. It was where Joshu had spent his working life, after all. My first reaction was to reject the idea – clubs are dark, subterranean caves that look cheap and tatty with the lights switched on. Leanne, whose life as Scarlett had made her almost as much of an expert as Joshu in the world of dance and DJs, couldn't think of a single one that wasn't a dingy dive at heart.

But neither of us could come up with an alternative. In desperation, I hit Google. There were a couple of top ten London club lists, and I took a look at them. 'Found it,' I yelped, turning the laptop round to show Leanne. 'Paramount. The thirty-first floor of Centre Point. Windows all round, it has to look good in daylight. It says there are amazing views down Oxford St and across central London. There's a dance space where we could have the memorial bit. They do food too. It's perfect, Leanne.'

She looked dubious. 'I don't think he ever did a gig there. I've never been there with him.'

'That doesn't matter. It's a club. That makes it a tribute to his working life.'

'It'll cost an arm and a leg. Look, there's a review that says the drinks are really expensive.'

I laughed. 'Do you seriously think Scarlett's going to be paying for it? By the time Georgie's sold the rights to *Yes!* and some shitty TV channel, we'll be in profit. Trust me, Leanne, this is the answer.'

Luckily both George and Scarlett agreed with me. We had a week to arrange the memorial service, and though I say it myself, we did a fantastic job. The guest list was a showbiz editor's wet dream. Everyone who wanted to be perceived as anyone was there, along with a full complement of paparazzi and red-top columnists. Scarlett had taken our words to heart and she'd spent most of the week resting in her room. On the day itself, the make-up artist was first to arrive at the house. Thanks to her subtle work, Scarlett managed the perfect combination of fragility and radiance, walking through the crowd to the podium holding Jimmy's hand, head held high. He looked heart-breaking, bewildered in a scaled-down black Nehru jacket and black trousers.

A couple of Joshu's more articulate and respectable friends spoke about his professional life then Scarlett reduced the room to tears with her personal eulogy. 'Joshu was the only man I've ever known who stopped the breath in my lungs. The first time I saw him, he was behind the decks under the arches at Waterloo. The way he moved, the smile on him, the glitter in his eyes, it was like he had a spark inside him that nobody else had. I knew right then he was going to be mine.'

Never mind that the glitter and spark had probably been from cocaine; nobody in that room could have doubted that she truly loved him.

'But loving Joshu came with a price tag. He had a head full of dreams, and it was like one life wasn't ever going to be enough for him. Being a DJ wasn't enough. He wanted to go beyond that, to become a record producer, to make films, to change the way people saw the world. Sadly for me and Jimmy, just being a family man wasn't ever going to be enough for him either. Joshu had a big heart and he needed more than a simple life could offer. I couldn't hold him down. I had to let him spread his wings, even though it broke my heart into little pieces.' Scarlett drew in her breath and quivered on the edge of tears, then gathered her boy to her. Jimmy clutched at her dress, peering out at the crowd with wide, sad eyes.

'The one thing that was enough for Joshu was being a dad. For all his faults, for all his frustrations, he loved his boy. He'd have thrown himself in front of a bullet for Jimmy. If there was one thing that Joshu loved without a second thought, one thing he would never have turned his back on, it was his son. And that's how I know what happened to Joshu was an accident, not a suicide, as some journalists who know nowt have tried to suggest. Joshu would never, ever have taken himself away from Jimmy. He might have had enough of me. He might have had enough of you lot. But he would never, ever have had enough of Jimmy. So let's raise a glass to my beautiful Joshu. Let's remember all the times he made us glad to be alive. To Joshu!'

It was irresistible. I didn't think there could be anyone in the room unmoved by Scarlett's words. From my position by the podium, I looked round the room, my own gaze misted with brimming tears.

And that's when my breath stopped in my lungs for all the wrong reasons. There, at the back of the room, leaning against the wall, was the man I'd spent so much time, money and energy escaping from. With a triumphant, ironic smile on his face, Pete Matthews tipped his finger to his forehead in a mocking salute.

What was it Faulkner said? 'The past is never dead. It isn't even past.' Once I'd struggled to understand that. Now I knew exactly what it meant.

39

The rest of the memorial passed in a blur for me. As soon as the formal part of the afternoon was over, I thought I'd try to escape without Pete spotting me. But I could feel his eyes on me, following me round the room. Although this wasn't my crowd, I knew enough of the media to attempt to use them as stepping stones to get across the room to an exit where I hoped I could make my getaway. But every time I looked up, there he was, on the fringes, stalking me as he'd done so efficiently after I'd walked away from our relationship.

Then I saw the one man who might possibly save me. Over by the buffet, his back to the impressive view of central London, Detective Sergeant Nick Nicolaides was using his height advantage to scan the room. I wasn't sure what he was doing there. But I was sure I could take advantage of his presence one way or another.

I weaved through the press of bodies, air-kissing a few of Scarlett's TV colleagues on the way. Nick looked mildly amused as I finally pitched up beside him. 'Are you here to give me grief for gate-crashing?' he asked.

Bemused, I shook my head. 'Why would you think that?'

'Because I understand you organised this—' He waved a

hand at the room, where the noise of chatter was rising incrementally, like the volume on one of Joshu's sets. '—and I wasn't on the guest list.'

'I didn't do the guest list,' I said. 'That was Scarlett and her agent. I hardly know anyone here.' *Apart from the bastard across the room whose eyebrows are drawn down in a dark frown now I'm talking to you.*

'Damn, I gave myself away.' He pursed his mouth in a self-mocking expression.

'Why are you here?' It occurred to me that his presence was a little puzzling.

He fiddled with the stem of his wine glass and shrugged. 'Call it curiosity. I don't often get the chance to have a window on this world. I like to take my chances when I can.'

'If this was an episode of *Poirot*, you'd be here because you didn't think Joshu's death was an accident.' I was teasing him, but he showed no response at all. Not a quirk of humour or a flash of seriousness. Just a blank.

'But it's not an episode of *Poirot*,' he said. 'And I'm a nosy copper who had nothing better to do on his afternoon off. How's the not-quite-widow taking it?'

'Harder than I'd have expected. She put on a good show of being over him, but it turns out she wasn't. Trust me, there's nothing fake about her grief. She's genuinely stricken. Partly it's on Jimmy's account. But she still had feelings for Joshu.'

Nick nodded. 'She's lucky to have you to take care of something as major as this.'

'I cracked the whip, that's all. It was other people who did the nitty gritty.' An idea was nibbling at the edge of my mind. 'I'm quite good at getting people organised.' I tried to project a winning combination of tentative and sexy.

'I imagine you are,' Nick said, not quite meeting my gaze.

'For example.' I shifted so that I had my back to the window. If he wanted to keep eye contact with me, he would have to move round, putting Pete firmly in his line of sight. 'You mentioned that you're a gatecrasher. But you're not really. If you had asked to come, we'd have been happy to give you an invitation. In your case, it's a technicality. But there are people here who are definitely not welcome. And someone like you would be doing Scarlett a huge kindness if you were to escort them off the premises. For example.'

He moved so he could see the section of the room that I'd been looking towards. 'Is there someone you had in mind?'

'Don't stare. But there's a guy beyond the bar, leaning against the wall. He's wearing a black jacket and a black shirt with a silvery tie.'

Nick stooped slightly, as if he were leaning down to hear my words over the background din. 'Dark hair? Kind of gaunt? Straight black brows?'

'That's him. His name's Pete Matthews.'

'And he's not welcome?'

'Definitely not.'

'I presume there's a reason you don't want to give him the bum's rush yourself?' Nick pushed his shaggy hair back from his face. In the vivid lighting, I could see one or two strands of silver among mixed shades of brown that reminded me of the colours of a female blackbird's wing. It made him seem more grown-up. More grown-up than me, at least.

'Yes.' *I'm desperate to run away from here and I want you to distract him so I can get a head start.*

'But you'd rather not share it,' Nick said. I don't think I imagined a note of regret in his voice. 'And by the time I've dealt with the problem, you'll be gone, right?'

Not just gorgeous and sexy, but smart too. I really hoped Nick would cobble together some vague reason to come and talk to us again about Joshu. I wasn't about to count on it, though. 'Something like that. My work here is done.'

'Hi, ho, Silver, away.' He grinned again. Damn, but it's a

great sense of connection when someone gets your cultural references. 'I'll go and chase your gatecrasher away, Stephanie. I'll consider it the price of admission.'

'Thank you. And thanks for coming.'

'I'm glad I did.' Nick dipped his head then slipped away from me through the crowd. As soon as he came between me and Pete, I walked quickly along the fringe of the room and through the door into the bustling kitchen area. A pink-faced woman in chef's whites said, 'Oi! You can't come in here,' as soon as she caught sight of me.

'I need to check out the back way in case Scarlett needs to leave quietly,' I said in as authoritative a tone as I could muster. 'You know, with the cancer treatment, she can't always predict how much energy she's going to have. And she doesn't want to make a fuss.'

'Oh, I get it. You're like the SAS, clearing the route for her.'

I tried not to roll my eyes. 'Something like that.'

Three minutes later, I emerged from a service lift at the back of the building. I didn't have my car with me – it was still at Scarlett's house, since I'd travelled to the memorial in one of the big black Daimlers Georgie had ordered to bring us from Essex in style. That didn't matter. The car could stay put until I needed it. I couldn't go back to Essex tonight. That would be exactly where Pete would come looking if Nick didn't put him off the whole idea of tracking me down. Somehow, I didn't think a word from Nick would wave a magic wand and end my persecution.

And assuming Nick did manage to buy me a few minutes, I knew I had to get out of the immediate neighbourhood before Pete emerged from the Centre Point tower. The one thing I had going for me was that clearly he still didn't know where I lived. That was why he was here today. An event he knew I'd be participating in, at a crowded venue where he knew I wouldn't want to make a scene. Then he could pick up my trail and follow me back to my lair. His mistake had been to show himself. If he hadn't been so cocksure, he could have kept watch in the street below and simply followed me when I emerged without a suspicion. Thank God for arrogance.

I looked around to get my bearings, then headed for Tottenham Court Road station at a brisk pace. Northern Line to Waterloo then Jubilee Line to London Bridge, then a train to Brighton. I would be safe behind my own front door in less than two hours. The very idea put a spring into my step. I'd thwarted the man who threatened my peace of mind.

It was a great feeling. Shame it didn't last long.

40

It had taken a while to get there, but Vivian McKuras figured they were finally getting to the heart of the matter. Pete Matthews was emerging as a man with a grudge against Stephanie Harker, and a man who didn't give up easily. 'Was that the first time you'd had any evidence that he was still trying to track you down?' she asked.

Stephanie nodded wearily. Her face had aged as the day had worn on, the markers of the years overwhelming the youthful elements of her features. Vivian had seen it before in those left behind by a crime. The damage became visible very quickly. Her voice had changed too. It had grown markedly less sprightly as her story had unfolded. 'Yes.' She sighed. 'I really thought he'd given up. But obviously he hadn't. The thing is, I don't lead a very public life. Other writers appear at literary festivals, or give talks at libraries. Ghost writers don't. If you don't know where I live, it would be hard to stake out anywhere I visit regularly. I seldom go to my agent's office – if we're seeing each other, we tend to do lunch and meet at the restaurant. Or if I'm auditioning for a book, we'll meet at the venue. And it's rare for me to attend launch events for books I've written. It's easier all round if I stay invisible.'

'Couldn't he track you down through property title or taxes, that sort of thing? Is that not possible in your country?'

'I didn't buy the house in Brighton in my own name. I set up a limited company and used it to purchase the property. I pay rent to the company, and the rent covers the mortgage. That way I don't show up as the owner at the Land Registry. My name is not on the public register of council tax, and all the utilities are in the company name. My bank statements and credit card bills all go to my agent's office address. I did everything I could to cover my tracks.'

'You had him tabbed as somebody tenacious then? A guy who wasn't going to give up and walk away?'

Stephanie looked fed up. 'Well, obviously. Given the way he started stalking me. And given what I knew about his temperament. He was an obsessive perfectionist at work. But I was equally determined not to make it easy for him to force his way back into my life. I thought he would give up if he couldn't make any headway.' She shook her head. 'I was wrong.'

Vivian pulled her laptop back in front of her and brought up the footage from the security area. She freeze-framed the image immediately before the kidnapper appeared. 'I want you to look at this very carefully and tell me whether you think this man could be Pete Matthews.' She turned the screen so that Stephanie could see it.

Stephanie's first reaction was to gasp at the sight of Jimmy. Her hand flew to her mouth, she drew her breath in sharply. Her other hand moved towards the screen. 'Jimmy,' she murmured. A single tear spilled from the corner of her eye and her face twisted in sorrow.

Vivian gave her a moment to compose herself. Either this woman was a consummate actress or she was entirely innocent of any involvement in the boy's disappearance. Vivian wished she'd thought of confronting her with the CCTV footage sooner, if only to clarify that issue.

Stephanie sniffed hard and wiped her eyes roughly with the back of her hand. 'It's OK,' she croaked, nodding and blinking. Vivian pressed play. The footage jerked into motion. The man came into shot, his cap obscuring his face. His legs were long compared to his torso, which looked strangely paunchy in contrast with limbs that seemed skinny. He bent slightly to talk to Jimmy, took the boy's hand, grabbed his backpack and passport and walked briskly away. Through it all, Stephanie held her breath. When they disappeared from sight, she released it in a soft moan.

'Is it him?' Vivian asked.

Stephanie frowned. 'I'm really not sure. I don't think it's him, but ... I don't know, there's something familiar about the way he moves.' Bewildered, she looked up at the FBI agent. 'I don't think it's Pete, but I couldn't swear to it.'

'What about his build? His height and weight? Look again, Stephanie.' Vivian ran the short segment for a second time.

Stephanie still looked doubtful. 'It's hard to be sure about his height. He's got that paunch, which Pete definitely didn't have the last time I saw him. But apart from that, he's got the same sort of build.'

It was enough for Vivian. She knew all about the reluctance of witnesses to make identifications that went against what they wanted to believe about people in their lives. Stephanie had taken a long time to get to Pete Matthews as a possible perp. She wasn't going to suddenly go all out to point the finger now. A possible ID was a pretty good starting point as far as Vivian was concerned. If Detective Sergeant Nicolaides couldn't positively place Matthews in the UK, she would happily promote him to number one on her suspect list. *Be honest, Viv, he's your only suspect right now.* She swung the computer back round to face her. Time to change tack.

'What happened when Detective Nicolaides told Pete to leave the memorial?'

'I didn't find that out till much later,' Stephanie said. 'All I knew was that Pete didn't show up in Brighton. And he wasn't waiting for me at Scarlett's when I went back to pick up my car. I really did think he'd finally got the message. To be honest, he hardly crossed my mind.' Her expression darkened again. 'There were other things happening that were a lot more important to me than whatever was going on in Pete's head.'

41

After Joshu's memorial, we all turned our focus back on Scarlett and her treatment. The chemo was almost over, then there was a brief course of radiotherapy. And then, miraculously, the all-clear. Simon told her that the treatment had been successful and although she would continue with drug therapy for the next five years, the chances were high that she was now clear of cancer.

We celebrated with a banquet out at the hacienda. It was a small party – Scarlett, Leanne, George and his partner, Marina, Simon and me. We'd hired a couple of chefs from the local Chinese restaurant and they presented us with a stunning sequence of irresistible courses that left us all groaning. We washed it all down with buckets of Prosecco, toasting Scarlett with every course. 'And my new book,' she said on the third or fourth toast. 'Now I've got the all-clear, we can publish, right, George?'

'Absolutely,' he said. 'I know Stephanie's all set with the typescript. And a very moving read it is too, girls. You've out-done yourselves with this one.'

Leanne, who'd had a few more drinks than the rest of us,

gave her cousin a sloppy kiss on the cheek. 'And for the first time in his sorry life, Joshu had perfect timing. Right, Scarlett?'

There was a moment of grisly silence as we all exchanged horrified looks. Then Scarlett said, 'For fuck's sake, Leanne, not in front of Jimmy.'

Leanne opened her mouth to say something, but Simon cut across her. 'We're here to salute the future, not brood on the past, Leanne. Let's raise a glass to our generous hostess and her son. To Scarlett and Jimmy!'

It was the perfect diversion and we all fell on it gratefully. It turned out to be the only sour moment in a sweet evening of celebration. Jimmy soon grew tired and, before he could become fractious, Marina whisked him away and miraculously got him to go to sleep. She was always amazing with Jimmy, much more so than any of the rest of us, including his mother. If I could have tempted her back to the UK to help me take care of Jimmy, I'd have done it in a heartbeat.

Simon had been right with the toast, though. It was time to look to the future. I was pleased that my friend had been granted time and health. Selfishly, I was also looking forward to having more time to myself. I didn't begrudge Scarlett a moment I'd devoted to her during the trauma of diagnosis and treatment. However, I needed to get on with my work, and with establishing my new life in Brighton. She'd always be part of my world, like any good friend. But I was beginning to make new connections – a book group, a pub quiz team – and I wanted that part of my life to grow too.

It turned out I wasn't the only one who was ready for change. It was about ten days later that I next saw Scarlett, and this time she came down to Brighton. 'It's not fair, you always trailing up to mine,' she said. 'It's nice to have a day out by the seaside, and now Jimmy's in nursery all day, I've got more time to myself.'

We wandered round the Lanes for a while, looking for

bargains and finding none. She did end up buying a Navajo blanket for the living room, paying about twice as much as I'd have done, even supposing I had her kind of money. And she was making good money by then – the TV shows, the merchandising, the endorsements for everything from kids' clothes to vitamin supplements. What the books earned was the icing on a towering layer cake. True to her word, a tenth of everything she earned was funnelled into the charitable trust she'd set up for the Romanian orphanage, and she planned to visit them again later in the year to see what practical use had been made of the money she'd raised. 'I'm going to set up a sponsored night swim,' she said. 'Sort of like the Moonwalk, only in swimming pools. From midnight till six in the morning. Women can form teams or do it individually.'

'That's a great idea.' I meant it. 'Will you take part yourself?'

'Course I will. I'll put a team together with the girls from the show. It'll be a laugh.' She gave me a wry smile. 'There'll be plenty waiting for me to fall on my arse. But they don't know I swim every bloody day, do they?'

'You show them,' I said. 'Plus, it's for a good cause. If they try to make you look bad, they'll end up looking pretty shabby.'

'True. Oh, and another thing about Romania. When Jimmy starts school, I'm going to pack Marina off back to Romania to be my eyes and ears out at Timonescu.'

I admit, I didn't see that one coming. 'Does she want to go back to Romania?'

Scarlett nodded. 'She talked to me about going home before I had my diagnosis.' This was how Scarlett divided her life these days. 'Before I had my diagnosis' and 'after I had my diagnosis'. She didn't speak of cancer in relation to herself. 'She misses her family and she feels homesick,' she went on. 'I persuaded her to stay on the promise that she could go back with a job once she's seen Jimmy off to school. She's going to work alongside the head of the orphanage and administer our funding. She'll be well paid and she'll have a job that's worth doing. I mean, face it, Steph, she's got skills and talents way above what she does for me.'

I couldn't help laughing. 'No kidding. She could run the bloody country. I hope you know what you're doing to Romania, letting her go back.'

Scarlett laughed too. 'She'll do a fantastic job for those kids.'

'But can you manage without her?'

'Of course not. It would be a bloody nightmare. My domestic skills are non-existent. But Marina's promised to send me a replacement. The daughter of one of her cousins, apparently. Marina says she's like a mini-me of her. So I'll be sorted and she'll be sorted and Jimmy will have somebody who knows how to make his favourite Romanian meatballs according to Marina's granny's traditional recipe.'

We both giggled. I'd picked up the frozen Swedish meatballs from Ikea often enough to get the joke.

We arranged for the shop to deliver the rug to my house later and walked down to the pier. She bought ice creams for us both and we walked along licking our cornets. 'I love being by the seaside,' Scarlett said. 'We never went on holidays when I was a kid, but somebody always took us to the seaside for a day out. Scarborough. Brid. Whitby, if we were lucky. Coming to see you now makes me feel like I'm going back in time to one of the few good bits of my childhood. I love the smell of fish and chips and candy floss. I love the neon and the old-fashioned signs on the rides and the bingo. I love the slot machines and the crappy grab-a-toy games that never let you win. And I love the way that even when it rains, people still walk along the prom and make the most of it. It's very British, isn't it?'

'I wonder if the next generation of kids will feel the same.

Brought up on Benidorm and Disneyland. Will they love this—' I waved my hand expansively, '—or will they see it as cut-price self-storage for pensioners?'

'God, what a depressing thought,' Scarlett said. 'I'm not giving thoughts like that house room any more. I am Miss Positive from now on. So much of the cancer stuff I read talked about mental attitude and the cancer personality. Like, storing up bitterness in your heart somehow turns into cancer in your body.' She held up a hand to stop me before I spoke. 'I know, it's probably all bollocks, but it gives me an excuse to make myself think positive and dump all the negativity.'

'Fair enough,' I said. 'I'm all for clearing the bitterness out of life.' We leaned on the railing and looked out across the glittering green and grey of the English Channel.

'Speaking of which,' she said, 'Leanne's off to Spain.'

That was the second bolt from the blue. First Marina, now Leanne. It was all change at the hacienda. 'That's a bit of a surprise,' I said.

'Why? I talked to you about it ages ago. Before I had my diagnosis.'

'You did. But she was such a support when you were having your treatment. And she had her hair cut, and people accepted her as your cousin. I thought you'd changed your mind.'

She gave me a look. Sorrowful. Almost pitying. 'You only ever saw Leanne's good side, didn't you?'

'I don't know what you mean.' And I didn't. I really didn't.

'Leanne only let you see the smiley, helpful, good side. Even when she ratted Joshu out, she made out that she was devastated, that she couldn't keep it to herself because she couldn't bear the thought of him doing the dirty on me. Am I right?'

'Yes. She was upset on your account.' I cast my mind back to that momentous night. I couldn't recall any reason to doubt the way Leanne had presented things to me. 'She wasn't sure what to do for the best, but she thought she owed it to you to let you know.'

Scarlett sighed and stared out across the sea. 'She was dying to tell me,' she said. 'Don't get me wrong. I don't think she said anything that wasn't true. She didn't lie about Joshu, though I wouldn't put it past her to make up a steaming great pile of shit about him if there hadn't been a truth to dish up. But she enjoyed every minute of seeing me hurt and humiliated.'

I was genuinely shocked by Scarlett's words. 'You think? I didn't see that at all. I saw her upset and worried. Scared and nervous about telling you.'

'You saw what she let you see.' Scarlett gave her ice cream one last lick then threw it out over the water, watching as the gulls squabbled over the disintegrating cornet. 'She knew what she was doing, Steph. I never had illusions about Joshu. I always knew he'd take it where he could get it if he thought he could get away with it. Although we never laid it out for each other in those terms, we both knew that was what the deal was. As long as he didn't rub my nose in it, as long as he never humiliated me, I never would have called him on it. Because I knew that deep down, he loved me. Leanne, she came from the same world as me. She knew the score.'

I was beginning to see an ugly picture I hadn't suspected existed. I didn't know what pissed me off more – the truth behind the game that had been played out with me as a piece on the board, or that I, who prided myself on being able to read people, had been so thoroughly taken in. 'Leanne knew that if she told you and made me part of spilling the beans that you couldn't ignore it. That you'd have to confront Joshu.'

Scarlett nodded. 'Nail on the head, Steph. I don't think she thought I would take it as far as I did. But I couldn't see any other way forward. Once he knew that I actually knew, there would be no need for him to keep the lid on his harem. I'd be humiliated at every turn. I had to throw him out.' She slid her big sunglasses down from her hat and covered her eyes. 'Me and Leanne, there's always been a bit of love/hate going on. Competition for lads' attention when we were kids. Which I usually won because I was older and smarter. She knows enough to make me look bad if she wanted to be spiteful. That's the real reason I wanted to keep her out of the first book. I knew I was taking a chance, bringing her into my life. But I thought it would be OK. And it was, for a while.' She sighed. 'Then she grassed Joshu up and I knew there was a message there.'

'What message?'

'She was reminding me that she knew a secret about me. Not in so many words, obviously. But the message was there. That's when I knew it was time she went to Spain. We both understood the terms of the deal. She stays in line and she gets the lifestyle she's always craved.'

'M-A-D,' I said. Scarlett gave me a puzzled, offended look. 'Mutually Assured Destruction,' I explained. 'It's what they used to say about the USA and the USSR during the cold war. Their nuclear weapons meant that if one of them started it, they'd both be finished.' I patted her arm. 'I wasn't suggesting you were mad.'

Scarlett looked relieved, then giggled. I realised she absolutely didn't want to have a reason to fall out with me. With Leanne gone and Marina going, she'd be very short on people she could trust without me. 'I never heard that before. I thought you were making out I was daft. See, I've still got a lot to learn before I can go head to head with the likes of you, Steph.' She gave me a sideways shoulder nudge.

'You do all right.' I licked the last of my ice cream off the cornet and flicked it into the air, watching it glide in lazy circles till the wind snatched it under the pier.

'Anyway, I realised the time had come for her to sling her hook when she said that thing at our celebration dinner.'

I didn't have to be reminded of Leanne's tasteless remark. 'She was pissed.'

'She was. And she gets pissed fairly regularly. Like most of the useless women in our family. And I don't want that loose mouth around me now. Like I said, I'm going for a positive outlook on life. I don't want her bringing me down. And Jimmy's getting to an age where he's like a sponge. I don't want him hearing shit like that about his dad. Plus, you never know. I might find another bloke one of these days, and the last thing I need is Leanne waiting in the wings to put the poison in.'

I couldn't argue with that. 'So she's off to do people's nails in Spain?'

'That's right.'

'How did she react when you told her it was time?'

Scarlett shrugged and turned away from the rail. 'Let's go and play bingo.' I followed her back down the pier to a bingo stall. 'She knew she was on borrowed time anyway. After I got my diagnosis, there was nothing for her to do in terms of impersonating me. I told her if I made it out the other side of the treatment, I'd put it about that I was changing my lifestyle to stay healthy. So the writing was on the wall.' We sat down on the padded vinyl stools and the stallholder immediately recognised Scarlett. There was the usual flurry of autographs and shots with camera phones before we could settle down for a game of bingo.

'Did Leanne go quietly in the end?' I said when we were alone again.

'Yeah, she knew she'd crossed a line. I think she quite fancies the weather, to be honest. And where she is, it's nice. It's not like *Benidorm*. It's up in the hills. A lot of expats and enough nightlife down by the sea to stop her pining for those fucking horrible clubs. I said I'd take Jimmy out for a holiday once she's settled.' She smiled. 'She loves the little bugger.'

'So, big changes all round.'

As we spoke, we were cancelling the numbers being called. I was always a beat behind, but Scarlett was sharp as a gull's beak, clicking off the numbers on her card the second they were announced.

'Yeah,' she said without a pause in her play. 'The only thing that doesn't change is the paparazzi always on my case. I thought the brand-new me would have been too boring for them. But they can't wait for me to screw up. You'd think I was Princess Diana the way they chase me around. It's totally out of hand.'

'I couldn't handle it,' I admitted.

Scarlett grinned. 'Yeah, but you're a ghost.' Then she grew serious again. 'I had that Madison Owen on the show the other day. You know, that Welsh kid that got her West End start from *Who Wants to Be a Thoroughly Modern Millie*. She reckons somebody's been hacking her phone messages.'

I snorted incredulously. 'You're kidding? How could anybody do that? And why would they want to? It's not like she's a big star or anything.'

Scarlett let her sunglasses slide down her nose and gave me a knowing look over the rim. 'She's not. But the geezer she's having an affair with is.'

'Really? Who?'

She pushed her glasses up and turned down the corners of her mouth. 'She wouldn't tell me. Only that he's a household name who makes a mega deal out of being the perfect family man. Anyway, she says that she hasn't told a living soul who he is. Not even her best mate. And obviously the boyfriend's not talking. They were supposed to get together last weekend. He'd borrowed a cottage in the Cotswolds from a mate of his. She was all set to meet him there. Except, when she arrives, there's a car parked in the lane. And she recognises the guy in the passenger seat because she'd seen him interviewing one of the judges on that stupid bloody TV talent show she won. She puts her foot down and shoots past. Only when she drives round the bend, she sees another guy in a field with a long lens pointing back towards the cottage. So she had to high-tail it out of there and text the boyfriend to tell him they were busted.'

'Maybe they were following the boyfriend? Maybe they'd had a tip-off?'

'She says he wasn't followed. He's sure about that. He's paranoid because of his wife and his reputation. Maddie says the only way anyone could have known about the arrangement was if somebody listened to her voicemail messages.'

It sounded to me like a tale that had the makings of an urban myth. Another case of a C-list celebrity who overestimated her importance. With my professional hat on, I'd heard a lot about the media's dirty tricks – eavesdropping on mobile phone calls with a scanner, for example – but this was a new one on me. I was dubious, to say the least. And not just because it would be illegal. Mostly I couldn't believe anyone could be arsed to hack the voicemail of people like Madison Owen on the off-chance of finding something more significant than, 'Hi, it's me, call me back when you get the chance.'

'I bet there's another explanation,' I said. 'This all sounds too far-fetched.'

'House!' Scarlett waved her hand in the air, all thoughts of invasion of privacy gone now she'd won.

The stallholder bustled over, delighted that she'd got a celebrity winner. 'You're supposed to get anything on the bottom shelf,' she said confidentially after she'd checked Scarlett's card. 'But since it's you, go on and have the pick of the stall. You deserve a treat after what you've been through.'

Scarlett gave her the hundred-watt smile. 'I wouldn't dream of it,' she said. 'You've got a living to make. I'll take one of those dolphins down the bottom. For my boy,' she added as the stallholder handed her a small stuffed toy in white and royal blue. 'He loves dolphins. He went swimming with them last year in the Bahamas.'

We slid off the stools and headed back into town. 'I've had a brilliant time,' she said when we turned into my street. 'Next time, I'll bring Jimmy again. When are you coming up to town again?'

I had an editorial meeting with a publisher the following week so we arranged to have dinner afterwards. I was glad that things seemed to be settling into an easy routine between us and when the day of our dinner rolled around, I made sure the meeting didn't overrun. Turning down the offer of a drink I knew would roll into the early evening, I took the tube to Hyde Park Corner and walked up Park Lane to the Dorchester. Once Scarlett had discovered there was such a thing as posh Chinese food, there had been no stopping her. Tonight, we had reservations at China Tang in the Dorchester where the food makes me want to lay my head on the table and weep. In the best possible way. I was already salivating at the thought of it. Unusually, everything had run according to time and I was half an hour early for our reservation. So I took a deep breath, mentally checked my bank balance and walked into the cocktail bar. There's a section of the bar that's cordoned off for private parties and I glanced in as I walked down the steps.

I nearly missed my footing, only just saving myself from a mortifying sprawl at the feet of the cocktail waiter. Scarlett was raising a glass of fizz to her lips and smiling at the person opposite her. None other than Dr Simon Graham, clutching the matching glass and gazing into Scarlett's eyes in an extremely non-medical way.

I carried on all the way down the bar and straight out the

street door, much to the confusion of the waiter. I needed a drink, but definitely not in the Dorchester cocktail bar. I crossed the forecourt and headed round the corner to the tall redbrick building that houses the University Women's Club. It's the only women-only members club in the country and it's my haven in central London. I first joined when I moved there and needed somewhere other than my horrible flat in Stepney to have meetings. Maggie recommended it and I was nervous at the thought of posh women with grand voices and even grander degrees looking down on me. But I couldn't have been more wrong. I warmed to it the first time I crossed the threshold and it's been my home from home in London ever since.

As soon as I walked in, I could feel my shoulders dropping in relief. I found a quiet corner and subsided in a comfortable wing chair with a Pimm's. The first welcome mouthful did the trick of calming me down. *Bloody hell.* Had I seen what I thought I had? Was that really a secret romantic tryst? Surely not. How could Simon be stupid enough to become entangled with a patient? And if they were an item, how crazy was it to be making eyes at each other in a public place? Even somewhere as discreet as the private area of the Dorchester bar? Especially after everything she'd said about the eyes and ears of the media upon her.

Which indicated that, whatever I thought I'd seen, I'd been mistaken. It was nothing more than two friends having a quiet drink together, enjoying each other's company. I was her dinner date, after all. It wasn't like they were making a night of it. What was wrong with me? Was I jealous of Scarlett having other friends? How old was I, for heaven's sake?

I took my time over my drink, then headed back to the hotel, walking into the restaurant precisely on time. Scarlett was already at the table, waving to me as I approached. She stood up to hug me in a waft of Scarlett Smile. 'Great to see you, you look fab, is that a new dress?' It came out in a rush and we both burst out laughing. 'Anyone would think we hadn't seen each other for months,' she said, settling back into her seat. 'Speaking of not seeing people for ages, guess who I just ran into?'

I shook my head, feeling irrationally relieved. 'No idea. That dishy cop?'

'Nick the Greek? You're blushing, Steph. You totally need to get stuck in there, girl. Give him a call.'

'I don't think so. Come on then, tell me who you bumped into.'

'Simon. Simon Graham. He was coming out as I was coming in, we chased each other round the revolving doors a couple of times. The doormen looked totally offended. Like, you don't do that kind of thing here.' She giggled. 'Anyway, he had time for a quick drink. I tried to persuade him to stay and have dinner with us, but he's meeting friends.'

'Small world.'

'Yeah. Six degrees of Kevin Bacon. It was nice to see him. When Simon says you're looking well, it really means something. Know what I mean?' She suddenly softened and I saw a reflection of the fear she always carried with her after her diagnosis.

But the moment passed, as did my misplaced jealousy of Simon. It was a good night, the first of many over the next few months. We'd meet in town or I'd go over to the hacienda and stay overnight. A couple of times she brought Jimmy down to Brighton and we had a typically English day at the seaside. She talked about her colleagues on the TV show, the people she was working with on her merchandising, Georgie and his team, Leanne in Spain and, of course, Jimmy. Choosing a school for him was high on her list of priorities and I lost count of the number of prospectuses and websites we looked at. But Simon never came up in conversation again.

The only time I ran into him after that was at Scarlett's

birthday party. Although she'd pretty much given up on the club scene, and in spite of her regular fulminations against the vile tabloid media, she understood that she still had to make her presence felt in the red-tops. So her birthday bash was in a new triple-decker bar on the South Bank with amazing views of the river from the roof terrace. As usual at Scarlett's shindigs, I knew almost nobody except the journos, and I wasn't in the mood for them that night. I found George leaning on the balustrade looking out at the river and the crowds walking past towards the South Bank complex and the London Eye. The music pulsed around us, quieter than it was on the dance floor below, but a presence nonetheless. 'Lovely evening for it,' George said.

'Perfect venue,' I agreed.

We stood in companionable silence for a bit, then he said, 'You've been terrifically good for her, Stephanie. She's a much improved piece of merchandise since you got your hands on her.'

'You are dreadful, Georgie.'

'It's the truth, sweetie. Look around you. At least half of the people here are perfectly respectable. Most of us have never been on reality TV. Our ugly duckling has turned into a swan, I rather think.'

'It's all been her own doing.'

Before George could say more, Simon Graham moved alongside me. 'Mind if I join you?' he said, both hands on the stem of his glass in an anxious posture. He gave a quick, nervy smile. 'I don't know anybody else here,' he added, throwing himself on our mercy.

'Neither do we,' George said.

'Liar, half of them are your clients,' I said.

'That doesn't mean I want to engage socially with them, Stephanie. I fear that I no longer number among the bright young things.'

'I never did, Georgie.' I smiled at Simon. 'You're welcome to hang out with the boring old farts, even though you are clearly not one of us.' And in truth, he did look more of a piece with the other guests than us in his low-slung jeans and body-hugging black satin shirt.

Still, he stayed and we made genial, forgettable conversation about this and that for quarter of an hour or so, then Simon's phone beeped. He dipped two long fingers into his tight pocket and pulled it free, then frowned. 'I'm sorry, I have to go. Work, I'm afraid.'

'That's a pity,' George said politely.

He gave a half-shrug. 'Goes with the territory. Nice to see you both again.' And he was off, weaving through the dancers and the drinkers and the talkers.

'He seems like a nice bloke,' I said.

'If a little dull.'

'There are worse things than dull.'

'Indeed, Stephanie. And I suspect both of us have had rather too much of them. Personally, I think dull rather a fine quality in a doctor. It suggests a devotion to his work which always inspires confidence.'

'Obviously worked on Scarlett,' I said.

George raised his eyebrows in an arch expression. 'Meaning what?'

'Only that she invited him to her party.'

George chuckled. 'I think she invited the entire contents of her phone contact list to her party.' He looked at his watch. 'Are you staying in town tonight?'

'I've got a room at my club.'

Now his smile was wholehearted. 'How very splendid. The University Women's, I assume? Are you ready to let me drop you off on my way back to Chelsea?'

I was ready. Maybe if there had been a handsome copper around, I'd have contemplated dancing till dawn. But I was out of luck on that score. Clearly his number hadn't made it into Scarlett's phone memory. We skirted the crowd, looking for Scarlett, fighting against the press of bodies and the growing volume of the music.

We found her near the top of the stairs leading to the dance floor, vaguely gyrating with a couple of fashion models. 'We're off,' I said. 'Great party.'

'Really?'

'Really. Are you having fun?'

'I'm having a ball,' she said, stepping away from the models and steering us towards the lift that would take us to the ground-floor exit. I noticed her wince as she turned.

'Are you OK?' I asked when we'd emerged from the crowd on to the landing. I gestured to her naked midriff. 'You made a face.'

'It's nothing. I think I must have put my back out picking Jimmy up. It's been bothering me the last couple of days. I've made an appointment with the osteopath. Little bugger's getting too heavy.' She pulled me into her arms and kissed me on the mouth. 'You're a total mother hen, Steph. You need to loosen up,' she scolded me.

'Be grateful somebody gives a toss about you, sweetie,' George said as the lift arrived.

We all laughed. And I went home and thought nothing more about Scarlett's back pain. More fool me.

42

I don't buy the red-tops unless it's for professional reasons. But I will glance at the headlines if someone on the train or in a café is hiding behind their paper. I'm only human, after all. And that's how I learned my friend was dying.

In fairness to Scarlett, she wasn't holding out on me. She'd only had the news confirmed the night before. She wasn't ready to share with anyone yet. She certainly wasn't ready for the whole bloody world to know she'd been diagnosed with terminal cancer.

The headlines screamed the story. SCARLETT'S DEATH SENTENCE. TV STAR HAS ONLY WEEKS TO LIVE. I'd only gone into Costa Coffee for a quick latte, but instead I'd been hit with the worst possible news.

I wanted to snatch the copy of the *Daily Herald* out of the hands of the plaster-stained workman reading it. But good sense prevailed and I ran out of the coffee shop and down the street to the nearest newsagent. I grabbed a copy off the shelf and threw a pound coin on the counter, not waiting for change.

I stood there on the street, the sun shining as if it had something to celebrate, and read the terrible news.

TV show host Scarlett Higgins has been diagnosed with terminal cancer. The former *Goldfish Bowl* star has been told she has only weeks to live.

Last year, Scarlett was treated for breast cancer. After undergoing surgery and chemotherapy, she was given the all-clear.

But doctors have revealed her body is riddled with secondary cancers which have invaded vital organs and her spine. The cancer is inoperable.

One of her medical team said, 'I'm afraid the news is as bad as it gets. The tests have confirmed our worst fears.'

Scarlett was not available for comment last night. Her agent, George Lyall, said, 'This is devastating news. I would ask that you respect Scarlett's privacy while she comes to terms with it.'

Only last year, tragic Scarlett's ex-husband, DJ Joshu, died from a drug overdose. *Cont p3–4.*

The rest of the article was a rehash of Scarlett's background and career, lavish with pics of Scarlett with Joshu, Scarlett with Jimmy, Scarlett (or possibly Leanne) falling out of a limo, Scarlett with shaved head and swimsuit promoting her charity swimathon for Timonescu. My eyes scanned the article, but nothing was really sinking in. I was appalled, numbed, shattered by the news.

I closed the paper and walked the short distance home. It was as if I had forgotten how to walk. Every step of the way needed concentration, like when I'd had to learn how to walk properly again after the accident.

I don't remember how I got there, but I seemed to come to on the doorstep, fumbling the key into the lock. I wasn't sure what to do when I got inside. My first instinct was to call Scarlett, but I didn't know if that was a good idea in my present state. I felt dazed and stupefied, unable to make the right connections in my head. Instead, I called George. He always knew what to do.

I had to hold for a couple of minutes. I barely noticed. And then his rich chocolate voice was on the line. I'd never noticed before how very comforting his voice is. But then, I'd never needed comfort from him before. 'Stephanie, my dear. You've heard the terrible news, I take it?'

'Is it true?'

'Lamentably true, I'm afraid. I'm so sorry, Stephanie. I know how fond you are of her. And she of you. We've no idea how the media got hold of it. Someone at the clinic must have leaked.'

'Some greedy selfish pig,' I said. 'What happened?'

'She was having back pain—'

'I remember, at her birthday party last month. She was complaining about it.'

'That's right. Her osteopath couldn't resolve it and she was concerned enough to suggest Scarlett consult a doctor. The only doctor she knows enough to trust is Simon Graham, so she went to see him. And because cancer is always Simon's first thought, he gave her an MRI. And the shocking truth was there to see.'

'Christ,' I said. 'And when was this?'

'A couple of days ago. Simon's very thorough and he insisted that she not panic until he'd carried out further tests. The results came through yesterday afternoon and he tried to call her. She wasn't answering her phone because she was on set. So he left a voicemail confirming that what they had feared was indeed the case.'

'That sounds suspiciously like the quote in the paper.'

'That's what Scarlett said too. She's convinced someone hacked her voicemail. But I think it's more likely that a nurse or technician overheard Simon leave the message and got on the blower to some hack at the *Herald*. These people sicken

311

me,' he said, sounding thoroughly disgusted. 'They know no boundaries of taste or decency. The woman has a child, for God's sake.'

His anger was shielding his sorrow. It's the only way men like George know how to express their pain. I was pretty sure George was as distraught as I was. How much worse must it have been for Scarlett? She'd fought through so much, but this was one battle she couldn't win. 'How is she? Or is that a stupid question?'

'Still stunned, I think. Is there any possibility you might get over there? I really think she ought to have someone with her who cares about her. I'm stuck here holding the fort. But if you could . . .'

'That was my first thought. But I wanted to check with you. I wondered if maybe she wanted to be left alone with Jimmy.'

George made a strange, choking sound, like a man struggling with his composure in the face of tears. 'Stephanie, if I was attempting to deal with what Scarlett has on her plate at present, I would want my best friend by my side. You know she won't ask. But she would be much better off with you there. Please, if you can, go to her.'

I didn't need telling twice. I wasn't sure whether I was fit to drive; I kept breaking down in tears and having to pull over on to the hard shoulder. Even so, driving would be a lot quicker than trains and cabs. And it would provoke less curiosity. Nothing attracts attention like sobbing on public transport. I really didn't feel up to dealing with the kindness of strangers. As it was, I had to convince one traffic cop that I wasn't having some sort of nervous breakdown.

Of course, when I got to the hacienda, it was even more of a media brawl than when Joshu died. Scarlett had a much higher national profile than her ex-husband and they all wanted a piece of her tragedy. There was something profoundly disgusting about their display. The hunger, the lack of

compassion, the blatant parasitism of their desire to feed off
Scarlett's suffering: it all made me feel tainted by my own tan-
gential connection to their world. The only real difference
between us was that I operated by consent. I drew a line that
respected what my subjects wanted to keep private. But we
were all in the business of satisfying an appetite that was
rooted in prurience. As I inched my car forward through the
press of press, I wondered whether I needed to reconsider how
I earn my living.

For a moment it seemed they were actually going to try to
follow me into the courtyard, but good sense prevailed and
they didn't spill in behind me. When I got out of the car I
could still hear them baying their questions in my wake.
Horrible.

The kitchen was empty and the house had the feel of a
place where nobody's home. At this time of day, Jimmy would
be at nursery, but Marina should be around somewhere, doing
housekeeper things. 'Hello?' I called. My voice echoed back at
me. No signs of life in the living room or in the guest rooms. I
carried on to what I always thought of as the leisure club,
wondering if I'd find Scarlett in the pool, relentlessly swimming lengths in spite of her pain. But she wasn't there either.

The gym was empty too. But when I peeped through the
window in the sauna door, there she was, hunched naked on
the top bench, her head in her hands. I stepped back before
she could sense my presence and went through to the changing room. I undressed quickly. My hand was halfway to a
swimsuit when I thought, *Fuck it. Meet her on her own terms for
once.*

Scarlett barely looked up when I walked in. When she took
in my nakedness, she gave a tired little smile and said,
'Fucking hell, it must be bad if this is how you show you're on
my side.' Her eyes were puffy and swollen, and she looked as
if she'd lost weight.

I climbed up beside her and put my arm around her. Thank God it wasn't too hot in there for once. It felt strange to be naked with another woman, but only because I'm a bit shy about my body, especially when I compare it to an impressive specimen like Scarlett. 'I'm so sorry,' I said, aware of how inadequate the words were. 'I'd take the bullet for you if I could.'

'I'd let you, an' all.' She groaned. 'It's Jimmy I feel for. First he loses his dad and now he's going to lose his mum.'

'It's not a done deal, surely? There must be some treatment they can try?'

'Simon came round first thing,' she said. 'He'd have been here last night instead of relying on a voicemail, only one of his patients was dying and he needed to be there.' She sighed. 'It's inoperable. I'm riddled with it, Steph. It's in my liver, my pancreas, my colon, my spine, my lungs. I'm a fucking walking cancer. They can give me chemo, but that's not going to give me more than a few months, and it'll be a few months of feeling like shit. You remember how it was before.'

'What's the alternative?'

'No chemo. Just pain relief. That way, at least I get a bit of time with Jimmy where I'm not throwing up or feeling too tired to be arsed with him. And I don't have to be in hospital either. I can stay here in my own home till the end. Simon's promised me that. I'll have to go into the clinic for check-ups a couple of times, but that's all.' She made it sound as insignificant as a trip to the supermarket. Her stoicism amazed me.

'If that's what you want,' I said.

She tilted her head back, squeezing her eyes shut. 'None of it's what I want,' she shouted. 'I want a life. I want to see my boy grow up. I don't want to die.' Her voice cracked and so did her fortitude. Tears trickled out from her clenched eyelids and her lips curled back in a rictus of anguish. I put my hand on her head and pulled her into my arms. I could feel myself choking up, and before long I was crying silently with her.

We stayed in the sauna for a while, sobbing and sweating and generally being maudlin and miserable. With good reason, it must be said. 'Where's Marina?' I eventually asked.

'I told her to take Jimmy off somewhere for a few days. Euro Disney or something. Just till the fuss dies down a bit. I need to get myself together. I don't want him to see me in bits. Or to have those fuckers outside snapping him every time he goes out the gate.' She shook her head. 'How the fuck did they find out so fast? They must have hacked my voicemail, it's the only thing that makes sense.'

'You think? Surely it's more likely that someone from the clinic leaked it.'

'They'd have known a lot more, though,' Scarlett said. It was a good point, one that I hadn't considered. 'I hate that I don't even have control over my own terminal bloody illness. I wanted to have a little bit of dignity about the whole thing. Not this bloody circus. I can't help thinking those fuckers created the stress that made me ill in the first place. Vultures. Can't wait to cash in.' She managed another tired smile. 'If anybody's going to make a bob or two out of me dying, it should be me, not some bloody hack or some Judas that works for Simon.'

It might sound strange that Scarlett was thinking about the cash implications of her announcement. But at that point, I thought I understood where she was coming from. Scarlett's working capital was her fame. Now it had a strictly limited shelf life. The swimathon might outlive her. But her fragrances and her endorsements would likely die with her. Unlike authors and musicians whose work carries on earning after their death, a celebrity's earning power dies with them. And Scarlett had a child she needed to provide for, as well as a charitable foundation whose work she presumably wanted to maintain. Of course she had half an eye on the bottom line.

She leaned into me. 'Are you up for another book? The last will and testament? The diary of a dignified death? It would be a bit classier than another pile of celebrity bollocks. Everybody's talking about going to Switzerland to that Dignitas place, whether we should be allowed to choose how we die. We could do a book about how I manage it.' Her enthusiasm might have seemed bizarre to an outsider. But to us it made perfect sense.

'Why not? If Biba wants it, we'll give it to her.'

When we couldn't stand the heat any longer, we moved to the pool. Scarlett lowered herself gingerly into the water. Already I could see the changes in the way she moved – normally she launched herself at the water in a running dive and broke the surface with a powerful overarm stroke. But today, a slow breast stroke was all she was up for. She seemed to be ageing in front of my eyes.

And that was only the start of it. Her decline was frightening. The weight seemed to fall off her. By the time Jimmy and Marina came back a few days later, I reckoned she'd already lost half a stone. She had no interest in food. 'It all tastes grey,' she said. And when she could bring herself to eat, she couldn't keep it down for long.

Leanne turned up the day after the news broke. I looked at her with new eyes thanks to Scarlett's revelations, but there seemed to be nothing artificial about her grief. That first night, after Scarlett had gone to bed, we sat up late in the kitchen, drinking brandy and railing against the injustice of it all. When we ran out of rant, I asked her how it was going in Spain. 'I like it,' she said. 'The weather's lovely and the people are friendly. It's quite nice to go to a place where nobody's made their mind up about you before you get there. It's like a clean slate.'

'I think we all fancy that sometimes. Ditch the past and start from scratch.'

'What? Even you, Steph? With your lovely life?'

I stuck my tongue out at her. 'Even me. It's not all loveliness. Remember all that hassle with Pete?'

'Yeah, but that's history now.'

I thought back to Joshu's funeral. 'I think so. I hope so. And business? How's that working out?'

Her smile was so open I couldn't believe it was anything other than the whole truth. 'Pretty good, actually. I'm starting to build up a nice little clientele. There wasn't any real competition. Before I set up, you had to go down Fuengirola or Benalmadena to get your nails done by somebody English. And let's face it, they all prefer somebody English. Bunch of racists, most of them. They act like the Spanish are trained monkeys.' She chuckled. 'Mind you, there's a lot of the Spanish play up to that. They've got the Manuel act off to a T.'

I was glad to see Leanne back at the hacienda. She had a sense of fun and she lightened the atmosphere. And if I'm honest, I was glad to have someone to share Scarlett's final journey with. It would have been a heavy burden to carry alone.

Leanne wasn't the only one picking up a share of the weight. The only doctor Scarlett wanted near her was Simon Graham. She trusted him, she said. And she needed someone medical that she could trust now the end was getting near. She insisted he take a leave of absence from the clinic, and he more or less went along with her demands. He generally went in to the clinic for a couple of hours in the late morning two or three times a week. But other than that, he was at the hacienda. He moved a single bed into her dressing room and spent the nights there, in case she needed help. She didn't want a stranger nursing her either. So Marina added nurse to her list of household jobs whenever Simon needed a hand.

Simon and Marina became part of the late-night kitchen set.

It was an odd group, brought together for the saddest of reasons. We started playing poker to pass the time and often we'd play for hours, trying to take our minds off the dying woman and the sleeping child upstairs. Simon bought a set of proper poker chips and we sat around the table trying to figure each other out. I'd learned to play poker with Pete and his musician buddies, and I'd found it an interesting way to gain an insight into people's personalities. Simon always took his time, weighing the odds (he claimed), before finally betting conservatively. Of all of us, he made the best decisions about when to fold. A man who would always cut his losses and come out even.

Leanne was more reckless, often playing no-hope hands down to the bitter end because she couldn't bear to be too far from the action. I could generally tell when she had something worth betting because she would shut up and follow the field. When she went out on a limb, I knew she had nothing worth a damn.

Marina was hardest to read. There was no tell when she looked at her cards. She always hung back on the first round but then there was no pattern to how she bet. As a result, she generally managed to out-bluff the rest of us. If we'd been playing for money instead of ceramic chips, she'd have fleeced us all.

Me, I bet my hand. I always bet my hand and I suspect that makes me pretty easy to read. I don't think my face gives me away; it's my inability to bet counter to the cards I'm looking at in my hand and on the table. I'm not good at bluffing – or lying, as I like to think of it.

Most mornings, I spent an hour or two with Scarlett in her bedroom that smelled of Scarlett Smile and antiseptic. Those were the gentlest interviews I've ever done. I'd suggest an avenue to explore and she'd talk for as long as she had strength. We covered all sorts of things – motherhood from both sides, coping with losing a parent, the double grief of her marriage ending followed by Joshu's death, putting her house in order for her own death. She shied away from nothing, openly talking of mistakes, regrets and missed opportunities. She did tire easily but she wasn't losing weight so rapidly now and she assured me that Simon was keeping her pain-free. 'It's bloody lovely, that bit of it,' she said. 'Morphine just makes me float. Only drug I ever took to.'

One morning, as I settled myself in the chair and laid out my recorder and notebook, she pointed to the machine. 'Leave that off a minute,' she said. 'I need to talk to you woman to woman. Not for publication.'

Wondering what was coming, I nodded. 'No problem. What's on your mind?'

She went straight to the point. Now she knew she was dying, there was no time wasted with small talk. 'You weren't keen on being Jimmy's godmother, I know that.'

I had a cold, sinking feeling in my stomach. I knew what was coming and I didn't know how to resist. 'You know I never wanted kids,' I reminded her. I had a horrible feeling I was wasting my breath.

'I know. But you've done a great job. You've got to know him, you've played with him and read to him and taken him out for the day. You buy thoughtful presents for him and you don't overindulge him. I couldn't have asked for a better god-mother.'

'Thanks.' I gave a half-shrug. 'I tried to do what was best for him.'

'Exactly. When we talked about this before, neither of us really believed push would come to shove. I was convinced deep down I was going to beat this fucking disease. And I think you were too. So it wasn't real, what we agreed.'

For one wonderful moment I thought I was going to get a reprieve. Scarlett had finally come to her senses and she was going to leave Jimmy in Leanne's care. Keep it in the family.

319

But no such luck. 'This time it is real,' she said. 'We both know I'm dying. So I'm going to say again what I said the last time. You're the person I want to take care of Jimmy. It's in the will.' She managed the ghost of a smile. 'You can't get out of it, Steph. I need to know that he's in safe hands, and that's you.'

'Leanne would be—'

'A disaster,' she said, slapping her hand softly on the duvet to make her point. 'You know that. I've not got the strength to argue with you, Steph. I need to know my boy's sorted. Promise me you'll look after him.'

What else could I say? 'I promise. I'll take as much care of him as I would if he was my own.'

And that was that. My life transformed in the space of quarter of an hour. Of course, I assumed there would be an inheritance for Jimmy. Not that I was in it for the money. Oddly enough, I was thinking of Jimmy. Thinking that he deserved as little disruption as possible, so I'd have to sell or rent my house in Brighton and move into the hacienda. Jimmy might have lost the people he loved most, but at least he'd be in familiar surroundings, which had to help. Hopefully there would be a bit of money to make it possible for us to carry on living here. And maybe enough left over to do something about the woeful décor. It never crossed my mind that she wouldn't leave her beloved boy a penny.

43

After three weeks of living under siege in the hacienda, I needed to go back to Brighton for a couple of days. I told the kitchen poker school I needed to pick up my mail and pay my bills. The truth was I was desperate for a few hours on my own, in my own space. I was looking at a future that held precious little prospect of that, with a child to raise. I thought I was entitled to a last sliver of me time.

I savoured every moment of those three days. Two nights in my own bed. Comfort food in my own kitchen. Early morning walks along the promenade. A pub quiz night. The sound of my own music on speakers rather than earbuds. Don't get me wrong, I didn't begrudge Scarlett my time and energy. I just needed to recharge my batteries. *Reculer pour mieux sauter,* as they say on the other side of the churning grey waves I walked beside.

When I got back, the landscape had changed. Simon was sitting in the kitchen on his own, reading a professional journal. No Marina, no Leanne. He tossed his magazine on the table and jumped up to greet me with air kisses on either cheek. He was wearing a ratty Boston Red Sox replica shirt and black cargoes that showed off slim, shapely calves. He had better legs than me, I noted, a tad bitterly. I let him mix me a gin and tonic to match his. 'Where is everybody?' I asked.

He pushed his hair back from his forehead and gave me the pained, boyish smile. 'Marina's sitting with Scarlett. They're watching some romcom. I bowed out on the basis that my genitals are on the outside of my body. And Leanne is, I believe, in Spain.'

'In Spain? Why? What happened?'

'They had a major bust-up. Leanne decided she needed to have a come-to-Jesus talk with Scarlett about the importance of family as far as bringing up Jimmy is concerned. Scarlett told her that it was already arranged and you are taking care of the kid. There was a bit of to-ing and fro-ing, then Leanne accused you of being a gold-digger. That you've only ever been interested in what you could make out of Scarlett and you only agreed to take the kid on because of his inheritance.'

'Ouch. Cheeky bitch. I hope Scarlett didn't fall for that.' I was genuinely outraged.

Simon smiled and patted my hand. 'Not for a nanosecond. She told Leanne not to judge other people by her own shitty motives. That she knew Leanne would stop at nothing to get what she wanted and she, Scarlett, had made bloody sure that she wouldn't get her clutches on Jimmy. Because if anybody was looking at Jimmy as a meal ticket, it's Leanne. And why didn't Leanne fuck off back to Spain instead of hanging round like a fucking vulture?'

'Ah. Not a friendly parting then?'

'Anything but. Leanne flounced out and got straight online. I took her up to Stansted yesterday morning. She was still sulking. She gave me hell for not weighing in on her side.' He looked plaintive. 'When I told her I thought Scarlett had made the right choice, she looked like she wanted to stab me. She had a few choice words for me, too. I tried to explain that it was not actually helping my career for me to take a leave of absence to care for Scarlett, but she kept on about me wanting to become the doctor to the stars.'

I gave a bitter laugh. 'She really has no idea how the world works.'

'None whatsoever. Me, I'd pay money not to become doctor to the stars. Scarlett's the exception. Mostly they are egocentric monsters. Anyway, Leanne has revealed her true colours. So the poker school is down to three.'

Which was fine by me, now that I knew what Leanne really thought of me. So the world had contracted to four of us revolving like satellites round Scarlett. Jimmy was the bewildered one, not really understanding what was going on and why Mummy was spending most of her time in bed. Scarlett tried to conserve energy for him every day, but the nearer she came to death, the harder it became. In the final few days, it was all she could manage to snuggle with him while he watched cartoons in bed with her.

When he wasn't at nursery, one of us would take charge of him. We'd play in the pool, kick a ball round the garden, watch videos or build rambling Lego structures across his bedroom floor. I used to sit on the window seat with him and work my way through his collection of picture books. I think he found me quite comforting to be with. When I look back on those few weeks, it's with a mixture of sadness and contentment; I think I did him a bit of good and built a bridge into our future.

The only interruption to our routine came when the team from *Yes!* magazine turned up for the final photo shoot, complete with stylist and make-up artist. I know there were people who thought it was pretty sick, but Scarlett wanted the world to see what a woman dying of cancer looked like. 'We shut sick people away so we don't have to confront the fact that we're all going to die,' she said. 'I want to show them that I'm still a human being, still the woman I always was.' Then that achingly sad smile. 'And it's a few extra quid in the coffers,' she added.

When the end came, it was very peaceful. We were all in the room when Simon loaded up the last bolus of saline and refilled the morphine pump. Jimmy kissed Scarlett and gave her a last cuddle. I held her in my arms for the last time, unstoppable tears running down my face. Her courage in the face of impending death had been remarkable. The final act of a remarkable woman. I walked Jimmy out of the room and took him to bed.

I was still sitting in his room, watching him sleep, when Simon came through to tell me it was all over. I stood up and wrapped my arms round him as he shook with the force of his tears. 'I'm sorry,' he kept saying. 'If only I could have saved her ... I'm sorry.'

'You did your best. Nobody could have given her better care.'

'She was special,' he gulped. He drew away from me, folding his arms over his chest, hands on his shaking shoulders. Somehow, he pulled himself together. 'I need to call the funeral director,' he said. 'They'll take her away and prepare her. And I need to sign the death certificate.' He bit his lip. 'I've lost my share of patients, Stephanie,' he said, 'but I don't think I ever minded more.'

44

The funeral was a circus. A perfectly orchestrated circus, but a circus nevertheless. Scarlett had left detailed instructions which it fell to George and me to carry out. And carry them out we did, even though our teeth were gritted for most of the time.

The media were frustrated by the lack of a grieving relict. We knew they would dog our every step until they got something for the front page, so we arranged for them to have a single pool photographer take a series of shots of Jimmy carrying a posy of flowers into the funeral parlour where his mother was laid out. In his second black suit of the year, he walked in with bowed head, not quite five and already apparently master of his own public image.

Once the media had the pics they wanted, they decamped from the hacienda. There was nothing to see now Scarlett was gone, after all. Their place by the side of the country lane was swiftly taken by the tributes left by Scarlett's army of fans. Bunches of flowers, cards and soft toys soon covered the verges and we all prayed that the rain would stay away. Banks of sodden tributes would be an eyesore that would provoke complaints to the council from the other residents of the lane, who had never approved of Scarlett or what she brought in her wake. It would be one more hassle we could do without.

The grown-ups went for a viewing before they closed the coffin. I barely glanced at her; I've never understood the need to mourn with the dead in your eyeline. From what I saw, they'd done a good job on her. She looked less gaunt than I expected, and Marina had chosen one of her signature hats to cover her baldness, the deep watermelon shade giving a welcome splash of colour to the interior of the woven willow coffin. 'It looks like we're sending her off in a giant picnic basket,' George said.

'It's what she wanted,' Simon said. 'She cared about the planet. Even if she wasn't going to be here, Jimmy's got to grow up in this world.'

George sighed. 'I know, I know. It just looks ... odd, that's all. I'm accustomed to a more traditional look.'

On the day of the funeral, George arranged for a driver to collect Scarlett's mother and sister from King's Cross Station. To her final days Scarlett had been adamant that she didn't want Chrissie and Jade at her bedside. She didn't want them to so much as set foot in her house. The instructions were to provide them with first-class return tickets from Leeds and a hotel room if they needed to stay overnight. George had booked them into a decent hotel near King's Cross. In an act that would have made Scarlett smile, he'd chosen one that had no bar or restaurant.

Marina, Jimmy and I were taken from the hacienda to the nearby funeral home by 1940s black Rolls Royce. I couldn't help feeling that Leanne should have been with us, but she hadn't turned up. The day after Scarlett's death, Simon said he'd called to try and persuade her to put the rift behind her and pay her last respects with the rest of us. But Leanne had been adamant that Scarlett hadn't wanted her there, so she would stay away. She wasn't going to be two-faced about it. It seemed a sad end to what had been one of the few important relationships in Scarlett's life.

There were two other vintage Rollers in the cortège, one carrying Simon and George, plus the two assistants from the agency who had worked most closely with Scarlett. The third was occupied by the team from Scarlett's TV chat show – her co-host, the producer, her stylist and a couple of others I hadn't met before. Chrissie and Jade were in a black BMW bringing up the tail.

The hearse itself was a horse-drawn carriage, all four bay horses with black plumes on their headbands. They were preceded by two professional mourners, their silk top hats beribboned and their black Crombie coats perfectly fitting their burly frames. You could hardly see the coffin for the floral tributes. MUMMY from Jimmy, of course. SCARLETT along one side from the TV channel and SMILE in the style of the logo from the perfume company. I hadn't seen a cortège that over the top since a fellow ghost writer had persuaded me to come with him to a Kray family funeral.

There must have been thousands of fans lining the half-mile route from the funeral home to the crematorium. They wept, they cheered. They threw flowers and, bizarrely, confetti at the hearse. Once we had passed, they abandoned the pavements and fell into step behind the cortège. The police, there to prevent any public order offences, were hopelessly outnumbered. They looked completely bewildered, taken aback by this outpouring of public sorrow for a Northern underclass underdog who had somehow won people's hearts.

The Prime Minister himself had jumped on the bandwagon. The local MP had got to his feet in the House of Commons and asked if the PM had plans to extend breast screening to younger women in the light of Scarlett's tragic death. The PM had put his serious face on and said, 'I was saddened to hear of the death of Scarlett Higgins, a brave young woman who demonstrated how it's possible in today's Britain to triumph over adversity and build a successful career. She brought delight to us all and she will be sorely missed. I will ask the Health Secretary to write to the Honourable Member in response to his question.' I hoped he was watching the live coverage on the satellite news channels, so he could see what popularity looked like.

When we reached the crematorium the funeral director emerged with a large wicker basket. As the pall bearers slid the coffin out and on to their shoulders, he opened the basket and released a dozen white doves into the blue sky in a flurry of feathers. The crowd gasped at the sight. A moment of pure theatre. I was making mental notes every step of the way; this would be the final chapter of the final Scarlett book, after all.

Outside the crematorium, there were giant screens relaying the service so the punters could share the grief. Inside, we followed the coffin down the aisle. Jimmy's hand gripped mine so tightly I knew I'd have tiny half-moon bruises across my palm from his fingernails. He was my responsibility now, and it weighed heavily on me. Again, I wished Leanne was here to share it with me. Marina was all very well, but she wasn't family. And besides, she would be leaving soon to take up the job Scarlett had promised her in Romania. I couldn't afford the cousin she'd offered Scarlett, nor did I have room in my small house for live-in help. I was going to have to get used to doing this by myself.

Inside, there were more flowers everywhere and the air was filled with the fragrance of Scarlett Smile. I was rapidly reaching the point where I never wanted to smell that bloody perfume again. The crematorium was crammed with faces from the pages of the red-tops and the slag mags. It was a paparazzo's C-list *collezione*. I hoped Maggie wasn't going to work the room at the wake. I'd had enough celebrity biography to last me a lifetime. Over the past couple of weeks, I'd come to a firm decision about my future. No more books with people who were only famous for being famous. From now on, there would have to be genuine achievement on the table to garner my interest.

The service managed to deliver more dignity than I would have expected. Liam Burke, whose rich Irish brogue delivered the pronouncements of Big Fish to the *Goldfish Bowl* contenders, read Christina Rossetti; the producer of *Real Life TV* spoke movingly about working with Scarlett – her creativity, her sense of what would please the viewers, her willingness to work hard, her sense of humour; George spoke about her rise from humble beginnings and the pleasure she'd given to everyone who knew her (an exaggeration that nobody was going to quarrel with that day); and the lead singer of a boy band she'd interviewed on her first show sang 'I'll Be Seeing You'. And yes, I cried.

Jimmy clung to me throughout the service, his little body trembling with an overdose of emotion. In the end, I scooped him up into my lap and he threw his arms round my neck as if he would never let me go. I rubbed his back and made soothing noises. I didn't know what else to do.

Once the service was over, George whisked us all back to the waiting cars. 'I'm not doing a bloody receiving line,' he said firmly. 'If we do, we'll have to include Jade and Chrissie and I am not having that.'

From a distance, they didn't look too bad. I said as much to George. 'I sent one of my girls up to Leeds to dress them and travel with them. So they're relatively sober and relatively straight. I have no confidence that state will survive the wake, however. We need to keep the bloody media away from them in case it all gets grisly.'

'What about Jimmy? Does he have to meet them?'

We'd reached the cars now. George looked around, uncharacteristically indecisive. 'I'll travel with you,' he said, getting in alongside Marina and me. Jimmy was still attached to me like a baby monkey. 'I'd like to keep him away from them if we can. My girlie said they're making noises about claiming Jimmy.' His mouth curled as if he'd encountered a bad smell. 'They see him as a meal ticket, of course.'

'I'll take him home,' Marina said. 'I don't need to be at the party.' She shrugged one shoulder. 'I don't know anyone and it's not necessary for me to remember Scarlett that way. Me and Jimmy, we'll go back to the house and take off our funeral clothes and have ourselves some fun.'

'You're sure you don't mind?' George said.

'I went to Joshu's memorial and I hated it,' Marina said. 'It's no loss to me. And better for Jimmy to go home and not be paraded like a prize pig.'

That wasn't quite how I would have put it, but I saw her point. And it was a relief, I had to admit. The last thing I wanted was a public tug of war over Scarlett's son. As it turned out, we couldn't have played it better. I was barely in the door of the hotel ballroom where the wake was being held when Chrissie and Jade Higgins swaggered up to me, drinks in hand. A space cleared around us as if by magic. One thing about slebs – they can sense handbags at dawn at fifty paces and they always like to give the antagonists plenty of room to make a show of themselves.

'Where's my grandson?' Chrissie wasn't about to bother with details like introductions. Up close, I could see the damage that distance had obscured. Her skin was rough, broken veins imperfectly covered by foundation. Too much mascara and shadow wasn't enough of a distraction from the yellow tinge to the whites of her eyes or the pouchy bags beneath them. Her teeth were yellow and chipped, and the closer she got, the more her rank breath sickened me. Her arms and legs were skinny, but her torso was round and hard, like a little barrel. If you'd been looking for Scarlett's mother, you wouldn't have picked her out of a line-up.

'You must be Mrs Higgins,' I said. 'I'm sorry we're meeting in such sad circumstances.'

She looked baffled by my politeness, like a bulldog confronted with a kid blowing bubbles. Not so Jade, who was hovering at her mother's shoulder, stick-thin and pale, junkie chic from head to toe. The sort who always looks grubby, even straight from the shower. 'Don't come the toff with us, you posh bitch,' she snarled. 'Where's our lad? What have you done with our Jimmy?'

Luckily for me, George was at my shoulder, the perfect mixture of urbanity and steel. 'In no sense is Jimmy yours,' he said. 'Scarlett made her intentions perfectly clear. If you are unhappy about that, I suggest you employ a lawyer.'

'A fucking lawyer? You think I need a fucking lawyer to tell me who my own family are? That boy's my grandson.' Chrissie pointed at me dramatically. I could hear cameras clicking all around me. 'She's got no claim on him. She's only after our Scarlett's money.'

'Greedy bitch,' Jade echoed.

I knew I was lost if I engaged with them. I'd be dragged down to their level and frankly they had more experience at the scummy end of the argument. But it was tempting. As if sensing this, George put a hand on my arm. 'I doubt you could even tell me the boy's birthday,' he said dismissively.

'Shut your yap, arsehole.' This from Jade. 'It's not you we're talking to. It's the scheming conniving bitch here that needs to answer to Jimmy's family.'

George shook his head. 'You're wasting your time. If you're trying to screw some hard-done-by deal out of a tabloid, let me say loud and clear, Scarlett put a roof over your heads and paid your bills for the last six years. In exchange, all she

331

wanted was for you to stay away from her. The boy is nothing to do with you. Now either you behave like civilised people or I will have you thrown out of here.'

Chrissie threw herself at him, fists flailing. Before she could make contact, Simon grabbed her from behind, pinning her arms to her side with the ease of practice. 'Time to walk away, Chrissie,' he said, backing her away from George. 'Come on, let's have a drink and a little talk about Scarlett.'

She gave in ungracefully. But as Simon started to turn her away from us, she hawked up a gob of smoker's phlegm and spat it full force towards George. Startled, he stepped back just in time and it splatted on the wooden boards centimetres from his shiny black lace-ups. He looked at the disgusting gobbet then stared at Chrissie and Jade in retreat. 'Excellent,' he said softly to me. 'Spitting is not a good look for the tabloids. Dear Chrissie's blown her chance of getting one of them in her corner. They know that moment's going to be all over YouTube by bedtime.'

'Do you think they will try to get custody of Jimmy?'

'They don't have a leg to stand on, which any lawyer worth their salt will tell them.' He sighed. 'Christ, I need a drink. This is like one of Dante's circles of hell.'

Nothing I could argue with there. Nor could I see much point in us being there. I was with Marina. I didn't need this in order to mourn Scarlett. It was an ordeal that had to be endured. And always at the back of my mind as I scanned the room and made Scarlett small talk with people I barely knew was the fear that Pete would use this event the same way he'd used Joshu's memorial – to get his claws back into me.

So I was only half-listening when one of the hacks button-holed me and started in on how wonderful it was of me to take Jimmy on. 'He's my godson,' I said. 'I was there when he was born and I've been part of his life ever since. I'm the lucky one here.'

'All the same,' she persisted. 'To take on someone else's kid when there's no financial provision is a big ask. You get top marks in my book.'

I must have looked puzzled, for she gave me a look of transparently fake concern. 'You didn't know? She's left everything to her charity. Every last penny. The kid doesn't get a shilling.'

45

I found George over by the buffet, delicately nibbling a sausage roll and surveying the room like a hawk waiting for prey to stoop. 'I've just had a very bizarre conversation with a *Herald* hackette,' I said. 'One of those where you have to pretend you know what they're talking about or else you look like a complete twat.'

George raised his eyebrows. I think it still surprises him when I use sweary words. 'How very awkward for you. What was she saying?'

'George, do you know anything about the terms of Scarlett's will?' Sometimes, taking a leaf out of Chrissie Higgins' book seems like the best line of approach. Especially when you're dealing with a master of diplomacy like Georgie.

His smile was pained. He wrapped the remains of the sausage roll in a cocktail napkin and put it down. 'Ah,' he said, reaching for his gin and tonic.

'So it's true then?'

He waved his free hand in a way that I think was meant to be nonchalant. 'I don't know what you've been told, Stephanie.'

'My friendly reptile reckons Scarlett left the lot to her charity. Everything goes to the TOmorrow charitable trust. The house, the cash, the merchandising rights. The whole lot. Is that right?'

'I was planning on sitting you down and telling you later in the week,' he said, his eyes hangdog.

'For fuck's sake,' I said. 'Jimmy doesn't get a thing?'

'Personal effects, that's all. Which essentially means jewellery.' His smile was like the grimace of a man going down for the third time. 'There are some rather good pieces.'

'You don't think I'm going to sell his mother's jewellery, do you? Christ, George, what do you take me for? And why am I only hearing about this now?'

'Please, keep your voice down, Stephanie. There are ears all around us. It's not good to air this in public. Let's walk.' He steered me out of the ballroom and down the hall through the hotel reception to the car park. We ended up in a hideous grotto, built, I suspect, for the benefit of wedding photographers. 'I'm sorry you were kept in the dark, but Scarlett was most insistent.'

'Why? Did she think I was like her scummy relatives? That I'd only take Jimmy on if he came stuffed with tenners? How do you think that makes me feel, George?' I was probably shouting by then but I was past caring.

'I entirely agree with you. And that's precisely what I said to Scarlett when she told me what she'd done. I knew you wouldn't walk away from the boy, whatever the financial arrangement.' Again the pained smile. 'Poor Scarlett didn't have the benefit of our experience. She still found it hard to trust people where money was concerned. That's why she paid Chrissie's utility bills directly rather than give her the money for them.'

I threw my hands in the air. 'I can't believe she's left nothing for Jimmy. What about a trust to pay for his education?' George shook his head. 'How am I supposed to explain that to him when he's old enough to understand?'

'All you can do is show him her will. I made her put a clause in explaining why she was doing what she did.'

'Really? There's an explanation? It's not just that her bloody cancer spread to her brain?'

George steered me over to a curved stone bench and sat down. He crossed one elegant leg over the other and took a cigar case from his inside pocket. He took out a small cigar and lit it with a match from a cardboard book advertising a bar in New Orleans. It was only the second or third time in our acquaintance I'd seen him smoke. A measure, then, of how stressful he was finding this conversation.

He exhaled a mouthful of aromatic blue smoke and fixed his sorrowful gaze somewhere in the middle distance. 'Her position goes thus. She started with nothing. Less than nothing, one might say, given her disadvantages. And purely by her own hard work and determination, she made it. Along the way, she saw a lot of spoiled brats. People who had wasted the opportunities their lives had laid on a plate for them. She talked about Joshu in that regard. A boy who had both brains and choices and who opted for what she called "arsing about with a set of decks". She was determined that her son would not go the same way. Scarlett worked for everything she had, and she valued it. She wanted him to have the same drive and the same satisfactions. Not to hand him the easy life on a platter. And that's why she decided not to make him a child of privilege.'

It made a twisted kind of sense. Scarlett knew the level I lived at – comfortable, but not lavish. She knew I could afford the upkeep of a child, but not the indulgences of the rich. I only wished she'd trusted me enough to share her decision. 'I can see her point,' I said. 'It would have been nice to hear it from her and not some tabloid hack, though.'

George blew a perfect smoke ring. Of course he did. I suspect George was born with the ability to blow perfect smoke rings. 'Scarlett didn't always observe the niceties of civilised intercourse,' he said wearily. 'She did well for someone who had such a deprived upbringing. And I don't mean deprived in the material sense. I mean deprived of all those elements that make you and me at home in the world. Stuff we take for granted. Like waiting for everyone at the table to be served before we begin eating. Like understanding that it's possible to cook a curry from scratch. Like always saying thank you when someone sends you a bunch of flowers. They live like savages, Stephanie. The way she described her childhood made me want to weep. So she didn't always understand the obligations of friendship. She should have told you. But I understand why she didn't.'

'I do too. And it makes me sad.' I stood up and patted George's shoulder. 'There is one good thing about Scarlett's will.'

'What's that?'

I smiled. 'I don't think we'll be hearing from Chrissie and Jade's lawyers.'

46

You'd have thought I'd had enough shit to shovel for one day. But it wasn't over yet. Not by a long chalk. I left George smoking his cigar in the ghastly grotto and headed back through the growing dusk across the car park to the hotel. I was almost home and dry when Pete stepped out from behind a parked SUV and blocked my way. 'Hello, sweetheart,' he said with the relaxed smile of a man who knows he's welcome.

My step stuttered and I recoiled backwards. But not fast enough. Pete moved more quickly than me and before I knew it, I had my back to the vehicle and he had an arm on either side of me. He stepped into me, pressing me close to the van. His familiar smell hit me and I felt sick. Impossible to remember now that once I'd revelled in the animal smell of him, loved that masculine fragrance that clung to his skin. Now I'd have settled for Scarlett Smile rather than this.

'Let me go, Pete,' I said, trying to sound calmer than I felt.

'I can't do that, Stephanie. It's been too long since I held you.' He rubbed his face against my neck. I felt the faintest shadow of stubble. He'd shaved before he came out and his skin was almost smooth against mine. There was something repulsive about the sensation.

'Let me go,' I insisted, turning my face away. 'You know this is wrong, Pete. It's over.'

'Don't be silly, Stephanie. You need me now more than you ever did before. I know about the kid, you know. A boy needs a father if he's not going to grow up a spoiled mummy's boy. And I'm the perfect choice for the job.' He was pressing me against the van. I could feel him growing hard against me. I was starting to feel genuinely afraid. This section of the car park was only overlooked by a few bedrooms and there were no lights on in any of them. His hot breath on my neck, his skin against mine, the pressure of his need combined to send a cold wave of fear through me. He'd never gone this far in his pursuit of me before.

'I don't need you, Pete. And I don't want you. This isn't right.'

'Of course it's right.' His voice was harsher now. 'You belong to me. You always have. Now we're going to be a family. You and me and Jimmy. We'll be together for ever.'

'No,' I shouted. 'Get off me, Pete.'

His hand shot out and slapped me. I gasped at the shock and pain, felt my eyes widening in fear and horror. 'Don't shout at me, Stephanie. Know what my trouble is? I let you get away with far too much before. I should have disciplined you more and indulged you less.'

'Stop it, Pete.' I didn't mind begging if it got me off the hook. I was terrified now, knowing how much stronger than me he was.

'"Stop it, Pete,"' he mimicked. 'Listen to yourself, Stephanie. You don't exactly sound like you mean it. In fact I know you don't mean it.'

'This is wrong, Pete.'

He gripped my cheeks tight in his hand, forcing my mouth into an O shape. 'Where's your policeman pal when you need him, eh? It's not so much fun when you've not got a tame copper to warn me off, is it? What did you think you were doing, Stephanie, setting that plod on me? Do you really think he scared me, with his "It's been pointed out to me that you are not an invited guest, sir. I'm afraid I'm going to have to escort you from the premises." Pompous prick.' He shook his head. 'What? You couldn't come and tell me yourself that I wasn't welcome?' He let go of my face, pushing my head back so it bounced painfully off the SUV's window.

'Like that would have worked,' I spat back at him. 'You can't take a telling, can you? I am not your girlfriend,' I said, syllable by angry syllable. 'I never want to see you again.'

I tensed for the slap that never came. Instead, I heard the familiar clatter of cowboy boots on Tarmac. Rapidly followed by Simon saying, 'What the fuck? Steph, are you OK?'

'Leave it out, pal, she's with me,' Pete snarled.

I tried to wriggle free, but Pete's weight told against me.

'I think you better step away from the lady,' Simon said. He looked more anxious than scary, but the bottom line was that he was a witness.

'And I think you better butt out.' To confront Simon, Pete had to turn sideways on to me. As he moved, I caught him off balance and pushed his hip forward as hard as I could. He stumbled away from me and that gave me enough time to get behind Simon. Forget feminism. At that moment I was more than happy to let a man protect me.

'Are you OK, Steph?' Simon didn't take his eyes off Pete.

'Thank you, yes.'

'You've picked the wrong fight, mate,' Pete said, eyes narrowing. 'Never come between a man and his woman. Did they not teach you that at your posh school?'

'He's not my man and I am not his woman,' I shouted. 'He's my ex but he can't get that bit through his thick skull. It's over, Pete. It's been over for years. Now leave me alone.'

Pete took a step towards Simon, hands clenching into fists.

What I could see but he couldn't was that George was moving up behind him, taking in the whole scenario with one long sweep of his eyes. To my astonishment, George set himself square on his toes behind Pete then with a swift one-two, he rabbit-punched him in the kidneys.

Pete screamed in pain, half-turning as he fell to his knees. George side-stepped and gave him a mighty kick in the balls. Pete screamed again and rolled on to his side, curled up like a baby. 'Leave her alone,' George said in his dry, precise voice as he stepped over Pete's moaning body, took my arm and swept me off towards the hotel.

Simon brought up the rear, exclaiming at George's pugilistic skills. 'That was well impressive, George,' he said for the third time as we turned into the foyer.

'I had no idea you were the James Bond sort of agent,' I said, squeezing his arms.

'I did a bit of boxing in the Guards,' he said. 'I train at a gym a couple of times a week, purely to keep fit. Haven't hit a man in anger for thirty years.' He winced. 'I may have kicked him a little too hard. These are definitely not the shoes for it.' He steered me away from the ballroom and into the hotel bar. We found a table in a corner and he sent Simon to the bar for large gins. 'That was your ex, wasn't it? The one you moved to Brighton to get away from?'

I nodded. 'That bit worked just fine. He doesn't know where I live. That's why he turned up today. And why he turned up at Joshu's memorial. He's still not given up.'

'That's not good,' he said.

Simon came back with the drinks. 'Bloody right it's not good. If George and I hadn't happened to be there, that could have turned very nasty.'

'Believe me, I know. And I appreciate it, guys.' I raised my glass and toasted them.

'What were you doing out there?' George asked Simon.

'I wanted some fresh air,' he said. 'I've been here for dinner with Scarlett and I remembered there was a little enclosed garden thing the far side of the car park. I didn't think anyone would find me there.' All of a sudden, he looked as if he would burst into tears. 'Sorry. I miss her, that's all. Not very professional, I know. But I'd grown very fond of her.'

George cleared his throat. 'Hard not to be when you got to know her.' He took a long swallow of his drink. 'Stephanie, I hate to put any more pressure on you, but you really will have to do something about that toerag. It's bad enough when it's just you he's stalking. But there's Jimmy to consider now. I shudder to think of the effect on that vulnerable little boy if he were to witness a scene like that. Or worse. I think you're going to have to talk to the police.'

I sighed. 'They won't take it seriously. Not until he actually does something. And no, that little incident in the car park doesn't count as something.'

We all stared glumly at our drinks in silence for a few minutes. Then Simon perked up. 'What about if you knew a friendly cop you could draft in to give him the hard word?'

'That would be worth a try,' George said. 'If you knew the right chap.'

'I was thinking . . . what about the one who ran the inquiry into Joshu's death? He seemed like a decent bloke. And you got on quite well with him, didn't you? You were talking to him at the memorial service, I seem to remember.' Simon smiled encouragingly.

And that is how Nick Nicolaides and I got to be an item.

47

Nick wasn't generally indecisive but standing outside Phat Phi D in the rain on the wrong side of midnight, he couldn't make up his mind what to do for the best. He understood only too well that the most important thing was recovering Jimmy alive and well. But he wasn't convinced that the best way of achieving that was by passing the latest information about Pete Matthews directly to Special Agent McKuras. OK, he wasn't an expert in the ways of foreign law enforcement, but the image of the Americans going in with all guns blazing hadn't become a cliché out of nowhere. He remembered Waco. He didn't want Jimmy literally getting caught in the crossfire. Or Matthews either, come to that, if he was completely honest with himself. The guy was a bully and a sleaze, but he didn't deserve to die.

He turned up his collar against the weather and walked back slowly to his car. Slumped behind the steering wheel, he mulled over his encounters with Pete Matthews. The first time, at Joshu's memorial service, he'd walked into something he didn't understand. Stephanie had said he'd be doing Scarlett a favour by asking Matthews to leave, and yet she hadn't denied it when Nick had suggested she was using him as cover to make her getaway. Which hadn't quite made sense. He wasn't even sure why he'd leapt to that conclusion. Something about her body language, he supposed. His psychology degree had included a fascinating module on kinesics. It seemed to Nick that kinesics codified what many people still thought of as intuition. He'd worked on absorbing the information till it had become second nature.

He hadn't needed kinesics to realise how pissed off Pete Matthews had been by his approach. Nick hadn't said he was a cop at first. He'd simply walked up to him and said, 'Mr Matthews, this is a private function to which you have not been invited. It would be much appreciated if you would leave.'

Matthews' eyes had widened and his mouth tightened in an expression of outrage. He glared at Nick and took a half-step towards him. When he realised Nick was not intimidated, he drew his brows down in a scowl. 'Who the fuck are you to tell me what to do? It's not your party, I know that much.'

Nick slipped his warrant card from his jacket pocket. 'Detective Sergeant Nicolaides. Met Police. This is private property where you have no right to be and you are being asked to leave. I'm sure the last thing you want is to make a scene when there are so many members of the press here.'

Matthews sneered at him. 'You have no idea what's going on here, copper. You've got yourself caught in the middle of a lovers' game. Whatever promises Stephanie's made to you, she's playing you. She's not going to deliver, because she's my woman. You understand? She's making a point to me, showing me she can get a mug like you to do her bidding.' He gave a harsh laugh, like one of those mynah birds they used to keep in the local pet shop when Nick was a kid. 'Sucker.' Then he held his hands up, palms out in the universal placatory gesture. 'It's OK, I'm not going to kick off and spoil Scarlett's party. Even if it is just a hypocritical bit of headline-grabbing.'

He shook his head. 'She's not shedding real tears, you know, copper. Ask Stephanie how many more copies of the latest book they'll sell now Joshu's popped his clogs. Scarlett would rather have the money than the man any day.' Then he looked over Nick's shoulder and swore.

Nick turned to follow his eyes and realised Stephanie was no longer where he had left her. He scanned the room but couldn't see her anywhere. When he turned back, Matthews was already near the door, pushing his way through the crowd. Whether it was, as Matthews claimed, a lovers' game, or something less romantic, Stephanie had clearly made her escape while he'd distracted Matthews. And whatever it was, it had diminished Stephanie's appeal where Nick was concerned. He wasn't interested in an involvement with a woman who was still entangled with another man. That was a scenario guaranteed to provoke sleepless nights and too many hours playing maudlin love songs.

And so he had put Pete Matthews and Stephanie Harker out of his mind. Nevertheless, he'd recognised her voice as soon as she spoke on the phone. 'Sergeant, I don't know if you remember me—'

'Stephanie Harker,' he said. Annoyed that she had made him blush.

'Wow,' she said. 'That's impressive.'

'I'm a musician, remember? I'm good at voices,' he improvised. 'How can I help you?'

'It's a bit awkward over the phone. Would it be possible to meet for a coffee? Or a drink?'

In spite of his determination to have nothing to do with trouble, he'd agreed. They'd met at a Costa Coffee near his office. She'd been sitting at a table away from the windows when he arrived, but she'd sprung up when she saw him and insisted on buying his espresso. When they'd settled down and got past the inquiries about how Jimmy was doing, he'd sat back and given her an encouraging smile. 'You wanted to talk to me?'

And out had spilled a tale that ticked many familiar boxes. A possessive man who won't take no for an answer, who convinces himself a woman belongs to him and only needs to be reminded of that fact enough times in order for it to become the truth. A man who stalks her with flowers and emails and letters and texts, who fills up answering machines and voice-mail boxes, who can't be invading her space because her space already belongs to him so how can that be an invasion?

Nick listened, his coffee untouched, a chill in his guts. He'd heard this story before. Too often, he'd heard it from the grieving family and friends of a woman already lying in the morgue because she'd stood up to her persecutor once too often. Or not managed to escape far or fast enough. When Stephanie stumbled through a halting account of her confrontation with Matthews in the Essex hotel car park, he felt a mixture of rage and frustration burning like indigestion in his stomach. He wanted to punch Pete Matthews until he cried like a brutalised child. And also knew that wasn't his way.

'I spoke to a lawyer when he began pestering me after we first split up and she explained that there wasn't much I could do unless he actually broke the law. But I don't know what the law is. And it seemed to me that the way he made me feel, the threat in how he was with me – well, surely there must be something the police can do about that?' She looked at him with a mixture of anxiety and apology that filled him with anger against the man who had put her in that place. But he also knew there wasn't much he could lawfully do about Pete Matthews.

'The lawyer was right, I'm afraid. If you kept a diary of his harassment, you could probably get a restraining order against him. But it wouldn't have the power of arrest. You couldn't just call the police if he breached it – you'd have to go back to court.'

'Which means it would be meaningless, in effect?'

'Yes. For us to take action, you would have to demonstrate that you have reasonable grounds to be in fear for your life, or at least in fear of serious violence. And from what you've said, he's been very careful not to threaten you in that way.'

She picked up the wooden stick and stirred her latte. 'What you're saying is, there's nothing to be done.'

And that's when Nick crossed the line. 'Officially, yes. Unofficially, there are possibilities.' He'd had no idea that was what he was going to say until he'd said it. He knew then that he'd decided to follow his desire rather than his head.

Stephanie looked alarmed. 'I didn't mean—'

'I know you didn't.' He pulled out his phone, summoned the notepad function and handed it to her. 'Give me his address and phone number and leave it with me.' Nick took in her anxiety and gave her a grim smile. He wiggled his fingers at her. 'Have you ever heard of a band called Jethro Tull?'

She'd looked completely baffled, but nodded. 'Vaguely. Big in the seventies?'

'That's the one. Their front man, Ian Anderson, played the flute. He was so paranoid about his fingers being damaged that when people put their hand out to shake his, he'd offer them his elbow instead. Well, I'm not quite that anxious, but I'm not going to do anything to Pete Matthews that would put my lovely fingers at risk.'

Her face lit up in a smile that made him fizz a little inside. 'When you put it like that . . .' She tapped the information into his phone. 'Thank you.'

'You're welcome. But there will be a price to pay.'

Now she looked anxious again. 'I'm not a free woman,' she said. 'I've got a child to take responsibility for these days.'

'You live in Brighton, right?'

'Yes, but I'm still staying at Scarlett's place in Essex till we sort out moving Jimmy down to my place. Because the house has to be cleared and sold, according to that bloody self-indulgent will.' She pulled a face. 'I'm sorry, I shouldn't whinge. I don't care on my account, but it would have been easier on Jimmy if he could have stayed put, at least for a few months.'

'On the other hand, probably better for you to be in Brighton rather than somewhere Matthews knows he can find you.'

She nodded acceptance of what he said. 'That's true.'

'So here's my price. Once you've moved back to Brighton, I get to come down on my day off and take you out to lunch while Jimmy's at school. How does that sound?'

Stephanie looked relieved, then delighted. 'That would be lovely. Thank you. For all of it.'

That same evening, Nick checked out Pete Matthews' address. It was the garden flat in a tall Victorian terraced house in Kentish Town, a couple of streets back from the main drag. The handiest thing about it was that the front door was down a shallow flight of steps, more or less invisible from the street above unless someone was standing on the pavement next to it. There was a sturdy chain holding the gate closed, but Nick reckoned it would yield to a decent set of boltcutters.

Matthews' flat was in darkness, so he took a chance on ring-ing the doorbell of the main house. The man who answered looked like a Regency fop gone to seed. His shortish dark hair was gelled into a wedge on the top of his head and his tight floral shirt did nothing to disguise a hard little pot belly. He wore white jeans deliberately cut to make him look hung like a horse. Nick, whose jeans were chosen for comfort rather than vainglory, had never understood the style. Mutton dressed as ram. The man pursed his lips waspishly, which provoked nests of wrinkles that would doubtless have mortified him had he known. 'Yes?' he said irritably.

Nick showed his warrant card and looked humble. 'Are you the householder, sir?'

'How very Edwardian. Technically, that would be my wife and I. But I am the man of the house.' He was, Nick thought, trying to sound posher than he was.

'I wonder if I might have a word?'

'Have we committed some unwitting crime, officer?'

'No, sir. I just wondered if anyone had been home this morning between nine and eleven. We're investigating an assault and we're looking for witnesses.'

Now the man looked shocked. 'An assault? Was one of the neighbours attacked?'

'No, nothing like that. We think the victim and the assailant knew each other and had a chance encounter on this street. Did you see or hear anything? You or your wife?'

He shook his head prettily, as if it were a matter of huge personal regret that he was unable to help. 'My wife Madeleine and I left the house together at ten to nine, as we always do, to go to work. I work at the BBC and she runs a charitable foundation round the corner from BH, so we travel in together on the tube. I'm afraid neither of us was at home.'

'What about your downstairs neighbour?' Nick pretended to consult his notebook. 'Mr ... Matthews?'

'I've no idea. He doesn't keep regular hours. He works in the music business, you see. You'd need to ask him and I've not a clue when he'll be back. Sometimes he's away for weeks at a time.'

Nick closed his notebook and smiled. 'Sorry to have bothered you. Thanks for being so patient.' He didn't wait for the man to close the door. He had what he needed. The upper part of the house would be empty during the day. And Nick had a day off on Wednesday, which gave him a whole day to make his arrangements.

Back at the office, he put a call in to an old mate in the Tactical Support Group. Nick had trained with Declan Rafferty and a bunch of other Greater Manchester Police recruits at the

Bruche training centre. They soon discovered they shared similar tastes in music. Like Nick, Declan would rather drive for an hour to listen to an obscure new band than head straight for the nearest pub and get rat-arsed with his fellow trainees. It doesn't take much in a quasi-military ambience like police college to forge bonds when you find common ground, and so it was with Declan and Nick. Although they'd chosen different paths and styles of policing, they still remained friends. At least once a month, they'd make pilgrimage to an unsung venue to hear music that barely made it on to the radar, even in these days of Internet accessibility to all. Discovering new acts before the herd was still a badge of pride for them both.

Once they'd sorted their next night out, Nick slid into the real reason for his call. 'You on the station van this week?' he asked, referring to the quick-response vehicle the TSG used as a mobile control and incident room as well as the wheels deployed to get their officers to the scene of trouble fast.

'I am. Not much happening, though,' Declan said. 'We've been kicking our heels. It's all gone very bloody quiet out there.'

'I wanted to ask a favour. Mate to mate. No blowback, you know what I mean?'

'If I can, I will. It'll only cost you a bottle of tequila gold.'

'Bloody hell, your tastes are turning expensive.'

'What's the favour?'

'I need to borrow the big key. And a set of heavy-duty dikes.'

Declan whistled. 'You don't ask much, do you? I take it this isn't official?'

'Definitely off the books.'

Nick counted eleven seconds of silence, a long time in phone years. Then Declan sighed. 'Where? And when?'

'Ideally, tomorrow morning around ten. In Kentish Town. But I don't want to meet you there. If it all goes pear-shaped, the last thing I want is any of the neighbours identifying a TSG officer on the scene.'

In the end, they agreed Declan would bring the steel battering ram and the diagonal cutters he'd asked for round to Nick's flat after dark that night. Provided they weren't needed in the interim – 'Not likely, we're like the Olympic torch these days. Never go out.' – Nick would return them to Declan the following evening.

The next morning at ten, Pete Matthews' street was as close as Kentish Town got to tumbleweed. Nick had been parked fifty feet away from Matthews' flat and had hidden behind his *Indy* when the sound engineer had emerged at a trot half an hour before. Nick watched Matthews hurry in the direction of the tube, but waited to make sure he hadn't just nipped out for milk and a paper.

Nick pulled on a pair of leather gloves then got out of the car and grabbed a holdall from the back seat. He walked confidently to Pete Matthews' gate and put the holdall down. Out with the heavy-duty bolt cutters, a matter of seconds and he managed to catch the chain before it clattered to the ground.

He hustled down the stairs and readied the Enforcer, sixteen kilos of tubular steel designed to generate maximum impact with minimum expenditure of energy. Declan had warned him to be careful with it. 'We don't call it the Big Key for nothing. It can deliver three tonnes of kinetic energy,' he'd said, as if he understood what that meant.

'You mean it's a bloody big bang?'

'I mean it's a helluva wallop. Do it wrong and it'll knock you off your feet.'

Nick braced and balanced himself, each hand gripping a handle. The door looked solid, but it was only wood. Even an amateur like him should be able to crack it open in a oner. He drew the ram back then let its own momentum carry it forward.

There was a dull crack and thud as the steel plate hit the door just above the lock. The door swung lazily open as if it had never been latched, never mind locked. 'Fuck me,' Nick said, admiring his handiwork. He packed the ram, the cutters and the broken chain in the holdall and took it back to the car. Still there was nobody on the street, not so much as a twitching net curtain to suggest there were any witnesses.

He walked back to the flat and this time he went in. The smell of coffee hung in the stuffy air. Nice place, Nick thought as he did the tour. Gig posters on the walls, vinyl and CDs shelved everywhere. High-end hi-fi system with slave speakers in every room. The furniture looked functional but comfortable. A dirty mug sat in the sink, an Italian Moka Express pot beside it. It seemed a shame, but it was time to give Pete Matthews a taste of his own medicine.

Nick began with the kitchen. He did what Stephanie had described to him. Emptied the cupboards and the drawers. Dragged his feet through the mess, trailing it through the house. He didn't deliberately break stuff, simply let it fall where it would. He moved into the living room, sweeping CDs and albums from their shelves, walking over the resulting piles and relishing the bullet-crack sounds from the shattering CD cases. In the bedroom, he strewed Matthews' clothes all over the floor, and in the bathroom he tossed the few toiletries into the toilet bowl.

Finally, he called Declan and said, 'All systems go.' It was the cue for Declan to call Matthews on his mobile and impersonate a bored copper telling a citizen that his neighbours had reported a break-in.

Matthews hurtled in twenty-five minutes later to find Nick sitting in his armchair reading the paper. He skidded to a stop like a character in a cartoon, all big eyes and open mouth and freeze-frame body. 'What the fuck?' was all he could manage when he recovered the power of speech.

'In my business, we call it restorative justice,' Nick said calmly, getting to his feet. 'This is a taster. You go anywhere near Stephanie Harker in the future and this will feel like spring-cleaning by comparison.'

Matthews looked around wildly, spinning from side to side, struggling to take it in. 'You can't do this.'

'It's no more or less than you did. But if there has to be a next time, I won't hold back.'

'I'm going to report you,' he shouted. 'You broke into my house, you trashed it. You bastard.'

There was no kindness in Nick's smile. 'Try it and see how far you get. There's a small matter of evidence. And you've got none. Anybody asks, I was in the area and saw someone running away. Looked suspicious so I investigated.' He shrugged and picked his way through the detritus to the door.

He heard footsteps coming for him and quickly sidestepped, throwing out his arm in a back-handed swipe that caught the sound engineer in the throat. Matthews gave a choking gasp as he staggered backwards. He crashed into an empty set of shelves, his temple catching the corner of the unit. A starburst of blood blossomed on his cheekbone. 'I warned you,' Nick said. 'Stay away from her or I swear to God, I will hurt you. And you won't see it coming.'

It had been harsh and contrary to his nature, but it had done the trick. When he called Stephanie a couple of weeks later, she reported that she'd heard nothing from Matthews. And in due course, they had their lunch in Brighton. Stephanie was struggling with the advent of Jimmy Higgins in her life and clearly felt protective of the kid, but it was also obvious that she was enjoying him too. Nick thought the pair of them were going to be OK, and he didn't mind the notion of having a relationship with a woman that also included a child. He liked Jimmy well enough, though he thought the kid had been spoiled. Stephanie, however, seemed intent on gently changing that.

In spite of his excitement, they'd taken it nice and easy. Now, Nick thought they were almost at the point where they could call themselves an item. He was pretty clear that he loved Stephanie. He just wasn't sure if he was ready to share his space. How much room would there be for the music if he had a live-in partner and a kid?

Nevertheless, he was totally committed to recovering Jimmy. And right now, he thought he had a better chance of blagging Pete Matthews' whereabouts out of a Detroit recording studio than Vivian McKuras.

Nick fired the engine into life and pointed the car towards his office. He wanted the quiet and security of a landline for this call, and work was closer than home. If it was up to him, this whole case would be tied up by breakfast. And Stephanie would be correspondingly grateful.

48

Stephanie looked down at her hands, her shoulders slumped. The colour had drained from her face. No more English rose now. It looked to Vivian as if the events of the day had finally caught up with her witness. There was only so much adrenalin the body could pump out. Realistically, she was going to have to decide what to do with Stephanie pretty soon. There was no reason to keep her in custody. There was no question that she was a material witness, but there was also no reason to suppose she would flee the country and refuse to give her testimony at any future proceedings. Vivian did not have Stephanie pegged as someone who would go on the run the minute she was a free agent.

Nevertheless it was clear from her story that there was going to be a media storm around her, even if it was only on behalf of the British media. Vivian wanted to provide Stephanie with protection on that score. Since taking her into custody would be an extreme overreaction, it might be best to book her into an airport hotel under an assumed name.

'How are you feeling?' she asked.

Stephanie shrugged. 'Drained,' she said. 'I'm exhausted, but I'm too wound up to sleep.' Not that she felt like trying. The last thing she wanted was to open the door to the nightmares Jimmy's disappearance might provoke. Her waking imagination was bad enough.

'Why do you think they chose to abduct Jimmy here? At an airport in the USA?' Vivian asked. 'I'm still curious. It seems unnecessarily complicated. Surely there must have been easier options back in the UK?'

Stephanie ran a hand through her hair. 'Christ, I don't know. Maybe they're trying to draw attention away from themselves.'

'What do you mean?'

'If Jimmy had been snatched in the UK, the authorities would have focused on a tight circle of suspects. Who knows him? Who hates me? Who had access to him? Over here, you're forced to consider a wider picture. It makes you think, "No, wait, it can't be as straightforward as it seems, otherwise why not do it in the UK?"'

Before Vivian could respond, a tap at the door was swiftly followed by Don Abbott's head and shoulders. 'Sorry to interrupt again,' he said. 'Can we have a word, Agent McKuras?'

Vivian raised a finger at Stephanie and scrambled to her feet. As soon as the door closed behind her, she raised her eyebrows in a question. 'News?' she asked eagerly.

'Kind of,' Abbott said. He rubbed his eyes. 'I tell you, the one thing I'm not going to do when I finally get home is watch TV. My eyes are fried.' He produced a tired smile. 'We've made a little bit of progress. We now know where he changed his clothes. The control room are sending a clip of CCTV footage to your computer. They eventually found the bathroom the perp comes out of in his TSA lookalike outfit. Then they had the pain-in-the-ass job of pairing up every guy who went in with the image of him coming out. I tell you, Vivian, you might think you got a tough assignment today, but you should be down on your knees thanking God that you haven't been staring at CCTV footage till your eyes bleed.'

'I'm grateful. Trust me. Did you get anything?'

He nodded. 'Guy comes in wearing a black tee and black trousers, ball cap, carrying a lightweight nylon backpack. But get this. He's got a beard and moustache. Doesn't look like the kidnapper worth a damn. And he never comes out again. It's our man, Vivian.'

She felt a bubble of excitement in her chest. 'That's terrific news! We need to get that image out there. Somebody must have sat next to him on a plane. We're on his trail now. What about the backpack? Where does that go? Have we got someone going through the trash from that bathroom?'

Abbott gave an exasperated sigh. 'You're right that he left the backpack behind. The bad news is that the bathroom was cleaned two hours after the perp was in there. The trash bag is somewhere in a mountain of crap. Assuming we had the bodies and the will to sort through it, and assuming we found it, the chain of custody's already up in smoke. We can't do anything worth a damn with it. It's gone, Vivian.'

'Shit. Are the guys in the control room backtracking to the gate he came into?'

'Even as we speak. But don't hold your breath for any substantial leads coming from that. This has run like clockwork. He's not going to have flown on his own ID. He'll have a fake driver's licence. Or something stolen.'

'I know. But it's all we've got.'

'Nothing to go on from the witness?'

Vivian shrugged. 'A couple of possible leads. But nothing that would hold up in a high wind. I'll let her take a look at the new CCTV material, see if she recognises anyone. Don't hold your breath, though.'

49

Nick Nicolaides was willing to bet he had one crucial advantage over his American counterparts. He did not believe any of them could have his degree of familiarity with the inner wheels of the music business. He was a good enough guitarist to have been enlisted several times by professional musician friends as a backing player on recordings, and he'd spent a fair few long nights sitting in studio control booths watching producers and sound engineers at work. He was at home in their world. He understood how to communicate with them. How to avoid pissing them off and how to win them over.

Nick fitted a hands-free phone headset and laid out notebook and pen. A few keystrokes and clicks of the mouse and he had a phone number for South Detroit Sounds. It was early evening there. Chances were the band was still working. Time to find out whether Pete was there or not. Nick keyed in the number and held his breath.

The phone was answered by a man with a slow drawl and a friendly tone. 'South Detroit Sounds, we are here to make music for you. How can I be of assistance?'

'I'm hoping you can help me,' Nick said in the sort of clear and polite English voice that makes Americans swoon. He was never going to sound like a TV toff, but after all these years in London, he could draw a veil over most of his Northern vowels when he had to.

'That would be my pleasure, sir. What can I do?'

'I believe one of my friends is running the desk for the Style Boys. Pete Matthews?'

'Sure, I know Pete. He's not here right now. They're taking the day off. He'll be in tomorrow, you want to call back then.'

Strike one for Pete Matthews, Nick thought. 'You're kidding me? I'm only in Detroit for one night. I've got a flight to St Louis in the morning.'

'That sucks. Maybe you can call him, fix up to get together.'

'I tried that first. But he doesn't seem to be using his UK cell. It's not even going to voicemail. Have you got another number for him?'

'Sure. Hold on, I'll be right back.'

Nick finger-picked the desk silently, listening to Bert Jansch in his head. In a few moments, the American was back on the line, reading out a mobile number. Two strikes. So far, so good. Now it was just a question of whether Nick could pull off the final finesse. 'That's brilliant, I appreciate it. Now, can I be really cheeky? My phone's getting low on juice, and if I can't get hold of Pete straight away, I'm worried he won't be able to get back to me. I don't suppose you've got an address for him? Then if I can't get through, I can go and check if he's home. If he's not around, at least I can leave a note.' There was no immediate reply. 'It seems a pity to be here and miss the chance to see him. Look, I totally get it that you don't want to hand out his address. If I can't get hold of him, I'll swing by the studio and leave a note.'

'No, you're OK. Let me see what I got.'

This time, the wait was longer. And the voice on the phone was different. More authoritative. 'You looking for Pete, yeah?'

'That's right. We're old pals.'

'How do you know Pete?'

'I did some fill-in guitar on the last Pill Brick set,' Nick said as nonchalantly as he could manage. But his spirits were sinking. 'We kind of knew each other before, but that's when we really became mates. Look, if it's a problem, I don't want to put you on the spot.'

'It's OK, you sound like the real deal,' the man said. 'And I don't think Pete's hiding out from anybody. You got a pen?'

And there it was. Strike three. An address for Pete Matthews. Something concrete to pass on to the people on the ground.

Vivian ended the call and tamped down the desire to jump out of her seat and do a little dance. It wasn't generally considered an appropriate response to positive news in the FBI, where high-fiving was barely acceptable. Stephanie had perked up during the conversation, even though Vivian had done her best to keep her end non-committal. Now she smiled. 'Detective Nicolaides is quite the operator,' she said. Seeing Stephanie's blush, she added, 'I'm talking professionally, of course. Stephanie, he's come up with a very exciting piece of information for us. Pete Matthews is not in London. He's not even in the UK. He's here, in America. Not only is he in America, he's in Detroit.' She sat back, a picture of determined delight.

Stephanie looked as if she hardly dare hope. 'I'm not very good on American geography. How far is that from here?'

'About five hours' drive up the interstate,' Vivian said, pushing back her chair and getting to her feet. She glanced at her watch. 'If it was Matthews who snatched Jimmy, he's had plenty of time to make it back to Detroit and send out for pizza by now.'

'I can't credit it,' Stephanie said. 'A few minutes ago, I felt like I was in the middle of a nightmare. A completely baffling mystery. And now ... It could really come down to that evil bastard? All this, because I said no to a bully?'

Vivian assumed a gentle expression and softened her voice. 'It's not your fault, Stephanie. You did the right thing in all of this. He's the one who carries the blame.'

'What now?'

'Detective Nicolaides really delivered the goods. He got us a cell phone number, and the address where Matthews is living. Now, what I propose is that we get on the road. I want you to come with me, because if we recover Jimmy tonight, as I hope we will, it's important that you are there to make him feel safe and secure again.' She made a scooping motion with her hands, indicating that Stephanie should get up and prepare to leave. 'Lia, I know Stephanie and Jimmy's bags have been scanned and searched. Can you have someone bring them to my office? We need to get going as quickly as possible.'

Lopez scowled. Clearly she didn't appreciate being treated like a bag handler. But there was no time to lose. A child's life could be at stake. She grunted and picked up Stephanie's carry-on then tramped out of the office, her feelings clear from the set of her shoulders.

'Follow me,' Vivian said, heading out the door and down the hallway. Her phone was already at her ear. 'Abbott, we're rolling. I've got an address for our prime suspect ... Detroit. Meet me at my office. I need you to drive us, I'm going to be making calls ... Sure. Thanks.'

Until this point, Vivian had only been able to demonstrate her people skills. And she had plenty of those. But what she loved was when events started to unfold and she could follow her instinct for action. Now, there were people to be organised, directives to be issued, a quest to be followed to its natural outcome. And kudos to be won along the way. That wasn't why she did her job. But it didn't hurt.

They'd barely made it to the office when Abbott appeared, rumpled and cheerful like a kid on the brink of a promised outing. Vivian walked Stephanie to her car then they drove back to the terminal kerbside, where Abbott was waiting with the luggage. He threw the bags into the back of the SUV, evicted Vivian from the driving seat and roared off towards the highway. 'We should have missed most of the traffic,' he said, gunning the engine and flashing the car in front to pull over.

'Just so long as you keep missing it,' Vivian said, phone in her hand again. Her first call was to her boss. Succinctly she outlined what they had and where they were going. 'I'm going to need local law enforcement to check out the scenario ahead of our arrival,' she said. 'And local tech support. We need to know if Matthews is there and, if so, whether he's alone. We might need listening devices ... Yes, sir. Five hours, maximum. I have the mother with me.' She ended the call and let out a huge breath. Turning to look at Stephanie through the gap between the seats, she said, 'My boss is talking to the local FBI office and the local cops. They're going to check out whether the house is occupied. If there's anybody home, they'll use listening devices and thermal imaging to see how many there are and where they are in the house. And if we think Matthews is there with Jimmy, we'll have a SWAT team mount a rescue.' Vivian spoke quickly, brimming with confidence. She could see her assurance leak into Stephanie, buoying her up and bringing her hope.

'Did you say we were headed for Corktown?' Abbott said, not taking his eyes off the road.

'Yeah. Why?'

'If we need a rendezvous, there's a great barbecue restaurant there.'

Vivian rolled her eyes. 'It's not always about your stomach, Abbott.'

'I'm just saying.'

Stephanie cleared her throat. 'I'm sure the barbecue in Detroit is lovely and I don't want to be difficult, but if we're going to be driving for five hours, I could use something to eat. It's been a long time since I ate anything other than a cold cheeseburger.'

'It's not an unreasonable request,' Abbott said. 'Soon as we hit an exit with some fast-food joints, we'll swing through and get supplies.'

'I'm sorry, Stephanie,' Vivian said. 'I should have been more considerate.'

'She gets carried away,' Abbott said. 'In a good way, I mean. We'll get you fed and watered, and with luck, we'll have your boy back in your arms tonight.'

50

The kid had finally gone to sleep. After Pete had slapped him for his whiny crying, he'd screamed a couple of times till it had eventually sunk in that the more he wailed, the more he got hit. He'd stopped crying then and crawled into the furthest corner of his bed, whimpering softly. Pete had stood above him, menacing and dark, not needing to say a word to inculcate wordless terror in the boy.

Then he'd remembered that the little shit would probably piss himself, so he grabbed his arm and dragged him to the half-bath under the eaves. He pulled down the kid's pants and sat him on the toilet. At first, the boy couldn't even manage a dribble of piss. But when Pete turned away in disgust, the urine streamed out, smelling strong and hot. The kid wiped himself clumsily and ran back to the bed before Pete could grab him. There, he cowered in the corner, big brown eyes wide and terrified.

Pete locked him in again and went downstairs, where he set his iPad to play a random selection of Peter Gabriel tracks. He lay on the sofa and let the music run over him like a river. When it came to 'My Body Is a Cage', he roused himself and sat up, concentrating on how the music was knitted together, figuring out the choices that had gone into the mix and wondering what he might have done differently. At the end of the track, he walked over to the player and searched till he found the Arcade Fire version of the same song. He listened with equal attention, working out why he found the original so much less powerful than the cover.

It would have been good if Stephanie had been there with him. He could have explained to her why small choices made big differences to a recording. But she wasn't here. It wasn't acceptable.

He took another beer from the fridge and went to check on the boy again. This time, he was asleep, sprawled across the bed, his thumb in his mouth and his hair matted with sweat. Pete didn't like the invasion of his space, but it wouldn't be for long. Then he could concentrate on working things out with Stephanie, restoring his world to its proper state.

That was the important thing, not this little bastard with his soft snoring and his twitching feet. Things had been out of kilter for long enough. Now it was time to restore equilibrium.

Pete yawned as he made his way down to the master bedroom on the next floor. An early night wouldn't be such a bad idea. He'd been short on sleep lately and the band were expecting a full shift out of him tomorrow. He took another swig of beer and sat on the side of the bed, pulling off his boots and letting himself fall back on the bed.

Soon he'd be back in England with Stephanie at his side. Soon.

51

By the time they joined the local FBI agents in the Corktown motel they were using as a centre of operations, Stephanie had lost count of how many hours she'd been awake. There had been a couple of times during the drive when she'd felt herself drifting away into surreal dreams, but every time she'd jerked awake before proper sleep took hold. It was as if her brain couldn't allow her to switch off, not while the possibility of finding Jimmy was so alive. But her body knew how tired she was. Her left leg ached with a low intensity that made her grit her teeth.

Vivian McKuras had been on and off the phone all journey. Stephanie had strained to hear her end of the conversations, but Vivian had been huddled round her phone and there was too much road noise from the SUV for her to be able to make out more than the occasional word.

The road signs showed names she recognised without really knowing why. Kalamazoo, Lansing, Ann Arbor. Soon after they'd passed Ann Arbor, Vivian leaned over to talk to her. Even in the dimness of the dashboard light, Stephanie could see she was looking pleased. 'I've got some very promising information from the team on the ground,' she said.

'Have they found Jimmy?' Stephanie felt shaky and gripped the seat in front of her.

'They've located the address Pete Matthews is renting. It's a row house—'

'What's a row house?'

'It's where the house is joined to the ones on either side. I thought you had them all over the UK?'

'We do, but we call them terraced houses. Not row houses.'

Vivian nodded. 'It's that old chestnut about being separated by a common language. Sorry. OK. So Matthews is living in this row house. He wasn't in work today. The band he's recording is taking a day off. We spoke to neighbours and engaged their cooperation. Thanks to thermal imaging and highly sensitive microphones, we've established that there are two people in the house. One on the first floor and the other in the attic room. Now, I don't want to get your hopes up too high but one of the neighbours reported that she thought she heard a child crying earlier this evening. Around eight o'clock.'

Stephanie cried out. 'Jimmy.'

'We've no way of knowing for sure if it's Jimmy. But the neighbour says this is the first time they've heard a child in the house. It's ... I'd have to say it's a helluva coincidence.'

'Why would there be a child there if it's not Jimmy? He had plenty of time to get back here by eight, right?' Stephanie was almost shouting in her excitement.

'He would have had time, yes. But I have to caution you, Stephanie. We have no way of knowing whether this child is Jimmy till we enter the house and retrieve him. And now I have to ask you a very important question. Do you know whether Pete Matthews is likely to have access to weapons?'

Stephanie felt the shock of the question as a physical tightening of her chest. 'Why would you think that? He's never shown any interest in guns or knives or anything like that. He doesn't even like action movies.'

'We have to ask. We'll be sending a team into that house and we need to be prepared for all eventualities. Are you sure he doesn't carry a weapon when he's travelling? Remember, this is a country where guns are not difficult to come by if you don't mind flouting the law.'

Stephanie shook her head vigorously. 'No way. It would never cross his mind. I don't know how to make you understand this, but although he threatened me and really frightened me, he's not the kind of man who responds violently. In all the time I've known him, he's never picked a fight in a pub, or got into a brawl or anything. He despises violent men. He's a bully, not a fighter.'

Vivian patted her arm. 'That's good to know, and I can pass that on to our people.'

'What's going to happen now?'

'We've got people staking out the house. We're going to meet with the leader of the team who will be mounting the rescue so he can reassure you as to Jimmy's safety. Then it's a waiting game, I'm afraid. Don will stay with you and I will go with the team. It's going to be OK, Stephanie.' That was hard to believe, but Stephanie clung to the words.

The motel was quiet. The night porter seemed bored, as if major FBI operations happened on his shift every other night. He directed them to a small meeting room down the hall, where two men were waiting. Stephanie felt like she'd fallen down a rabbit hole and landed in the *Die Hard* franchise. Both men were tall and broad, dressed in black fatigues and body armour and utility belts that would have put Batman to shame. Both had square jaws and steady eyes. The only thing that distinguished them was the top half of their heads. One had an auburn buzz cut, the other a scalp so closely shaved it was impossible to estimate his hair colour. Two helmets lay discarded on the conference table. The introductions passed Stephanie in a blur. All she cared about now was getting Jimmy back. She could almost feel him in her arms.

The agents began to discuss the operation, but she wasn't following the conversation. After a few minutes, she interrupted. 'Can I come to the house? I promise I won't get in the way. But I want Jimmy to feel safe as soon as possible. I should be there when you bring him out.'

'That's out of the question, ma'am,' Auburn said.

She had a sudden inspiration. 'You'll need me if you get into a hostage situation,' she said craftily. 'It would save time to have me there.'

Vivian gave a wry smile. 'She has a point. I say we take her.'

The men in black put their heads together. Neither looked happy but they finally agreed. Stephanie could remain in one of the command vehicles.

Feeling pleased with herself, she trailed in their wake back to the car park. They drove for less than half a mile and parked behind a large nondescript van. The two men in black peeled off and melted into the night while Vivian knocked on the van door. She showed her ID and they both climbed inside. Two men and a woman were hunched over a battery of screens and comms equipment, headsets jammed close. Vivian explained who Stephanie was and the woman grunted a welcome, gesturing towards a jump seat in the far corner with her thumb. 'Sit down there. You're here on sufferance, so don't get in the way.'

Stephanie did as she was told. The screens told the sort of story that could be read by anyone who'd seen enough TV cop shows. The long view of a street of attractive brick-built terraced houses illuminated by street lighting. The front and back views of one house in particular. The multi-coloured thermal image of a house with two indistinct shapes inside. A screen that showed a constantly shifting series of scenes of men preparing their protection and weaponry, pulling on gas masks and goggles, all clearly streamed from a helmet cam.

Presumably all the men were equipped with similar cameras.

The woman said, 'Stand by,' and the kaleidoscope of the assault team clarified itself into a view of the front stoop. Brusquely, she said, 'Go, go, go.'

And then it was like a movie, only without the soundtrack. Front and back door smashed open, a flash-bang stun grenade rolled down the hall. The men poured in from front and back. Stephanie imagined the noise and the smoke and the smell and the shock of it all. Jimmy would be terrified. But so would Pete. And that thought did make her smile.

Their booted feet pounded up the stairs and into a bedroom. Through a haze of smoke, she saw Pete clutching the covers to his chest, scrambling back against the wall, his mouth opening and closing in silent yells. She watched spellbound as three of them dragged him naked from the bed and threw him to the floor, guns pointed at his head. They cuffed him and yanked him back to his feet.

The image changed and now they were climbing another flight of stairs. A bundle of bedclothes huddled in a corner of the room. One man stepped forward and lifted it bodily into his arms. All Stephanie could see was the top of a shaggy head of dark hair and a child's arm reaching out to cling on to the FBI agent's neck. But that was enough.

Before anyone could stop her, she had wrenched open the van door and was running down the street, oblivious to anything except the house she had seen on the screens. She ran, tears streaming down her cheeks, her mouth wide in a glorious smile. As she grew near, the officer carrying the child emerged from the doorway and descended to street level.

Stephanie hurled herself at the man, pulling the blankets back from the child's head. Big brown eyes wide with fear and bewilderment gazed into hers. But instead of throwing her arms round him, Stephanie recoiled, her face a mask of horror.

Whoever the boy was, he wasn't Jimmy.

PART 3

pursuit

1

Heathrow Airport, London, three days later

Stephanie hauled her two suitcases off the luggage carousel and dragged herself towards the 'Nothing to Declare' channel. She was about to enter when a man in a suit stepped in front of her. 'Miss Harker? Miss Stephanie Harker?'

Not again. Not now. 'Yes, that's me,' she said, almost too worn down to speak.

'If you'd like to come this way?' He gestured back towards the baggage hall.

'Who are you?'

'I'm with the immigration service. If you'd follow me?'

'Do I have a choice?' It wasn't a challenge, merely a token and he knew it. Stephanie turned and followed him through a door into another airport back corridor. It was an environment that made her feel like throwing up. All those hours with Vivian McKuras, and for what? Embarrassment all round and a triumphant Pete Matthews crowing about the figure he was going to sue the FBI for.

The man opened a door and stepped back, indicating that

she should enter. And for the first time in days, Stephanie's spirits lifted a fraction. For it wasn't a stranger sitting at the table in the interview room. It was Nick Nicolaides, and when she walked in, he sprang to his feet and pulled her into a tight embrace, his hand stroking her back in a timeless gesture of comfort. He leaned his head on top of hers and said, 'I'm sorry, love. Sorry for your pain, sorry for Jimmy, sorry you had to go through it all by yourself.'

Stephanie closed her eyes and drank in the very particular smell of him. Even fresh from the shower, Nick smelled like himself. It was comfort beyond measure. For three days, she'd had nothing to anchor her to her life, only a deepening sense of misery faultlined with crisis and disaster. 'Thank you,' she mumbled.

They stood wrapped around each other, not speaking, for as long as it took. Then Stephanie gently tapped on his shoulder and they moved a little apart, holding hands as if they couldn't quite let go of each other. 'Thanks for coming to meet me,' she said.

'I told my boss you needed a police escort, and he agreed with me.'

She gave a dry laugh that had no mirth in it. 'Good line.'

Nick stretched his face in a grimace. 'It's not just a line, Steph. There's a media mob out there with your name on it. No reason why you would know, but Jimmy's abduction has been the only show in town for the last three news cycles. And everybody wants your story on how it happened. So I'm here to take you out the back way.'

She groaned and leaned her head against his chest again. 'I suppose that means I can't go home either?'

'Not unless you want to be doorstepped from dawn till dusk.' He half-turned his head as if he didn't want to meet her eyes. 'You could stay at my flat. You'd be very welcome. And if you wanted to be alone, I could bunk down with a mate.'

This time there was warmth in her smile. Nick's bachelor flat was far from ideal for two, but that was the least of her worries. 'There's nowhere I'd rather be. And I don't want to be alone, thanks all the same. I've had enough of feeling isolated these last three days to last me a lifetime.'

'Sorted, then. Come on, time to get moving. We can talk in the car.'

Ten minutes later, they were heading for London without any discernible tail. 'I bet it's been like a rat's nest over there, everybody looking for somebody else to bite,' Nick said.

'I think part of the problem is that there isn't anybody to bite. It was nobody's fault, not really. Just a bizarre coincidence.' So bizarre it had taken hours to sort out. Hours of Pete screaming that he wasn't a paedophile, that the kid was not his son, that he was just a fucking babysitter. Even though he was at the other end of the hallway in the FBI Detroit office, she could hear him bellowing like a baited bull.

The story, when it emerged finally, was stupidly straightforward. While he'd been in Detroit, Pete had taken up with Maribel, the day receptionist at South Detroit Sounds. When they spent the night together it was usually at her place because it was easier for her than finding overnight care for her six-year-old son Luis. But her mother up in Traverse City had been rushed into hospital with a suspected stroke and Maribel had turned to Pete for help. She hadn't given him the chance to say no, simply handed him the kid and the keys. Pete had decided to go back to his own place, which had a better TV and music system and where he could bed Luis down in the spare room. Hence the report of a crying child and the two bodies on the thermal image screen.

The following day had consisted of an endless rehash of what had gone wrong. And of course the media got hold of the abortive raid and ran it as the day's bleakly comic item. In the midst of it all, Stephanie kept telling anyone who would listen that they needed to redouble their efforts to find Jimmy. When Vivian managed to escape the inquest, she assured Stephanie that efforts were continuing but that they had no leads.

'We now know the kidnapper flew to O'Hare from Atlanta. But that's another major hub airport. He could have come from anywhere. And if he doesn't try to take the kid out of the US, they can just disappear.' Vivian looked harried and haunted. Probably by the ghost of her career, Stephanie thought.

They'd sat down to look at the CCTV footage that had been isolated of the bearded man who had become the fake TSA officer. Stephanie had no idea who he might be. 'He could be anybody behind that beard,' she complained.

'What about the way he walks? It looks like he has a limp to me.'

Stephanie shook her head. She'd spent months in physiotherapy after her accident, trying to walk properly again. She knew the difference between real and fake when it came to leg injury. 'He's putting that on to hide his own gait. It's not consistent. See, there? Look, he dodges out of the way of that little girl running down the concourse and he forgets himself. He recovers almost immediately, but I think he's only pretending to have a limp.'

And that was how they'd left it. No further forward, waiting to see if any of the calls to the Amber Alert hotline panned out. They hadn't wanted her to leave the US, but Vivian told her how Nick had fought Steph's corner with her boss. The bottom line he kept returning to was that Stephanie was a victim first and foremost. That she was a respectable citizen who would happily return to a US court to testify in any future trial. When the chips were down, they had no reason to hold her, and unless they were going to send her to Guantanamo Bay, they'd better put her on a plane home. There had been impish pleasure in Vivian's eyes when she mentioned Nick playing the Guantanamo card. Stephanie formed the distinct impression Vivian wasn't in love with the concept of legally questionable detention.

So here she was, feeling curiously bereft in spite of the fact that she'd only had Jimmy in her care for nine months. Not even long enough to complete the adoption process. Her next interview with the social worker would be interesting. 'Sorry, I seem to have mislaid the kid . . .'

'There is one silver lining,' Stephanie said.

'Really? I'm impressed that even an optimist like you can find anything good in this mess,' Nick said.

'I think Pete's finally decided chasing me is more trouble than it's worth.'

Even in profile he looked sceptical. 'I hope you can still say that in six months' time.'

Nick had filled his fridge with fruit, salads, cheese and cold meat. The bread bin was stacked with ciabatta rolls, bagels and croissants. And Stephanie knew there would be as much good coffee as she could possibly want. Food and drink were, apart from guitars and gigs, his only extravagances. But what she wanted more than brunch was a long hot shower. The FBI had installed her in a safe house that Stephanie reckoned was as much about keeping her under surveillance as protection. It wasn't conducive to anything other than quick showers hunched over like a self-conscious teenager after school swimming class.

When she emerged, she felt almost normal. Nick had set out a selection of food and she made herself a ciabatta sandwich with hummus, corn salad and sun-dried tomatoes. Armed with food and coffee, they sat on opposite sides of the breakfast bar. There wasn't anywhere else to eat in the flat; the living room, with its stunning view over Paddington Basin and west London, was only comfortable if you were a guitar. Or a guitarist.

'What's happening now? Are you still working with the FBI?'

Nick blew out a stream of coffee-scented air. 'In theory, yes. But they're not very impressed with the standard of our intel.' His smile was wry.

'It wasn't your fault.'

'No, but we're far enough away to be a useful scapegoat. They're not sharing much with us except outcomes. So, all the tips to the hotline that don't pan out – they tell us about those. Active leads, nada.'

'Maybe they don't have any active leads. Without communication from the kidnappers, they wouldn't have much to go on.' Her own words struck cold in her heart. She pushed her sandwich away, no longer hungry.

'I did get a message from Vivian, asking if we could check our databases for the name he flew under. He used the alias William Jacobs, but they don't have any record of the ID he used to travel. The name doesn't ring any bells with them or with us. Which means it's another dead end.' Nick took a bite of a bagel with peanut butter and cream cheese and chewed so hard she could see the muscles in his jaw working.

'Is there anything I can do to help?'

'Technically, there's nothing any of us over here can do, unless we're asked directly for international cooperation.'

'Even though Jimmy's a British citizen?' With Nick, Stephanie didn't have to hold back on letting her indignation show.

'It's a difficult one. We can offer support, which we have done, but unless they ask us, we can't interfere in somebody else's jurisdiction.'

'If it was your case, what would you do?'

Nick pushed his hair back from his forehead and thought for a moment. 'I'd go back to the crime itself and strip away all the externals and ask myself what actually happened.'

'What do you mean?'

'Leave aside all the emotional stuff that a child abduction generates. Disregard everything except the offence itself.'

'I'm still not sure I understand.'

Nick looked over her head while he figured out how to explain himself. She remembered that one of the things she really liked about him was that he didn't use his intelligence to browbeat her or make her feel stupid. He wanted to share. Not to dominate. 'Maybe it's best if I talk you through the process. What happened here? A child was kidnapped. Was this a spur-of-the-moment crime, an opportunist act?'

'No, obviously not.' Stephanie resigned herself to the role of doltish sidekick.

'Was it planned, but random? In other words, did the kidnapper know what he planned to do, but not specifically who he was going to target?'

Stephanie frowned. 'That's a more difficult one to answer.'

'But I think we can get to an answer. The middle of the day is far from the busiest time at a major airport. There are fewer travellers, so there's more chance of our fake TSA guy being spotted by the real thing. Of those fewer travellers, I don't imagine too many of them are adults travelling with young children. Which means relatively few targets. When you factor in the percentage of those adults likely to set off the metal detector, the number shrinks further. If you were going for a random kid, there are far better choices he could have made. Plus, he flew in from Atlanta. Which, as I understand it, is almost as busy an airport as O'Hare. Why travel to achieve something you could do just as well at the place you started from?' He chinked his cup against hers, pleased with his demonstration of logic.

'It wasn't random.'

'And if it wasn't random, it was specifically targeted at capturing Jimmy or causing you pain. Which we will come back to in a moment. Before that, I need to figure out who knew your travel plans.'

Stephanie looked startled. 'Nobody knew the details. I mean, there were people who knew I was going on holiday, and the dates. But not things like times and flight numbers.'

'OK. So who knew you were going away?'

'Maggie, of course. My lawyer, because I had to have the right paperwork for the court to allow me to take Jimmy out of the country. My pub quiz team, my book club.'

'And me,' Nick reminded her.

'Oh yeah. Obviously, you are in the pay of this gang of international kidnappers.' Stephanie giggled. 'It's all been part of your evil plot, getting me into your bed.'

'Took you long enough to figure that out. But joking apart. Any of those people could have told someone else.'

'But why would you? It's not likely my pub quiz team are dying to find some dodgy character they can sidle up to and go, "Stephanie Harker's taking her kid to America a week on Monday," is it?'

'If you were trying to find an opportunity to kidnap Jimmy, you might well choose to befriend someone in that position. Or you might join the pub quiz with a team of your own.'

Stephanie sighed. 'It's all very far-fetched. And if you wanted Jimmy that badly, why not snatch him here in the UK? I'm sure there must be opportunities in the school playground, or when I'm at the park with him. Why make it so complicated?'

Nick scratched his chin. 'That's an interesting question too. And I don't have an answer.'

'I might,' Stephanie said slowly. 'You don't really move in the same world I do, so it wouldn't necessarily occur to you. But most of my clients inhabit a world where they get recognised all the time. In the supermarket. Walking down the street. At the leisure club. If the kidnapper has any kind of public profile, it would make sense to go for Jimmy when he's out of the UK.'

Nick grinned. 'Brilliant! That makes total sense. You're right, it would have taken me a long time to get that. So let's keep that in the back of our minds. But just backtracking a moment – how did you organise your travel plans?'

'I booked the flights direct with the airline, I organised the accommodation through an owners' rental website recommended by Maggie, and the car hire I did on the 24/7 website.'

'Where you gave them details of your incoming flight?'

'Only the one from Chicago.'

Nick nodded impatiently. 'But for someone who knows you're coming from the UK, it's not hard to work out roughly when you'd be going through security for that onward flight. Have you got an account at 24/7?'

'Yeah, I've had it for ever. I use it all the time. It's brilliant for weekend trips. We should do that one of these days.' She could feel herself blushing. This relationship still felt new enough for it to be novel for her to suggest the kind of activities that went hand in hand with commitment.

'I'd like that. But am I right in thinking pretty much anyone in your circle would know you use them?'

'I suppose. I never gave it much thought.'

'And what's your password?'

'Dignan97. That was the first ghosting job I did, and the year I did it.'

'And pretty much anyone in your circle could figure that out.' He bit into his sandwich fiercely.

A sense of unease made Stephanie uncomfortable. 'Nobody I know would be involved in this,' she said.

'You thought Pete might be,' Nick said through a mouthful of bagel.

There was a long silence. 'I don't make a habit of creating enemies,' Stephanie said. 'Apart from Pete, I can't think of anybody I've pissed off in the sort of way that would provoke this kind of response. I mean, when I annoy someone, it's usually because I've said no to a project. And that's just business,' she added, upset that Nick could imagine her life as a landscape studded with angry, vengeful people.

'I don't mean to suggest that you go around hurting people,' he said. 'But there are a lot of fucked-up minds out there. Weirdos who look at the world differently from the rest of us. Who see slights and insults everywhere. It's not impossible that somebody like that has found their way into the fringes of your life.'

Stephanie sighed. 'That's a horrible thought. I don't want to start looking at my friends like they're suspects in a major crime.'

'Nobody does. But somebody did this, Steph. Somebody has taken Jimmy. And I think there's still every chance we can get him back alive. Here's another silver lining for you. Because this was targeted and not random, I think it's very unlikely that Jimmy's been taken by a paedophile killer. For those people, any kid will do. For whoever took Jimmy, his identity was important.'

'That's why I wondered about Megan the Stalker. I know you said she's out of the picture, but there must have been other nutters obsessed with Scarlett that we don't know about.'

'Which is why I'm interested in people who are relatively new to your circle,' Nick said. 'If they saw Jimmy as the continuation of Scarlett, if they saw you as the way to Jimmy, they could have hacked your 24/7 account and found out the details of your trip weeks in advance. Plenty of time to get their ducks in a row.'

Stephanie got up and refilled her coffee. 'I hate the very idea of this. That you think someone has wormed their way into our lives just to steal Jimmy away ... it's vile, Nick.'

He couldn't meet her eyes when she sat down again. She imagined he knew too much about what human beings were capable of, that this plugged into all his worst nightmares. 'It is vile. Who else besides you would know of anyone who had an unhealthy interest in Scarlett or Jimmy?'

'Marina would be the obvious one. She looked after Jimmy from the start. Scarlett relied on her for everything practical. She was effectively the housekeeper.' Stephanie absently picked up her sandwich and took a bite. 'And Leanne, I suppose.'

Nick frowned. 'Remind me about Leanne. I don't think I ever heard the full story.'

So Stephanie told him. The body double, the loose lips, the exile to Spain, the final argument over Jimmy and the refusal to embrace hypocrisy to come to the funeral. Nick listened attentively. Then he spoke in careful, measured tones. 'You're telling me she thought she should have custody of Jimmy?'

'I don't think she meant it,' Stephanie said. 'In that respect, she was like Chrissie and Jade. She saw it as a way to get her hands on Scarlett's money. She already had the house and the business, but she wanted more. She loved her life in Spain, and having a kid would have seriously cramped her style. Both work and play.'

'All the same, we should check her out. Have you got contact details?'

Stephanie nodded. 'I haven't spoken to her since she stormed back to Spain, but I don't expect she's moved. She had the perfect set-up there.'

Nick looked slightly worried. 'You didn't call her when Scarlett died? You didn't ask her to come to the funeral?'

'It was Simon who spoke to her. I meant to give her a ring, but everything was too chaotic, I never got round to it. I had a Christmas card from her, though. She said she was having a good time and that we should come and visit.'

383

Nick nodded slowly. 'You know what, Steph? I think you and me could really use a weekend break in Spain.'

She could see the way his mind was working and, though it made her uncomfortable, she couldn't blame him. Once he met Leanne for himself, he'd see that organising a subtle and complex abduction simply wasn't her style.

Of course he would.

2

Stepping out of Malaga airport was like walking into a blast furnace. The dry heat almost took Stephanie's breath away. By the time they got the air conditioning cranked up on the hire car, her dress was sticking to her back and she could see a trickle of sweat running down Nick's hairline. She wondered whether it was racist to consider that his looks were better suited to Mediterranean sunshine than grey English weather. Whatever. She thought he definitely looked more glamorous in his white linen shirt and cargo shorts, sunglasses pushed back on the top of his head. Whereas she probably just looked hot and bothered.

Thanks to Google maps, they'd easily planned their route to Leanne's house in the foothills behind the coastal strip. Nick had reckoned it would take about half an hour. Stephanie, who had spent a while in Spain interviewing a golfer, a retired soap star and a comedian, thought it would probably be nearer an hour, given the Spanish roads and the tourist drivers. At least it would be pretty once they'd cleared the airport and its immediate surroundings.

The villa Scarlett had bought for Leanne was on a quiet side road in a small township which had clearly grown around an elderly village. A couple of streets of old buildings had been ambushed by brilliant white houses with terracotta roofs. The turquoise glint of swimming pools caught Stephanie's eye as they neared their destination. It looked like a prosperous settlement, somnolent in the late morning heat.

The gates of Leanne's house were open, which didn't surprise Stephanie. After all, Leanne was running a business from here, albeit there was no sign at the gates to indicate that. Maybe she was trying to avoid the local taxman, working word-of-mouth and cash in hand. They pulled in next to a silver Mercedes A-class. They'd agreed not to phone ahead and put Leanne on her guard, so it was a relief to see signs of life. 'Must be money in this manicure business,' Nick said.

The heat was less oppressive now they were on higher ground, but Stephanie still felt it was better suited to lying on a sunbed than playing at private investigations. Then she thought of Jimmy, ripped out of his old life and facing who knew what terrors, and mentally scolded herself. Whatever the rigours of a hot day in Spain, they faded into insignificance beside the catalogue of loss Jimmy had known. She had an unbidden flash of memory – the delight on his face when, zipped into his first wet suit, he'd swum in the sea off Brighton. He'd splashed through the gentle swell then thrown himself into her arms, giggling in delight. All she wanted was a collection of moments like that. For both of them.

Spurred on by the thought, she paid proper attention to what she was looking at. The house was cared for, the stucco clean and fresh, the gravel raked and the terracotta pots well stocked with geraniums. Bougainvillea was trained up trellises on either side of the mock-medieval nailed wooden door. 'Looks like she's got good help,' Stephanie said. 'I can't see Leanne keeping all this in order.'

Nick pressed the doorbell and they waited. He was reaching out to push it again when they heard the shuffle of sandals on tile. The door opened to reveal a short, squat man with skin tanned lizard brown. He wore nothing but riotously patterned shorts and flip flops. Where there should have been a six-pack was a taut firkin. A shock of thick white hair protected his head from the sun that had turned the rest of him mahogany. He looked mildly surprised to see them.

Not as surprised as Stephanie and Nick were to see him. 'We're looking for Leanne,' Stephanie said. 'This is the right house, isn't it?'

The man scratched his head. 'Right house, wrong year. We bought the house after she moved out and we've been here, what ... nine months?' His accent was Liverpudlian with the edges scuffed off.

'I'm sorry, Mr ...?' Nick pulled his wallet out of his back pocket.

'Sullivan. Johnny Sullivan. And you are?'

Nick showed his warrant card. 'Detective Sergeant Nick Nicolaides, Met Police. And this is Stephanie Harker.'

'I'm not with the police,' Stephanie said. 'I'm an old friend of Leanne.'

'Well, like I said, she's not been here for a long time now. We bought the house, all above board. Never met her, like. It was done through the lawyers.'

'Can we come in, Mr Sullivan? I'd like to ask a couple of questions.'

Sullivan drew his eyebrows down in a considering frown. 'I don't see why not. I've got nothing to hide.'

They followed him down a cool hallway and into a big kitchen that looked out over a small kidney-shaped pool. Beyond it was a small building. Sullivan cocked his head towards it. 'She used to run a nail-bar business out there. According to the wife, she was well thought of among the ex-pat women. Did a good job and she wasn't dear. She was cousins with that Scarlett lass, the one off *Goldfish Bowl* that died of cancer. But you'd know that, with her being your mate, like.' He gestured at the patio with his thumb. 'In or out?'

'In will be fine, Mr Sullivan.' Nick stood with his hand pointedly on the back of a chair.

'Take a seat,' Sullivan said. 'You want a glass of water? Or a beer? I've got the local brew, it's not bad.'

They accepted a glass of water each and began the business of extracting information from Johnny Sullivan. He was forthcoming to a fault, apparently holding nothing back. A year ago, he and his wife had been renting an apartment in the village, looking for somewhere to buy. Leanne had taken off one day without warning, causing some annoyance to her customers, who had all forgiven her when they heard her celebrity cousin had been diagnosed with terminal cancer. Nobody could argue with that as a reason for cancelling a pedicure.

What had been more surprising was that Leanne hadn't come back. Someone had obviously been to the villa to pack up her clothes and personal effects, but they'd been in and out without anybody seeing them. 'People assumed she'd decided to stop in the UK.' He shrugged. 'Some folk get homesick, like. They miss the food and the weather.'

A few weeks after her departure, the villa had been quietly put on the market. Johnny and his wife heard about it through the network of property lawyers. 'I won't lie to you, we pounced on it. The price was fair and it was exactly what we were looking for.'

'You bought it from Leanne herself?' Nick asked. Stephanie was fascinated to watch him in action. He asked things that wouldn't have immediately occurred to her, but she could see how important the questions were. They were both expert interrogators, but because they started with different goals, they took very different routes.

'Well done, young man. You put your finger on the one unusual thing about the whole transaction. The property wasn't in Leanne's name, it was owned by some charitable trust.'

'Was it the TOmorrow Trust, by any chance?' Stephanie was pretty sure she already knew the answer, but she had to ask.

Johnny Sullivan pointed his finger at her like a pistol. 'Got it in one. I assumed it was a tax dodge. It usually is round here.'

'Did she leave a forwarding address?'

'Only the lawyer. She didn't get much post, but when anything does come, we pass it straight on to the lawyer.'

'Do you know if Leanne was particularly friendly with anyone in the village?' Nick leaned back in his chair, the picture of relaxed, sociable interest.

'She had a bit of a thing for Paco. He runs the bar in the main square. She was pally with a British couple, Ant and Cat. The three of them used to hang about in the bar nattering to Paco. But I don't think they're in touch with her any more. Ant and Cat got married at New Year and they sent her an invitation via the lawyer. She never so much as sent a card or a wedding present, let alone turned up. They were really pissed off with her.' That was the last nugget of useful information they got from Johnny Sullivan.

As they waved goodbye, Stephanie said, 'It sounds like Leanne had really had it with Scarlett. To turn her back on all of this, just because they had a row.'

Nick grunted noncommittally. 'It's interesting,' he said. 'I want to see what Paco and the famous Ant and Cat have to say.'

They found the bar without difficulty. Better yet, the three people they wanted to speak to were all there. It was a typical village bar; simple décor, basic menu and a friendly ambience. But as soon as they mentioned Leanne's name, the temperature dropped. 'Walked out on us without a word,' bleached-blond

Ant said, curling his lip in contempt. He rolled his shoulders, deliberately displaying his weight-room muscles. 'She was Cat's best mate but she just used you, pet. As soon as she was back with her celebrity pals, we were history.' Paco nodded, polishing a wine glass with vigour.

Cat, statuesque with an Amy Winehouse mane of raven hair that owed everything to the skills of her hairdresser, nodded sagely. 'Dumped Paco there like he had the pox. Not so much as a postcard or a text. I lost count of the number of times I texted her and got nothing back.' Ant patted her hand.

'And voicemail,' Paco chipped in. 'She ignore my voicemail twenty time or more. She love that life in London, I know this. But I think she will come back because we have something good.' He finished polishing the glass and replaced it on the shelf. 'I love her. But is no point.'

'That's right, Paco. No point. How could we compete with the likes of Scarlett?' Cat pouted, petulant as an adolescent.

'After Scarlett died, did you not expect her to come home?'

'Course we did,' Ant said, flexing his forearms. 'But she must have hooked up with some bloke with more money than sense.'

'She always had an eye for the main chance.'

It was, thought Stephanie, an odd judgement. Living in a small Spanish hill town and painting women's nails for a living didn't seem to her to demonstrate an eye for the main chance. What it had always said to her was that Leanne was a woman who knew her limitations and was happy to work within them. If she'd been a gold-digger or someone who was only out for what she could get, she'd had her chances when she'd been living at the hacienda. She'd had power over Scarlett and Joshu and she'd never chosen to wield it. But Ant and Cat had constructed their story as deliberately as Stephanie built the biographies of her clients and this was the version of Leanne that would be handed down now and for ever.

A second beer in the bar produced nothing else of significance. It was clear to Stephanie that Leanne had made a life here then promptly burned her bridges behind her. But Nick saw a different set of possibilities.

They weren't the sort of possibilities that would fill anyone's heart with joy.

3

They walked back to the car in silence, both lost in their own thoughts. Nick didn't start the engine immediately. Instead, he said, 'You have Leanne's phone number, don't you?'

'Yes.' Stephanie dug out her phone and thumbed through her contacts. 'There it is. A Spanish mobile.'

'I'd like you to send her a text.'

'Saying what?'

'Saying you're planning to bring Jimmy out to Spain for a holiday soon and you'd love to get together. And then we'll sit back and see what happens.'

Stephanie gave him an odd look. 'What do you think will happen? Jimmy being abducted has been in all the British papers. They do get them out here, you know. And it's been all over the Internet. If she wanted to get in touch with me, she would have done it by now.'

'Maybe. But I think you'll get an enthusiastic text back saying something like, "What a great idea, when are you coming?" And when you give her dates, oh bugger, that'll be exactly the week she's booked to go to Thailand with friends.'

She wasn't stupid. She understood what he was saying. The realisation sat like a lump in her chest. This was the last thing she'd expected to discover on this trip. 'You think someone else has her phone. You think she's dead.'

He reached for her hand. 'I'm sorry. I can't see any other explanation. We know she left to spend time with Scarlett before she died. Then they had a row and she walked out. She'd built a life here. This was the obvious place for her to come back to. But she didn't. She walked out of a house in Essex and she was never seen again.'

'But Simon spoke to her when Scarlett died. To ask her to come to the funeral.'

'Did he? Did he actually speak to her? Or did he text her? We know her phone was live for some time after she disappeared. Paco left voicemail messages. If someone killed her, it would make sense to keep the phone live, to confuse the issue of where Leanne was. It would be easy enough to impersonate her in a text.' Nick's voice was gentle, but there was no sugar-coating his words.

Unbidden, the tears started, fat and heavy on her cheeks. Stephanie began to shake, her teeth chattering. Nick pulled her close, waiting out the storm. When the first shock passed, her eyes and nose were swollen and sore. 'I can't believe it,' she said. She put her hand on his chest and looked up into his troubled face. 'You suspected this before we came here, didn't you?'

He sighed. 'It did cross my mind. Bad things sometimes happen to women who storm out into the night.'

'You think some evil bastard picked her up? Took her somewhere and killed her?'

Nick nodded. 'Something like that. I think I need to talk to Essex police when we get home. The trail's pretty cold by now, but they need to set up a murder inquiry. If the phone's still live, it might give them a starting point for a search.'

'Poor Leanne. She wasn't the sharpest knife in the box, but she was a decent person.' Then suddenly Stephanie sat bolt upright. 'Wait a minute. You're not being straight with me, Nick.'

Startled, he pulled back. 'What do you mean?'

'You know what I mean. It wasn't some stranger that killed Leanne. It must have been someone at the house. Because her place in Spain was sold and the money went into the trust.' Stephanie's eyes were wide with horror. 'Was there an accident? Did Leanne die in the house?'

'Whoa,' Nick said, twisting in his seat and gently gripping her shoulders. 'You're getting way ahead of yourself here. There's other explanations, ones that make a lot more sense.'

'I can't think of one.' Chin up, Stephanie was back in control now. She wanted answers and there was no fending her off.

'What was Leanne's job? What did she do for Scarlett?'

'You know that. She was her body double, her impersonator.'

'Exactly. To someone who was obsessed with Scarlett, Leanne was as good as the real thing. They might even have taken her in the mistaken belief that she *was* Scarlett. Now, the fact that you're delusional in one area of your life doesn't necessarily prevent you functioning like the rest of us in other respects. Our mystery man grabs Leanne and holds her prisoner. Sooner or later it dawns on him that this isn't Scarlett. Which means he's got to get rid of her and cover his tracks. He finds out about the house and business in Spain and realises the alarm will be raised if Leanne appears to abandon everything. He goes there and clears out her personal stuff under cover of night. Then he impersonates her in letters or emails or texts and sets up the sale of the villa. He doesn't care who it belongs to or where the money goes because he's not interested in money. He's interested in Scarlett.'

Stephanie shivered. It made such clear and terrible sense. There had often been obsessive fans hanging around outside the hacienda. The same faces showed up again and again whenever Scarlett did any public appearances. Sometimes they got too close and had to be warned off. One or two, like Megan the Stalker, had gone out of control. But what about the others, who managed to hold it together on the surface but who were mad as a box of frogs underneath? Nick's theory answered all of the questions raised by Leanne's disappearance much more convincingly than the notion that Scarlett or one of her circle could have anything to do with her death.

'And in all the fuss and confusion around Scarlett's death, nobody was paying much attention to detail,' she said. 'The trustees probably didn't notice the money from the sale of the villa in amongst all the other cash that was coming in from realising Scarlett's assets.'

'Who are the trustees?' Nick asked.

'Simon, Marina and George.'

'Maybe it's time to talk to George,' Nick said.

'As soon as we get back to London. Do you still want me to send that text to Leanne's phone?'

'Oh, I think so. It'll be interesting to see what a text from a dead woman looks like.'

4

It was after midnight by the time they returned to Nick's flat. They fell into bed exhausted, but not too exhausted to take comfort in each other. Afterwards, when Nick had slipped into sleep, Stephanie lay awake, gripped by an abiding sadness. Jimmy was seldom absent from the front of her mind for long. She had imagination enough to create endless scenarios of misery and anguish for him. In spite of everyone telling her not to blame herself for what had happened, Stephanie could not escape the guilt that washed through her in regular waves. If they didn't find him alive and well, she would feel tainted by her failure for the rest of her life. She'd made a promise to Scarlett and she had not kept it.

Eventually, she drifted into restless sleep and morning rolled around far too soon. By some miracle, Stephanie's whereabouts hadn't leaked to the media. Nick was insistent that while the flat was still a safe house, they shouldn't do anything that meant her breaking cover. That included turning up at George's office or eating in the sort of restaurant where waiters had paparazzi numbers on speed dial. 'Poor George was completely stumped,' Stephanie told Nick after she'd spoken to the showbiz agent. 'I suggested he could come here.

You'd have thought I was suggesting he walk through South Central LA waving a wallet full of dollars.'

Nick grinned. 'I take it he's coming here, then?'

'Of course he is. He said he'd be with us around eleven. He'll expect biscuits.'

Nick crossed to the kitchen cupboards and produced a bag of cantucci and a packet of Florentines. 'Will these do?'

'Another demonstration that men are from Mars and women are from Venus,' Stephanie said. 'I couldn't have these in the house. Well, I could. But they wouldn't be there the next day. And if I'd known they were there, they wouldn't be.'

Nick grinned. 'I'll bear that in mind. By the way. I had an email overnight from Vivian McKuras. They're running headlong into a brick wall over there.'

'All the technology we've got now, and yet one man can walk off with a little boy and there's no way of tracking him?'

'The trouble with technology is that criminals understand what it can do just as well as we do. So they figure out ways to circumvent it. In a case like this, unless they get a reliable, quantifiable witness sighting, their best chance of tracing the perp and the victim is when they make contact about the ransom or the terms of release. No contact ...'

Stephanie bit her lip, stricken.

Nick slapped a hand against his thigh in anger at his stupidity. 'Jesus, listen to me. Could I be any more insensitive? I'm sorry.' He spread his arms out.

She didn't move towards him, but she shook her head. 'It's OK. I don't want to be wrapped up in cotton wool. I need to know the reality of what's going on. It's hard, but I don't want to be an ostrich about this.'

'OK. But I'll try to be a bit more considerate about how I express myself. One good thing – I asked McKuras to confirm to my boss that she still needs my input, so I'm cleared to carry on doing whatever unorthodox investigation it is that we're doing.'

Now she moved into his arms. 'That's good. When are you going to talk to the Essex police?'

Nick looked over her head towards the glass wall with its spectacular rooftop view. 'I wanted to discuss that with you,' he said slowly. 'Technically, I should speak to them asap. Suspicion of murder is not something a cop's supposed to sit on.'

'No, I can see how they'd take a dim view of that,' Stephanie said, acid in her tone. 'I can hear a "but" coming though.'

'This is a pretty cold case now. And my primary concern is getting Jimmy back. While we're still stumbling around in the dark on that, I don't want to do anything that might provoke the abductor.'

'You think the kidnap and the murder are connected? How? That doesn't make any sense.'

Nick moved away from her and started preparing the coffee machine. 'I don't know what I think. At the moment, it's all one big confused jumble. For all I know, some demented obsessive is snatching people who were connected to Scarlett. Like a mad souvenir collection.' He banged the worktop with his clenched fist. 'Call it superstition, if that helps. I just don't want the people we're talking to about Jimmy to freak out because they're getting calls from cops about a possible murder. There's nothing more calculated to make people shut up about anything.'

'So you want to wait? Not talk to anyone at Essex police about Leanne until we've got Jimmy back?'

She saw his back stiffen and knew he was already preparing himself for not getting Jimmy back. Stephanie wished she didn't know that. Because there was no way she could let herself concede there was the slightest chance that would happen. Someone needed to keep the flame alive. If that isolated her from Nick, hard though it would be, she'd still make that call.

'That's what I'm thinking.' He turned back to her and raised his eyebrows in a question.

'You'll get no argument from me. Nobody but us seems to have noticed Leanne's missing. I don't think it'll make any difference if we sound the alert today or in a month's time.'

Nick's reply was cut off by Stephanie's phone jittering on the worktop. 'It's from Leanne,' she said, grabbing the phone. Nick leaned over her shoulder so he could read the text along with her. 'Don't thnk its a gd idea 2 get 2gethr. 2 sad 4 Jimmy & 4me. Soz. Lx.'

Stephanie felt her heart contract. Nick's guess had been in the ballpark. 'You got it right,' she said bleakly. 'That's not Leanne.'

'But it's someone who wants us to think Leanne is still alive and well. Somebody who doesn't know we've been to Spain.'

'That doesn't exactly narrow it down.'

'It does in a way, Stephanie. It lets her Spanish friends off the hook. Word of our visit will have gone round like wildfire. If any of them was responsible for her death, they'd never have answered your text. Whoever got rid of Leanne, it happened in England, before she went back to Spain.'

Before Stephanie could respond, the entryphone beeped. Nick buzzed George up and went to the door to greet him. George walked in, tentative as a cat on new territory. Stephanie had positioned herself by the glass wall so George would get the full-on smack-in-the-face of the view as soon as he walked in. But he seemed oblivious to the panorama, crossing straight to her. He took her hands in his and gave her his most searching look. 'My dear Stephanie,' he said, his voice velvet with concern. 'You must be beside yourself. What a terrible experience for you.' He looked over his shoulder at Nick. 'I'm sure Nick's already got the bases covered, but if there's anything at all I can do to help, all you have to do is ask. I am at your command.'

Stephanie squeezed her eyes shut to fight the tears that welled up in response. 'For God's sake, George. Can you stop being quite so nice? I can take anything but kindness at the moment.'

He chuckled and pulled her into a chaste embrace. 'That's my girl.' He stepped away and looked around him for the first time, taking in the dozen or so guitars hanging on the walls or sitting on stands. 'Do I take it you are something of a musician, Sergeant Nicolaides?'

'Call me Nick, please. Yes, I play a bit.' He waved George towards the squashy leather sofa that was his only concession to living-room furniture. 'Please, have a seat. Coffee?'

George caught Stephanie's eye, one eyebrow raised in a question. 'Yes, George, it's safe.'

Nick busied himself with coffee and biscuits while Stephanie took George through the story of the abduction and the disastrous FBI operation against Pete Matthews. The account of Pete's experience gave him a moment's grim satisfaction. 'Serves the bastard right,' he said. 'Perhaps now he'll realise that stalking you is rather more trouble than it's worth.'

When Nick returned, George got down to business. 'How can I help you find Jimmy?'

'We need to talk to everyone who was close to Jimmy or Scarlett. Somebody knows who's done this. But they might not realise the significance of what they know,' Nick said. 'The roots of this offence probably run deep. That's why we need to dig into the history.'

George puffed his cheeks up and blew out a stream of air. 'I don't think I can be of much help,' he said. 'To be honest, I had as little to do with Jimmy as I could get away with. I'm of that generation of gay men for whom childlessness was a given. I am not a lover of children. Especially when they are still in the age of intractability. Scarlett knew that and she didn't impose him on me. Either in person or in anecdote.' He pulled a face. 'Why do people always think stories about their dull children are endlessly fascinating?'

'It's OK, George. I've seen your face when Jimmy made a beeline for you,' Stephanie said. 'We didn't really expect you to have noticed anyone behaving oddly around him. But we do need to talk to Marina and Simon. Obviously, we can reach Simon at work, but we don't have contact details for Marina. I know you're one of the trustees for TOmorrow, so I reckoned you must know how to get in touch with her.'

George produced his best 'cat who's got the cream' smile. 'My, but you are out of touch, Stephanie. You won't find Simon at the clinic these days.'

'No? Has he got a new job?'

'New job, new country. He's joined Marina in Romania. Simon is now the medical director of the TOmorrow project. He takes care of all the little orphans.' Seeing Stephanie's astonishment, his smile widened. 'That's surprised you, hasn't it?'

'I'm gobsmacked,' she said. 'Are he and Marina an item, then?'

George pulled a face. 'You know me, darling, never one to gossip ... But there would have to be something quite pressing to make one abandon a well-paid job in a private London clinic for the wastes of Transylvania, wouldn't you say?'

Stephanie looked up at Nick, perched on a high guitarist's stool. 'I never saw any signs,' she said. 'They kept that well under wraps.'

'They were rather thrown together during Scarlett's final illness.'

'I know, but I didn't have her pegged as his type.'

George's expression fell somewhere between mischief and

distaste. 'Some men find the more pneumatic sort of woman quite irresistible. I suspect Simon had never met anyone quite like Marina before. And she's a bright girl. She has a degree in economics from Bucharest.'

For the second time in their conversation, Stephanie was completely wrong-footed. 'She never mentioned that.'

'I don't imagine it came up.'

'She was always very reticent about herself,' Stephanie said, feeling the need to defend herself against her own guilt at not taking enough interest in Marina. 'I used to have this fantasy that she was escaping a chequered past. That she worked so hard for Scarlett as a form of atonement.' She blushed, embarrassed at revealing what felt like silliness.

'She always seemed very capable to me,' Nick chipped in. 'Not that I had much to do with her.'

George winked. 'She's certainly proved herself capable of whisking Simon off from under our very noses. Are you thinking of going to Romania to see them?'

His words snapped Stephanie back to the reason for their conversation. 'The FBI are getting nowhere. We're clutching at straws, George. Marina – and Simon too – are the only people we can think of who might be able to come up with a lead. So yes, we'll go where we need to.'

'And Leanne? Have you spoken to her?'

'We've been to Spain,' Nick said. 'We went to her house – to make sure Jimmy wasn't there.'

George finished his coffee and stood up, shaking the creases back into his trousers. 'Splendid. Mind you, from your description of what happened, one would have to conclude it was far beyond Leanne's mental capacity to organise.' He moved towards the door. 'I will have Carla email you the contact details for my fellow trustees when I get back to the office.'

'How's the trust going?' Nick's question was apparently casual, making conversation on the way out.

'To be honest, I don't pay much attention,' George said. 'I'm really only there to make up the numbers. Marina and Simon do all the donkey work. After the estate was settled, there was a lot of money swilling round in the trust – something approaching five million, I believe. They're doing great work out there, and Simon's got a team of volunteers organising another Scarlett Swimathon. Which of course has a marvellous knock-on effect on the book sales, as you know, Stephanie. It looks like the Swimathon might become an annual event. There's a lot of interest.'

'Good for them. Thanks for coming over, George.' Nick clapped him on the shoulder.

George turned and waggled his fingers at Stephanie. 'Bye, darling. Don't be a stranger, now. I have a couple of projects in the pipeline that are right up your street. I'll talk to Maggie.'

It was the last thing on her mind then, but Stephanie knew she couldn't ignore work indefinitely. Bills had to be paid, obligations met. 'Thanks, George.'

The door closed behind him and Nick leaned against it. 'So,' he said. 'Simon and Marina. Are you thinking what I'm thinking?'

Stephanie took a deep breath. 'There's only one thing stopping them from being the perfect happy family?'

5

Paddington Basin to Luton Airport at the crack of dawn; a surprising amount of traffic on the road, but no hold-ups, no anxious panic because of an inexplicable clot of standing traffic. Airport shops; a lightweight daypack, a water bottle, a waterproof jacket, a pair of trainers and some socks. Luton to Cluj; three hours of dozing uncomfortably above the clouds, not talking about what was on their minds in case anyone overheard. Finally, the hire car – a make and model neither of them had ever heard of – a Google map print-out and they were on the final leg of the journey Stephanie prayed would bring Jimmy back to her.

They'd spent the previous afternoon and evening formulating plans, discarding them, reforming them, refining them and finally coming up with a tentative course of action that they both knew would have to be infinitely flexible. The important thing was that they were clear about their primary objective – they were there to locate Jimmy. Everything else depended on that.

And, because Nick maintained it never hurt to go belt and braces, they'd sent another text to Leanne's phone. 'Totally understand, I know how fond of Jimmy you were. Maybe I could come on my own? Get my nails done for old times' sake? Sx' Nick had read it and nodded. 'I bet you don't get a reply at all this time.'

Once they were clear of the airport and sure they were headed in the right direction – south-west into the mountains – they pulled off at the first petrol station, a low brick building that looked like a refugee from the 1950s, its modern pumps wildly out of time. Nick went into the kiosk and returned with bottled water, chocolate, two packs of sliced salami and a packet of plain biscuits. While he was inside, Stephanie put on the socks and trainers. Phase one of their plan was to find the orphanage then walk past as if they were hikers. The drawback to this plan was that the only clothes Stephanie had with her were the ones she'd packed for a Californian holiday. Strappy sundresses and shorts were fine for Disneyland and the beach but not very appropriate for walking in the Transylvanian mountains, even on a fine spring day like this. Hence the airport shopping. With her one pair of jeans and an old plaid shirt of Nick's, she looked almost credible.

As they climbed higher, the air coming through the vents grew a little cooler. The landscape changed from lush green rolling hills dotted with rangy sheep to wooded slopes punctured with rocky outcrops. It was easy to see how Bram Stoker conjured Dracula against this dramatic and mostly empty backdrop. Occasionally they passed through villages that barely earned the title – a few houses clinging to a hill, or a clutch of cottages occupying a small plateau – but there was nothing to tempt them to pause in their journey.

After an hour and a half of driving up twisting narrow roads, Stephanie realised they must be closing in on Timonescu. Her stomach felt simultaneously tight and fluttery. 'Take me through the plan again,' she said. 'This is not the kind of thing I do. I'm not a woman of action. Not like you.'

Nick grinned. 'I'm not a woman of action either.'

She gave his upper arm a playful punch. 'Nobody loves a smartarse. You know what I mean.'

'It's simple. We're going to drive past the orphanage, but not so slowly that we attract attention. We'll carry on a bit further and find somewhere discreet to leave the car. Then we'll put on our backpacks and walk back past the orphanage, scouting as we go for vantage points where we can watch the place.'

'And then we sit tight?'

'That's right. Till Simon or Marina or both of them emerge. Then we try to follow them. And see where that takes us.'

'It's not exactly watertight, is it?' Stephanie tried not to show how nervous she felt about Nick's plan. The truth was that what had seemed like a brilliant idea in the security of his flat was scarier than sitting in an interrogation room with Vivian McKuras. Much scarier.

'We have to be flexible. We'll stay in touch on our phones. At least on these roads they won't get much of a head start. And it's not like there are a lot of side roads to turn off on.'

Stephanie breathed deeply. 'And if we manage to follow Simon and we find Jimmy with him and Marina, what do we do then?' When she'd asked this before, Nick had been evasive, saying they'd cross that bridge when they got to it. Well, as far as she was concerned, they were on the approach road to the bridge now.

'We assess the situation and decide the best way to make sure we walk out of there with Jimmy,' Nick said.

'Can't we just call the police and tell them?'

Nick negotiated a hairpin bend with a twist of the wrists, then nearly ended up in a ditch avoiding a horse-drawn cart coming down the hill in the opposite direction. 'I don't trust the local law enforcement. The TOmorrow trust is funnelling a lot of money into the local economy. They're going to have more clout than a Scotland Yard detective walking in on their patch without any kind of agreement. Even if it only takes a few hours to sort things out, Simon and Marina could take off with Jimmy and be on their way to anywhere in central Europe. We've got to do it ourselves. We've got to physically remove Jimmy and get him away from there.'

'Then what do we do? I don't have his passport, and if the locals are in Marina's pocket, how can we possibly get away on these roads?'

'We do what they don't expect. They'll expect us to head for the airport. But I say we head on over the mountains and down the other side to Bucharest. We'll take Jimmy to the British Embassy and they can sort out an emergency passport. We're the guys in the white hats here, after all. We are the rescue mission.'

Stephanie was not reassured. 'You think they'll hand Jimmy over? Just like that?'

'No. I think we'll have to make some unpleasant noises. Simon's the weak link, though. He's a doctor. If he ever wants to practise anywhere again, he can't afford to have an international warrant for his arrest floating around out there. As far as I can tell, he's a nice middle-class boy with no experience of being on the wrong side of the law. He's the one who will cave, trust me.' He gave a wry smile. 'You've never seen my dark side, Stephanie. But don't forget, I'm the one who kicked Pete Matthews into touch for you. I can do this. I can get Simon to see how much better off he will be if he hands Jimmy over in exchange for no legal pursuit.'

'You'd do that? You'd let them get away with it?'

Nick's jaw tightened. 'It goes against all my instincts, but yes. I'd do it to get the kid back. I'd do it for Jimmy's sake. The kid needs stability and familiarity, not to be transplanted to a foreign country and given a foreign identity. Because they'll have to do that. They can't risk Jimmy Higgins reappearing. He'll be given the identity of some Romanian orphan. So yes, I'd do it for the kid. And for you.'

'And what if Marina won't play? What if Simon goes along with you and she says no?'

'Then it'll be three to one.' His mouth clamped shut. Stephanie realised she was going to get nothing more out of Nick on this subject. He didn't want to rehearse with her a situation he was determined to avoid. He peered at the odometer. 'According to this, we're only a couple of miles away. Keep a look out for any signs.'

They passed through another hamlet – a cluster of mean houses with steep roofs huddled round what appeared to be an inn – then the forest seemed to grow thicker as they climbed through a series of tight bends. As they rounded the last hairpin they looked across a tumultuous stream that surged along the roadside to a meadow. At the heart of the meadow was a high wall surrounding a grim stone building. Four storeys high, twelve windows per storey, it sat foursquare behind tall iron gates. The cream stucco and the steeply pitched dark roof looked in good repair, but the overall impression was forbidding. There was a large paved area at the end of the driveway where several cars were parked, but the remainder that they could see was covered with grass. Nick slowed down and they passed a bridge over the stream. A large signboard proclaimed Orfelinat Timonescu.

'Jesus,' Nick said. 'It's big.'

Stephanie looked back and from this perspective she could see the beginnings of a children's play area that looked well equipped. 'What if they live in?' she said. 'What if Jimmy's stuck in there with all the other orphans?'

The road swung round in a broad curve. On the right, what appeared to be a logging road split off. Nick turned into it at the last moment and drove round the first bend. He turned the car around and when he finally stopped, they were about fifty yards from the road but out of sight to the casual observer. 'Why would they want to? If they've gone to these lengths to build a new life, I don't imagine they're spending their down time in an orphanage,' he said. 'Like I said last night, we have to be prepared to be flexible.' He reached for her hand and squeezed it. 'We have to hope. Somebody has to stand up for Jimmy,' he said.

Stephanie smiled. 'You think you can play me like a six-string,' she said, no sting in her voice. 'But I can see through you. I know why we're here, but that doesn't mean I'm not going to be apprehensive.'

'Apprehensive is good. It means you don't do stupid, heed-less gung-ho shit.' Nick opened the car door and unfolded himself, stretching his arms up to unkink his back. Stephanie joined him and in silence they organised their backpacks. Still without speaking, they set out down the track to the road.

'There's a path along the top side of the meadow,' Stephanie said. 'I caught sight of it out of the corner of my eye. I think you must get to it via the bridge that leads to the orphanage.'

And so they walked back down the road and crossed the bridge. There was no sign of life from the oppressive building behind the wall, no sound of children playing. It was early afternoon by now, and Stephanie was surprised that every-thing was so quiet and still.

They soon spotted the narrow path that cut across the meadow to the treeline. It looked exactly like the sort of path two hikers would be attracted to. They paused while Nick pre-tended to consult the map. 'Once we get to the trees, we'll look at the map again and act like we made a mistake. Then we'll go back the way we came. But as soon as we reach the bend, you slip into the trees and keep an eye on the orphan-age. I'll go back to the car and wait for you to tell me when I need to make a move.' He slipped off his backpack and took out a pair of binoculars. 'You'd better have these.'

They walked across the meadow purposefully, continuing along by the trees for a few hundred metres. Suddenly, the sound of children shouting and laughing drifted their way on the light breeze. A little further on, they turned and retraced their steps. There was a gap in the wall of about twenty metres where the stone had been replaced by tall spiked railings. Behind it, they could see children engaged in a typical assortment of childish activities – throwing balls, skipping, chasing games or just mooching around. Some of the children were clearly disabled, but they joined in nevertheless, making the most of the spring sunshine and their freedom. None of them was Jimmy, Stephanie was sure of that. Three women in dark trousers and the kind of white tunics worn by nurses and hospital orderlies sat on a bench, legs crossed, eyes on the children, smoking fiercely and talking animatedly. They paid no attention to Nick and Stephanie, who kept up their brisk pace all the way back to the road. 'It looks like the kids are having fun,' Stephanie said. 'Scarlett did something good. When she first came here, it was like all the horror documentaries after the fall of Ceauşescu. Kids chained to their cots, babies lying in their own filth, disabled children with bedsores weeping pus. Looks like they've had a transformation.'

'That's another reason to try and sort this out without bringing the police into it. I don't want to drag Scarlett's charity through the mud. The media would have a field day with the irony of that – the charity set up by his mother is exploited to hide tragic kidnapped Jimmy,' Nick said, making the quote mark signs in the air with his fingers.

They walked on and as they rounded the bend, Stephanie slipped in among the trees. Nick kept on walking, leaving her alone among the slender trunks of the conifers. The trouble with this kind of woodland was that there was no undergrowth to use as cover. Nothing grew under the dense canopy of needles. She flitted through the trees then moved closer to the road, where bracken was starting to unfurl among the coarse grass and unfamiliar hedgerow plants. If she sat on the carpet of needles at the edge of the trees, she reckoned it would be hard to spot her. Spreading her waterproof jacket on the ground, Stephanie settled down for what she knew might be a long watch. It was almost four in the afternoon; she had no idea when it would get dark, but she was determined to stick it out.

For Jimmy, it was the least she could do.

6

The sun had disappeared behind the wooded summit and with it the warmth of the day. Nick's plaid shirt was no match for the sharp chill on the breeze that came with the early evening. But if she put on the waterproof jacket in an attempt to keep warm, the damp from the ground would soon seep into Stephanie's bones, making her even colder than before. It was a conundrum that had no satisfactory answer, but mulling it over kept her mind off what might lie ahead of them.

The front door of the orphanage had opened a couple of times, startling her into sudden attention, the binoculars rammed against her eyes. The first time, a man and a woman emerged in the apparent uniform of dark trousers and white tunic. The man went to one of the cars while the woman jogged down the driveway, undid a padlock and opened the heavy iron gates. The man drove through, then waited for the woman to close and lock the gates again. It was an unwieldy process, but Stephanie liked the time it took. The next departure, about ten minutes later, featured a grey-haired woman in a pink button-through overall, who mounted a motor scooter hidden behind the cars and repeated the performance at the gate.

'Come on, Simon,' Stephanie muttered as the scooter grumbled past her up the hill. To relieve the monotony, she called Nick and told him about the people who had left. 'It takes a while to open and close the gates,' she reported. 'So if he does come out, you've got a few minutes' warning.'

'Are they all going down the hill?'

'No. One each way.'

'OK. Then I'll stay put till you know for sure which way he's headed.'

There was nothing else to say. Neither of them had any appetite for small talk. Stephanie returned to her vigil, wrapping her arms around her torso to preserve what warmth remained.

And then the door opened again. Even without the binoculars, she recognised Simon. Shirt over his straight-leg jeans, the distinctive walk provoked by his cowboy boots. She could almost believe she heard the clatter of his boot heels on the stone steps. He didn't close the door behind him and he paused at the foot of the stairs, turning to look back, as if he was calling someone.

When Jimmy came barrelling through the door at full speed, Stephanie stopped breathing. A tightness gripped her chest and her throat closed as if there were a sob trapped within. The boy caught up with Simon, who ruffled his hair as she'd done so many times. They walked hand in hand to a Mercedes saloon and got in. At the gate, Simon went to unfasten the padlock and Stephanie recovered herself enough to stab the button on her phone to call Nick.

'It's Simon,' she blurted out. 'He's got Jimmy with him.'

'Bloody hell.' She could hear the engine catching as Nick turned the ignition key. 'Are they heading up or down?'

'I don't know yet, Simon's only just driving through the gate. Hold on . . . ' She watched, the tension in her body growing with every passing minute. Simon drove through the entrance then dawdled over closing the gate. He acted as if he had all the time in the world, which only made her feverish impatience worse. When he finally set the car moving again, the indicator light signalled he was turning left. 'Down,' she practically yelled. 'They're going down the hill. Come and get me.'

As soon as Simon's taillights disappeared round the first bend, Stephanie was on her feet, plunging through the narrow strip of hedgerow on to the road. Already she could see Nick's headlights glimmering through the trees. The day was dimming fast now; at least they would have Simon's lights ahead of them to make tailing him easier.

Nick's car rounded the bend and skidded to a halt next to her. She threw herself into the passenger seat, surprised to realise she was panting. Nick grinned and thrust the car into gear. Nervous relief made him crack wise. 'Isn't this where you're supposed to say, "The game's afoot, Holmes"?'

In spite of herself, she giggled, a hysterical response to his silliness. 'Just remember, it was Inspector Lestrade of Scotland Yard who was the real dummy in the Sherlock Holmes stories, Detective Sergeant Nicolaides.'

Nick hurtled round the bends as fast as he dared, catching occasional streaks of scarlet light through the trees ahead. Then at once the red disappeared. They corkscrewed through another couple of bends and suddenly the hamlet was in sight. Stephanie strained to catch a trace of the Mercedes, and suddenly yelped, 'There, past the inn. The road that goes into the forest. They're driving down there.'

Nick threw the car into a screaming turn and they shot past the houses and the inn, bucketing from side to side as they went from tarmac to rough track. He tapped the brakes, trying to slow down safely to a manageable speed. 'Fuck,' he said, intense and savage as he wrestled with the inadequate car.

Up ahead, the red lights intensified as the Mercedes braked.

Then it suddenly turned right. Nick slowed down. 'It's a gateway,' Stephanie yelled. 'Stop, Nick.'

He turned off the headlights and managed to stop the car fifty metres from the gateway. Switching off the engine and the sidelights took seconds, then they were both out on the track, leaving the car doors open. They ran to the gateway, Nick crouching low and crossing to the far side.

Stephanie peered round a rough stone pillar topped with a bear rearing up on its hind legs. The Mercedes had drawn to a halt in a pool of light about thirty metres away. The light came from floodlights mounted on the front of what looked like a hunting lodge crossed with a castle, complete with stone turrets on each corner. Jimmy and Simon were already out of the car and heading for the front porch, Jimmy skipping ahead.

The door opened and a woman emerged, running down the steps, arms thrown wide to greet the boy. She swept him into her arms, spinning round with him. As Simon joined them, she paused to kiss his mouth. It was the perfect image of a family reunited at the end of the working day.

Only the woman was wrong.

Stephanie's knees gave way beneath her. She crumpled to the ground with a soft moan, unable to believe the evidence of her eyes. Her eyelids fluttered and for a moment, she wondered whether she was going to faint. Then Nick was on his haunches next to her, his comforting arms around her. 'Bloody hell,' he said. 'Did I just see what I think I saw? Bouncing down the steps of a place that looks like Dracula's weekend retreat? Was that Scarlett?'

'I can't believe it,' Stephanie said. 'I was with her till right before she died. I saw her in her coffin.' She shook her head, as if to clear it of craziness. 'It can't be Scarlett.' Then the light dawned. 'Think, Nick. Who's missing? Who's not where she's supposed to be?'

Relief broke over him, lightening his expression. 'Leanne. It's Leanne.'

'The devious, twisted bastards,' Stephanie said, sounding almost admiring. 'They've been plotting this ever since Scarlett told Leanne I was going to be Jimmy's guardian. She'd grown to love him. She was desperate to keep him. And the selfish, greedy bastards figured out a way to do it that means they get access to a chunk of the money as well, with Simon set up as

416

the doctor in the house. With Simon and Marina controlling the trust fund, I bet Simon and Leanne are sitting pretty out here in their castle in the woods.'

Nick stood up. 'Thank Christ I didn't go to Essex police with our theories about Leanne being murdered. I'd have been a bloody laughing stock. Nick the Greek with egg from head to toe.'

'They're still criminals, Nick. They abducted Jimmy and, like you said, they must be living high on the hog off the back of the TOmorrow trust. We've got as much leverage against Simon and Leanne as we had against Simon and Marina. We can still get Jimmy back.'

Nick's answering smile was grim. 'Damn right. I'm ready when you are.'

Fifteen minutes later, they set off up the short paved driveway. Nick had insisted they wait, sitting in the car with the doors open. 'Don't close the door. The click of the lock, that's the kind of artificial sound that really carries in places like this. We'll give them a little bit of time to settle into their normal routine. That way they'll be nice and relaxed and not expecting the shit to hit the fan.'

Then he had a better idea. 'Let's push the car across the gateway. That way, if they decide to make a run for it or call reinforcements, they're fucked.'

And so he let off the handbrake, and with scarcely a sound, they pushed the tinny little car forward until it completely blocked the entrance to the house. To get through themselves, they had to treat the car itself as a kind of passageway they had to scramble through.

Nick must be able to hear the thudding of her heart, Stephanie thought as they approached the house. It felt like wading through a fairy story. The house gleamed with recent maintenance, its shutters immaculate, its stucco spotless, its metalwork rust free. Window boxes filled with flowering bulbs perched on every sill and balustrade. Warm light glowed through the blinds in the ground-floor windows. The Brothers Grimm meet a TV makeover show.

They climbed the four steps to the porch as quietly as possible. Then, ignoring the doorbell, Nick hammered with his torch on the heavy wooden planks of the door. They heard no footsteps approaching, so closely did the door fit its frame. Without warning, it swung back on its hinges. The woman who answered it wasn't facing them. She was looking over her shoulder, laughing at something someone inside had said or done.

Stephanie thought she was going to throw up.

The woman turned to them and all the animation and colour drained from her face. Lot's wife must have looked a lot like that, Stephanie thought irrelevantly. Time itself seemed to slow as she struggled to make sense of what – or rather who – she was seeing. 'Hi, Scarlett,' she said. She heard Nick's sharp intake of breath behind her. 'Aren't you going to ask us in?'

8

Stephanie's words galvanised Scarlett into action. She tried to slam the door on them, but Nick was too fast and too practised for that. His arm shot out and he leaned his whole weight against the edge of the door for maximum leverage. Scarlett was forced to give ground. As she skittered backwards, Stephanie and Nick pushed their way inside.

'How could you?' Stephanie said, her voice scarcely above a contemptuous whisper.

The sound of chopping came from a brightly lit room to the right, followed by Simon's voice. 'Who is it, love?'

Stephanie carried on into the warm kitchen. Simon stood at a wooden butcher's block dicing onions. Seeing her, he stopped in mid-action, the knife clattering to the board, his mouth flapping like a panicked goldfish. At the same moment, Jimmy saw her and clambered out of his chair, hurtling across the short distance between them. 'Stephie,' he shouted happily. 'I love you.' He threw his arms round her legs, laughing and whooping. 'Are we going home soon?' he added, oblivious to the stunned and horrified faces around the room.

'Steph's just come to visit, to make sure you've settled in,' Scarlett said, sweeping past Stephanie and grabbing Jimmy. In one seamless motion, she handed him off to Simon. 'You go and play upstairs with your Lego with Simon. I've got things to talk about with Steph.' Her smile was as convincing as an octogenarian's toupee.

'I'll go with the boys,' Nick said, following Simon.

'Stephie,' Jimmy's voice was sharp with longing as he was carried out of the kitchen, arms stretching over Simon's shoulder.

'Later,' Scarlett said, shutting the kitchen door behind them. For a dead woman, she appeared in remarkably good health. She was lightly tanned and looked fit, eyes sparkling and skin smooth. Her hair had grown back, a thick and multi-shaded blonde that spoke of expensive visits to a good hairdresser. Probably not in the local village. It was loosely fastened with a silver hairclip. She spread her arms in an invitation to embrace. 'I am so sorry, Steph. You have no idea how much I hated keeping you in the dark.'

The warmth of Scarlett's approach almost wrong-footed Stephanie. Almost, but not quite. Struggling to speak, the blood pounding in her ears, she finally found her tongue. 'How dare you? After what you've put Jimmy through. How dare you try to shrug this off like it's no big deal?'

Scarlett took a bottle of Prosecco from the big American-style fridge and calmly popped the cork. 'Jimmy's fine. You saw that for yourself.' She reached into a glass-fronted cupboard for a pair of champagne flutes. As she poured, she shook her head in a more-in-sorrow-than-in-anger way. 'You know better than anyone how bloody impossible my life was, especially after the cancer. I couldn't go anywhere, do anything without a pack of paps on my tail. I couldn't live like that. Nobody could. I'd had it up to here, Steph. The stress made me ill. Literally, they nearly killed me.'

Sweat prickling the back of her neck, Stephanie was struggling to find an even keel in this conversation. Scarlett was so matter-of-fact. Offhand, almost. Not like a woman who has been caught out faking her own death and abducting her own child a continent away. And her own emotions were swinging wildly between relief that her friend was still alive and rage at what Scarlett had done. 'You could have retired from public life. Moved abroad where nobody knew who you were.' Stephanie gave a bitter little laugh. 'Somewhere like bloody Transylvania. I bet you can shop here no trouble without being mobbed.'

Scarlett held a glass out to Stephanie, who waved it away. Scarlett put it down on the counter close to her instead. 'As it happens, I can. And we did think about that. But it was complicated. A doctor like Simon doesn't make a lot of money in Romania. And even though it's cheap to live here, it still cost us a bomb to do this place up. Then there's other things that don't come cheap. Satellite Internet, multichannel TV, that kind of thing. And if you want anything better than the basic shit, you have to pay through the nose. So we needed to make sure the money kept coming in. I earned the right to a decent life, Steph. But those fucking jackals were robbing me of it.'

There was something shocking about Scarlett's complete lack of shame. 'So you set up the terminal cancer and the Swimathon to make sure the TOmorrow Trust would keep you in the style to which you've become accustomed?' Anyone else would have flinched at Stephanie's bitter sarcasm, but Scarlett merely smiled and tipped her glass towards her former friend.

'Pretty much, yeah. Obviously, the orphanage gets a bloody good cut too. Otherwise there would be no reason for them to go along with the set-up. Marina is the go-between. She makes sure everybody's happy. And they get Simon's services for next to nothing, which is a big deal when you've got as many disabled kids as they have to deal with. You make it sound like we're on the make, Steph, but we're doing a lot of good here.'

'You pretended you were dead.' The tide of anger had risen high enough to sweep away Stephanie's initial shock. 'I wept for you. I held your son while his little body shook with sobs because he'd already lost his dad and now he'd lost his mum too. Do you have any idea the grief you caused to the people who loved you?'

Scarlett's mouth quirked in what might have been embarrassment. 'It's not like there were many of you. Not that knew me. Really, it was only you and Jimmy and George that I gave a shit about. Obviously Simon and Marina were in on it, so they were only pretending. Look, I've said I'm sorry, and I meant it. If there had been another way to do it, I would have gone for it, believe me. But I had to keep you in the dark. Somebody's grief had to be authentic. So Simon and Marina could figure out how to react.'

Stephanie's mouth fell open. The notion that her personal pain had meant nothing more to Scarlett than a control in a psychological experiment was beyond her comprehension. How could someone treat another human being like that, let alone one who was supposed to be their best friend? 'You callous bitch,' she said, her voice quiet, almost strangled.

Scarlett drained her glass and refilled it. 'I was playing for high stakes, Steph. I've always done what it took to get where I needed to be. Don't act like it's a surprise. You wrote the book, after all.'

Stephanie felt like her brain was slowly dragging itself up to speed after being mired in a swamp of lies. 'I saw you dead. I saw you in your coffin.' Scarlett smiled like a poker tournament winner released from the tyranny of keeping a straight face, and Stephanie suffered another moment of terrible understanding. 'Oh my God,' she gasped. Her hand flew to her mouth, as if by stopping the words emerging she could kill the knowledge.

Scarlett nodded. 'She was fucking impossible, you know

that. She wanted Jimmy, she wanted me to sign over the Spanish property to her, she wanted an income. Like any of that would have happened, even if I had been dying.' She shook her head in disgust. 'Silly cow thought she could threaten me with exposure.'

'If she had talked it would only have been a nine-day wonder, Scarlett. You could have called her bluff. By then, you were the brave cancer heroine. The fact that you'd used Leanne as a body double bad girl might actually have earned you a few Brownie points.' Stephanie's bitterness leaked into every word.

But Scarlett looked puzzled rather than upset. 'It wasn't the body double thing I was worried about. It was Joshu.'

9

Now it was Stephanie's turn to look baffled. 'What about Joshu?'

'Leanne knew about the morphine.' Scarlett rolled her eyes as if she was dealing with a particularly stupid pupil.

'What about the morphine?' Stephanie persisted.

'Joshu didn't *steal* the morphine from Simon. Simon gave it to him. He made out that he was doing it as a favour, so Joshu would leave me alone. But he'd swapped the labels. Joshu thought he was shooting up a low dose, but it was really the highest one legally available. Leanne had seen Simon in the kitchen doing something with the labels and when Joshu died, she put two and two together. But she thought at first it was Simon trying to get Joshu out of the way so he could have a clear run at me. She didn't realise we were already head over heels in love with each other by then.' Scarlett smiled sweetly at the last memory, as if that erased the awful truth she'd just revealed.

'You ... You set up Joshu, knowing those doses of morphine would kill him?'

'What would you have done? He was a nightmare, you know that. He was off his face half the time, and if I had died, he would have never let go until he'd got his hands on Jimmy and he'd have completely fucked him up. I couldn't chance that, Steph. You've lived with Jimmy, you know what a sweetheart he is. I couldn't leave him in Joshu's hands. I'd tried everything to get him to back off. But he wasn't having it. I didn't have any choice.'

Stephanie reached for the glass of Prosecco and drank it in one. Scarlett laughed with delight. 'That's more like it. More like old times, Steph.' She refilled the glass, reaching over to squeeze Stephanie's arm. Stephanie flinched and drew back but Scarlett didn't seem to mind. Stephanie had understood Scarlett's single-mindedness, the drive that had taken her from a no-hope background to the high life. But understanding how it had turned into this cold-blooded ruthlessness was still a step she was finding it hard to make.

'You killed Joshu to protect Jimmy. Then you killed Leanne to protect yourself.'

Scarlett looked put out. 'Well, how would anyone have been better off if Leanne had grassed us up? We'd have been sent to jail in disgrace and Jimmy's life would have been over. And Leanne would have been sitting pretty even though she was as guilty as us.'

'How do you work that out? Leanne being guilty, I mean?'

Scarlett shrugged prettily. 'She saw what she saw and she didn't tell the cops at the time. She tried to blackmail me later. In my book, that makes her as much of a criminal. She had no right to get off scot free and with my son thrown in. And I won't deny that her last job as my body double saved us a lot of aggravation about what to put in the coffin.' She grinned at her own cleverness.

'But Leanne supposedly went back to Spain weeks before you "died".' Stephanie made contemptuous quotation marks in the air. 'What? You kept her prisoner all that time?'

'It wasn't hard. Simon had the drugs. He kept her sedated in the dressing room where he was supposedly kipping down. The weight fell off her, which made it look even more authentic. Then when we were ready for my big death bed scene, he upped the dose. She didn't know anything about it. You could say she spent her last couple of weeks totally blissed out. People pay good money for that kind of thing, Steph.'

If that was an attempt at humour, it fell flat on its arse as far as Stephanie was concerned. 'And the text I got this morning, supposedly from Leanne? That was you too, was it?'

Scarlett looked ridiculously pleased with herself. 'Of course it was me. I had to think on my feet with that one.'

'Not fast enough,' Stephanie said. 'We already knew Leanne wasn't in Spain. We met the delightful chap you sold her house to.'

Scarlett looked mildly disconcerted. Capitalising on that, Stephanie went on the offensive. 'And Jimmy? What was that about? You kidnapped Jimmy. You've put me through hell this last week. I've been insane with worry. I've hardly slept. I've been terrified for him.'

For the first time, Scarlett looked as if contrition might be within her emotional range. 'Yeah. I felt really bad about that, Steph. If I could have found another way round it, I would have. But I couldn't just ask you for him back, could I? You'd never have been able to explain that to social services, and they'd have thought you'd murdered him or sold him or something.' She gave a weird little half-laugh. 'So I had to kidnap him off you. We did it in America to draw attention away from anything that might point to us. Simon did the dirty deed. Lots of heavy-duty disguise and totally different shoes to change the way he walks. Simon drove up to Canada with him, got him across the border with a couple of Romanian passports, and then they flew back from Toronto. Piece of piss, really.'

'But why? Why make it so complicated? Why didn't you

426

just make Simon Jimmy's guardian in the first place? Or even Marina, if she was in on it?'

For the first time, Stephanie thought she saw something shifty flit across Scarlett's face. 'Either of them, tongues would have wagged. The hacks would have been all over it. Why was some Romanian nanny getting custody of Scarlett Higgins' kid and taking him off to Romania? What sort of life was he going to have? Or why was some doctor getting the kid? Was he Scarlett's secret lover? And why was he taking the kid off to Dracula's back yard?' She sighed. 'Questions, questions, questions. I don't want to sound mean, Steph, but you were the boring option. My mate, my ghost writer, the woman who was there when Jimmy was born, the person who more or less lived with us through the cancer. You're his godmother, and that made you the obvious person to take care of him.'

'And I did take care of him.' Stephanie's chin came up in defiance. 'I couldn't have taken better care of him if he'd been my own. You want to know the truth, Scarlett? He feels like my own. Never more so than this last week, after you took him off me.'

Scarlett dipped her head in acknowledgement. 'I'm glad to hear it. But now I need him here with me. I'm sorry. When I asked you to take him on, I didn't mean it to be temporary. I'd convinced myself I could let him go. Told myself he'd be better off without me, just with you.' She was serious now; there was emotional depth to what she was saying, unlike when she'd been talking so nonchalantly about murder.

'What changed things?'

Scarlett twirled the stem of her glass between her fingers, making the bubbles dance in the glass. Outside, it had started to rain, the rising wind throwing handfuls of drops against the windows. To Stephanie, it felt like a film set. It was hard to believe she was living through this disturbing scene for real.

427

Any minute now, Nick was going to burst in with Simon and Jimmy, telling her she'd fallen for a grotesque practical joke.

'What changed things?' She sighed. 'We thought there would be more kids, me and Simon. Giving Jimmy up – I'd squared that with myself on the basis that we'd have kids together. But once we'd been here a few months and nothing was happening, Simon ran a few tests. Turns out that the chemo I had for the breast cancer fried my eggs as well. I've got more chance of flying to the moon than I have of conceiving again.'

'So you wanted Jimmy back. Since you couldn't make a replacement, you thought you'd just snatch him back.'

She folded her arms across her chest. 'He is mine, after all, Steph. Not yours.'

'No, he's not mine. But he's not yours either. He's not a possession. He's a little boy we both owe a duty of care to. He's the one both of us should have the honesty and the decency to put first. What's best for Jimmy, that's how it should be.'

Scarlett's old smile was back. The lopsided, charming one that always provoked an answering smile in whoever was the target. This time, the old magic failed. 'And that's how it's going to be from now on. I made a mistake, letting him leave my world. Now I've fixed it. He's going to stop here with me, Stephanie. You just have to accept that.'

The icy certainty in Scarlett's voice made Stephanie's skin crawl. The unspoken threat was in her level gaze. This was a woman who had organised two cold and calculated murders already in pursuit of what she wanted. Implicit in her words was the menace of what she would exact from Stephanie if she didn't simply walk away from a boy who was, after all, not her son. Nobody had to know what had happened here.

Except Nick, of course. Honest, passionate, inconvenient Nick.

As if to bolster up what she hadn't said, Scarlett added

casually, 'You'll have to stay the night. The roads round here are bloody awful. Even the locals regularly come off those bends and plunge to their deaths. You and Nick would be taking your lives in your hands if you went off in the dark in the middle of a storm.'

It was, Stephanie thought, like being trapped in a Brothers Grimm tale. Most of which, if she remembered rightly, didn't have a happy ending. If they stayed the night, would they make it to morning? Would their food be drugged? Would their throats be cut in the night, their bodies fed to whatever wildlife roamed the forest? She was sure there must be wolves, or at least wild boars. And everybody knew that pigs ate anything and everything. Would wild boars be any different?

Or would they be doped up and put in the car, sent crashing down a sheer drop to certain death? Such a terrible tragedy, and all arising from a desperate desire to talk to that nice nanny and that helpful doctor who were closest to the boy who'd been mysteriously kidnapped. Simon had always been so convincing with her, he'd have no trouble with the local police who, she was sure, were understandably close to the local orphanage and its benefactors.

Thus far, Scarlett had always done what was necessary to achieve her goal. She kept it simple, but she kept it ruthless. Letting her believe her plan was working might be the only way to survive this. Stephanie let her eyes drop. 'OK,' she said, hoping she sounded defeated. 'We'll be gone in the morning.'

'You think you can convince Nick the Greek to keep his mouth shut about Jimmy? It's not like we have to tell him about the other stuff, after all.'

Like he's not smart enough to work it out for himself. Stephanie managed a sly smile. 'He'll go along with whatever I say. It's not like this is an official visit or anything. He's got no authority here.'

Scarlett appeared to accept what Stephanie had said, but Stephanie caught another of those flashes of ice behind her eyes. Scarlett was keeping the peace, that was all. They weren't safe, her and Nick. Quite the opposite. They were like Damocles, sitting at dinner waiting for the hair suspending the sword above his head to snap. All they could be certain of was that at some point, they would be killed.

Knowing what she knew now, there was no way Scarlett could allow them to leave alive.

10

'That's settled, then.' Scarlett topped up both glasses. This time, Stephanie joined in the celebratory clinking of glasses. 'You've no idea how much I missed you, Steph. The one good thing about not having to keep things hidden from you any more is that you'll be able to come and visit. There's even a little outbuilding on the edge of the forest with a wood stove. You could come out here to write, if you wanted to.' There was nothing to distinguish her cheerful expression from the one Stephanie had grown used to over the years.

'That might be fun.' It was beyond bizarre, she thought, desperately trying to come up with a plan that would mean safety for Jimmy and life for her and Nick. Nothing she could think of worked. Whether they went with or without him, they'd never feel safe again. Scarlett was cunning, clever and ruthless, and Simon appeared to be entirely in thrall to her narcissism. Stephanie and Nick would never know the day or the hour. The only thing they could be certain of was that their knowledge was a death warrant where Scarlett was concerned.

But Stephanie had meant what she said about Jimmy being her primary concern. By any measure, putting the child first meant ensuring he didn't grow up in a household where murder was high on the list of approved solutions to complex problems. They had to walk out of here with Jimmy. She had a feeling that if she said as much, Scarlett would laugh and say, 'Over my dead body.'

Well, maybe that could be arranged.

Stephanie, who had never done anything more violent than set a mousetrap, let her mind race through the dramatic climaxes of films she'd seen and books she'd read. Scarlett turned away from her and opened the fridge. 'I'm sure there's olives and cheese in here, we can have some nibbles while Simon finishes cooking,' she said. 'You two must be starving.'

Stephanie knew she'd simply have to act without thinking about it. In one smooth movement, she picked up the knife Simon had been using on the onions and stepped up close behind Scarlett. With her left hand, she grabbed the thick tail of hair, twisting it round her hand and yanking it backwards. Scarlett yelped in shock as her head jerked back, exposing her soft throat to the sharp blade that Stephanie drew from left to right. The knife was so sharp that neither woman felt the impact of the cut.

A sudden gusher of crimson spurted forward, staining the packed contents of the fridge and splattering against the brilliant white interior. Stephanie pushed Scarlett away from her and stepped back. Her former friend crumpled to the floor, blood spreading in a pool from the grinning gash in her throat. Air gurgled in the blood, a gruesome sound Stephanie thought she would hear for ever in her nightmares. Spasms racked Scarlett's body and her hands twitched and contorted as they tried to reach the wound.

Stephanie threw the knife down. Then she remembered all those TV dramas and picked it up again, taking it to the sink. She grabbed a nearby towel and rubbed the handle clean, then ran it under the hot tap. It would be identifiable as the murder weapon, but it wouldn't have her fingerprints on it. She did the same with her Prosecco glass. She didn't think she'd touched anything else, but she kept hold of the towel. She felt like she was outside her body, watching herself do these things but not actually part of them.

She glanced down at her clothes, checking for obvious bloodstains, but saw none. The blood had all spurted forward, leaving her clean. She took a deep breath then turned back to the mess she'd made. The blood wasn't flowing any more, just seeping. It was amazing how fast someone could bleed out. And how much mess that blood could make.

Stepping carefully to avoid contaminating herself with Scarlett's blood, Stephanie made it to the door. Using the towel, she opened it and stepped into the cosy hall, carefully shutting the door behind her. Ahead of her, a wide wooden staircase rose to the upper floor and Stephanie climbed carefully, taking her time over each step. She remembered having felt like this on the one occasion she'd smoked dope; her body didn't seem to be a living thing any longer. It was more like a giant robot suit inside which she was manipulating the controls.

On the upstairs landing, light and noise spilled from a doorway. Stephanie walked unsteadily to the doorway and made herself smile. 'You look like you're having fun,' she said. Jimmy and the two men were putting the finishing touches to building a Lego railway, testing the motors in the trains and the levers that moved the points.

'It's the most fun I've had in years,' Nick said, looking as if he meant it.

'I'm sorry I've got to break it up,' she said. 'Jimmy, we need to go home. If there's anything you want to take with you, grab it now, because we really do need to be on our way.'

Nick was first to react. He scrambled upright and hoisted Jimmy into the air. 'What do you say? Anything you can't live without, Jimmy?'

'Wait a minute,' Simon said, struggling to get to his feet in the tight corner where he was penned by Lego and a toy chest.

Jimmy looked around, frowning. 'My DS,' he said, pointing to the small Nintendo console lying on the bed. Nick scooped it up and headed out the door. Stephanie moved back to block the exit.

'Wait a minute,' Simon said, lunging towards the doorway. But Stephanie didn't budge, and his reluctance to hit a woman bought Nick and Jimmy valuable seconds. He gripped her upper arms and tried to shift her bodily out of the way, but Stephanie resisted. 'What have you done, you mad bitch?' he shouted. 'Where's Scarlett? Scarlett?'

Finally, he used his superior weight against her and simply pushed her back. He ran down the stairs, shouting Scarlett's name. The yelling stopped abruptly as soon as he opened the kitchen door. By the time Stephanie had recovered her balance and made it to the bottom of the stairs, he was kneeling in Scarlett's blood, cradling her head in his lap. 'She didn't leave me any choice,' Stephanie said. 'It was me or her. You know that.'

Simon didn't even turn his head. 'My love,' he kept repeating, his voice cracked and broken.

Still moving like a woman in a trance, Stephanie carried on out the front door towards the little car. She was only a ghost, after all. She'd never been here. A single thought kept reverberating inside her head. *You can't kill someone who's already dead.*

You can't kill someone who's already dead.